★ THE GUNSMITH'S GALLANTRY ★

Susan Page Davis

BARBOUR
PUBLISHING

For more information about Susan Page Davis, please access the author's Web site at the following Internet address: www.susanpagedavis.com

Cover design: Müllerhaus Publishing Arts, Inc., www.Mullerhaus.net

Published by Barbour Publishing, Inc., P.O. Box 719, Uhrichsville, OH 44683, www.barbourbooks.com

Our mission is to publish and distribute inspirational products offering exceptional value and biblical encouragement to the masses.

 Member of the
Evangelical Christian
Publishers Association

Printed in the United States of America.

The son shall not bear the iniquity of the father.

<small>EZEKIEL 18:20 KJV</small>

★ CHAPTER 1 ★

Fergus, Idaho
May 1886

Wait, Hiram!"

The gunsmith paused on the board sidewalk and turned around.

Maitland Dostie left the doorway of his tiny office and shouted at him, waving a piece of paper. "Got a message for ya."

Hiram arched his eyebrows and touched a hand to his chest in question.

The gray-haired telegraph operator smiled and clomped along the walk toward him, shaking his head. "Yes, you, Mr. Dooley. Just because you haven't had a telegram in the last five years and more doesn't mean you'll never get one."

Hiram swallowed down a lump of apprehension and reached a cautious hand for the paper. "What do I owe you?"

"Nothing. It was paid for on the other end."

It still seemed he ought to give him something, but maybe that was only if a messenger boy brought the telegram around to the house. Hiram nodded. "Thanks. Where's it from?"

"Why'n't you look and see?"

Hiram wanted to say, "Because if it's from Maine, it's probably bad news." His parents were getting along in years, and he couldn't think of a reason anyone would part with enough hard cash to send him a telegram unless somebody'd up and died.

But Hiram rarely spent more words than he had to, and Dostie had already gotten more out of him than usual. Besides, if someone in the family had died, the telegraph operator would know it. Wouldn't he look a little sadder if that were so? Hiram nodded and tucked the paper inside his vest so it wouldn't fly away in the

5

cool May wind that whistled up between the Idaho mountains. He walked home, stepping a little faster than previously, certain that Dostie watched him.

At the path to his snug little house between the jail and a vacant store building, he turned in and hurried to the back. Maybe he ought to look. If it was bad news, he'd have to tell his sister, Trudy. Undecided, he mounted the steps and opened the kitchen door. A spicy smell of baking welcomed him, along with Trudy's smile.

"Just in time. I'm taking out the molasses cookies and putting in the dried apple pies." She bent before the open oven.

The woodstove had warmed the kitchen to an almost uncomfortable level. Hiram hung his hat on its peg and headed for the water bucket and washbasin. No use trying to get cookies from Trudy unless he'd washed his hands.

"Did Zachary Harper pay you?"

"No. He says he'll come by next week."

"Humph."

Hiram shrugged. Trudy got a little mama-bearish on his behalf when folks didn't come forth with cash for his work on their firearms, but he knew Zach would pay him eventually. It wasn't worth fussing over. As she peeled hot cookies off the baking sheet with a long, flat spatula, the soap shot out of his hand and skated across the clean floor. Thankful it hadn't slid under the hot stove, he walked to the corner and bent to retrieve it. The paper in his vest crackled.

"Oh, I 'most forgot." He corralled the soap and returned it to its dish. After a good rinsing, he dried his hands, fished out the folded yellow sheet of paper, and laid it on the table.

"What's that?" She stopped with the narrow spatula in midair, a hot, floppy cookie drooping over its edges.

"Telegram."

"What's it say?"

He rescued the crumbling cookie and juggled it from one hand to the other. "Don't know." He blew on it until it was cool enough that it wouldn't burn him and popped half into his mouth. The warm sweetness hit the spot, and he felt less anxious.

Trudy set the cookie sheet down and balled her hands into fists. She put them to her hips, though she still held the spatula in one. "What's the matter with you? Why didn't you read it?"

He shrugged. How to tell his younger sister that he hadn't wanted to be smacked with bad news while the telegraph operator watched him?

"It's windy out."

She scowled at him.

"I didn't want it to blow away. Read it if you want." He reached for another cookie. "Is Ethan coming over tonight?"

"What do you think?"

Hiram smiled. The sheriff spent a disproportionate amount of time at the Dooley house these days, but he didn't mind. Ethan Chapman was a good man.

Trudy still eyed the telegram as though she expected it to rear back and sprout fangs and a tail rattle.

"Go ahead and read it," Hiram said, feeling a little guilty at putting the task off on her.

"If it's addressed to you, then you do it."

He sighed and laid his cookie aside. It would be better with milk, anyway. He wiped his hands on his dungarees and picked up the paper. As he opened it, he quickly scanned the message for the "from" part and frowned. Why on earth would Rose Caplinger send him a message all the way from Maine?

"What?" Trudy asked.

He held it out to her. "It's Rose."

"Violet's sister?"

Hiram nodded. "She wants to visit, I guess." He should have read it more closely, but the idea of his opinionated sister-in-law descending on them was enough to make a bachelor quake. He and his bride, Violet, had traveled west twelve years ago, in part for the opportunities that beckoned them, but also to escape her pushy family. If Rose hadn't bothered to come after Violet died, why on earth would she take it into her head to visit a decade later? "We'll have to tell her not to come."

Trudy's eyebrows drew together as she studied the paper. "Too late, Hi. She's already in Boise."

Libby Adams lowered the bar into place inside the door of the Paragon Emporium. After a long day tending the store, it was a relief to close up shop. She threw the bolt and turned the OPEN sign to CLOSED, but before she turned away, a man appeared outside and tried the door handle.

Surprised, Libby gestured for him to wait, removed the bar, and unbolted the door.

"I'm just closing, Cyrus. Do you need something tonight?" She stood with the door open a few inches, peering out at the stagecoach-line manager, whose office lay a few yards down the boardwalk.

"I came on a social call." The tall man's smile stopped short of his gray eyes. "It's been a while since we've talked. Thought I'd invite you to dinner—say, Friday evening?"

Libby caught her breath. Cyrus and her husband, Isaac, had been friends. After Isaac's death, Cyrus had made overtures to Libby, but too soon in her widowhood, she'd felt. Cyrus's wife, Mary, was also deceased, so she supposed there was nothing improper about it. Back then, she'd told herself that his timing alone had prompted her to turn him down.

Now it was more than that. Her sharp grief was past, but she knew without any rumination that she didn't wish to form a social alliance with Cyrus. She found his authoritative manner overbearing and repulsive. Actions she'd observed over the past few years confirmed her suspicions that she would not find happiness in the Fennel household. No, if she ever married again, it would be to a far gentler man than Cyrus.

She opened the door a bit wider so as not to appear rude, but she determined not to budge on her answer. "I don't think so, Cyrus, but thank you for asking."

His face hardened. "Why not?"

"I'm content with my situation the way it is."

"Oh, come on, Libby." He leaned closer, and she drew back, shocked that his breath smelled of liquor. "Aren't you tired of being alone? We've both had enough of that. Do you enjoy living by yourself and working all day to earn a living? I'm offering you a chance to put this behind you." His nod encompassed the emporium and Libby's entire life.

His implication that she lived a bleak and pointless existence annoyed her. "I'm not ready to—"

"Of course you're ready. Neither of us is getting any younger. Now's the time, while we can enjoy life together."

She shook her head. "I'm not interested in changing my situation just now, Cyrus."

His eyes narrowed, and he studied her thoughtfully. "Not interested in me?"

"If you insist that I say it, then I suppose not." Her pulse quickened at the angry twitch of his mouth. "We've known each other a long time, Cy. To be frank, I don't think we would suit each other."

"We could have good times, Libby."

"Ah, but we might differ on what constituted good times. I think we'll do best to remain friends and not try to make more of it than that."

He swore softly, and she stepped back.

"You'd best go home. I expect your daughter will have supper waiting when you get there. Good night." She shut the door quickly and once more shot the bolt. Cyrus raised his hands to the door frame and peered in at her. "Good night," she said again and plopped the bar into place. She turned away and hurried up the stairs to her apartment.

As she took out bread, preserves, and cheese for a cold supper, she shook her head. "Drinking, this early. He never did that when Mary was alive." She wondered how his daughter, Isabel, liked that. Isabel taught the village school. A thin, colorless young woman, she'd always kept to herself. Libby had made a point of drawing her out. She'd known Isabel's mother and felt a nebulous duty to make sure Isabel wasn't forgotten and isolated after her mother's death. For the last year, Isabel had taken part in the Ladies' Shooting Club against her father's wishes. Cyrus had declared the club a menace to the town, but he'd backed off somewhat when the ladies' organization had proved its worth. He still wasn't keen on it—which was one more difference between her and Cyrus. Libby loved the shooting club and saw it as a benefit to the members and an asset to the town.

She took her plate to the parlor and sat down on the French settee Isaac had imported for her. She ought to entertain more. What good was all this fancy furniture with no one else to enjoy it? But she was always too tired in the evening. She did well to carve out time for shooting practice.

Cyrus's renewed interest surprised her. She'd assumed he'd given up the notion of wooing her. A couple of years ago, she'd made it clear—or so she thought—that she didn't want a new husband, even if he was the richest man in Fergus and a member of the town council.

She bent over and unlaced her shoes, then kicked them off and leaned back on the cushions. For a moment, she allowed herself to imagine life at the Fennel ranch. Cyrus would ride into town every morning to run the stagecoach line. Isabel would go to the schoolhouse. And Libby—Libby would clean the house and bake and sew, she supposed. Maybe tend the hens and a vegetable garden. She'd probably not see another soul all day, except perhaps a ranch hand or two. None of the bright visits she enjoyed now with her customers. It struck her that, as owner of the emporium, she was privileged to see nearly every resident of the town at least once a month. Who else could claim that?

She tried to conjure up a picture of Cyrus as a loving husband. She'd counted Mary Fennel as a friend, but Libby suspected she'd harbored a deep unhappiness. Without tangible proof, she held the keen memory of a night twelve years ago when she'd been called with Annie Harper to Mary's bedside. Mrs. Fennel had miscarried a baby that night, and she'd wept long afterward.

Libby, in her own awkwardness, had tried to soothe Mary, but she would not be comforted. In a moment alone, when Annie had gone to the kitchen, Libby had patted Mary's shoulder and said, "There, now. You have Isabel. She's a good girl, and perhaps the Lord will give you another child yet."

"No," Mary wailed. "He's punishing me. Cyrus wanted a child of his own, but it's never to be. God won't let me give him that."

Shocked into silence, Libby had listened to her weeping for hours. She had never told anyone of Mary's words, but many times she had pondered them. Her own barrenness had brought on deep sorrow and feelings of inadequacy from which she'd never recovered. But Mary. . .something odd lay behind those words. Though she and Mary visited many more times, Libby had sealed her lips and never brought it up again.

Now Cyrus had come to her door and invited her to dinner—offering much more than that. She shivered. If God had another husband for her, she would consider it. But not Cyrus. Never would she tie herself to that unhappy family.

⭐ CHAPTER 2 ⭐

Isabel Fennel brushed back a wisp of light brown hair that clung to her damp forehead. A cloud of steam engulfed her as she drained the water off the pan of green beans she'd cooked for supper.

The spring term of school was drawing to a close, and she looked forward to the coming break. She found teaching exhilarating—except when Willie Ingram started cutting up. But coming home to her sullen father's dark moods and having to prepare supper for the two of them tired her out. She found it nearly as exhausting as running the boardinghouse on Main Street, as she had for a few weeks last summer between school terms.

She set the bowl of beans on the table and opened the oven to spear the baked potatoes. When everything was on the table, she went to the hallway that ran the length of the ranch house. Her father had come in twenty minutes before and settled in the parlor to read.

"Papa?"

"Here!" His muffled voice and the rattle of newspaper reached her from the front of the house.

"Supper."

She heard his chair creak as he rose. She'd begun to turn back to the kitchen when a peremptory knock sounded on the front door. Likely one of the ranch hands, though they usually came around back. She glanced at the kitchen table, laden with steaming dishes, and hoped whoever it was wouldn't keep Papa talking long. A sudden reminder that most of the ranch hands were off on spring roundup sent her to the doorway to peer down the hall.

Her father shuffled out of the front room, glanced her way, then went to the door and opened it. "Yes?"

She couldn't see past her tall father's form, but she heard a deep male voice say, "Cyrus? Is that you? My, you've aged, h'aint you?"

She frowned and cocked her head so she could hear her father's reply better.

"I...do I...?"

"It's me," the other man crowed. "Kenton."

"No! Kenton? It can't be."

Isabel shook her head, thinking, *Well Papa, obviously it* can *be, whoever Kenton is.* She racked her brain for the name and came up dry.

"Come in." Her father ushered the man inside and steered him into the front room. Isabel barely caught a glimpse of him, but she had the impression of a limping man about her father's age or older. Cyrus Fennel was in his midfifties. This visitor must be someone he'd known many years ago, perhaps from his gold-mining days.

She heard their muffled voices but could no longer make out their words. Wondering what to do, she lingered. After a couple of minutes, with no one advising her and the voices still rumbling in the far room, she scurried about to cover the hot dishes with linen towels, hoping to save a little of their warmth. At least she'd baked a couple of extra potatoes, thinking she'd use them in a hash for tomorrow's breakfast.

If she was expected to put on a company meal, some drop biscuits might be a good addition to the menu. She quickly stirred them up and popped a pan in the oven, hoping it was still hot enough to brown them. The kitchen was so warm, she didn't want to add more fuel to the cook fire.

Ten minutes later, she decided the biscuits were as done as they'd ever be and was placing them in a basket when her father entered the kitchen with a grizzled man limping behind him.

"Isabel, I'd like to introduce you to your uncle Kenton."

Isabel nearly dropped the biscuits. "My uncle?" She stared at the man. His wrinkled face and small, dark eyes held nothing familiar and showed no resemblance that she could see to either side of her family. His dark hair was liberally sprinkled with gray, and his spotty beard reminded her of the old coyote's pelt one of their ranch hands had nailed to the bunkhouse door last winter. His shirt, none too clean, sported frayed cuffs and collar, and his scuffed boots had seen better days.

"Yes dear. This is your mother's brother, Kenton Smith. He's come all the way from back East, and he wanted to meet you."

Isabel felt her face flush. If her mother had a brother named Kenton, she certainly had never heard about him. The whole scene made little sense to her, but she hastened to untie her apron and fling it over the back of her chair. Hesitantly, she approached the man and held out her hand.

"Mr. Smith."

"Oh please, just call me Uncle Kenton." He grinned, exposing a row of crooked teeth and a gap where one should have been on the bottom left side.

"U—uncle Kenton," Isabel managed.

"My, what a fine young lady Mary's little girl grew to be."

His overly enthusiastic smile sickened Isabel, and she turned away. Snatching her apron from the chair, she crossed to her peg rack and hung it up.

"I've invited Kenton to take supper with us," her father said jovially, but his mirth didn't make it as far as his steely eyes.

Isabel walked to her cupboard and took down an extra plate, cup, and saucer.

"There you go, sir." She turned to fetch his silverware, but he held up one finger.

"Uh-uh-uh. Uncle Kenton." Again the sugary smile showed his neglected teeth.

"Uh, yes." She threw him a fleeting smile and scurried to the chest of drawers near the door, where she kept linens. She took her time choosing a napkin for him and sliding it through a pewter ring. When she turned back to the table, Kenton and her father were waiting beside their chairs. She handed Kenton the napkin.

"Thank you, niece."

Her father pulled out her chair, something he almost never did. Was he trying to impress her uncle?

She sat down and looked to her father expectantly. He bowed his head, and so did she. Though she didn't peek to see if Uncle

Kenton imitated them, she had the feeling he did not. Instead, she had the distinct impression that his gaze bored into her all during her father's brief blessing.

"Amen," she said on the heels of her father's. She shook out her napkin and spread it in her lap. "So, Mr.—Uncle Kenton, why is it that I've never met you before or even known of your existence?"

Her father cleared his throat, but Kenton gave a low chuckle.

"I expect I can explain that. Your parents left the area where I lived before you were born, and I've never come to Idaho before. I did try to keep up a correspondence with my. . .sister, but I'm afraid we let it lapse over the years. My fault, really. I never was much of a one to write letters."

"Mary did speak of you now and then, I think," Cyrus said vaguely as he served himself some meat and handed the dish to Kenton.

"Oh, this looks mighty fine." Kenton took a large slice of beef and passed the platter to Isabel. "Have you been keeping house for your pa since your mama died?"

"Yes, she has," Cyrus said.

"I also teach school," Isabel put in, aggravated that her father had neglected to mention it.

"You don't mean it!" Uncle Kenton seemed tickled beyond expectation. "Little Isabel, a teacher. Now ain't that something?" He accepted the dish of green beans from Pa and heaped most of its contents on his plate.

Throughout the meal, Isabel watched the man. Something didn't add up. Her mother had been dead three years, but Isabel had enjoyed her company for nearly thirty, and certainly she would recall if Mama had ever mentioned a brother. Instead, Isabel was certain that Mary Smith Fennel had told her on several occasions that she had no brothers whatsoever, not even a half brother or a stepbrother. She had mentioned an older sister many times. The sister had died of diphtheria at the age of fifteen, when Mary was but nine, and she grieved over dear Leola all her life. But brothers? Nary a one.

"So you lived with Mama and her parents on the farm back in Waterville?" she asked as she cleared their plates and brought the coffeepot.

"Waterford, my dear," her father said quickly, spoiling her attempt to trip up the guest. She'd thought it a clever ploy, but not with Papa there to catch it before the alleged uncle had time to open his mouth.

"Oh yes, of course." Isabel turned a smile on the stranger. "You'll have to forgive me, sir. I was born after my parents came west, so I don't remember that place at all."

"Think nothing of it." Uncle Kenton picked up his cup and sipped his coffee, giving no indication that he intended to answer the question.

"Er. . .so you were Mama's older brother?"

"By a few years."

"Oh." Isabel was certain that her mother would have extolled a brother who fell between her and Leola in age—as certain as she was that the Ladies' Shooting Club met on Monday and Thursday afternoons. Possibly more so, since the club occasionally adjusted their schedule to accommodate funerals, butchering days, and the club president's recent catarrh.

While the guest continued to sip his coffee, Papa scowled at her, his eyebrows nearly meeting in the middle of his brow to form a miniature windbreak. His hard, gray eyes sent such a chilly look her way that Isabel shivered. She turned quickly away and set the coffeepot on the stove. After taking a moment to collect herself, she returned to the table, bearing half a mince pie.

"Would you gentlemen like dessert?"

"Oh, now that looks fine. Pert' near scrumptious." Kenton's lips spread in a wolflike grin.

"Yes, thank you," said Papa.

She cut generous slices for them both but none for herself. She sat down again and stirred her coffee, which didn't need it, and pondered the situation. When the men's cups reached half empty, she jumped up and refilled them.

"Well!" Papa wiped his mouth with his napkin and threaded it through his napkin ring again. "Kenton, what do you say we go into my office and talk things over? Bring your coffee along."

"Certainly." Uncle Kenton rose, nodded to Isabel, and followed her father into the hall.

Isabel sat still at the table, her mind and heart racing. The men walked down the hallway to the small room Papa called his office, and the door closed. Of course, Papa had a larger office in town, where he used to have his assay business and where he now sold tickets for the Wells Fargo line. But he kept a room at the ranch house for himself—a place where he could smoke a cigar, or read, or go over the accounts for the ranch or for one of his businesses in town.

What was the man doing here? Had he truly come to meet his niece? Then why closet himself with Papa? And why had he evaded her questions?

She rose and put away the leftover food, washed and dried the dishes, swept the floor, and filled the water reservoir on the cookstove, but the two men did not emerge from the office.

At a gentle tapping sound, she hurried to the back door. One of the ranch hands stood there with an armload of kindling and stove wood. Five of their six hired men had ridden out that morning for the roundup, leaving only Brady behind to tend to chores at the ranch house.

"Come in, Brady. Thank you." Isabel swung the door wide. Brady had been with them since before Mama died. Older than most of the other hands, he usually hauled firewood and water for Isabel each evening, as he had for her mother. She appreciated that.

Brady walked to the wood box and dumped his load of sticks.

"Saw a horse out front. Your pa got company?"

"Yes."

Brady lingered, and she knew he expected more. He wasn't being nosy, exactly. After all, the ranch's business was his business. Isabel wondered if he wished he was out on the roundup with the others, or if the middle-aged man was glad he didn't have to sleep on the cold ground tonight. Regardless, she could see that he wanted an explanation.

"My uncle is visiting. They're. . .they're talking in Papa's office."

"That right?" Brady frowned but said no more about it. "Thought I'd butcher a couple of hens tomorrow, since we're about out of fresh meat."

Isabel trusted Brady's judgment on such things. Judah, the cook, was off with the other hands to prepare their meals on the roundup, and he usually supervised the butchering. But with the warmer spring weather upon them, they'd used all the frozen meat and all the smoked hams and fish. Only a side or two of bacon remained in the smokehouse. But Brady would keep her in small lots of meat until the other men came home and Judah butchered again.

"Fine. I'll be at school all day, but you can leave them in the lean-to. I'll cook them when I come home."

Brady would hang the chickens where no dogs or other critters could get at them. He nodded and picked up the empty water pail from beside the stove. "I'll get you some more water and coal, Miss Isabel."

When he'd gone out, she went to the hall door and listened. Papa's voice and Uncle Kenton's rose and fell. She wondered if she could distinguish what they said if she were, say, three yards farther down the hallway.

As she turned this over in her mind, Brady entered again through the back door and set the full bucket of water beside the stove. He dumped the coal into the scuttle by the wood box. Isabel was thankful that her father was blessed with enough resources to buy coal. The town of Fergus had long mourned its dashed hopes of getting a railroad spur. Coal must be hauled in by freighters and cost more than some of the town's one hundred or so residents could afford. Firewood was hard to come by, but some scoured the mountains for it in the dead of winter. Old-timers told of when dried buffalo chips were available on the prairie a few miles distant, but that era had long since closed.

"Is the gentleman staying over?"

Isabel stared at him, dismayed at the thought. "Oh, I...I think not." But where *would* Uncle Kenton stay the night? She supposed Papa might send him a mile to the boardinghouse, but was that polite, to shuffle a relative off like that? She certainly hoped Papa wouldn't invite him to stay at the ranch.

"Anything else you need tonight, Miss Isabel?"

"No, thank you."

"I was going to ask the boss if I could ride into town for a bit."

Isabel looked away. Of course Brady would want to stop in at the Nugget saloon. She hated the place, but her own father patronized it. He let his hands go to town on paydays. She knew Papa would say yes tonight if Brady asked him, since it was a quiet evening. The seasoned cowboy rarely overindulged, but he liked a glass or two and some company.

"I hate to disturb them." She nodded and met his gaze. "I'm sure it's all right, Brady."

"Thanks. I won't be gone but an hour."

The cowboy touched his hat brim and disappeared, shutting the door behind him. Isabel shivered. The kitchen was no longer overly warm. No doubt the temperature would drop even farther tonight. Spring took its time settling into these mountains, and they still had to keep a fire all night. Her father, being the richest man in Fergus, wouldn't feel the bite of cold.

Kenton Smith, she reflected, looked less prosperous than his brother-in-law. A thought oozed into her mind that he might have come looking for a job or a leg up in the world. Kin was kin, and one didn't turn family away.

She looked at the clock. Quarter to eight. Should she wait to see if the men came out and joined her for further conversation? She didn't want to spend any more time with Uncle Kenton. He had none of her mother's sweetness and charm. He didn't even look like Mama. And if Mama had been proud of him, she'd have told her daughter about him.

Maybe she could quietly retire and avoid seeing him again. But just in case, she'd better check the linens in the spare room. She blew out the lamp on the table.

As she tiptoed down the dusky hallway, she heard Uncle Kenton's voice rise in pitch to rival Bertha Runnels' soprano.

"No, you listen to me!"

Isabel gasped and backed up against the wall across from the closed office door, her pulse throbbing. Her father's voice came, calmer and firm.

"Sit down, Kenton. We can work this out."

Isabel didn't want to hear any more. Papa said people in town were always asking him for money for one thing or another. Probably this no-account uncle she'd never heard of wanted some, too. Come to think of it, that might explain why she'd never heard of Uncle Kenton. Maybe he was a leech, and Mama hadn't wanted him to find them and beg for a handout.

She wrapped her arms around herself and hurried toward her room, passing the door to the spare room. Better take a look.

A quick glance told her the chamber was ready if her father decided to put her uncle in there, but she hoped he wouldn't. Feeling a bit selfish and uncharitable, she sent up a quick prayer. *Lord, if Thou carest about my comfort, please do not let that man stay the night in this house.*

Guilt crept over her, and she stopped praying as she walked to her own room. He was her mother's brother, after all. She set her spectacles on the dresser and took her time brushing her long, light brown hair and thinking about tomorrow's lessons. The fourth graders would multiply fractions, and she had no doubt Will Ingram would have trouble with the concept. In the end, he would probably *make* trouble to distract her from the arithmetic lesson.

No sound of the stranger's leaving had reached her. Not for the first time, she wished she could see the front dooryard from her window, but her room was on the back side of the house. Finally, she drew the curtains and undressed. If Papa came out of his office this late and expected her to play hostess, shame on him.

She cracked the window open, turned out her lamp, and crawled under the quilts. Once or twice, she heard their voices, but when she raised her head, the tones had dropped again. After a long lull, she drifted into near sleep, but suddenly she opened her eyes. A regular crunching sound came to her, not from down the hall, but from outside. Hoofbeats?

Isabel sat up in the dark.

The sound continued but got no fainter or louder. She rose and went to her window. It seemed to come from the direction of the barn. She stuck her feet into her shoes and grabbed a big shawl. Wrapping it around her, she crossed the room, opened the door, and stood listening. She heard nothing from within the house. A faint glow showed that a lamp still burned somewhere at the front of the dwelling. She walked down the hall, her shoes clumping a little since she hadn't buttoned them all the way up.

The front room was empty, and the table lamp burned low.

"Papa?"

No one answered.

She stole to the kitchen and opened the back door an inch. Again she heard the *crunch-crunch*, with a bit of a metallic clang to it.

After a quick look around, she gathered the heavy flannel skirt of her nightdress and tiptoed across the yard between the house and the barn. A pause in the noise made her flatten herself against the rough boards of the barn siding. Her breath came in deep gulps. She made herself exhale slowly and quietly, though her heart raced. A clack came from behind the barn, and then a moment's stillness. Measuring the distance from her position to the kitchen door, she wondered just how foolish she was.

The crunching began again, and she edged toward the back corner of the barn. A glow brighter than starlight and lower than the heavens spilled around the edge of the wall. She sneaked one step closer and another, until her icy fingers touched the boards at the back corner.

Crunch-splat. Crunch-splat.

She knew what made that sound. To confirm her inkling, she peeked around the corner.

A kerosene lantern sat on the ground near a small heap of dirt. Her father, tall and broad-shouldered, cast a huge shadow against the back wall of the barn as he wielded a spade.

Isabel pulled back around the edge and leaned against the boards with her eyes shut. What did it mean? Her father was digging a hole in the night. . .for what? And where was Uncle Kenton? Maybe he was there, too, and she hadn't seen him in the shadows.

Slowly, she leaned forward, until one eye passed the corner. No Uncle Kenton. Her father scooped up another spadeful of dirt. A cold breeze caught the fringe of Isabel's shawl and her loose hair. She drew back, not wanting to think about the scene. She gathered her nightdress and sidled along to the front of the barn wall. As quietly as she could, she fled across the barnyard to the kitchen door. Once inside, she ran down the hall to her room and closed the door behind her. She sat down on her bed, panting. There was no doubt.

Her father was not opening the hole; he was filling it in.

★ CHAPTER 3 ★

Are you going to Boise to fetch Rose?" Ethan asked as he shuffled two biscuits from the serving plate to his own.

Hiram shook his head. He'd thought about Rose's telegram for the last two hours, and the more he considered its implications, the more they troubled him.

As she often did, his sister spoke for him. "She's taking the stagecoach tomorrow."

"That road has been open only a few days." Ethan frowned as he buttered his biscuit. "The stage had trouble getting through from Reynolds yesterday."

"Well, if the stage can't get through, chances are a wagon couldn't either," Trudy said.

"True." Ethan shot a troubled glance at Hiram. "What'll you do? Will she stay here with you?"

"I don't suppose we could send her to the boardinghouse." Trudy frowned.

The idea of boarding Rose elsewhere hadn't occurred to Hiram, and he looked eagerly to Trudy.

"Don't look so hopeful. We couldn't do that, and you know it."

Hiram shrugged and put his knife to his venison steak.

"She's family." Trudy nodded as though that settled it. She picked up half her biscuit and smeared it with butter. "It's just plain rude to expect kinfolk to pay for their lodging."

Hiram eyed her sidelong. He and Trudy had been alone too long. She had an uncanny way of reading his unvoiced thoughts.

"Not even if we paid for it," she added.

Hiram drooped in his chair and turned his attention back to his food. His little sister was a good cook, and he would miss that if she married Ethan and moved out of the house. For eight years—no, nine—she'd been his cook, housekeeper, and nearest companion. She understood him. She let him grieve when he got in the sorrowful mood over Violet's passing, and she left him alone when he needed it. She even helped him in his business, testing people's guns after he'd fixed them.

She'd started that shortly after she came. Folks had brought Hiram a passel of work in some misguided attempt to keep him too busy to think of how Violet and their baby boy had died. Hiram had worked on those guns day and night. And as they piled up, repaired, Trudy had asked him if she should take them back to their owners.

"I'll need to fire them first," he'd said.

"I could do that for you. Just make sure they shoot okay?"

She'd taken on the job from that day, and her frequent practice had made an excellent shot out of her. So good that other women came to her now for lessons.

Ethan cleaned his plate before he addressed Trudy again. "So, you expect her on tomorrow's noon stagecoach?"

"Probably. I'm getting the front bedroom ready."

Hiram cast a worried glance toward the parlor, where the stairs went up. He was glad he'd be down here in his bedroom and Rose would stay in the bedroom upstairs. The front room was nicer than his sister's little room at the back, but Trudy didn't like the noise from the street and the saloon at night, so she used the snug room under the eaves, above the kitchen.

"How long is she staying?" Ethan asked.

Good question, Hiram thought—one he'd like answered, too.

"We don't know yet," Trudy said. A little frown settled between her eyebrows. The unspoken implication hung in the air. Like Hiram, she hoped Rose wouldn't extend her visit beyond a few weeks.

"Well, if there's anything I can do, let me know." Ethan's gaze left Trudy's face long enough to include Hiram, and he nodded his thanks.

After a cup of coffee and two pieces of pie, Hiram sat back

with a sigh. He surely would miss Trudy's presence, and not just in the kitchen. That was, if the sheriff ever got around to popping the question. The two walked out in the evenings and had made eyes at each other for nearly a year now. Even though it meant giving up his housekeeper, Hiram thought the time had come. Of course, he'd never say as much. Like him, Ethan took his time to come to a decision and even longer to act on it. But from the way those two looked at each other, everyone in town could tell the decision was as good as made. The only thing lacking was the formal proposal.

"Well, I'm glad Rose gave us a day's warning and didn't show up unannounced." Trudy had a faraway look, and Hiram figured she was ticking off the cleaning chores she'd do before Rose arrived. She stood. "More coffee?"

Hiram shook his head.

"No, thanks," Ethan said. "Want to walk tonight?"

"It's a little windy."

Ethan nodded reluctantly. "It's chilly." He waited, watching her, obviously hoping she'd brave the cold and the gale for him.

"I'd make a fire in the parlor," Hiram offered.

Ethan flicked a surprised glance at him. Hiram wished he'd stayed quiet, as usual. But if Trudy didn't want to go out into the cold. . .

"Thanks, Hi, but I'll wear my cloak and bonnet. Let me wash up these dishes first."

"I'll dry." Ethan started carrying plates from the table to the dishpan on the sideboard.

Hiram stood and gathered his own dishes. Trudy poured hot water into her dishpan and added soap. Hiram made a silent exit into the front room, where he had a half-finished gunstock waiting for him. If Ethan needed more time alone with Trudy to get his proposal out, Hiram would do all he could to provide it. He took a last glance back through the doorway into the kitchen and saw Trudy laughing as she tied an apron around the sheriff's waist. Hiram smiled and went to his comfortable chair.

A few minutes later, Trudy came to the doorway.

"We're going to walk down toward the river and back."

Hiram lifted a hand in salute. He wouldn't worry about her in

Ethan's care. Besides, it was too chilly for them to stay out late.

The back door shut on the laughing pair, and he sat in the comfortable quiet of the house, sanding the wood he held. He was happy for Trudy. She'd come as a gangly sixteen-year-old girl, powerless to help him in his fresh grief. Over the last nine years, she'd grown into a beautiful woman. She'd held off potential suitors until Hiram had wondered if she would remain a spinster for his sake.

Then he'd realized she was waiting for Ethan. For a long time, Ethan Chapman had glided along in self-made isolation, ignoring everything but his own hurt. Last summer the town council had thrust sheriffhood upon him. And he'd finally sat up and taken note of the town and Gertrude Dooley.

Hiram's contented smiled soured when he remembered the telegram. Rose Caplinger was as unlike her younger sister, Violet, as a buzzard was unlike a swallow. She might be handsome— Hiram couldn't really remember—but she had the sharpest tongue in Boothbay Harbor, Maine. That he recalled quite clearly. More than once, she'd been informally censured in the neighborhood for gossip. She had none of Violet's gentle spirit and always sought the limelight for herself. If Rose wasn't the center of attention, then the day was not worth living.

He looked about the room once more, regretting the extra work her visit would cause Trudy and the intrusion into their happy existence. What would happen to his peace when Rose arrived?

Isabel had the coffee scalding hot and the eggs nearly set in the pan before her father came to the kitchen. As he did every weekday morning, he appeared for breakfast fully dressed in the clothes he would wear to town. He was a somewhat snappy dresser, as men's fashions went in Fergus. With the Reverend Phineas Benton and Dr. James Kincaid, he completed the roster of men who wore a coat and tie every day.

He pulled a watch from his trouser pocket and consulted it before taking his seat. "Seven-oh-four."

"Are you sending out both coaches today?"

"Yes indeed. Winter's back is broken, and the line is open for business in both directions." He flapped his napkin out and laid it in his lap.

Isabel filled a plate with eggs, two leftover biscuits, and two sausage patties, and placed it before him.

"Papa?"

"Yes? That looks good."

"Thank you. Papa?"

"Yes?"

"Tell me about Uncle Kenton."

"Kenton?" Her father looked up at her briefly with a small frown. He picked up his fork. "What about him?"

"Well. . .where is he?"

"He left last evening."

"Obviously, but where did he go?" Isabel turned to get him a mug of coffee.

"Oh, I believe he's traveling about. He said he may come back again after a bit. You'll see him again, I'll warrant."

She set the steaming mug beside his plate and took her seat opposite him.

"Papa?"

"Hmm?"

She waited until he looked into her eyes.

"Why have I never heard of Uncle Kenton until last night? Mama told me many times that she never had a brother—only her and Leola."

Her father coughed and covered his face with his napkin for a moment. When he revealed it again, he looked rather blotchy and uncomfortable.

"My dear, I can only tell you the truth."

"Please do."

He sighed and returned the napkin to his lap. "You're grown up, and you deserve to know it. The fact is, I advised Mary to tell you years ago—certainly by the time you turned twenty-one. But no, she wanted to protect you."

"Protect me? From her brother?"

Papa cleared his throat and toyed with his fork. "Yes, actually. She didn't want you to ever know about his. . .his past. And she thought that as long as we were in the West and he was in the East, you would never know about him and the disgrace he brought on her family."

Isabel stared at him. Her mother had never hinted at disgrace or regret concerning the Smith family. She'd spoken with longing about her parents and her childhood home, the happy days with her sister until the frail Leola sickened.

"I. . .don't understand."

Her father gave a big sigh and reached across the table for her hand. "It pains me to tell you this, my dear, but your Uncle Kenton spent several years in prison."

Isabel swallowed hard and wished she'd poured herself some coffee. "What for?"

"It's just as well if you don't know the details. Your mother was mortified by the scandal, and her family rarely talked about Kenton. She figured you'd be happier not knowing he existed." Papa ate his eggs, and Isabel watched him, unsatisfied.

After a moment's silence, she got up and fixed her own plate, though she didn't feel like eating. The memories badgered her as she sat down again and nibbled at her food. She didn't recall much about her early years, though there had been a farm in Nebraska. When she was seven, Papa left her and Mama there and came ahead of them to Idaho Territory, prospecting for gold. A year later, he'd sent for them, and they'd ridden the train as far as they could. Papa had met them in Salt Lake City and brought them to the boom town of Fergus, where by then, he ran the assay office.

Isabel ruminated on her father's words. She had a criminal for a relative: a man who'd done something so dire her father wouldn't even name the deed. What else did she not know about her family?

Her father took a second watch from his vest pocket and opened the case.

"Would you like more coffee?" she asked.

"No, I think I'll leave now and stop at the sheriff's before I open the stagecoach office." He stood and reached for his hat. "Want me to drop you at the schoolhouse?"

It was early yet. Though she could use some extra time to prepare in the classroom, Isabel had her domestic chores to think of, too. "Thank you, but I'll stay and do the dishes first. Oh, and Papa, I'll be going to the shooting club after school."

Her father scowled. Any mention of the Ladies' Shooting Club of Fergus put him in a foul mood. It was Isabel's one rebellion, and she stuck to it with a bit of pluck that surprised her.

"I thought they met during school hours."

"They do, but Trudy and the others agreed to meet at three now that the sun sets later. I appreciate their doing that for me."

He said nothing but clapped his hat to his light brown hair. She thought him quite handsome with the touches of gray at his temples. Not for the first time, she wondered if he'd thought of remarrying. Of course, he had a built-in cook and housekeeper. Should she ever leave him, he had the means to hire someone to do for him, as he had hired the Thistles to run the boardinghouse and the cowboys to do the ranch work. Did he ever long for companionship beyond what he got from her and his male friends in town? Once she'd thought he'd eyed Libby Adams wistfully, but she didn't know if he'd ever approached the beautiful storekeeper.

"I'll be here for supper," she said as he stepped toward the door. "You'll be home to eat, won't you?" It wasn't the question she wanted to ask, but she needed what information he was willing to give. The other would have to wait, perhaps forever. She would not dare ask.

"I'm not sure."

She sighed as his footsteps echoed down the hall and the front door closed. Would he linger in town and visit the Nugget before he came home? She'd have to prepare supper and have it waiting in case he did show up to eat it.

The question she'd stifled several times during their conversation overcame all other thoughts and reared up, dark and threatening. In the darkness of the night, what had Papa buried behind the barn?

★ CHAPTER 4 ★

Ethan Chapman entered the jailhouse whistling. No prisoners, which meant he'd slept in his own bed and had a good breakfast with his two ranch hands, brothers Spin and Johnny McDade. The sun shone on Fergus, though a cool wind blew down from the mountain passes. The river ran high from snow melt on the summits. And Trudy was in her kitchen—he could smell her baking from next door. Gingerbread. With the wind out of the south, he was pretty sure he knew what he'd have for dessert at noontime.

The office, cell, and back room retained the same neat condition he'd left them in yesterday. Not much call to stick around this morning. When he wasn't needed at the jailhouse, Ethan liked to walk about town to let himself be seen. His visits with the business owners reassured them that Fergus would remain peaceful. They hadn't had a serious crime since last summer, when the Penny Man had kept them all on edge for a few weeks.

He turned northward first and strolled past the boardinghouse. Mr. Thistle, a one-armed Civil War veteran, worked at washing the windows fronting on Main Street.

"Morning, Sheriff."

"Good morning, Mr. Thistle. How's business?"

"Pretty good since the stage started running again. We expect some guests to come in today. Rilla's fixing lamb stew for luncheon if you're interested."

"Thank you. We'll see." Ethan watched him adroitly wring out his rag with one hand, then ambled on past one of Cy Fennel's vacant buildings left over from the town's boom period and past the

29

Nugget. The saloon was quiet now, but in twelve hours or so, things would heat up. Ethan would return then, with his damping influence on the party atmosphere. He could hear a rhythmic ringing from the smithy and crossed Main Street, since the Nugget was the last business on the west side of that end. As he stepped into the smithy, his friend Griffin Bane glanced up from his work and nodded.

"Ethan."

"Howdy, Griff."

The blacksmith hammered fussily at the edge of the hoe blade he was shaping, then plunged it into a tub of water. The sizzle and sharp-smelling cloud of steam comforted Ethan. Everything was right in Fergus.

"Livery busy these days?" he asked.

"Tolerable." With his tongs, Griffin seized a new piece of bar stock and stuck it into the forge. "We've got two coach teams to switch out today."

"So I've heard. That's good." When he went outside again, Ethan looked toward the livery stable, which Griffin also owned. The towering smith had bought it when the original owner moved on to a more prosperous town. For now, things looked quiet. The six-mule replacement teams for the stagecoaches were probably grazing out back.

Ethan wandered down the board sidewalk on the east side of Main. Beyond a vacant building was Charles Walker's feed store. He stepped inside, hoping to see Walker, but an employee was there alone, counting bags of oats. Ethan said a quick 'Good morning' and went out again.

Next came the stagecoach line's office. Cy Fennel was unlocking the door.

"Oh Sheriff, I was thinking of walking over to see you this morning."

"You're in town early, Mr. Fennel."

"Yes, well, things are picking up now, and I have some bookwork to go over. But I wanted to ask you something. Step in for a minute, won't you?"

Ethan followed him into the small office where Cyrus sold stagecoach tickets. He avoided looking at the discoloration on the board floor near the stove, which marked the spot where a corpse had once lain. He didn't like remembering that.

Cyrus sat down behind his desk and laid his keys and a ledger on the surface.

"What is it?" Ethan asked.

"I wondered if you know who owns the Peart place now."

Ethan raised his eyebrows, which made his hat ride up a little. "Frank and Milzie Peart's land?"

"That's right. Who's the owner?"

"Well, I don't rightly know."

"Didn't you have to contact the heirs when Milzie died?"

Ethan shook his head. "I reported it to the marshal and took an inventory, but I'm no lawyer."

Cyrus stroked his chin. "Maybe I'll take a look next time I'm in Boise. There must be an heir."

"My understanding is that they had no will and no surviving children. When I went through Mrs. Peart's belongings, I didn't find any evidence that she had living relatives. No letters or anything like that."

Cyrus shrugged. "Well, now that we've got us a preacher and a doctor, maybe we should try to entice a lawyer to come to Fergus."

The idea startled Ethan. His pa had always said lawyers were more trouble than they were worth. And he wasn't sure he wanted Cyrus poking into the Peart estate. Cyrus had already bought up more property in and around town than any one man ought to own. He cleared his throat. "I guess I could look into it a little more. Write some letters, maybe."

Cyrus stood and hung up his hat. "Good. Let me know if you find out anything, Sheriff."

Ethan was dismissed, no question. He turned and went out, but his complacency had wilted. Cyrus had that effect on people. And he usually got them to do what he wanted.

Across the street, smoke rose from the Dooleys' chimney, reminding him of the gingerbread. Of course. Trudy. She and her friends would rise to the challenge. He would invite the Ladies' Shooting Club to help him discover Milzie Peart's heir.

★ CHAPTER 5 ★

Hiram removed his hat as he entered the emporium with his sister shortly before noon. The smells of cinnamon, soap, leather, and vinegar hit his nostrils with a not unpleasant mix. Libby Adams kept the store tidy, and people tended to gravitate there to have a chat with neighbors and get the latest news.

Hiram hung back as Trudy approached the counter. His stomach rumbled because they'd put off lunch until after Rose's arrival on the stagecoach, and he wouldn't want the lovely Mrs. Adams to hear such an embarrassing sound. But he could watch with appreciation as she measured out a pound of coffee for Bertha Runnels. When Mrs. Runnels had paid for her purchase and turned away, Libby greeted Trudy with a broad smile, and Hiram inhaled carefully. Seeing Libby smile was as good as watching the sun rise from the top of War Eagle Mountain.

After a moment, he looked away and found some hardware to study, lest people notice him watching Mrs. Adams for an inordinate length of time. Couldn't have folks drawing unwarranted conclusions, and Hiram was not one to go about staring at women.

"How may I help you today?" Libby asked his sister.

After Mrs. Runnels was out the door, Hiram sneaked another glance. Libby's rose-colored dress set off her golden hair and blue eyes. She had to be at least his age, maybe a year or two older, but she was still the beauty of Fergus. Looking at her gave him the same lightheaded appreciation as when he'd first handled a .44-caliber six-shooter.

"I need some extra ammunition for this afternoon," Trudy told her. "Don't forget we're meeting an hour later than usual so Isabel can join us after school lets out."

"Of course. I'll remind any of the ladies who come in this morning." Libby took a small box from beneath the counter and set it down. "Anything else for you or Hiram?" Her gaze beamed across the room and caught him looking. Hiram gave a quick nod and turned to examine the hammers and pry bars on the display behind him.

"I'm sure there's something I should be getting," Trudy said. "Hi's sister-in-law is coming in on the Boise stagecoach, and there's bound to be something we'll need during her visit."

"Oh? You didn't mention that you expected a visitor."

Trudy gave a dry chuckle. "That's because we didn't know. She sent a telegram yesterday afternoon from Boise."

"Oh my."

"Yes." Hiram looked over his shoulder in time to see his sister grimace. "I expect we'll get by. Let's see. . . . Maybe I'll take some tea and extra sugar. Rose might not like to drink coffee."

Libby fetched the items. "Do you have plenty of cream?"

Trudy frowned. "I'll have to ask Annie Harper to send some with the milk tomorrow morning. Unless you have some. . ."

"I have a can in the icebox." Once again Libby obliged and poured a pint into a glass bottle.

"I guess that's all." Trudy turned and beckoned to her brother. "Can you carry these things for me, Hi? I didn't bring a basket."

"Take one of mine," Libby said. "You can return it later."

Before either of the Dooleys could speak, she had placed Trudy's purchases in a light carrying basket woven of willow sprouts.

"Thank you. That's a lot like my market basket," Trudy said.

"Well, it was Violet's, but I've used it ever since I came."

The mention of his deceased wife reminded Hiram of Rose's imminent arrival, and he glanced toward the front window. No sign of the stagecoach yet.

Trudy picked up on his anxiety. "We'd best get over to the stage stop. Thank you, Libby."

"Will you bring your guest to the shooting club?" Libby asked.

Trudy's eyes darkened. "I'm not sure yet. Though what we'll do with her if she doesn't care to go, I'm sure I can't imagine."

Libby's gentle smile eased Hiram's own misgivings on that very topic. He didn't like the idea of sitting home with Rose while Trudy had fun with the club members. Unfortunately, gentlemen were not welcome at the club meetings.

"I'm sure things will work out."

Trudy nodded. "I expect so. I've been praying ever since Hi brought that telegram home."

Another customer came to the counter and stood behind them. Hiram glanced her way and nodded. Mrs. Storrey, her arms full of yard goods and notions, nodded back. Hiram reached for the basket.

"I'll see you this afternoon," Trudy said to Libby, and Hiram followed her out the door. He put his hat on as they gained the boardwalk and strolled beside Trudy toward the Wells Fargo office with the basket dangling from his hand.

Cyrus Fennel stood just outside his office door, looking anxiously northward, past the Nugget and the smithy, toward Boise.

"Good day, Dooleys." Cyrus barely looked at them as he eyed the road and then his pocket watch. To Hiram's amusement, he pulled out a second watch and compared it with the first.

"Stagecoach late?" Trudy asked.

"Not yet." Cyrus's lips thinned to a grim line. "That Bill Stout had better get the coach here in one piece. Folks have been waiting months for regular service to Boise to resume."

"Still snow in the passes." Hiram gazed off toward Boise, too, but he couldn't see farther than the mountains beyond the end of Main Street.

"They got through on Tuesday."

The only traffic on the north end of the street consisted of Ted Hire walking from the smithy to the Nugget, where he worked. Hiram set down the basket.

Cyrus eyed them with sudden interest. "Do you folks expect someone coming in today?"

"Yes sir," said Trudy. "We look for Mrs. Caplinger of the state of Maine."

Cyrus whistled. "She's had a long trip. Relative of yours?"

Trudy glanced at Hiram, and he shrugged. It would get around town soon enough, anyway. They'd already told Libby, who was not a gossip but definitely a link in the Fergus news chain.

"Our sister-in-law," Trudy said.

Cyrus's eyebrows flew up. "Oh? That would be the late Mrs. Dooley's sister?"

"Yes." Trudy's face brightened. "Oh look. Here comes the sheriff."

Hiram exhaled, feeling extra friendship for Ethan for arriving in time to curb an awkward conversation. The sheriff emerged from Gold Lane, the dusty little side street that sprouted westward between the jail and the boardinghouse. He caught sight of them and smiled, veering across Main Street to join them. Hiram wondered if he'd planned to go to their back door and beg some lunch. A glint of sun caught Ethan's badge on the front of his jacket. The tall, broad-shouldered young man did make an impressive figure of a lawman, and it was no wonder Trudy admired him so—though Trudy had lost her heart to Ethan long before he began wearing the star.

"Howdy," Ethan said, mainly in Trudy's direction, but swinging his head enough to include the men. A wagon rolled up the street, and rancher Arthur Tinen Jr. and his wife, Starr, stopped in front of the emporium.

"Hello," Starr called, waving as her husband reached to help her down from the wagon. Trudy, Ethan, and Hiram waved back, and the Tinens entered the store.

"You got the time, Chapman?" Cyrus asked.

"Nope, 'fraid not."

Hiram looked up at the sun, where it hovered on the edge of a noncommittal cloud. Cyrus wouldn't bother to ask him if he had a watch.

"They're late." Cyrus snapped the case of one watch shut and stuffed it into his vest pocket. "If Ned Harmon and Bill Stout were out drinking last night, I'll fire them both."

Trudy gritted her teeth, her eyes smoky gray. Cyrus chafed Hiram's sensibilities, too. He arched his eyebrows at his sister in a silent signal. Someday he might do battle with the mighty Fennel, but today's snappishness wasn't worth fussing over.

Ethan stepped closer to Trudy. "Say, would the ladies of the club be willing to help me out? Mr. Fennel was asking me this morning about the Peart place. I may need to write several letters to get information. Do you think the ladies would be interested?"

"I know they would," Trudy said.

She and Bitsy Shepard, owner of the Spur & Saddle saloon, which rivaled the Nugget, had served as temporary sheriff's deputies for a brief time last summer, and the ladies took their duty to the town seriously. Ethan's expression cleared at her ready acceptance, and he shot a satisfied glance at Fennel. Sometimes Cyrus wanted more than folks could give him, and Hiram knew some of the wrangling Ethan had gone through with the stubborn man. But if the shooting club helped, Ethan could rest easy. A heap of work would be accomplished, whether the ladies got the information he wanted or not.

But the fact that Fennel wanted someone to investigate the ownership of poor old Milzie Peart's land troubled Hiram. He caught Ethan's eye. Ethan nodded unhappily, but by unspoken agreement, they said no more in front of Cyrus.

Trudy pushed back a strand of her light hair. "I'm sure we can help if it's a letter-writing campaign you need. I'll mention it at this afternoon's meeting."

"Thank you kindly," Ethan said.

A drumming of hoofbeats and a rattle of wheels pulled their attention to the north end of the street once more. Hiram exhaled. The stagecoach. He squared his shoulders and drew Trudy back from the edge of the boardwalk. She was apt to be so busy casting sweet glances at Ethan that she wouldn't think to corral her skirts and get out of the way.

The coach had advanced up the street at a good clip and was nearly upon them. Cyrus stepped forward, still holding one watch open and glaring at the driver.

"Whoa!" Bill Stout pulled the horses up so that the coach door sat even with his boss. The leather straps creaked, and the coach swayed. The horses panted and shook their heads.

"You're ten minutes late." Cyrus's harsh tone cut through the cool air.

Bill sighed and shook his head. "It's heavy going through the passes, Mr. Fennel. I told you that day before yesterday."

"I expect you to maintain the schedule."

"When humanly possible," Bill said evenly. "I hope we've got mules for the next leg."

By this time, Ned, the shotgun messenger, had stowed his weapon and leaped down from the box to open the door for the passengers.

The first person to fill the doorway, in a flurry of lavender skirts, pleats, soutache braid, and covered buttons, was Rose Caplinger. The woman's dark hair was swept up beneath a large hat, and her snapping brown eyes critically surveyed what she could see of Main Street. Cyrus stepped forward quickly, but Ned already had extended a hand to her.

"Watch your step, ma'am," Ned said.

When Rose's dainty feet in patent leather shoes hit the boardwalk, Cyrus edged Ned aside.

"Welcome to Fergus. I'm Cyrus Fennel. I trust you had a pleasant journey with the Wells Fargo line?"

"Pleasant?" Rose blinked up at him. "Not unless your idea of *pleasant* is bouncing over every rock in Idaho Territory at high speed and being jostled by a drummer and a herdsman stinking of sheep, while a quartet of Chinese miners stares at you from across the coach."

Said drummer and shepherd were staggering out of the coach while the miners hung back; whether out of courtesy or intimidation, Hiram couldn't tell. But the time had come when he must step up and rescue Rose from Cyrus's arrogance—or perhaps rescue Cyrus from Rose's ill temper. At any rate, he forced one leg forward, then the other, until he stood next to Cyrus.

Rose's gaze lit on him, and the sour cast fled from her face. Her eyes softened. Her lips trembled.

"Hiram Dooley!" With only this brief warning, she flung herself at him.

★ CHAPTER 6 ★

My dear, dear brother-in-law." Rose entangled her arms about Hiram's neck, pushing him back three steps so that Trudy had to jump aside, nearly upsetting the willow basket. Rose placed a heartfelt smack on Hiram's jaw. It probably would have landed higher if Hiram hadn't had the presence of mind to raise his chin as her puckered lips reached toward him. Trudy felt her face flush in sympathy for her brother.

"Uh, good day, Rose." Hiram's voice sounded somewhat constricted. He held his hands inches from Rose's back, obviously trying to avoid placing them on her person, darting desperate glances toward Trudy and Ethan.

Not one to neglect her duty, Trudy came to the rescue.

"Rose, how lovely to have you here." She touched Rose's shoulder, and the newly arrived lady gave a reluctant sigh and released Hiram.

"Gert." Rose turned and eyed her from head to toe. "My, how you've grown."

Trudy's strained smile congealed on her face. "I go by Trudy now, if you don't mind."

"What? Oh." Rose's gaze had already strayed to Ethan, who stood comfortingly close to Trudy. "And who is this dashing gentleman? A lawman, I see."

Trudy's heart beat faster. Flirting was not the norm in Fergus. Fluttering lashes and coy smiles tended to occur behind the doors of the Nugget or the Spur & Saddle. She felt like taking Ethan's arm and staking her claim. Ethan, however, seemed not to mind the pretty woman's admiration.

"Hello. You must be Violet's sister." He held out his hand, and Rose took it eagerly.

"Yes, I am."

"Rose Caplinger, this is our sheriff, Ethan Chapman," Trudy said dryly. "Ethan, Mrs. Caplinger."

"How *do* you do?" Rose's eyes flicked back and forth between Ethan and Hiram. "My, I can see that this town is the place to find handsome gentlemen."

At that moment, Ned Harmon plopped a large valise and a carpet bag onto the boardwalk beside them. He pushed back his wide-brimmed hat. "Where do you want your trunk, ma'am?"

"Trunk?" Trudy squeaked. She looked at the roof of the stagecoach, where a huge black steamer trunk was roped down.

"Oh anywhere, thank you," Rose said with a smile. "I'm sure my brother-in-law has a conveyance nearby."

"Uh, no, actually, we live just across the street and down a bit." Trudy fixed Ned with a meaningful frown. "I don't suppose you and Bill could drop it over there for us?"

"Well. . ."

Hiram slid a coin into Ned's hand.

"Surely." Ned tipped his hat to the ladies, nodded at Hiram, and turned to the clutch of men waiting for their bags.

"Well then," Trudy said, "Let's get you over to the house. You must be famished, and I have luncheon ready."

Ethan helped Hiram with the luggage, and Trudy picked up the basket. By the time they'd walked to the Dooleys' house, Bill Stout had brought the coach down the street. Hiram dropped Rose's valise on the tender grass beside the path and hurried to help Ned lower the trunk to earth. The question of just how long Rose intended to stay niggled at Trudy's mind, but she said nothing.

Ethan scooped up the valise, which more than counterbalanced the big carpet bag he already carried, and followed the two women around to the back door.

As they wound around the rear corner of the cozy little house, Rose gazed about, and her nose crinkled. "Oh, you have livestock."

"Just a few hens and two horses." Trudy opened the kitchen door and held it for Rose. Ethan had to turn sideways to get in with the luggage. He looked questioningly at her, and Trudy said, "In the front room, if you please."

Rose removed her hat and looked about for a place to settle it. "Oh, my hatboxes. I must have left them in the coach."

"Here, let me take that." Trudy took the hat, a feathery, red velvet creation that was more stylish than even Libby Adams would wear, and placed it on the rack near the door. It hung there next to Trudy's second best cotton sunbonnet and Hiram's battered "barn hat," appearing so flamboyant beside them that in Trudy's mind it walked a narrow line between elegant and tawdry, barely coming down on the fashionable side. She couldn't help being reminded of one of Bitsy Shepard's hats.

Ethan edged into the kitchen from the parlor minus the bags.

"Would you mind going out and asking Ned to see if Mrs. Caplinger's hatboxes are still in the coach?" Trudy asked.

"Don't mind if I do." Ethan bolted out the door so fast neither woman had time to thank him.

Rose turned to Trudy instead. "Thank you, Gert. I can't do without my hats."

"I go by Trudy now."

"What a quaint kitchen. Don't you have electricity?"

"No, we don't. It will probably be a long time before they bring electric lines up these mountains."

"But you have telegraph wires." Rose arched her shapely dark brows. "You did get my message?"

"We did. But we still don't have electricity."

Rose nodded and gazed toward the work counter and woodstove. "And no pump?"

"It's out back."

"Oh my dear. You still have to haul all your water?"

Trudy shrugged. "It's not so bad."

"But on wash day. And to think of all the trouble when one wants a bath. . . ." Rose looked hopelessly down at her dust-coated clothing. "Oh my."

Trudy pulled in a deep breath. "I'm sure you'd like to freshen up before we eat lunch. I put a pitcher of water in your room upstairs. Let me take you up. Hiram will bring your luggage up, and. . ." She hesitated, but duty took precedence over personal comfort. "I thought we could heat water this evening so you could have a bath if you'd like."

"Ah. And wash day is. . . ?"

"Monday. Unless you need something right away."

"No, I think I can get by until then."

Trudy mounted the stairs before her sister-in-law and showed her into the front bedroom.

"Well, this isn't so bad."

Trudy tried to view the room through Rose's eyes. She'd given her the flying geese quilt that Violet had stitched ten years ago. A small box stove stood under the eaves, with a stovepipe flue poking out through the ceiling. A chair, washstand, and small chest of drawers completed the furnishings. Plain white curtains edged the window.

"Aunt Sal warned me to expect rustic conditions," Rose said.

"You spoke to Mama before you left home?" Trudy couldn't hold back the eagerness in her voice.

"Yes. Actually, she tried to discourage me from coming, but I was ready for new vistas." Her face puckered up. "It was so dreary after my Albert died. I needed a change of scenery. So I thought, what better than a visit to my brother-in-law in the West?"

"Indeed." Trudy could hear Hiram thumping slowly up the narrow stairs with some of Rose's luggage.

"I had no idea how vast the West is," Rose proclaimed as he appeared in the doorway, laden with the valise, the carpet bag, and a hatbox under each arm. "Oh, thank you so much, Hiram. Right there, near the dresser." She glanced about. "I suppose there's no closet."

"No, but we have hooks." Trudy nodded to the peg rack.

"I see."

"Did you want that big trunk up here?" Hiram asked doubtfully.

"If it's not too much trouble."

He winced. "Ethan stayed in case you wanted it. . . ." He cast a pleading glance at his sister.

"It might be easier for you to unpack it in the parlor and carry small lots up here," Trudy said with a determined smile.

Rose tapped her chin and looked about. "No, I think I'll put it right there under the window so that I can sit on it if I wish and look out." She walked over and pushed the curtains back. "Oh."

Trudy and Hiram exchanged a troubled glance. "Is everything all right?" Trudy asked.

"This window fronts on the street."

"Well yes. But it's by far the larger of the two bedrooms up here."

"May I see the other?"

Trudy swallowed hard. "The other one is my room, and as I said, it's not nearly so spacious as this one."

"Nevertheless, I'm afraid the dust from the street will affect my sinuses. I do have delicate sinuses, you know."

Trudy looked down at the rag rug and mustered her dignity. If Mama were here, she would do the ladylike thing.

Hiram surprised her by speaking up. "I don't think you should ask Trudy to give up her room."

"It's all right, Hi." Trudy smiled out of affection for him and appreciation of his small gesture of chivalry. "If Rose prefers it, we can switch."

She led Rose across the landing and swung open the door to her room. Rose entered and looked about the cozy but small chamber. The eaves came down on both sides, making slanted walls to within a yard of the floor. The one windowsill at the back was only inches above the floor. Yellow wallpaper with nosegays of darker yellow and orange flowers brightened the room.

Trudy's bed was narrower than the one in the front room, but she preferred this room to the bigger one Hiram and Violet had shared. Hiram, too, seemed unable to sleep there and had moved downstairs before Trudy arrived nearly nine years ago. They never discussed it, but the front bedroom remained vacant except for the rare occasions when they entertained a guest. Trudy could count those on one hand.

Rose cleared her throat. "Perhaps you're right, dear. I can see that you're comfortable in here. I'll manage across the hall, I'm sure."

"If you need anything, just let me know," Trudy said.

Hiram gazed at her, his eyebrows hiked up under the hair that spilled over his forehead.

"What is it?" Trudy asked.

"Ethan's still waiting."

"Isn't he staying to lunch?"

Hiram raised his hands and shoulders and cast a glance after Rose, but she had already stridden across the landing, and the sound of drawers being opened reached them.

Trudy stepped closer to her brother. "What do you think?"

He gulped audibly, and she would have laughed had she not felt like doing the same. He said softly, "Ask me again after she unpacks that trunk and plants a garden."

Trudy drew in a quick breath. "You don't think she'll stay all summer?"

"Well. . .she sure brought a heap of stuff."

"Hiram, you don't think. . . ?"

His face drooped into a forlorn mask.

"Come," Trudy said. "We've got to convince Ethan to stay and eat with us."

"And you'll take her with you this afternoon?" His hangdog expression gave her a maternal pang. Sometimes it was hard to remember that Hiram was nine years older than she.

"We'll see. She may want to rest from her trip."

"If she does, I'm heading over to the livery to keep Griff company."

"Good plan." Trudy walked out to the head of the stairs and called, "Rose, I'll have lunch on the table in five minutes."

"I'll be right there," came the muffled reply.

Ethan sprang up from a chair when Trudy and Hiram entered the kitchen. "What's the word on that trunk?"

Trudy glanced at her brother, but he was no help. "Let's leave it in the front room for now. If she insists on having it upstairs, I'll ask her to take the heavy stuff out first."

Both men sighed, and she chuckled. "Come on, fellows, you must be hungry."

"Starved," Ethan admitted. "Are you sure you want me, though, with your company and all? 'Cause I could go over to the boardinghouse."

"Would I have set four places at the table if we didn't?" She looked pointedly toward the extra place setting. As much as she loved him, sometimes Ethan needed things spelled out for him.

He smiled and sank back into the chair. "Thanks."

A few minutes later, Rose came down and joined them. She'd brushed her dress off and combed her hair. Hiram held a chair for her, and Ethan held Trudy's. When all were seated, Hiram nodded at Ethan.

His friend, having known Hiram's quiet ways for years, bowed his head and began to pray.

After the blessing, Rose smiled brightly at Ethan. "Sheriff, I didn't realize you were joining us for the meal. How delightful."

"Thank you, ma'am." The tips of Ethan's ears turned pink.

"Are you a particular friend of Hiram's?"

"You might say that." Ethan's gaze darted to Trudy's, and she imagined she read apology there.

It's all right, Trudy thought. *I know you care for me.* She held his look and tried to communicate that thought to him. Ethan's ears became red.

"Uh, how long can we expect to enjoy your company, Mrs. Caplinger?" He tore his gaze from Trudy's and looked back to the visitor.

"I haven't decided yet. If I like Fergus and dear Hiram thinks it's a good idea"—Rose turned her beaming face toward her stunned brother-in-law—"I may decide to make this my new home."

Hiram dropped his fork. It clattered off his ironstone plate onto the floor. The others all stared at him. Hiram's face went three shades redder than Ethan's.

★ CHAPTER 7 ★

Libby and her clerk, Florence Nash, dashed out of the emporium at half past two.

Annie Harper and her daughter, Myra, were just driving out of Harper Lane, where their farm lay. Annie's husband, Zachary, one of the town council members and occasional deputy for Ethan, allowed her to take the wagon to shooting club meetings and carry several of the other women who lived within the town limits. They usually drove out to a ranch near Ethan's to practice their marksmanship.

Trudy came from her house, carrying her brother's Sharps rifle, and Apphia Benton, the minister's wife, bustled up the sidewalk from Gold Lane, where she and her husband rented a little cottage from Cyrus Fennel. From the Spur & Saddle, at the south end of Main, came the owner, Bitsy Shepard, and two of her saloon girls.

Each woman carried her weapon of choice to the practice sessions, or whatever she was able to lay hands on, ranging from Bitsy's tiny Deringer pistol to prewar muskets used by some of the outlying ranchers' wives. Libby had begun selling a variety of firearms the summer before, and several ladies had purchased pistols that would fit into their handbags.

Annie stopped the wagon and waited for the various club members to climb in at the back. Libby placed her handbag in the wagon bed, carefully lifted her skirts, turned, and gave a little hop onto the edge. Florence's mother, Ellie Nash, ran down the steps of her house, where her husband kept the post office, her skirts hiked up above her ankles.

"We'll wait for you, Mama," Florence called. "Don't get all in a dither."

"Isn't your sister-in-law coming?" Libby asked as Trudy settled beside her and smoothed her skirts over her ankles.

Trudy shook her head. "She wanted to take a nap, and I can't say I blame her. She's had more than a week's travel by train and stagecoach."

"Poor thing must be exhausted," Libby said.

"Your sister-in-law?" Florence asked. "I didn't know you had one."

"She's come to visit us from Maine." Trudy's strained smile told Libby she would rather not discuss it—indeed, would probably rather not be hosting the woman. But in a small town like Fergus, news of a newcomer always interested folks.

"Is she your brother's kin?" Annie asked, looking over her shoulder at Trudy.

"That's right. Rose is the sister of Hiram's wife, Violet."

"Poor dear," Annie murmured.

Trudy's lips tightened, and she busied herself with resting the Sharps so that it wouldn't jostle on the ride. Libby considered Trudy her best friend. Their experiences of the past year had bound them together in spirit, though Trudy was younger by a decade, and Libby could read her friend quite well by now.

"I remember Violet," said Bitsy. "She was a dainty thing, comely and pert." Bitsy was a shrewd business owner, and she made up for her diminutive size by wearing bright colors, startling makeup, and when she felt the occasion warranted it, shocking fashions. For the moment, she wore her bright red bloomer costume, which, where Bitsy was concerned, exhibited the height of modesty.

Her two girls were also apt to show up sporting what some ladies would deem inappropriate clothing. This time their skirts hung short enough to reveal their shoe tops and sheer, clocked stockings with a suggestion of ruffled satin petticoats—a sharp contrast to Mrs. Benton's proper two-piece, black bombazine dress. But the club members had welcomed them into their ranks and their hearts. Their friendship and prayers had borne fruit, and Goldie and Vashti now regularly attended the Reverend Mr.

Benton's church services. Bitsy, however, had come to church only once. Libby had not given up praying for her.

"I wish I could have known Violet," said Apphia, the newest arrival among them. "I've heard she was lovely in spirit as well as in form."

"I sort of remember her, but I was only a tyke when she passed on," Myra said as Annie clucked to the horses. "Is her sister as pretty as Violet was?"

"Rose is. . ." Trudy cleared her throat and shot a glance at Libby. "Yes, she's very pretty."

Libby determined to have a moment alone with Trudy before the day was over. Something had clearly gone wrong with the visit, and the young woman's insecurities had resurfaced.

"And what's Hiram up to this afternoon?" Apphia asked gently, but Libby had to wonder if she asked to make sure that Hiram had not stayed home alone with Rose. That wouldn't be proper, though most of the people in Fergus wouldn't give a hoot.

"He's gone over to the livery to help Griffin Bane," Trudy said. The wagon was now nearly even with the smithy on the right, and beyond it lay Bane's livery stable. All the ladies gazed toward it.

"Mrs. Harper!" A high female voice reached them from the other side, and all those in the wagon swung around and looked toward the Nugget saloon. Opal, one of the employees at that establishment, hurried out the door and ran toward them carrying a shotgun. "Do you have room for me?"

"Surely. Pile in at the back." Annie stopped the horse and waited for Opal to climb in. She handled the shotgun with utmost care. One of the first things Trudy taught each new club member was gun safety, and carrying loaded guns in wagons was forbidden.

"Miz Adams, I'll need more shells for this when we're done," Opal said when she'd caught her breath.

"Save your empty shells for me, and I'll give you a discount." Libby had recently made a practice of buying back used shotgun shells and spent brass casings from the women.

"Ted doesn't like me taking it, but he said if I buy my own ammunition, it's all right. I'm saving up for a pistol like yours."

"Take your time," Libby said. "And be sure to thank Mr. Hire for letting you use his shotgun."

" 'Tisn't his, really." Opal shook her head as though nothing made sense anymore. "Since Mr. Morrell was—" She broke off and cast an uneasy glance at Trudy. "Well, since he died, Ted's just kind of taken over the Nugget. I don't think he really owns it."

"I'm told he has rights," Trudy said. "I asked the sheriff about it myself. He said Ted Hire has contacted Jamin Morrell's kin. Morrell has two sisters in Philadelphia, and Ted is negotiating with them to buy the business. He's putting aside a percentage of the income from the Nugget in an account for the family."

Libby wondered if Ted kept honest records for the ill-fated saloon owner's sisters, but that was none of her business. Ted seemed decent enough—he always kept short accounts with her at the emporium. But he was shrewd. He'd managed to keep undisputed control of the Nugget when the owner died. And he never came to church, unlike Augie Moore. The big man who tended the bar at Bitsy's saloon attended services faithfully and even carried his own Bible. Funny, Libby thought. If she needed help and had only the rival saloons' men to give it, she'd pick big, muscular Augie any day over cold-eyed Ted.

"I'm glad the snow's off and we can shoot out to Thalens' ranch again," Florence said. "It was all right meeting out behind your place now and then in the winter, Trudy, but it's so much nicer to get out away from town."

"And to be able to shoot without your gloves on," her friend Myra added.

"Yes," said Ellie, "and to be back on the twice-a-week schedule. My aim suffered over the winter."

When they arrived at the ravine where they practiced in good weather, four ranchers' wives awaited them, and Isabel Fennel was walking over the hill from the schoolhouse.

As the other riders climbed down, Trudy waited, standing in the wagon bed.

"Ladies," she called, and they all gathered around and looked up at her. "Sheriff Chapman has requested help from our membership. It's not a dangerous task, and it's one that any of you could take part in if you have the time and the desire."

The women's eyes glinted with interest. After the quiet winter in Fergus, they were ready for some action.

Trudy cleared her throat. "You all remember our dear, departed member, Millicent Peart."

The ladies murmured, "Oh yes" and "We surely do." Tears sprang into Libby's eyes just thinking about the old woman.

Trudy nodded. "Of course you do. We all do. Well, it's been brought to the sheriff's attention that Millicent had no will, and no one in town seems to know whether the Pearts had an heir who can claim their property."

"How can we help?" asked Starr Tinen.

Trudy nodded at her. "Afternoon, Starr. The sheriff asked if some of our members could help write letters. He'd like to inquire of town officials and law officers back East, in the area where the Pearts came from, to see if we can find a trace of any relatives back there."

"I'll help," said Emmaline Landry. Several other women raised their hands.

"Wonderful," Trudy said.

Libby rummaged in her bag. "Would you like me to take names?"

"I'm not sure we need to." Trudy raised her voice. "Any of those willing and able may gather this evening at my house. Come after supper—six thirty or so. Bring your pen and ink. If you can spare an envelope and a sheet of writing paper, bring those, too. The sheriff is asking around town for information about Frank and Milzie Peart's background. He'll come by tonight and tell us what he knows so that we can begin our task."

"Maybe we could send some telegrams," Bitsy said. "It would be faster."

"But explaining the situation may take quite a few words."

Ellie frowned. "That could get expensive."

"Yes, I think it's best if we write letters," Trudy said. "There's no big hurry, and Sheriff Chapman can help us word our inquiries discreetly." She looked over the club members. Isabel nodded soberly, and Trudy hoped the schoolteacher would come to the gathering, though she lived outside town. "All right, then. If there's no other business, let's get started. Mrs. Benton, would you open our meeting in prayer, please?"

After the prayer, Libby went to the back of the wagon to offer Trudy a steadying hand as she climbed down. "I can't come tonight, but I'll send a dozen envelopes over with Florence."

"Thank you." Trudy brushed off her skirt and straightened.

Libby shrugged. "It's not much." She wished she could go. She always enjoyed visiting with Trudy and her brother. The other ladies would liven up the evening for sure. But she kept the emporium open until six every night, and afterward she straightened the store and worked on her bookkeeping. Like Bitsy and the saloon girls, she would have to bypass the gathering. "I wonder why anyone cares about that place. The Pearts' cabin burned flat, and the mine never paid much. The land is practically vertical."

"I know, but. . ." Trudy's brow wrinkled above her blue gray eyes. "Ethan told me Cy Fennel was the one who asked about the property."

Libby looked over her shoulder to see if Cyrus's daughter was within earshot, but Isabel had already gone to her shooting station. "He's already bought up every parcel available. Doesn't he own enough land?"

"Apparently not."

★ CHAPTER 8 ★

Ethan made his rounds that evening at a measured pace. He'd just come from an enjoyable half hour in Trudy's kitchen, instructing the ladies on how to frame their inquiries about the Pearts. Some of the old-timers of Fergus had given him a few scraps of information. Several folks had recalled that Frank Peart was from New Jersey, and Ethan had probed the memories of those who had been in town the longest.

Charles Walker, the former mayor of Fergus, remembered the name of a town Frank had talked about. Ethan had borrowed a geography book from Isabel during the school's lunch hour and found that the town was just outside Elizabeth, a fair-sized city. He'd decided to inquire of the city clerk as well, in case some of the Peart family records were filed there. A wire to the U.S. marshal in Boise might turn up something, and he'd passed the name of an attorney in the territorial capital to Trudy. She would write to the lawyer and explain the situation, asking for any advice the man could give the sheriff. Ethan was confident that within a few weeks they would learn something.

He mounted the steps to the Spur & Saddle. Nine months ago, he'd cringed to enter the saloons. Now it didn't bother him. It was a regular part of his job. Bitsy's place wasn't bad, anyway. Inside, it looked like a swanky hotel lobby. Bitsy'd had the piano and two velvet-covered settees hauled all the way up here by mule train. She did all right. Lots of regular patrons came here once a week or more.

Now, the Nugget, at the other end of Main Street, sang a

different tune. The plain, square building held a few tables, a rustic bar, and short benches. Men didn't go in there for the atmosphere. The former owner had made plans to improve the place, but right now, Ted Hire was running the Nugget. He seemed to be doing all right, but who could really say? Maybe Oscar Runnels, who freighted in the liquor for him. But Ted kept his business affairs to himself.

Ethan took only a few steps into the Spur & Saddle. On a Thursday evening, things weren't too lively. About ten men sat in the cushioned chairs or on the settees with their drinks in their hands. Three played a quiet poker game. The rest conversed with each other or the ladies serving drinks. Funny how he thought of Bitsy, Goldie, and Vashti as ladies now. A year ago, he'd have blushed scarlet to think about the saloon women. Now he considered Bitsy a friend and ally, if an eccentric one, and he knew Trudy cared about Bitsy and her girls as well.

Augie stood behind the bar and waved. Ethan nodded to him. Bitsy sat at a table, engaged in conversation with a gentleman Ethan didn't recognize, but he had the look of a salesman. Probably staying overnight at the Fennel House, the boardinghouse owned by the number-one landlord of Fergus, good old Cyrus.

Vashti, the dark-haired girl, caught his eye as she sashayed across from the bar to the poker players, balancing a tray with three glasses on it. She smiled broadly, and Ethan had to admit the girl had a pleasant face. He turned away before he could form any impressions of the rest of her. Augie and the ladies had everything under control. He rarely had to take action at the Spur & Saddle.

He strolled across the street and passed the end of Harper Lane and the Walkers' house. Lamplight streamed from the parlor windows of the yellow house. Ethan thought of stopping in to see how the former mayor was doing, but he shrank from the almost certainly sour reception Orissa Walker would give him. Charles hadn't fully recovered after being shot last summer, and he'd had to give up his position as mayor. Just couldn't keep up with things anymore. Orissa seemed to take it personally that she was no longer the mayor's wife, but no way could she keep that position when her husband couldn't serve.

After the shooting, Ethan had wondered if Cyrus Fennel

would manage to get himself named mayor, but the folks had demanded a vote. They'd elected a man everyone truly liked: postmaster Peter Nash, Walker's next-door neighbor. Things had been quiet since, to Ethan's relief. He'd spent a quiet winter on the ranch, riding into town most days and taking his time courting Trudy. Life in Fergus was good these days. Good and peaceful.

He sauntered on, checking locked storefronts and peering into vacant buildings left over from the Gold Rush of twenty years ago. He even moseyed along the side streets. Quiet. Absolutely, pin-droppingly quiet.

Outside the livery, he found Griffin and Hiram sitting on a couple of hay bales shooting the breeze.

"What are you doing out here, Hi?" Ethan asked.

Hiram rolled his eyes heavenward.

Griffin laughed. "He's got a kitchen full of women, and he says it's your fault."

"Oh yeah." Ethan leaned against the wall and guffawed. "I expect the ladies will be finished before long."

The big blacksmith ran a hand through his beard. "He don't like being booted out of his own house. Can't say as I blame him."

"That so?" Ethan eyed Hiram, but he only grimaced and looked skyward. "Tell Trudy. Maybe next time they can meet at Preacher Benton's house."

"Yeah," said Griffin, "or how about Bitsy's place? She's got plenty of room."

Hiram sat up and glared at Griffin.

"Take it easy, now." Ethan clamped his hand on Hiram's shoulder. "You know he's just teasing. We wouldn't want our womenfolk meeting in a saloon, would we, Griff?"

"Oh, I dunno. Bitsy's all right. And her bar girls come to church now. I can't see why it would matter if they had a meeting at the Spur & Saddle."

"Well, I can."

Hiram spoke so rarely that both his friends stared at him in surprise.

"Okay," Griff said. "I won't suggest it."

"But I will suggest to Trudy that they might want to meet at someone else's house next time," Ethan said. "They can spread the fellowship around. And you know they're doing this for a good cause."

"What? So Cyrus can buy up more land?" Hiram shook his head and shoved his hands into his pockets.

Another touchy subject, Ethan realized. Ten years ago, Cyrus had bought the ranch Hiram had had his eye on.

Ethan looked toward the rising moon. "Think the ladies are done writing their letters?"

Hiram shrugged and kicked at a pebble on the ground.

"What about that sister-in-law of yours?" Griffin asked. "She writing letters, too?"

Hiram looked uneasy. "She came in the parlor as soon as Ethan left, so I slipped out."

"Maybe she's not the sharpshooter type," Griff suggested.

"Come on," Ethan said. "It's getting dark. Let's go around to your place, Hiram. I've a mind to take Trudy walking tonight."

Griffin chuckled. "I'll see you boys around."

The two friends walked in silence past the smithy and across the street. Lamplight shone from the windows of the Nugget. Several horses rubbed stirrups at the hitching rail. The men headed up the boardwalk. As they passed the jail, Ethan threw a cursory glance toward his office. Quiet and dark, just the way he liked it.

Annie Harper and her daughter, Myra, emerged from the path that led to the Dooleys' back door.

"Evening, ladies," Ethan called, and Hiram tipped his hat in silence. "Are you finished with your meeting?"

"Hello again, Sheriff," Annie said. "Yes, we're the last to leave. Gert—I mean, Trudy—has all the letters ready to be mailed."

"That's fine. I appreciate your help." Ethan smiled and watched them cross the street. Myra looked back over her shoulder and gave a coy wave.

"Ha! She's waving at you, Hiram."

"Not me."

"Well, surely not me. She knows who I'm sweet on, and I'm not ashamed to say so."

"Yeah, you been sweet on Trudy for a long time."

"So?"

Hiram shrugged. "You coming in?"

They ambled around to the back. Hiram mounted the stoop first and opened the kitchen door.

"Oh, you're back," Trudy said when her brother entered. "You want coffee? We've got some cookies, too. Ellie Nash brought them, and there are some left over." She looked past Hiram and met Ethan's gaze. Her voice dropped a pitch. "Hello, Ethan."

"Trudy."

They stood looking at each other for a long moment. Hiram plopped his hat on its peg and walked to the woodstove. He opened the coffeepot and peered into it. After a moment, he held it out toward Ethan, his eyebrows arched.

"Thanks," Ethan said, "but if Trudy wants to go walking..."

"Surely." She turned her gaze to Hiram. "Go ahead and drink that. I'll put on more so that Ethan can have a fresh cup with you when we get back."

From the next room, the sound of footsteps on the stairs reached them. Hiram caught his breath, his face freezing in a panicky mask.

"She won't kill you," Trudy hissed. "We'll be back in half an hour. Right, Ethan?"

"No more than that."

Hiram shook his head violently.

"Twenty minutes," Trudy amended.

Ethan gritted his teeth. How was a fellow supposed to court a girl in twenty-minute increments? But anyone could see Hiram did not want to be left alone with his sister-in-law. Light footsteps crossed the parlor toward them.

"Well, let's head out." Ethan hoped they could leave before—

"Why, Sheriff! I didn't expect to see you again tonight."

Too late.

"Uh..." Ethan shot a glance at Trudy and back at the elegant brunette framed in the doorway. She wore a different dress than she had this afternoon, pink and frothy, and her hair was neatly coiffed. "Trudy and I were just going to take a stroll."

"Yes," Trudy said. "We'll be back shortly. Help yourself to coffee if you want some."

"Oh, I'd love to see the town by moonlight," Rose said with a broad smile. She walked over to Ethan and laid a hand on his forearm. "Maybe you could point out the sights to me."

"Uh. . ."

"Ethan's courting Trudy," Hiram said testily.

They all turned and stared at him. He still stood in front of the stove with the coffeepot in his hands.

Rose's jaw dropped. "Well, I never! How. . .exciting. Perhaps Hiram and I should go along as chaperones."

"They don't need no chaperone," Hiram said.

Ethan was surprised Trudy hadn't spoken up and given Rose what for. Hiram's outburst must have shocked her into silence. He cleared his throat, not sure what Trudy's reaction would be, but knowing what his mother would have demanded that he do. "Mrs. Caplinger, I'm sure we'd be happy to have you accompany us if you'd care to come along."

Rose smiled sweetly at him. "Thank you. That's very kind of you. But since Hiram says it's all right, I'm sure you have an understanding with him. And with Gert, of course. I think I'll stay here and keep my brother-in-law company. We haven't had a chance to discuss the folks back home. I need to catch him up on all the doings in his old neighborhood."

Trudy opened her mouth and closed it.

Ethan said, "Well then, if you're sure you don't mind, we'll be going. Trudy, do you want your shawl and bonnet? It's a little cool out tonight."

While she gathered her wrap and put on her bonnet, Ethan looked over Rose's shoulder at Hiram. His friend's face was gray.

"We'll see you in half an hour," Ethan said. Hiram scowled. "Or less."

"Take your time," Rose said. She took down one of Trudy's teacups. "We'll be right here when you return. Won't we, Hiram?"

Hiram's shoulders drooped. He walked to the table, poured Rose's teacup full of coffee, and took a mug for himself from the cupboard. A small stream of coffee trickled from the pot, then gave out. Hiram gazed at it mournfully.

If Trudy noticed, she would stop to start a new pot. Ethan scooted her out the back door and pulled it closed behind them. "Guess it'll be a short stroll this evening." He put his hat on.

"It had better be." She frowned up at him. "I feel guilty leaving them together."

"Hiram does seem a little on edge around her."

"You heard her this noon. She's talking about staying here permanently. Hiram's petrified. He thinks that somehow he fits into her future plans."

Ethan reached for her hand. "Let's not think about that now. What do you say we walk down to the river?"

"No, that would take too long. I'm sorry, Ethan, but I'm worked up myself. If I thought I could get away with it, I'd ask her to stay at the boardinghouse. She's making Hiram very uncomfortable. But if I did that, she'd wire her mother, and her mother would tell my mother, and then I'd be in trouble. No, we've got to be good hosts. But somehow we've got to disabuse her of the notion that we want her to live with us."

Ethan squeezed her hand. "I'm sure it will work out. Do you want to walk out Harper Lane?"

Trudy stopped on the boardwalk. "No. No, I don't. I don't know why I'm even out here with you. I should be back there with them. We may not need a chaperone, but Hiram does."

"Aw, that's a little extreme, don't you think? Twenty minutes..."

She put her hand up to his cheek, warm and gentle, and Ethan's hopes rose. For about three seconds.

"I'm sorry, Ethan. Any other time, I'd love to be out here walking with you. But my brother needs me. Please, let's go back."

★ CHAPTER 9 ★

Rain began after midnight and fell incessantly through dawn. Isabel's father drove her to school in the wagon. The schoolroom was cold, and she decided to keep her cloak on for a while. When it was too chilly, the children couldn't concentrate on their lessons. They never worked sums quickly if their hands were cold.

The door crashed open behind her, and Will Ingram bounced in. "Morning, Teacher."

"Good morning, William. Please close the door more gently than you opened it."

"Yes ma'am. My ma said to come early and see if you wanted a fire built in the stove this morning."

"Yes, please. I was just going to do that, but you may have the task." She went to her desk and arranged her books and lesson notes.

Will puttered about at the stove and went out for a minute to bring in an armful of wood from the shed.

"Not much wood left," he said when he came in. Water dripped off his clothes, and he left wet footprints from the door to the potbellied stove halfway along one wall of the large room.

"Thank you. I'll inform the school board. I expect they thought we were done needing a fire this spring."

The other children filtered in by twos and threes. Most days they stayed outside until she rang her bell, but on days of rain or extreme cold, they were allowed to enter the schoolroom as soon as they arrived. All knew the rule, however, that they must remain quiet.

At precisely eight o'clock, Isabel stood and rang her handbell softly. "Good morning, students."

"Good morning, Miss Fennel," they chorused.

She opened the school day by taking the roll, offering prayer, and reading a psalm. Then began the round of arithmetic classes. At the blackboard, she set problems for the older children to work while she drilled addition and subtraction up to tens with the two first graders. No second graders attended the Fergus school this year, and the third and fourth grades had only one pupil each. She generally called them together for their arithmetic.

She erased the older children's problems from the chalkboard and began to write two examples each for Julie Harper and Paul Storrey. Behind her, the stove door creaked open. Will must be adding fuel to the fire, though the classroom had warmed up nicely. She thought she heard a whisper. Isabel turned around with a stick of chalk in one hand and her open arithmetic book in the other. Will was sliding into his seat beside Nathan Landry.

Pow! Bang!

Girls screamed and jumped up, knocking books and slates from their desks. Isabel's chalk flew from her hand, and the book tumbled to the floor. Children scrambled in a tangle of pantalets and fallen benches away from the stove.

Pow!

The older boys had remained in their seats. Will held one hand across his mouth, Isabel's brief impression of his expression was not horror, but rather an ill-hidden smirk. The girls continued to shriek. Six-year-old Millie Pooler wailed. Her classmate Ben Rollins, whose seat was near the stove, appeared to have wet his pants.

"Children! Calm yourselves."

The room stilled. Julie Harper caught a prolonged sob and hiccupped.

Isabel glared at Will. His gaze met hers, and he dropped his hand to his side and sobered. "Want me to check the stove, ma'am?"

"No William. I think you've done enough for today. You will go straight home and tell your father what you've done." She looked at the watch pinned to her bodice. "I shall come around to see your parents this afternoon, and I shall ask them what time you reached home. If you have not arrived there by nine-twenty, I shall ask them to increase whatever punishment they have meted out for this act of yours."

"But—"

"Go. Now. Anything you wish to say to me may be said this afternoon at your home."

He held her gaze only a moment longer then lowered his chin. "Yes ma'am." He walked slowly toward the cloakroom, and a few seconds later the outer door slammed behind him.

Isabel surveyed her class. "Children, pick up the mess and resume your seats, please." She walked to Ben and touched his shoulder. "Ben, you may be excused. Tell your mother I said you may return to school after you change your clothes."

Ben hung his head. His eyes full of tears, he murmured, "Yes ma'am," and headed for the door.

Before going back to the blackboard, Isabel eyed the stove. When it cooled off, she would examine the contents, but she thought she knew what she would find.

"No one is to go near the stove," she said firmly. Stooping, she retrieved her arithmetic book.

"Here's the man you want to ask," Libby said, nodding toward the door. Hiram Dooley had just entered the emporium, letting in a chilly draft. He stopped on the rag mat and wiped his boots, but rainwater dripped off his hat brim onto the floor as he looked downward.

"Yes, a good idea," Isabel said.

"Mr. Dooley, may we have a word with you?" Libby called.

Hiram looked up with widened eyes as though shocked that a woman would speak to him. He glanced down at the small puddle on the floor, as if he suspected that prompted the attention they gave him.

"Don't worry about that, Hiram. Folks have been tracking in mud all day, and a little more water won't hurt. I intend to mop the whole floor this evening after closing."

He slid out of his slicker and hung it on one of the hooks near the door, then walked toward the counter, eyeing Libby and the schoolmarm cautiously.

"What can I do for you ladies?"

Libby smiled, hoping to put him at ease. A quiet man who always seemed a little on edge around women other than his sister, Hiram had become one of her favorite neighbors. Since the start of the shooting club, she'd furthered her acquaintance with both Dooleys, and she liked what she found beneath his self-effacing exterior.

"Miss Fennel was just telling me about a prank one of her students pulled today. It seems while she had her back turned, one of the boys tossed a few cartridges into the school stove."

Hiram frowned. "The boy ought to know better."

Isabel nodded, her pale blue eyes snapping. "So I told his father twenty minutes ago. Mr. Ingram assured me he will deal with the boy, but he also said something I had to wonder about. Mr. Dooley, is it true that putting a bullet in a stove is not dangerous? Mr. Ingram seemed to think it was a harmless joke his son played."

Hiram rubbed the side of his neck thoughtfully. "Well now, I expect it set off the powder charge and made a pretty big bang, depending on what caliber shells you're talking about."

Isabel winced. "I confess it frightened me. It scared us all and put the classroom in an uproar."

"Which is just what Will Ingram wanted," Libby said.

"I suppose so."

"Well ma'am, it's like this," Hiram said. "The powder would make a big boom, for certain, and the cartridge case would move, but it would stop when it hit the side of the stove's firebox. Not being confined in the chamber of a gun, it wouldn't shoot off so hard or go in a particular direction. I reckon the blast was a lot of noise without much force behind it, and the lead bullet pretty much stayed put inside the stove."

"I suppose that's a good thing," Isabel said gravely. "I'm glad to know there wasn't as much danger to the children as I at first feared. But it certainly disrupted the class."

"It's a bad trick to pull," Hiram said. "And you never know. If the stove door weren't shut tight. . .well, we could imagine circumstances where it could result in tragedy."

"Yes," Libby said. "If another child went over and opened the stove door, for instance, just before the powder caught."

"True." Hiram set his lips together in a tight line.

"Mr. Ingram will probably tan his backside," Libby said.

"I hope he does." Isabel colored slightly. "Perhaps as his teacher, I shouldn't admit that, but Will has been a handful this spring. It took an extreme situation like this for me to go directly to his father. And I'm not sure yet that one of the other boys didn't supply the bullets. Mr. Ingram agreed to get the entire story out of him. But I'm glad to know there was little danger to the other children. Thank you, Mr. Dooley."

He nodded.

Libby had been keeping an eye on the other customers browsing throughout the store. Laura Storrey looked her way from the section where kitchen utensils hung on a pegboard. Libby glanced at Isabel and Hiram. "Can I get either of you anything? I see Mrs. Storrey looking my way as though she'd like assistance."

"I just came for a can of cinnamon for Trudy, but I can find it, thank you." Hiram gave the cinnamon the same sober nod other people would give a coffin, but Libby remembered when he had been more lighthearted. She was sure that the gentle gunsmith needed only the right circumstances to banish his gloomy aspect. Of course, the arrival of the widowed sister-in-law he so disliked hadn't helped. As she hurried to assist Mrs. Storrey, she resolved to add his name to her prayer list. It might seem frivolous to some, but to Libby it made perfect sense to pray that another person's dejected spirits be lifted.

The rough benches in the old haberdashery building filled quickly on Sunday morning. More than half of Fergus's one hundred–plus residents had signed the church's new constitution and become members. The holdouts lay low on Sundays, and some slunk into the saloons after sundown.

Hiram looked about with satisfaction while Rose engaged Trudy in a whispered conversation. He hoped they'd build a proper church this summer. Mayor Nash had already spoken to him about leading the building crew.

Libby had stopped halfway up the center aisle to speak

to Vashti and Goldie, the two girls who worked at the Spur & Saddle. He found it hard to take his eyes off Libby. Her golden hair picked up rays of sunlight that reached in through the front windows. She always radiated a sweet spirit, and he couldn't think of a kinder, more competent woman. She'd done a lot for Trudy this past year by befriending her and prompting her to organize the shooting club for the women.

As he gazed at Libby, she straightened and glanced his way. Hiram's chest tightened as he realized she'd caught him staring. But she only smiled, that gentle, thoughtful smile he'd come to admire. He allowed himself to answer it and give a half nod, remembering his conversation with her and Isabel just a few days ago. He'd managed to keep from making a fool of himself then, largely due to the serious topic and Isabel's presence. Libby turned to find her seat, and he lowered his gaze to his hands, thankful that Rose hadn't noticed the silent exchange.

All the men Hiram considered friends sat in the benches facing the podium—Ethan, Griff, Peter, Josiah Runnels, and many others besides. He could only think of two women in town who weren't at church, aside from outlying ranchers' wives. That would be Bitsy Shepard and the new girl at the Nugget. He didn't even know her name, but her arrival on the stagecoach had drawn everyone's attention. She wore a fur stole over a dress with no shoulders. Or at least that's what Griff had told him. Hiram hadn't gone over to the stage stop to get a peek. But Ted Hire hadn't wasted much time replacing the bar girl who'd been arrested last summer; that was certain.

Rose, who sat between Hiram and Trudy, chose that moment to leap to her feet. "Oh, Mr. Fennel. So nice to see you again."

Hiram automatically rose. He'd been taught since childhood to stand when a lady stood. Cyrus had paused at the end of the bench, beyond Trudy. Rose gushed like a schoolgirl and allowed him to shake her hand.

"I trust you've recovered from your arduous journey, Mrs. Caplinger."

"Yes, I believe I have. This mountain air is quite invigorating."

Cyrus smiled at her. Hiram didn't like the way his gaze darted to Rose's figure. He felt the blood infuse his cheeks and wondered for an instant whether a man could be embarrassed for another when the other man should be ashamed and wasn't. It was an interesting train of thought, but a flash of color as the door opened again distracted him from it.

He wished he were standing beside Trudy, without Rose and her poufy dress between them. He'd have nudged Trudy to be certain she noticed the new arrivals.

Augie Moore, the bartender (and some said the cook for the Sunday chicken dinner) at the Spur & Saddle had just entered, which was not unusual. In the crook of his left arm, he cradled his black leather Bible. In the crook of his right arm lay Bitsy Shepard's bejeweled hand.

Bitsy hung back a little, but Augie tugged her gently forward. The dyed feathers on her cobalt blue hat bobbed. At the next-to-last bench, Augie stepped aside and let her enter the row ahead of him. They sat down next to Ralph and Laura Storrey. Bitsy kept her chin down, but Hiram could see her dark eyes flicking back and forth beneath the net veil of her hat. Her dress, black with touches of bright blue on the sleeves and bodice, would have been as modest as Trudy's if it had contained about a half yard more fabric. Still, for Bitsy, it was quite ladylike.

The real shock was her presence in a church meeting. Trudy and the other shooting club members had invited Bitsy for months, but except for one time last summer, she'd always said no. What had changed her mind?

Pastor Benton stepped up to the pulpit, and Cyrus moved quickly down the aisle to his seat beside Isabel. As their guest settled her skirts about her, Hiram met Trudy's gaze over Rose's head. Trudy's grayish eyes sparkled with the reflected blue of her Sunday dress. Hiram could tell from her suppressed energy that she'd seen Bitsy come in. Months of prayers answered—that's what Trudy's look said. He nodded and resumed his seat. Now maybe they could turn their prayers to the family problem and seek guidance for what they should do with Rose.

She leaned toward him and murmured near his ear, "I declare, some folks' mothers never taught them how to dress appropriately for church services, did they?"

Hiram pretended he hadn't heard and hoped no one else had.

★ CHAPTER 10 ★

On Monday afternoon, Libby noticed that Isabel looked a little peaked at shooting practice. She drew her aside while others were firing their rounds and invited her to tea after the meeting ended.

"Won't you have to go right back to your store?" Isabel's eyes held a flicker of hope, though her tone was doubtful.

"Some days I make time for a tea break. Florence can take over the store for half an hour. . .if you'd like to talk, that is."

"Yes, I think I would."

The schoolmarm rode back to town with the rest in Annie's wagon, and she got out with Libby and Florence at the Paragon Emporium. Josiah Runnels reported that business had been spotty, which was normal during shooting club hours. Half the town's women had been improving their marksmanship.

"Florence, you'll be all right for a short while?" Libby asked as she removed her bonnet.

"Yes ma'am."

Libby smiled and led Isabel up the stairs to her private quarters. She quickly built up the fire in her cookstove and set the kettle on. While they waited for it to heat, she took out delicate pink and white china cups and silver teaspoons. Snowy linen napkins and a cut glass plate followed. Isabel watched so avidly that Libby wondered whether the young woman was starved for beauty. Libby loaded the plate with small shortbread cookies, dried figs, and chocolate-dipped wafers. Not homemade, but she supposed Isabel would understand.

"I don't have much time to cook, so I let the store keep me in refreshments for my few guests."

"You needn't apologize. Those look heavenly." Isabel carried the plate to a drop-leaf table while Libby poured the hot water into a teapot that matched the cups. She brought it to the table and sat down.

"How have you been, Isabel?" she asked. "School is nearly out, isn't it? You must be ready for a break."

"I am. And I hope I'll be able to rest a bit. Not like last summer." Isabel scrunched up her face.

"Ah yes, the boardinghouse."

"It's a good venture on Papa's part," Isabel said quickly. "The Fennel House was profitable last fall, but I'm glad Papa hired the Thistles to take it over."

"Yes. It was too much for you when school resumed." Libby carefully filled their teacups.

"Of course, they barely had any boarders all winter, but now that the stage line is running again, the drivers bunk there, and passengers go there for dinners. We had quite a few wanting overnight accommodations last summer and fall."

Libby nodded with a smile and wondered how long it would take Isabel to get around to the real issue. "Are you getting enough rest now?" she asked.

"Oh yes, I suppose so. The end of a school term is always hectic. But we'll have the final program and recitations in a few weeks, and then we'll have six weeks off. I do look forward to it." The lines on Isabel's forehead didn't smooth out as she took a sip of her tea.

"I'm glad you get some time off. Of course, I imagine you'll have a garden to tend and a lot of other things to catch up on."

"Yes, I always have projects I've put off during school, but a change is as good as a rest, they say."

Libby reached for a cookie. "Please help yourself, my dear. I'm glad you were able to rejoin the shooting club this spring. It always refreshes me to get out of the store and have a chance to talk to other women."

Isabel nodded hesitantly. Until she'd joined the club, she hadn't mixed much with other women in town. Lately Libby had begun to know Isabel a little better. Beneath the prim, correct exterior, she found a lonely woman grieving the loss of her mother.

"Mrs. Adams—"

"Yes?"

Isabel's gaze fell. "Nothing. It's just. . ."

"You can speak freely."

Isabel swallowed and looked up at her. "I've worried about Papa lately."

"Have you? Is his health declining?"

"No, it's not that." Isabel picked up her teaspoon and laid it down again. "May I confide in you, Mrs. Adams?"

"Of course, but please call me Libby."

"Thank you. You knew my mother."

The turn of conversation took Libby by surprise, but she nodded and smiled. Better to discuss Mary than Cyrus. "Of course. Mary was a lovely lady."

"Did she ever talk to you about her family back East?"

"Maybe now and then." Libby frowned, trying to remember. "She was from Massachusetts, wasn't she?"

"Yes. Waterford. And she had an older sister, who died at the age of fifteen. Consumption."

"Oh, I'm sorry." Libby waited, sensing that there must be more to come.

Isabel sighed. "Yes, Mama grieved for her sister to her dying day. I was always told it was just the two girls in the family. But. . ." Her face tightened, and she caught her breath.

"But what, my dear?" Libby asked gently.

"A man came to call last Wednesday evening. He said he was her brother."

"Oh my." Libby sat back and studied her guest. "Was your father at home?"

"Yes, for which I was thankful. But. . .but Papa talked to him for a long time in his study. The man stayed for dinner, and he seemed glad to meet me. But you'd think I'd have known I had an uncle, wouldn't you?"

"Yes, it does seem odd. Did you speak to your father about this?"

"The next morning I asked him point-blank why I'd never

heard of Uncle Kenton before." Isabel lifted her teacup with trembling hands and took a sip.

"What was his explanation?" Libby asked.

"He told me Kenton had been to prison, and my mother was ashamed of him."

Libby pondered that. "Perhaps it's true."

"Perhaps. But it seems odd that my parents kept up this rather elaborate lie for nearly thirty years. Mother even told me once she wished she'd had more siblings. It was always her and Leola in the stories she told, never any boys. This Kenton said he was a few years older than Mother, and by the look of him, it fits, but. . ." Isabel shook her head. "I'm confused. Papa said he wanted to tell me when I reached my majority, but Mama discouraged him, so he kept it quiet."

Libby reached across the table and patted her hand. "I'm sorry you found out so abruptly. I'm sure your father didn't mean to shock you."

"I suppose not."

"Many people come out West to make a new start, hoping no one will ever learn of their somewhat checkered past."

"That's true, but when I was younger, we got letters now and then from my grandparents in Massachusetts. They never spoke of Kenton. It's strange."

"Yes, it is." Libby considered all she knew about Cyrus Fennel and the way he treated people. She suspected Isabel had not experienced the closeness of a doting father. Mary's cryptic words after her miscarriage came to mind, but this was not the time to bring up that sad memory. "I'm sure he felt it was in your best interest not to know about this unsavory uncle, and that you would be happier not knowing."

"Perhaps."

"And if you decided to marry someday and have children of your own, you wouldn't feel burdened to pass on the family's dark secret."

Isabel huffed out a bitter chuckle. "Not much chance of that happening."

"Oh, come now." Libby smiled, hoping to draw her guest into a lighter frame of mind. "Women your age, and even mine, have been known to find husbands."

"Do you mean you would consider marrying again?" Isabel stared at her with huge eyes.

Libby smiled and gave a delicate shrug. "I haven't ruled out the possibility. If the right man should take notice."

"I know what you mean."

"Do you?" Libby suspected she knew the man Isabel longed to have notice her. The schoolteacher had cast yearning glances at Griffin Bane for years, but the blacksmith had never seemed to take the hint. "There are several good men in Fergus who are eligible, and it's more than two years since my Isaac died."

"You don't have someone in mind, do you? Oh, forgive me." Isabel blushed a becoming pink. "That was too nosy of me."

"Not at all. I'll confide in you as well. There is one man in town who interests me. Perhaps one day both of us will find romance."

Isabel smiled for the first time all afternoon. "I hope so for your sake. I fear it's not in my future. But now I'm wondering. . . ."

"Yes?" Libby prepared for a direct question as to where her heart lay. She wasn't ready to reveal that, though it might set Isabel at ease to know they were not both attracted to the same man.

Instead, Isabel looked up, the strain showing in her thin face. "There's something else."

"Concerning your father?"

"Yes."

Libby took a sip of her tea and braced herself for a mention of Cyrus's drinking habits. What on earth would she say?

Isabel inhaled deeply and met her gaze. "I wasn't going to say anything about this part, but. . ."

"What you say will go no further than this room," Libby said.

"Thank you. I fell asleep Wednesday evening. Uncle Kenton was still in Papa's study with him. I'd overheard what sounded like an argument, but I couldn't make sense of it. I was afraid Papa would invite him to spend the night, and I didn't want to face him again, so I went to bed. Some time later, I awoke to a strange noise."

"What sort of noise?"

"Digging."

"Digging?"

Isabel nodded. "I couldn't imagine at first what it was, but I went outside. All of our ranch hands were away. I was terrified."

Libby knew well the shiver of fear that could come over a woman alone, especially at night. "What happened?"

"You mustn't tell anyone."

"Of course not."

"I...I went out around the barn, and I saw my father burying something."

Libby sat back quickly and thought about that. "What was it?"

"I have no idea."

The silence hung between them. Libby didn't like where her thoughts led her.

"Was your uncle with him?" she asked at last.

"No, he wasn't. I hadn't heard him leave, but as I said, I'd fallen asleep."

Libby reached for her cup. "Let's think about this logically, my dear. Did the man arrive on horseback?"

"I don't know."

"And you haven't seen him since?"

"No. I asked Papa about him the next morning. He said Uncle Kenton would stay in the area and might visit us again, but he hasn't so far."

"It's been less than a week," Libby noted. "Still..."

"Yes," said Isabel. They sat looking at each other. Finally, she picked up her cup.

"Let me freshen that for you," Libby said.

"No, thank you. I should let you get back to work. But thank you for listening."

"Isabel, you can't think..." Libby stopped, not wanting to put it into words.

"That my uncle is in the hole behind the barn?" Isabel grimaced. "I'm trying not to think it. I expect I'm being silly. But I haven't dared ask Papa about that hole."

Libby reached for her hand. "Let me go with you to your father's office. We'll confront him together, and he'll tell you this is a huge mistake. There must be a sensible explanation."

Isabel bit her lip and shook her head quickly. "I daren't, Libby. He would be angry with me for suggesting something so foolish, don't you see? That might—probably would—be worse than the truth we would learn."

Libby sighed and drew back her hand. "I'm sorry. Do you think...?"

"What?"

"I don't know. Perhaps we should tell someone. Sheriff Chapman, for instance."

"Oh no!" Isabel's cheeks grew rosy. "I'm risking Papa's anger just by telling you. You mustn't let anyone else know what I saw, Libby. You promised."

"Yes, I did," she said reluctantly. "I'll keep my word. But you must make me a promise."

"What?"

"That if you're ever afraid, you will come to me. Or go straight to Ethan Chapman. His ranch is close to yours."

"Oh, I couldn't—"

"Now you're being silly. My dear, if you ever think there's a remote possibility that you're in physical danger, you must act. Come here anytime, day or night. Give me your word."

"All right." Isabel inhaled deeply and let out a shaky breath. "I know it can't be true...what we're both thinking. But even if it's not, I can't help wondering where Uncle Kenton is and what is buried out back, and...Libby, what else has my father not told me?"

★ CHAPTER 11 ★

Hiram slid his checker forward with one finger. He looked up into Ethan's eyes and chuckled. Ethan scowled but crowned his playing piece with another checker.

Hiram sat back and waited for his friend to consider his next move. One good thing about Ethan: He was there when you needed him. The Dooley house had gotten a little too congested for Hiram during the past week. Females in and out all the time, what with the welcome tea the preacher's wife had helped Trudy host for Rose, and the shooting club ladies coming to consult Trudy on everything from guns to quilting bees these days.

The jailhouse had become his hideaway, and Ethan didn't seem to mind. After all, the sheriff had spent enough evenings in Hiram and Trudy's kitchen. The way Hiram saw it, he'd called the loan, and Ethan was paying him back by giving him a quiet place to get away from the petticoats.

Scrambling footsteps on the walk jostled them both from their reverie. Ethan stood as they looked toward the door.

"Sheriff! Come quick!" The dark-haired saloon girl, Vashti, stood panting in the doorway.

"What is it?" Ethan reached for his hat as he spoke.

"A bunch of tough cowpokes are likely to tear up Miss Bitsy's place. She told me to get you pronto."

"Where they from?"

"I never seen 'em before. Augie went for his shotgun, but the leader drew on him before he could get to it."

Ethan touched his sidearm as though making sure it was there and strode to the door. "Stay here, Miss Vashti, or go to Dooleys' and stay with Trudy."

Hiram followed him down the path toward the street. No way was he staying behind with the flashy bar girl.

Ethan dashed up the boardwalk, and Hiram stuck to his heels. Not that he wanted to get involved in a brawl, but if Ethan was headed for trouble, he might need someone he trusted at his back. He couldn't let Trudy's suitor get shot up before he'd gotten around to proposing either. What would he tell his sister?

Hiram had never been into the Spur & Saddle, not even for the Sunday chicken dinner. But he knew from what people told him that the place mostly stayed quiet and orderly compared to the Nugget. Miners and ranch hands favored the noisier, roughneck place. Tonight was only Friday, in any case. Saturday night was when most cowpokes cut loose.

A gunshot rang through the cool evening air. Ethan picked up speed, and so did Hiram. Bitsy had invested a lot in her business. Even though it was a saloon, everyone would hate to see anyone hurt or the only piano in town get damaged.

Nearly a dozen horses were tied outside the Spur & Saddle, and sharp voices burst from inside. A rancher tore out the door and nearly collided with Ethan.

"What's going on in there?" Ethan grabbed Micah Landry's jacket to steady them both.

"Sheriff! Good thing you're here. Bunch of toughs giving Bitsy a hard time. Wanting more drink and getting personal with the girls. She told them to take it to the Nugget, but they won't leave."

"Who fired the shot?"

"One of them. Augie went for his piece, but he wasn't fast enough."

Ethan pulled his .45. "How many customers inside?"

"Maybe ten or a dozen."

Bitsy's strident voice came from within. "Leave her alone. You all just get out of here. You're not welcome anymore."

"Get away, Micah." Ethan mounted the steps and cautiously peered through the half-open door.

Micah stared after him then looked at Hiram. "You're going in with him?"

Hiram shrugged and climbed the steps to stand behind Ethan. He wished he had a gun.

From inside, a man snarled, "We don't leave 'til I say we leave. And you, Mr. Bartender—you can just step away from where your gun is and pour the whiskey. Me an' the boys want another drink."

Hiram caught a deep breath and shot off something like a prayer as he peered over Ethan's shoulder. The well-lit room seemed full of people. It took him a moment to realize half of them were reflected in the mirror behind the bar. That must be the one Oscar Runnels had packed all the way up here by mule train ten years or more ago.

A big cowboy seemed to be the one speaking. He faced away from them and toward Augie, whose fists were clenched on the surface of the bar. So far the leader hadn't noticed Ethan and Hiram in the mirror.

Three other men stood near the interloper with their hands hovering over their holsters. One of them held Goldie, the blond bar girl, close to him, with his arm clamped about her waist. Hiram didn't let his gaze linger on that travesty. The poor girl must be terrified. Bitsy stood to one side, next to a table full of regulars—two town councilmen and a stagecoach driver.

Ethan stepped into the room. Before he could reason himself out of it, Hiram followed. He sensed someone close behind him and flicked a glance rearward. Micah had changed his mind. The odds felt better.

"All right, folks," Ethan said, "Let's settle down and put the firearms away."

The big cowboy spun toward him with a heavy Colt Dragoon pistol in his hand.

"Well now, it's the law." The man's teeth gleamed white in the lamplight. He held the pistol loosely in his hand, as though he'd forgotten it was there, but the muzzle pointing toward Ethan didn't waver. The sounds Hiram expected in a saloon—clinking glass, soulful music, and friendly laughter—all were absent.

"Put it away," Ethan said. Everyone in the room stood still. Ethan held the cowboy's stare. "Unless you want to spend the night in jail, be quick about it."

At the extreme range of his vision, Hiram caught movement. Zach Harper was scooting around the edge of the room toward the door. Now that the attention was off him, Augie cautiously stooped and slid his hands beneath the bar.

"You heard the sheriff." Bitsy stepped forward in all her shimmering evening finery. The jeweled choker about her snowy neck caught the lamplight. "Drop the gun."

The big man made as if to lay his pistol on the nearest table then whipped it toward Ethan. At the same moment, one of the other roughnecks leaped toward Hiram with his fists raised.

A pistol roared. Hiram didn't pause to think about it. He ducked, avoiding the cowboy's swing, and landed a solid blow in the assailant's midsection. The cowboy grunted and swayed. Hiram took the opportunity and threw his weight behind the next punch. He hit the man square on the jaw.

Shouts and screams erupted around him. Chairs scraped the floor. Hiram was aware only of the man he'd punched sagging backward and spreading his arms as he hit the floor.

Another shot rang close behind him, and Ethan yelled. "That's it, folks. We're done."

Hiram sucked in a breath and pulled his throbbing knuckles to his mouth. When he was a kid, it never hurt like that to hit someone.

Ethan continued to speak in a firm but soothing tone. "Easy now. You fellows just keep your hands high."

Hiram turned slowly. Acrid smoke hung in the air. Ethan covered the two remaining strangers with his pistol. The one who'd started the trouble lay sprawled on the floor near a tipped chair, bleeding on Bitsy's nice oak floor. Goldie had escaped the men and huddled at the end of the bar near Augie, who now held his shotgun up where all could see it.

Didn't Ethan look fine? Too bad Trudy couldn't see him, with his dark hair falling down over his forehead and his eyes blazing. Their sheriff had proved his mettle tonight. The two unscathed cowpokes shook in their boots at the sight of him.

Bitsy stepped forward. "Want I should disarm them, Sheriff?"

"Thank you, ma'am." Ethan held his ground with his gun trained on the cowboys.

Bitsy stepped toward the first one, staying as far away as she could and still ease his pistol out of his holster. When she had both the men's sidearms, she laid them on the bar.

"All, right, you two," Ethan said, "you didn't draw your weapons, so go on. Get out of here, and don't come back."

"What about Eli and Sandy?" one of them asked. He looked toward the man Ethan had shot and shuddered.

"I don't expect that one is going anywhere. As to the other fella, he'll spend the night in the jailhouse." Ethan nodded toward the man Hiram had laid out on the floor.

"Wait a minute, Sheriff." Bitsy strode toward the man who had spoken. She glared at him for a moment, drew back her hand, and slapped him. "That's for Goldie. She ain't that kind of girl." She turned her back and walked over to embrace Goldie. "It's okay, honey."

Ethan looked at the cowpokes and nodded toward the door. "Go on. Tell your boss he can come bail that one fella out if he wants him back."

The two glanced toward their six-guns.

"You can pick those up tomorrow at the jail, provided you're sober."

The men walked meekly out the door. Ethan exhaled and closed his eyes for a second.

Micah clapped him on the back. "Good job, Ethan."

The men who had been playing poker before the incident started clapping. Bitsy, Goldie, Augie, and the other patrons joined the applause.

Hiram grinned at Ethan. "Want me to fetch Doc Kincaid?"

Ethan caught his breath. "Yes, get him quick. There may be help for that fella."

Augie was already bending over the wounded man. The one Hiram had hit stirred and moaned. He raised his hand to his jaw.

"Hiram Dooley, you surprised me!"

Hiram turned and found Zack Harper beside him.

"You sure conked that no-account. I wouldn't have believed it if I hadn't seen it."

"Yeah, Hi, where'd that punch come from?" Micah asked. "You weren't a boxer in your salad days, were you?"

Bitsy walked over and squeezed his arm. "I never thought of you as pugilistic, Hiram. Goes to show you never know a person as well as you think. And I thank you for assisting the sheriff."

Hiram opened his mouth to speak and closed it again. Truth was, he felt a little shaky.

Ethan was conferring in low tones with Augie, but he turned to the second cowboy, who had rolled over and pushed himself up on his knees.

"Okay, mister, get up nice and slow. Put your hands out where I can see 'em." Within seconds, Ethan had the cowboy's wrists tied with a short length of twine supplied by Augie. "No need for the doctor, Hi."

Hiram nodded and looked again at the dead cowboy as Ethan herded his prisoner toward the door.

"Death certificate?"

"That's right," Bitsy said. "Now that we have a doctor, we should get him to look at all the dead bodies and write out death certificates."

The others stared at her.

"That came out wrong," she said. "You know what I mean. We went a long time with no doc to make it official."

Hiram nodded with the rest. They all remembered deaths in Fergus that had gone unrecorded.

"I'll fetch him." Hiram hurried out the door in spite of his wobbly knees. The fresh air revived him. He ran along the boardwalk ahead of Ethan and the prisoner, past the jail to the boardinghouse. Dr. Kincaid sat in the parlor, reading by lamplight.

"Can you come to the Spur & Saddle, Doc?"

Kincaid rose, his lithe, athletic form seeming out of place among the fussy cushions and doilies of Mrs. Thistle's parlor. "I'll get my bag."

"You won't need it," Hiram said.

"Oh?" Kincaid arched his eyebrows.

"The fella's dead. Sheriff Chapman shot him."

"I see."

"We need you to. . .well, look at him."

"I'll go right along. Anyone else hurt?"

"Well…one fella got a little bruised up, and…" Hiram realized he was kneading the knuckles of his right hand. He held it out sheepishly. "Looks like he's not the only one."

Kincaid reached for Hiram's hand and drew him closer to the lamp. He probed the joints. "Does that hurt?"

"Yes sir."

The doctor studied the hand for a moment longer, feeling it gently. "Flex your fingers, please." After Hiram complied, he nodded. "You'll be sore for a week or two. It's swelling. Soak it in Epsom salts. Sometimes wrapping it helps. And a nip of whiskey—"

"Oh, I can't have whiskey."

Kincaid nodded. "Well then, willow bark tea may ease the pain if it's bad enough for you to want something. Tell your sister."

"Yes sir. Thank you."

"All right, I'll go along to the Spur & Saddle. Where do they want the body?"

"Griff Bane can lay him out at the livery."

"Who is it, anyway?"

Hiram puzzled for a moment. "I don't rightly know. There were four of them. Cowboys, not miners. They were wearing spurs. But they never said what outfit they work for."

"I'll ask the sheriff." Kincaid headed for the stairs.

Mrs. Thistle stood in the doorway between the parlor and the dining room. "What happened, Mr. Dooley?"

"Just a little fracas at the saloon, ma'am."

"Thank heaven it was the one down the street for a change."

"Yes ma'am."

"Did I hear you say you hurt your hand?"

"Oh, it's nothing." He shoved his hand into his trouser pocket and tried not to wince. He was eager to get home and try that willow bark tea and Epsom salts.

"Well, between your sister and Mrs. Caplinger, the womenfolk will know what to do, like Dr. Jim said."

Hiram gulped. The last person he wanted hovering and fussing over him was Rose.

★ CHAPTER 12 ★

Libby totaled the order for Annie Harper. Coffee, sugar, saleratus, and a length of dress goods.

"Let's see, now. I believe that with the eggs and milk you've been supplying me, you haven't used all your credit, Annie."

"That's wonderful. Zack's been a little short on cash lately. Say, did you hear about the dustup at Bitsy's place last night?"

"No. What happened?" Libby reached under the counter for a roll of brown paper. "Let me wrap your material for you."

"Thank you. Seems Sheriff Chapman and Hiram Dooley stood off a half dozen gunfighters."

Libby let the roll of paper thump onto the counter. "They *what?*"

"My husband saw the whole thing. He said a bunch of strangers rode in and were drinking too hard. They started tearing up the saloon. Ethan marched in there and shot the leader dead, and Hiram got into fisticuffs with one of the others. Laid him out cold on the floor."

Aware that her lower jaw was hanging, Libby snapped it shut. She could scarcely credit what she was hearing, but still. . .Zack Harper wouldn't lie about something like that. Though he might exaggerate.

"I thought I heard a gunshot or two, but when I opened my window, I didn't hear anything more," she said. "Is. . .is the sheriff all right?"

"I expect so. Zachary said he was right as rain when he left the saloon last night, and I haven't heard otherwise."

Libby finished wrapping the parcel, and Annie went on her way. Only a few customers had come early to the emporium. Libby took off her apron and beckoned Florence to the counter.

"I need to step over to Trudy's for a minute. Will you be all right?"

"Yes ma'am." Florence, at nineteen, was one of the beauties of Fergus. Her red hair and green eyes drew all the young men's attention, and she sometimes had to choose whom to allow to sit beside her at church. She was a good girl and a steady worker, and Libby had trained her well over the past two years.

"Say, did your father mention anything this morning about some unpleasantness at the Spur & Saddle last night?"

"No, but Mr. Harper and Mr. Bane came to see him as I was leaving to come to work. Papa was still at breakfast."

So, the council members were making sure Peter Nash, the mayor, knew about the latest doings. "I won't be long." Libby grabbed her bonnet and shawl and hustled out the door. She dashed across Main Street and down the boardwalk to the path beside the Dooleys' house. When she knocked, Rose opened the back door.

"Oh, Mrs. Caplinger." Libby paused to catch her breath and consider how to word her inquiry. "Is Trudy about this morning?"

Rose's pretty nose wrinkled. "She's feeding the livestock. Mr. Dooley injured his hand, and his sister felt obliged to do the chores for him."

"Oh my. It's not serious, I hope."

Rose lowered her thick, dark eyelashes and sighed. "The doctor examined him, and he assured Mr. Dooley that he would recover in a few weeks."

"Weeks?" Libby caught herself. She'd save the questions for Trudy. "Well, I hope this won't keep him from his work. I'll just step over and..." She turned as a door creaked across the barnyard. Trudy was just coming from the barn, carrying a basin of chicken feed.

"Hello, Libby! What are you doing here?" she called.

Libby gathered her skirts. "Thank you, Mrs. Caplinger." She turned and hurried toward Trudy. "I came to ask you a question." She lowered her voice and looked back toward the kitchen, but

Rose had already withdrawn and closed the door. "Is. . .is the sheriff all right? I just heard about the brawl at Bitsy's."

Trudy gave a rueful smile. "Ethan's fine. He's taking it hard that he killed a man. But I wish I'd been there to see it when he stood up to those fellows. Hiram, too."

"Yes. Your sister-in-law said Hiram was injured."

Trudy shrugged and opened the gate to the poultry yard. "He'll be all right. But next time I expect he'll think a little longer before he lambastes a tough cowpoke."

Libby gasped. "His hand. . . ?"

"Bruised pretty good. All colors of the rainbow this morning."

"Will he be able to work?"

"It may be a few days before he does fine work. I'm tending the horses this morning only because Rose insisted he shouldn't carry a pail of water from the pump to the trough. As if he couldn't lug it with his left hand. But I don't mind. Hiram's done a lot of chores for me." Trudy flung handfuls of cracked corn to the dozen chickens in the yard, and they scrambled about her feet to get it.

Libby noted that Rose's mothering of Hiram stopped short of offering to do the work herself. "Well. I'm glad he's all right. If you need anything. . ."

"Doc Kincaid said to soak it in Epsom salts, and we did that last night. I may need another package, though."

"I'll bring it over this afternoon. No charge."

Trudy's eyes widened. "Why, thank you, but there's no need to bankrupt yourself on our account."

"You said your brother may be unable to do close work for a while, so he'll lose some income. Besides, a man who defends our town ought to be treated special, don't you think?"

Trudy lowered her empty basin and grasped Libby's sleeve, her eyes gleaming. "Libby, you know Hiram wouldn't want anyone to fuss over him—he'd be so embarrassed—but I've got to tell you, from what Ethan says, Hi is a real hero. He jumped right into the fray to support Ethan. Those men would have ruined Bitsy's place and maybe killed some innocent people if Ethan and Hi hadn't stepped in." Her grave expression smoothed out, and she gave a conspiratorial smile. "Rose asked Hiram whatever ailed him to walk into danger like that. Know what he said?"

Libby shook her head, amazed at how eager she was to hear the answer.

"He said he'd heard Miss Bitsy had a great big mirror and lots of pretty furniture in there, and when he saw it was true, he couldn't bear to let those rowdies stave it up."

Libby blinked at her. "That doesn't sound like Hiram."

Trudy laughed. "I think he was trying to get Rose to ease up. She practically swooned when she saw what he did to his hand. I think he was afraid Ethan was going to get himself killed. He went in there for his friend's sake. Well, and maybe a little for Bitsy, too, since she was so good about helping defend the town when we needed it. Hiram and I pray every day that she'll come to know the Lord."

"So do I." Libby felt tears spring into her eyes. She'd known Hiram was a praying man, but it touched her deeply to hear of his faithful pleas for the saloon owner. "Do you and Hiram pray together? He's so quiet."

"Usually I pray, and he just says, 'amen.' But I know he prays inside." Trudy frowned. "Since Rose came, we've quit reading scripture together. Used to do it after breakfast every morning, but now. . ." Trudy sighed. "Rose being here sort of puts us off kilter. She makes Hi nervous as a cat."

"I'm sorry about that. Any indication of how long her visit will last?"

"Not yet." Trudy fastened the gate to the chicken yard. "She made gingerbread yesterday because she remembered he used to like it, and she's talking about piecing a wedding ring quilt, of all things."

It was a bit blatant, but Libby couldn't bring herself to comment on Rose's choice of quilt patterns.

"Now that she sees my brother as a wounded hero, who knows?" Trudy asked. "If she had her way, I think she'd make mollycoddling him her life's mission, if you know what I mean."

Libby knew all too well what she meant.

★ CHAPTER 13 ★

Ethan slid his prisoner's breakfast through the slot at the bottom of the cell wall. It was a little late, but the Thistles had fed their roomers first before bringing flapjacks and bacon for two to the jailhouse. He poured himself a mug of coffee, set the pot back on the small woodstove, and went to his desk to eat his own meal from the tray. He'd left the door of his office open, since the stove had heated things up all too well.

He'd just finished the stack of flapjacks and wished there were more when the prisoner decided to talk.

"You gonna keep me here all day?"

"Maybe." Ethan shoved the tray aside and tilted his chair back, resting his boots on the desktop. He sipped his coffee. "How's the headache this mornin'?"

"Tolerable."

Ethan grunted and drank more coffee. So far all he'd gotten out of the prisoner was his name—Eli Button. Didn't sound like a real name to Ethan. Probably made it up, though he'd met some folks with strange names. But none of the current wanted posters had a name like that.

When he'd drained his mug, he lowered his feet to the floor with a thump and stood. "You want more coffee, Button?"

"Much obliged."

"Slide your cup out here."

When the prisoner had stood back from the bars again, Ethan picked up the tin cup he allowed inmates and took it with his ironstone mug to the stove. He poured Button's drink first and took it back to the cell. "There you go." When he had his own refilled mug in hand, he went back to his desk. "I can't let you go until I know who you work for. I need to notify your boss about your dead partner."

Button scowled. "I'm sure the other boys told him."

"We'll see." Ethan settled his boots on the desktop again. "I'm not letting you go until I see your ranch foreman in here." He hadn't voiced the thought that perhaps Button wasn't really employed at a local ranch at all. He'd never seen any of the men who'd caused trouble at Bitsy's last night. Odd for a rancher to hire an all-new crew, and even odder for the folks in town not to hear about it.

"We h'aint been here long." Button's voice bordered on whiny. "The fella that owns the ranch is named Fennel."

Ethan froze with his mug an inch from his lips. After a moment, he set it down. "Cyrus Fennel."

"That's right."

"You don't work on Fennel's main ranch, though." Fennel was a close neighbor of Ethan's, and they saw each other almost daily on the road or in town. Ethan couldn't believe he wouldn't know if Cyrus had doubled his crew overnight.

"Naw, it's about ten miles from here. But he owns it."

"Who's the foreman?"

"Eastern fella, name of Smith."

Ethan let out a short puff of air, just short of a snort. Smith sounded even more bogus than Button.

The doorway darkened, and he looked up. Griffin Bane, the big blacksmith, filled the space.

"I can stay for an hour. No more."

"Shouldn't take that long." Ethan swung his long legs down off the desk. "I don't expect trouble, but it's possible someone from the ranch where this hothead works will come by to bail him out."

"Where you going to be if I need you?"

Ethan stood and reached for his hat. "Over to Mayor Nash's house. The council's meeting. I don't know why they need me there." He gritted his teeth, hoping they weren't going to give him any grief over last night's shooting.

"Glad I'm not on the council this year." Griff plopped down in Ethan's chair and eyed his mug speculatively. "You done with this coffee?"

"Yeah. Help yourself to more. See you shortly."

Ethan hoofed it for the Nashes' home, where Peter kept the post office on the boarded-in front porch. He'd hoped to catch Cyrus as he left his office, but the Wells Fargo station was empty when Ethan passed.

He walked into the post office—you never knocked on the outer door—and rapped on the door to the house. Ellie Nash opened it.

"Good morning, Sheriff. The council is all here, I believe. They're in the parlor. Can I bring you coffee?"

"Just had some, thank you, ma'am." Ethan pulled off his hat and entered the small parlor. Though it wasn't so fine as the Walkers', it felt cozier. Meetings here always seemed more cordial than the ones last year, when Charles Walker had presided.

Ethan nodded at Libby Adams, the newest member. Folks had debated long and hard last fall over letting a woman sit on the town council. Since they hadn't achieved statehood yet, the town pretty much made its own rules. The Ladies' Shooting Club of Fergus had strong opinions that they lobbied for, one of them being that women should be able to hold town offices and vote on local questions.

A lot of men had protested, but in the end, the ladies and the minority of men supporting them had won. Bitsy had pointed out that widows and unmarried women who owned property were already allowed to vote on special property-tax issues in the territory. It was only a small step, she declared, until they gained equal suffrage with men. Throughout the territory, the push for women's voting rights was strong.

Personally, Ethan was glad they had a female council member. It kept Cyrus, Oscar, and Zack from swearing and smoking those infernal cigars they liked so much.

"Welcome, Sheriff," Peter said. "Take a seat. We have several items to discuss, but we'll put the one that concerns you first so you can get back to your duties."

"Thank you." Ethan tried to ignore the tickle in his chest.

How bad could it be?

"First of all, as the current leaders of the town, we would like to thank you for the boldness you exhibited last night in protecting the lives and virtue of our citizens and the property of one of our leading business owners."

Ethan looked down and adjusted his position in the chair. What other town would commend a man for defending a saloon? "It's part of the job, I reckon."

"Nevertheless, we extend our gratitude to you as sheriff. This council is in agreement that we ought to raise your pay a dollar a week."

Ethan jerked his chin up and met Peter's gaze. A dollar a week would go a long ways. Because of all the time he spent in town fulfilling his duties, he'd had to keep his ranch hands longer in the fall and hire them back earlier this spring.

"Why, thank you very much. I appreciate your confidence."

Libby said, "And we appreciate your valiance."

Oscar frowned as if puzzling over that word.

"Thank you, ma'am," Ethan said.

"Did you find out who the fella you plugged is?" Zack asked.

Libby winced, and Ethan felt his face flush in sympathy.

"Not yet. The prisoner's pretty tight-lipped, but"—he glanced at Cyrus—"Mr. Fennel, if I might have a word with you when you're finished here, I'd appreciate it."

Cyrus cleared his throat. "Are you implying that I had something to do with last night's shootout? Because I haven't set foot in the Spur & Saddle since—"

Ethan held out one hand. "No sir, not at all. It's just. . ." He looked around, wondering how much he should spill in front of the others.

"Spit it out." Cyrus glared at him.

"All right. The prisoner—that is, the man Hiram Dooley knocked out during the fracas—says he and the other troublemakers work on one of your ranches."

"What—" Cyrus stopped abruptly and clamped his lips shut in a bitter frown. "I see."

"Do you? Because I don't, Mr. Fennel."

Cyrus harrumphed and took a gulp from his cup.

Peter looked around at the others, and his gaze came back to Cyrus. "If you can shed any light on this situation, Cy, we'd appreciate it. Zack said the four roughnecks were all strangers, but if you know them..."

"I don't know them." Cyrus shot Ethan a dark glance then heaved a sigh. "I suppose they're out to the old Martin ranch."

"You don't know?" Oscar sat up and poked a stubby, accusing finger toward him. "You mean to tell me you don't know who's living on your property? That don't sound like you, Cyrus."

Fennel rubbed the back of his neck and met Peter's gaze. "The truth is, I have a tenant out there now. Didn't know he would hire a bunch of rabble-rousers. I had no idea until this minute that those men came from out there." He turned toward Ethan. "You sure that's where they're from?"

"No sir, but the prisoner says it's about ten miles from here."

Cyrus nodded reluctantly. "That's about how far it is to the old Martin place. My most remote property." He sighed again and slumped in the armchair. "I haven't been able to do anything with the place. A fellow came along wanting to lease with an option to buy. He seemed like a decent man, and I agreed to let him live out there. He said he'd run some beef on the land."

"What's his name?" Libby eyed him keenly.

"Uh...Smith."

Ethan wondered at the little frown that puckered Libby's smooth brow.

"I don't know where he got his hands. Maybe some fellows who had worked for him someplace else. Anyway, I'll ride out there this afternoon after the stagecoach comes in. You can be sure this won't happen again."

"I should hope not," Peter said.

"I'll lay down the law to him." Cyrus reached for his coffee.

"You want me to let the prisoner go?" Ethan asked.

Zack let out a whoop of laughter. "Still can't believe Hiram Dooley put out his lights. Never would have expected him to do that, him being such a quiet man."

"Does the prisoner owe anything?" Cyrus asked, ignoring Zack.

Ethan shrugged. "I generally charge a buck a night, to save the town from paying their expenses. He had a couple of dollars on him. I can take it out of that if you want and pay the Thistles for his meals. But someone ought to pay for the damage at Bitsy's."

"How bad was it?" Oscar asked.

"Not much. I had her give me a list this morning. She says they broke one chair and three glasses, and the man that fired the gun made a hole in the wall. A couple of dollars ought to cover everything."

"I'll stop by the jailhouse later and pay you," Cyrus said. "And I'll speak to my tenant about making sure his hands stay out of trouble."

"Oh, and the other two—the ones I let go—I've got their six-shooters over at the jailhouse. You could return them, I guess, if you get a pledge they won't come fixing to bust up the town again."

"All right. I'll see you after lunch."

Ethan nodded. "We done?"

"I guess so," Peter said, glancing around at the other council members. "And again, Sheriff, we thank you for your excellent service."

Ethan left the house, wondering if Cyrus would be able to control his tenant's hired hands. He didn't want to walk into another gunfight anytime soon.

★ CHAPTER 14 ★

Late Saturday afternoon, the Ladies' Shooting Club met at its customary practice range. Libby almost skipped the extra practice session, but knowing her store could be the next place targeted by ne'er-do-wells spurred her to ask Josiah Runnels to take charge while she and Florence attended.

"This is awfully good of you," Bitsy said to her as they climbed down from Annie's wagon. "I know it's hard to leave off during business hours."

Libby put her arm around Bitsy's shoulders and gave her a squeeze. "The ladies rallied around me last year when I needed help. I think it behooves us all to be ready."

"I admit I was a little on edge last night. When Trudy said we ought to hold an extra meeting and show we can't be scared by a bunch of tough cowpokes, well, it seemed the right thing to do."

"I agree," Libby said. "It makes me feel stronger when we get together to shoot."

"Shooting is a skill every woman should learn, like plucking a chicken or making soap." Bitsy picked up the handful of bright rags they had brought along. The orange wool Annie had donated clashed with her red bloomer costume. "Don't like men messing up my place, though. Sometimes I wonder if I'm in the wrong business." She gave Libby a rueful smile.

"Shall we set up the targets?"

While Trudy gathered the other women for a safety review, Libby and Bitsy walked across the new green grass to fasten bits of cloth to sticks for the ladies to use as practice targets. Libby's mind roiled with possible comments. *Of course you're in the wrong business,* she wanted to scream. But that wouldn't help Bitsy or their tenuous friendship.

As Bitsy worked a scrap of orange fabric into the end of a split stick, Libby said cautiously, "You're such a good businesswoman. You've been on your own a long time, and you've made a success of it."

"Yes, I have." Bitsy pushed the other end of the stick into the soft earth. "Twenty years and more I've had my own place. Yes, twenty-three now. I came here at the height of the boom in these parts."

"About the time my Isaac came."

"True enough."

They walked a few yards to the spot where the next team would aim. Libby stood up the fallen stick they'd used to hold a rag on Thursday. "Do you ever think of doing something else?" she asked.

"Not really. What else could I do? I know liquor, and I know men. Oh, I know how to turn a dollar all right. But what else could I do now? Everyone knows I'm a saloon keeper."

"You could carry the same success into a new venture." Libby swallowed her jitters and went on. "I was glad to see you in church Sunday."

"Augie and the girls have been pestering me to go for months." Bitsy shrugged. "I still don't think I belong there."

"Why not? God welcomes anyone who comes." Libby expected a sharp rebuff, but Bitsy's expression softened.

"Maybe I'll go again. But if I go tomorrow, folks will expect me to be there every Sunday morning, and then who will set up the dining room? We were barely ready to serve dinner on time last week, and then only because Augie got up an hour early to bake his pies and biscuits."

Libby smiled. "I'm going to come over there for dinner one of these Sundays if I can get a handsome man to escort me."

"Naw! You wouldn't."

"Why wouldn't I?"

"You know why."

A flush tingled Libby's cheeks. It was true, she and a few

others avoided the saloon, even though the chicken dinner was served without alcoholic beverages on Sunday. Many families went. She'd heard the meal complimented by her customers. But the Sunday dinner had been instituted at the Spur & Saddle after Isaac died. Libby had never felt it proper, as a single woman, to be seen there.

"I wouldn't be embarrassed to come into your place for a meal. As I said, I'll just have to find someone. . ." She eyed Bitsy thoughtfully. "I don't suppose you've ever thought of going into the restaurant business?"

Bitsy waved a hand in dismissal. "There ain't enough folks in Fergus to support another eatery. Miz Thistle serves three meals a day now at the boardinghouse. I think she kinda resents us offering dinner on Sunday."

"Well you were here before she was." Libby smiled. "Come on. One more target."

As they set up the last one, Bitsy frowned in concentration. "You know, you're not the first to suggest I clean up my act, so to speak, though if I do say so, my place is always clean as a whistle."

"I'm sure it is." Libby waited, hoping she'd continue.

Bitsy straightened and brushed her hands together. "There. All set. I think Augie would like it if I switched to another line of work. He's not a jealous man, but he doesn't like it when drunks come in and point guns at him."

Libby arched her eyebrows. "You surprise me. I mean. . .I didn't know."

"About me an' Augie?" Bitsy shrugged. "He's been with me eight years and trying to get me to marry him for seven."

"Really!"

"Yup." Bitsy winked at her. "Didn't know I could keep a secret so good, did ya?"

"Well, no, I didn't." Libby opened her mouth again and then closed it. She was dying to ask Bitsy why she didn't marry Augie if he was so keen on it. The muscular, bald bartender seemed like a reliable man, and he'd shown more than once that he would protect Bitsy and work hard to help her succeed. Libby had always figured he was a loyal employee whom Bitsy paid well to tend bar and run out rowdies. No more. Now she'd discovered that he cooked the succulent meals people raved about and secretly wooed his boss. Quite a character, Augie Moore.

Bitsy smiled. "Looks like the teams are ready to shoot, Miz Adams. Let's git on over there. And you come by any Sunday. I promise you won't be embarrassed."

"I'm sure I won't, Bitsy."

"Nope. No risky paintings in my place. And my girls are good girls."

"Papa, I heard something today that disturbs me." Isabel set the platter of pork roast down on the table and faced her father, determined not to let him evade her questions.

"What was that?" He spread his napkin in his lap and waited for her to take her seat.

"That those wild cowboys who started trouble at the Spur & Saddle last Friday evening live on your property. People are saying it was one of your tenants that Sheriff Chapman shot."

Her father speared a baked potato and put it on his plate, then reached for the dish of mashed squash.

"Is it true, Papa?" She sat down and cut slices of meat for both of them.

Papa cut his potato open and smeared a generous slab of butter over the steaming pulp. "The men in the saloon weren't tenants. They were employees of a tenant."

She watched him cut his meat, certain there was more to the story than he revealed.

He stopped chewing and fixed his gaze on her. "Who are these people that you gossip so much with, anyway?"

Heat climbed from her collar to her hairline. "It seems everyone in town is talking about it."

"Yes, but it's those shooting club women you got it from, isn't it? I tried to tell Charles Walker last year that it meant trouble, letting women get together and shoot guns instead of tending their families like they'd ought."

"Well, Mayor Walker would be dead if it weren't for the shooting club. And maybe you, too."

Her father's whole face drooped. She felt a pang of guilt,

reminding him that his friend had been injured so badly he'd had to step down as mayor last summer. Walker had only recently resumed his activity at the feed store. But the truth could not be denied—without the patrols taken on by the women in time of crisis, the town of Fergus would have seen more murders.

They ate supper in gloomy silence. Isabel wondered how long she could endure this dreary existence. Uncle Kenton's appearance had brought new anxiety, and she had not forgotten about the hole behind the barn.

Since her mother's death, life at the ranch had become nearly unbearable. Only her teaching position and the new friendships she'd made through the shooting club kept her going. She'd nearly given up her girlhood dreams of marriage and a family of her own. She blamed that on her plain looks and living outside town, where she didn't get to know the other young people. Fergus hadn't even had a minister or regular church services until last July.

No suitors had ever approached her father for permission to court her. There'd been a day when she longed only for one man, but she'd never told anyone. Griffin Bane, the big, bearded blacksmith, though not as educated and refined as might be desired, had captured her heart long ago. If only he knew it. But she didn't expect him ever to ride out to the ranch to call on her.

"What's the matter now?" Her father stared at her with those cold gray eyes.

She realized she had let out a plaintive sigh. "Nothing, Papa. Would you like more pork?"

★ CHAPTER 15 ★

On Thursday afternoon, Trudy and Libby rode on horseback to the shooting club site. They'd started out early so they could set up new targets as a surprise for the women—animal shapes that Myra Harper had painted on muslin. Trudy had sewn them into bags and stuffed them with hay, so now the ladies would be able to shoot at a hare or a coyote or even a pronghorn for practice.

When they arrived, they ground tied Trudy's horse, Crinkles, and Hiram's laconic gelding, Hoss, who suffered Libby to ride him on occasion. Each horse was burdened with two of the bulky new targets, and they stood still while the women removed them.

"I'm glad I was able to get four done," Trudy said. "Each team will have one this way."

"The ladies will be so pleased." Libby helped her prop the first one up with sticks. "What's Rose up to these days?"

"Working on her quilt and cooking everything she thinks Hiram will like."

"Oh dear. At least it saves you some work if she does the cooking."

"Ha. Did I say she does the dishes afterward?" Trudy scowled as she prepared to hammer the stick into the ground. "That woman can dirty more dishes making a cake than the folks at the boardinghouse use in a week. Why, I might have to come over to the emporium and buy more dishes just so she can have enough to make an apple pandowdy."

Libby smiled, but she didn't feel any jollity. "She still won't come to the club?"

"Nope. Too mannish, she says. She thinks all the men in town are going to swarm around her because she's too delicate to pick up a gun."

"Oh." Libby swallowed hard as Trudy pounded in the stake. "I...thought she was only interested in Hiram."

"That doesn't keep her from harping on what a bad example I am and how uncouth western women have become. She's sure the men of Fergus would like their women to act feminine for a change." Trudy shrugged. "Between her nagging and Hiram's complaining, I don't much enjoy sticking to home these days."

"Hiram's..."

"He thinks I ought to be able to get Rose to leave him alone. Don't ask me how. She's got him running as scared as a rabbit that stumbled on a timber wolf rendezvous."

"Really?" Libby couldn't explain the warm feeling that washed over her, but she smiled as they carried the remaining targets to the next spot.

"She keeps wanting to change things in the house. She asked him if he wouldn't like Violet's sampler better between the windows instead of beside the door. Or if he wouldn't like her to make him a new blue shirt for Sundays, to bring out the blue in his eyes. Yesterday she went up in the attic and got into the trunk full of Violet's things. She said at the supper table she wanted to shorten one of Violet's skirts for herself."

"What did Hiram say?"

"He wasn't happy. But Rose said that since I hadn't made use of her sister's things in ten years, why shouldn't she? And Hiram gave in."

"Did you want the skirt?"

"No. It's taffeta, and I'm not a taffeta-wearing woman."

Libby smiled. "You would look lovely in the right taffeta dress. Though I can't for the life of me think where you'd wear it in Fergus. How is Hiram's hand?"

"Better, I think. He was working on Lyman Robinson's musket last evening." Trudy slipped a stick inside the cloth bag of a coyote target and stood it up. "Pound that in m'dear. But be ladylike about it."

Libby laughed and raised the hammer. "I'll be delicate, I

promise. Watch your thumbs, though."

When they finished situating the last target, Trudy wiped her brow. "It's getting right warm today."

"Summer will be here before you know it." Libby eyed her cautiously. "So what does your brother do when you're here at the club?"

"Goes wandering all over town to keep out of Rose's range."

"Ha!" Libby clapped her hand over her mouth after her unmannerly laugh. "Oh dear, forgive me."

"What is there to forgive? Hiram actually asked me this afternoon if there wasn't some way I could steer her off toward some other gent so she'd leave him alone."

"Say, that might not be a bad idea," Libby said. The more she considered it, the better she liked it. She studied Trudy. "I mean, if Hiram doesn't see the need to marry, why should he let a woman pester him?"

"Hiram's not against marriage. He wouldn't have married Violet in the first place if he were." Trudy's eyebrows drew together. "I think it's more that he doesn't want someone else deciding for him when he'll like a woman—or which woman he'll like."

Libby nodded. "Yes. Do you think. . ."

"What?"

"That he's finished his grieving? I know I still ache sometimes when I think of Isaac. And if someone else came along and told me it was time to be done with it and move on, I might resent their interference."

Trudy's face grew somber. "Hiram's grieved long and hard. I can't really say whether he's done or not."

Libby looked off toward the mountains. "I didn't mean to suggest he'd ever forget about Violet, but I think there does come a time for most folks when they realize. . .well, that God's left them here after their loved one went, and there's probably a reason for that. It makes you ready to open your eyes a little wider and try something new. Not a new marriage, necessarily, but *something*."

"Yes. But Rose won't be that something for Hi. So a distraction for Rose might be just the thing."

"Do you think so?"

"Well, he's the one who said it first." Trudy tugged at her

bonnet strings. "Maybe the shooting club could come up with a plan that would set her off in a different direction."

"It wouldn't surprise me a bit. We have some very imaginative ladies in the club. Surely if we put our heads together. . ."

"Well, I don't know. Hiram probably wouldn't like it if every woman in town was in on it. He doesn't like everybody else knowing his business, you know?"

"Hmm. What if you and I and one or two others attacked the problem?"

Trudy nodded slowly. "But not Mrs. Benton."

"Oh?"

"Not that there's anything wrong with the plan, but the preacher's wife might see it as. . ."

"Underhanded?"

"Well, do you think it's wrong to try to do a little matchmaking for the sake of someone you love?" Trudy studied her with somber blue gray eyes.

"Not wrong, but perhaps it would be best to keep Apphia out of it. That way, if anything backfires, she can tell her husband honestly that she knew nothing about it. How about Bitsy?"

"Bitsy's idea of the right man for Rose might not measure up to ours."

"True." Libby looked up at the sound of hoofbeats. "Here comes Starr. Looks like she's alone today."

The young woman cantered up on her husband's pinto with her dark hair tumbling down her back below her sunbonnet.

"Hello!" Starr pulled the mare to a halt near Crinkles and Hoss and leaped down. "Am I early?"

"The others will be here soon," Libby said.

"Where's Jessie?" Trudy asked.

"Oh, she's staying home with Hester today. I think our little gal's got the croup."

"That's too bad. But it was nice of your mother-in-law to stay with her and let you get out." Trudy looked over at Libby and raised her eyebrows.

"Oh, look! Are we going to shoot at those?" Starr had spotted the animal targets and strode toward them.

"Aren't they delightful?" Libby asked, walking after her. "Myra painted them, and Trudy stitched and stuffed them."

"I think they're absolutely darling. May my team shoot the bear?"

Trudy smiled. "I don't see why not."

Libby halted beside the young woman as she examined Myra's handiwork. "Starr, since we have a few moments alone, Trudy and I wanted to get your opinion on a matter."

"Oh?" Starr turned toward her eagerly. "I'll do anything for the club, if it's not too time-consuming. Arthur doesn't like me to be gone from the ranch for hours and hours."

"We just need to ask you something," Libby said.

"Yes," Trudy added. "It concerns my brother."

Starr looked from her to Libby, clearly intrigued. "I can't imagine what it could be, so you'll have to tell me."

Trudy cleared her throat. "Well, as you know, my sister-in-law has been visiting us for the past couple of weeks. Her visit has presented a. . ."

"An interesting challenge," Libby said quickly.

"If you mean how she follows Mr. Dooley around all the time and stares at him in church—" Starr laughed at Trudy's abashed expression.

"That's exactly what we're talking about," Libby admitted. "Is it that obvious?"

"About as obvious as the new red and gold sign at the Nugget."

Trudy expelled her breath and shook her head.

"Whyn't they put some clothes on that woman?" Starr asked.

"I'll inform the town council that a resident raised an objection to the Nugget's new sign," Libby said. She knew it was too early to give up on the plan to help Hiram, and she refused to be sidetracked by the Nugget's lurid sign, though she'd already complained privately about it to Mayor Nash. "Perhaps it's just as obvious to you that Mr. Dooley does not return Mrs. Caplinger's regard. Not that he disdains her, you understand, but he's just not. . .not in the same frame of mind she seems to be in."

"He doesn't want to marry her."

"Er, yes." Libby glanced at Trudy to see if Starr's bluntness had upset her. Trudy's mouth sagged, and she kicked at a clump of grass.

"So what do you want to ask me?" Starr's brown eyes twinkled.

"We had a thought." Libby smiled gently. "Not that we generally try to manipulate people's lives, of course..."

"Of course not." Starr waited, obviously enjoying the conversation.

"It occurred to us that if Rose were distracted, that is, if her attention were deflected onto another gentleman—one on whom she could fix her affections..."

"And one who doesn't mind," Trudy said with a scowl. "One who doesn't feel like running and hiding every time he sees her coming, which is pretty often if she's staying at your house."

"I see." Starr blinked and inhaled. "Let me contemplate the problem."

"Oh dear, I'm afraid Annie and the others are here." Libby looked toward the road, where the Harpers' team was approaching with the wagon full of petticoats and firearms.

"Maybe we can talk about this later," Trudy said. "My brother doesn't want to be the object of gossip."

"Griffin Bane," Starr said.

Libby and Trudy both stared at her.

"Of course!" Libby grinned at Trudy, though she felt a flicker of protest on Isabel's behalf.

"Griff is the perfect man for the job," Starr insisted.

"I don't know." Trudy scrunched up her face. "If he hasn't found a wife all these years, what makes you think we can wish one on him?"

"My dear, you make him sound ancient." Libby pressed her arm as the wagon drew nearer. "He's my age, which isn't much beyond Rose's years. And trust me, he's lonely."

"That's the important thing," Starr said. "Trudy, if you get Ethan to whisper a hint in his ear, and if Libby mentions his manly good looks to Rose and tells her what a thrifty and diligent businessman he is..."

"Yes," said Libby. "If we do that, I'll warrant we'll soon see some stares beaming in a different direction during church."

Starr giggled. "I think it would work!"

★ CHAPTER 16 ★

Isabel dragged her feet as she walked toward the ravine. She wasn't sure she wanted to face the other women today. Usually a shooting club meeting buoyed her. They were all so nice. But she'd had a trying day at school, and her family situation wasn't helping any. She felt more like going home, crawling into bed, and covering her head with Mama's tumbling-blocks quilt. The boys in her class refused to learn their lines for the closing program. And Papa drove her insane some days, though she loved him. Ever since he'd dug that mysterious hole behind the barn in the middle of the night, their relationship had carried a strain, like barbed wired stretched tight between two posts and ready to shear off and hit someone. More than ever, she wanted to get away from him.

But what chance did she have of that?

She might be able to get a school in another township for next winter. But then she'd probably have to live with a strange family. She'd certainly have to get used to a new town, new students, and a new school board that might want things done differently than she'd done for the past decade in the little school at Fergus. Could she adapt so readily? She wasn't sure.

The only other acceptable option was marriage, and that seemed unattainable. A plain spinster with a domineering father didn't command a lot of attention from bachelors. And if a man did come forward by some miracle, marriage would demand even more changes than a new school would. Maybe it was best she didn't have the opportunity.

The other women had already gathered, and the teams

were forming up to shoot the first round when she joined them. Starr Tinen was Isabel's group's leader. As usual, she looked as pretty and wholesome as a ripe peach. Everyone liked her, with her friendliness and a dash of derring-do. But on days like this, surrounding herself with beautiful, clever women only dampened Isabel's spirits. She sighed and rested her handbag on the tailgate of Annie's wagon while she rummaged for her pistol and box of ammunition.

"Bad day?" Starr came to stand beside her, smiling sympathetically.

"Sort of. The children are eager for school to let out for the summer break. I'm not sure Will Ingram and Paul Storrey will last another two weeks."

"That's rough. Are you ready to practice? We have new targets."

Isabel looked toward their shooting range. "Ah. Those are clever."

"Aren't they? I adore them." Starr giggled. "Trudy told me that they'll keep her from sinning."

"Oh?" The idea startled Isabel. "How so?"

"She says she usually pretends she's shooting at someone she doesn't like, and that's how she aims so well."

Isabel caught her breath, a bit startled. "Really?" Trudy was such a pleasant, friendly young woman.

Starr's shoulders quaked. "Not seriously. I expect her idea of someone unlikable is John Wilkes Booth or the porcupine that gnawed into her grain bin."

"Of course."

"Well, Trudy's got other things to think about right now, anyway."

"Oh?"

Starr nodded. "The big thing is her sister-in-law. That Rose Caplinger appears to have set her cap at Hiram, and Trudy says he wants none of it. She's cooking up a scheme to save her brother."

"What sort of scheme?" Isabel managed a sketchy smile, but she didn't feel the spirit of the plan or quite see the humor of it.

"She's going to try to match Rose up with the blacksmith. Get her out of Hiram's hair."

Isabel's mouth went dry. She could see her second nonoption evaporating into thin air over the distant peak of War Eagle Mountain.

Starr grinned. "Come on, let's get you set up to shoot."

Isabel supposed she could pretend the pronghorn painted on her target was Rose Caplinger. The very thought shocked her, and she quickly offered a silent prayer of repentance. She fired her rounds and squinted through the haze to see if she'd aimed well. The acrid smoke of the pistol she'd bought against Papa's wishes left a bitter taste that lingered on her tongue.

When she left the practice an hour later, Isabel couldn't stop thinking about what Starr Tinen had told her. The women of the shooting club, whom she had actually begun to think of as friends, planned to do their utmost to marry off the man she loved to Hiram Dooley's shrewish sister-in-law. She couldn't bear it. For years she had carried a secret adoration of the big, brawny smith. Griffin Bane was all that she imagined in a good husband. Unlike her father, he was forthright and plainspoken. No devious schemes for Griffin. He lived a simple life, open for all to read. Honest, hardworking, not to mention handsome. And he'd proved faithful in church, too, since they'd begun having church.

She marched home and straight to her bedroom. Papa wouldn't be home for another couple of hours, provided he didn't stop at the Nugget first. In that case, who knew?

She sat down on the edge of her bed. Her heart felt heavy in her chest. Had she made a fatal mistake in never revealing her feelings for Griffin? No one knew except her mother, and she'd taken the secret to her grave. Isabel had dreaded anyone finding out. If Griffin learned of her love and rejected her, she wouldn't be able to stand the sorrow. It was better that he didn't suspect. Yet she'd said nothing all this time, and now she stood a good chance of losing him forever. If she didn't act swiftly, Starr and Trudy would throw Rose Caplinger at him. But if she let the facts be known?

The very idea terrified her.

She'd nearly told Libby a week ago when they'd talked about her father. If she had, would Libby have put a stop to this wild plan?

Tears streamed down Isabel's cheeks. When she reached for a handkerchief, her hands shook. She gave in to her sorrow and buried her face in her pillow. She'd never really thought Griffin would come courting. But the notion that he couldn't—ever—if Trudy Dooley's plan went forward, opened a black chasm inside her. She sobbed with abandon. The knowledge that no one would hear her only magnified her loneliness. She cried harder.

Twenty minutes later, she sat up and dried her eyes. If Papa discovered she'd cried over a man who barely knew she existed, he'd tell her she was foolish, and perhaps he'd be right.

"Are you just going to let this happen?" she asked aloud.

Continuing to live unloved and unacknowledged suddenly loomed a larger danger than the humiliation she might suffer if she took action.

Before she could change her mind, she washed her face and grabbed her shawl and bonnet. She walked quickly the half mile to town, hoping the cool breeze would even out her blotchy complexion and repair the mottling her weeping session had caused. Instead of dissipating with the exercise, her indignation grew. When the livery stable came into view, she headed straight for it, not allowing herself to think about whether anyone else saw her. The townsfolk would assume she went on business for her father, anyway. No one would ever imagine her walking into a man's place of business on a personal errand.

Smoke poured from the stovepipe on top of the smithy next to the stable, and she veered toward it. The sun would set soon, and Griffin would stop his work. She was glad she'd caught him before he left for the evening. The ringing of steel on steel beckoned her.

When she shoved the door open, he looked up from his anvil, where he was shaping a horseshoe. Despite the chilly May air outside, the smithy was warm, and Griffin stood near the forge wearing his denim trousers, leather apron, and one of the men's cotton loomed undervests that Libby sold in the ready-mades section at the emporium. His suspenders hung in loops from his belt, and perspiration glistened on his noble brow. Isabel's knees wobbled suddenly. She grasped the doorjamb and hauled in a deep breath to stave off a swoon.

"Miss Fennel. What can I do for you?" Her sudden appearance in the doorway of the smithy startled Griffin.

"What can you do for me?" Isabel's voice shook.

"Does your father need something?" Cyrus had already been over here twice today to grouse about the quality of the new team Bill Stout had brought in for tomorrow's stage run. Griffin had stood the man's griping only so long. Then he'd told Cyrus it wasn't his fault if someone had bought inferior livestock for the stage line, and maybe the division agent—Cyrus himself—ought to take over the task of buying the replacement horses. Then Griffin had politely but firmly asked him to clear out so *some* people could get their work done. And now Cyrus was sending his daughter over to bother him? He lowered the hot horseshoe into the tub of water by the forge.

The steam plumed up between them. Isabel stared at him with her pale eyes. She seemed colorless, standing there in her dress the hue of dust. Any tints her clothing caught came from the glowing coals in his forge.

"Mr. Bane..."

She swallowed hard, and his heart tripped. Was she bringing bad news? Her visit was unprecedented, and she wore an expression that bespoke resignation. Maybe someone had died. He almost turned to look at his friend, who sat in the shadowy corner to her left, but she began speaking again.

"I'll tell you what you can do for me." She squared her shoulders. "At the very least, you can notice I'm alive."

Griff straightened with the three-pound rounding hammer in his hands and cocked his head to one side. "I beg your pardon?"

"Griffin Bane, we've been acquainted more than ten years, and I don't think you've ever once noticed me."

He tried to get out an answer to that, but no sound was capable of passing his constricted windpipe.

Isabel balled her hands into fists. "I'm a good cook and a woman of faith. Do I need to remind you that I'm also intelligent, or that my father owns a great deal of property? When he passes on, I shall inherit it all. Every acre. I may not be the handsomest woman in Fergus, but I daresay I'm among the most eligible."

He cleared his throat. "Yes ma'am, I expect so."

"Do you? Well then, do something about it. Or do you prefer to be sacrificed to *that woman*, so that Hiram Dooley doesn't have to think about getting married?"

A sudden movement in the corner drew a startled gasp from her. Hiram leaped from his perch as Isabel whirled and stared at him. She lifted one thin hand to her lips and sobbed. Lifting her skirt, she turned and ran.

Hiram raised one hand as though to stop her, but she was gone. He looked around at Griffin. For a long moment they stared at each other. Hiram shrugged.

The quiet gunsmith's bewilderment reflected his own, and Griffin began to shake. A huge laugh worked its way up from his belly to his chest. Unable to stop, he let it out in a whoop. Hiram's eyes flared, but he soon chortled sheepishly. Griffin laughed until tears rolled down his cheeks and sputtered on the coals in the forge.

At last he pulled his bandanna from his back pocket and wiped his eyes. "I ask you, what on earth was that all about?"

Hiram gulped. "I have no idea. But her eyes were kinda wild and scary looking."

Griffin rubbed the back of his neck and lowered his eyebrows. "I don't know what got into her. It was like. . .like a mare that's been in the loco weed."

Hiram looked toward the doorway and shook his head. "Don't think she even knew I was here, at first."

"Me neither," Griffin said. "But what do you suppose she meant, me being sacrificed at your weddin'?"

Hiram's face froze. "She didn't say that."

"What *did* she say? Some babble about how I'd ought to respect her pa's money. Do you think she wants me to take on shopping for a new team for him? Because I told him I don't have time to go to the horse auction in Boise."

"That's. . .not the impression I got." Hiram hesitated. "I can't say for certain, but it sounds to me like she thinks one of us ought to marry her."

Griffin's hand went slack, and the hammer clattered to the

floor. "Ow!" He grabbed the toe of his boot and hopped about the smithy on one foot. When he at last stood still again and gingerly tested his weight on his injured foot, Hiram's face had gone all sad, the way he'd looked most of the time since Violet died.

"Griff?"

"Yeah?"

"Seems to me there's an awful lot of nuptial thinking going on in this town."

Griffin gulped. "You think she was serious? Maybe we ought to do something about it."

"Like what?"

"Maybe ask the sheriff to put a moratorium on weddings?"

Hiram frowned. "Ethan can't do that."

"Well then, the preacher maybe?"

★ CHAPTER 17 ★

Libby knocked on the door of the small house and looked around appreciatively. Lilies bloomed below the front windows, and the fresh white paint on the board siding made the dwelling stand out from the weather-beaten gray buildings on either side.

The Bentons had come to town less than a year ago, but they'd made a lot of improvements in the little rental. The pastor had purchased paint, nails, and various other items at the emporium, and Libby wondered if the landlord—Cyrus Fennel—had reimbursed the couple for enhancing his property. She also wondered if he'd followed through on his original promise to let them buy the house if they wanted to, after the six months' free rent he'd grudgingly given them had expired. On the Reverend Mr. Benton's small salary, she doubted they could afford it. Perhaps she should bring the matter up at the next town council meeting.

Bitsy cleared her throat, and Libby glanced over at her. Her companion eyed the door through narrowed eyes and twisted the chain handle of her mesh reticule between her hands.

Before Libby could assure her there was no need for nervousness, Apphia opened the door, her face glowing with pleasure.

"Ladies! Do come in. I'm so happy to see you both."

"I hope we're not interrupting your supper," Libby said.

"Not at all. We just finished. Are you here to consult my husband or to visit with me?"

Bitsy jerked her shoulders back and shot a panicky glance at Libby.

"You, please," Libby said, and Bitsy huffed out a quiet sigh.

"Delightful. Won't you come and sit in the parlor?"

Libby stood aside, beckoning for Bitsy to precede her. Her friend hesitated then mounted the steps and followed Apphia, pulling her shawl across the deep neckline of her bright yellow satin dress. Libby came last, closing the door.

The tiny house had no entry hall, and the front door opened on what the hostess had so glibly called a parlor. The cramped room held two chairs and a cushioned bench, a small table bearing a kerosene lamp, and a bookshelf consisting of rough boards stacked on large tin cans painted a jaunty red. Two potted plants and a framed miniature sat atop the shelves, and one wall held a sampler portraying a cross wreathed in roses and silk-floss letters, reading: BUT MY GOD SHALL SUPPLY ALL YOUR NEED ACCORDING TO HIS RICHES IN GLORY BY CHRIST JESUS.—PHILIPPIANS 4:19.

Mr. Benton peered in a doorway at the back, which Libby knew from previous visits led to the kitchen.

"Good evening, ladies."

"Hello, Pastor."

"May I serve you three ladies something?"

"No, thank you," Libby said quickly, and Bitsy shook her head, not meeting the preacher's gaze.

"That's kind of you, Phineas, but we seem to be content." Apphia nodded to her husband with a smile, and he withdrew. "Please sit down." She indicated the two chairs and took a seat on the bench.

"I do hope we're not intruding," Libby said.

Bitsy seemed more on edge than before. She wriggled in her chair, arranging her skirt and shawl to expose as little of her flesh as possible.

"Not at all. I didn't get a chance to congratulate you this afternoon on your fine shooting," Apphia said to Bitsy. "Earning the 'personal best' ribbon is an honor."

"It surely is." Bitsy touched the bit of sky blue ribbon pinned to her bodice. "I think I hold this more valuable than my onyx eardrops."

"The shooting club has helped us all to grow inwardly, I think."

Libby nodded, and silence descended on them. Apphia obviously waited for a cue from her as to the nature of their visit.

The pastor's wife wouldn't want to make presumptions, yet she mustn't enjoy seeing Bitsy so uncomfortable in the parsonage.

"Bitsy and I were talking today, and she had some questions that I couldn't answer concerning spiritual matters. Do you mind if we present her inquiries to you?"

"Of course not—unless you'd prefer to speak to Mr. Benton. He is much more knowledgeable than I am."

Bitsy's eyes darted toward the door. Perspiration beaded on her powdered brow.

"I think we'd prefer you for this errand," Libby said.

"Of course." Apphia waited, an expectant smile hovering at her lips. "Bitsy, let me say again how glad I am to have you here."

"Oh, I. . ." Bitsy cleared her throat and studied the crocheted doily beneath the lamp. Libby wondered how many invitations from Apphia the saloon owner had turned down in the past year. But she was here now, and that was what counted.

"Bitsy is very interested in the scriptures, and more pointedly, the matter of salvation."

Bitsy drew in a deep breath. "I'm convinced now that God can save me. Didn't know for sure, but Libby's shown me lots of places in the Bible where it says He can."

"Oh yes, most assuredly He can," Apphia said.

After a quick nod, Bitsy plunged on. "Well, here's the thing. If I got saved, would God make me close the saloon?"

Apphia blinked twice. "To be honest, I'm not sure. But I believe the Lord *is* going to save you, my dear, and I also believe that if you come to Him, you'll want to do whatever will please Him."

Libby let out a pent-up breath. She'd known there was a better answer than her poor brain had come up with.

"But how will I know what He expects me to do?" Bitsy leaned forward in her earnestness, letting the edges of her shawl slip.

"He makes that very clear in His Word." Apphia reached to the bookcase and took out a black-covered Bible. "Let me show you some verses."

Libby watched quietly as Apphia turned to Acts 16:31. " 'Believe on the Lord Jesus Christ, and thou shalt be saved.' "

"Hmm." Bitsy bit her bottom lip. "I thought He expected us to do good deeds."

"That comes after," Apphia said. "If you believe Jesus died to pay for your sins, you'll want to do things that please Him. But that's not what will save you and get you into heaven."

Bitsy frowned. "Funny. I always heard that it did. When someone died, folks would say, 'He's surely in heaven, he was such a good person.' But you're telling me different."

Apphia smiled. "If there's one thing I want you to understand, Bitsy, it's that all the good deeds in the world won't amount to a thing if you don't trust in Jesus. The first and most important thing is that you believe on Him. Doing good doesn't save you. But after you are saved, you will want to do good to please Him."

Bitsy's frown deepened, and she shook her head. "See, that's what I was afraid of. If I listen to this, I'll have to change my entire life and start being good."

Libby smiled involuntarily. "Bitsy, you already do good deeds. I don't know many people as generous as you."

"But my business. How would I live?" Bitsy shook her head. "I'll have to give it some thought."

Apphia said gently, "If God is calling you, then you won't be able to resist. But you needn't be afraid. He wants only what is good for you."

"That's what Augie says."

Apphia said nothing but shot a surprised look Libby's way. "Let me share another scripture with you. It tells a little bit of what God expects from us after we believe in Him."

"Yes, I'd like to hear that." Bitsy settled back and waited while Apphia turned the pages.

"Here. This is in Micah 6:8. 'He hath shewed thee, O man, what is good; and what doth the Lord require of thee, but to do justly, and to love mercy, and to walk humbly with thy God?' You see? God wants us to walk with Him. He wants us to do kindnesses to others and to be merciful."

"I expect I could work on it," Bitsy said doubtfully.

"That's one of the best parts," Libby told her. "God will help you know what's right through reading the Bible. And He'll give you the strength to do it."

"That's right." Apphia began turning pages again.

At that moment, male voices could be heard outside the front door, and a firm knock resounded throughout the house.

"Excuse me." Apphia laid her Bible aside and hopped up to answer it.

"Hello, ma'am." Griffin Bane's deep voice was filled with humility. "We're sorry to disturb you this evening, but Mr. Dooley and I wondered if we could have a word with the parson. If he's not too busy, that is."

At the mention of Hiram's name, Libby tuned her ears to the conversation. She leaned over to try to get a look, but Griffin's large figure completely cut off her view of anyone accompanying him.

"Certainly, Mr. Bane. Won't you both go on through to the kitchen? I believe my husband is out there studying his sermon."

"Oh, we don't want to bother him," Griffin said.

"It's no trouble. He's here to serve you in any way he can." Apphia stood back, and he ducked and entered the room, which seemed instantly to grow smaller.

As Griffin cleared the doorway, Hiram appeared behind him, hat in hand. Standing next to the huge smith, Hiram looked almost scrawny, though Libby knew he was several inches taller than she was. Her past surreptitious scrutiny had told her he didn't want for muscles, though he didn't have Griffin's brawn. Griffin looked toward the women and hesitated.

"I'm entertaining a couple of my dearest friends," Apphia said.

"Good evening, ladies," said Griffin.

To Libby's surprise, Hiram spoke. "Nice to see you, Bitsy. Libby." His gaze lingered on her, and Libby felt her cheeks color.

"How do you do, gentlemen?" she asked.

"Howdy," said Bitsy at the same time.

"We're good." Griffin looked expectantly at Apphia.

"Right this way," she said.

Mr. Benton came to the kitchen doorway. "Well, look who's here. I thought I heard more company. Gentlemen, will you join me for some coffee?"

"Thank you, sir," Hiram said.

"Since you two are having some, why not?" Griffin's loud voice echoed off the walls and low ceiling.

The three men shuffled into the kitchen. Apphia waited until all were well out of the parlor then shut the door between the rooms.

"There, now. This seems to be a busy place tonight."

"I ought to get going," Bitsy said. "Thursday nights can get busy. You just never know. But. . ." She looked wistfully to Apphia. "I hope we can talk about this again sometime."

"Of course we can," Apphia said. "Come anytime. If you have mornings free, drop by whenever it suits you. I'm usually here."

Bitsy nodded soberly and stood. "Thank you. I need to think some on what you told me. And. . .could you write down those scriptures you read? I think Augie could find them in his Bible for me. I mean, all Bibles are the same, aren't they?"

Libby's heart bubbled with joy as she watched Apphia write the references for Bitsy on a scrap of paper. They had made it to the door and were saying their good-byes to Mrs. Benton when the parson emerged from the kitchen.

"Ladies! I'm glad I caught you."

Libby turned toward him, curious about why he had detained them.

"My two guests just departed out the back door," the pastor said, "but they came to me on an odd errand. I wondered, Mrs. Adams, if you could possibly shed any light on it."

"If I'm able, I'll be most willing."

"Mr. Bane told me a strange tale." He eyed Libby and Bitsy sternly. "Now, this is not for distribution. I'm sure you understand that we must keep it confidential. But since you ladies are friends of Isabel Fennel's—"

"Isabel's?" Bitsy jerked her chin back. "They came to discuss Isabel with you?"

"Er. . .well, it's a delicate matter." Phineas Benton glanced uncertainly at his wife.

"I'm sure these ladies will practice utmost discretion," Apphia said.

"Yes. Well, it seems Miss Fennel entered the smithy earlier this evening in high dudgeon and let loose at Mr. Bane. Something about Mr. Dooley not wanting to get married again. Mr. Dooley overheard it all, and both men were puzzled by what she meant. Remembering that the shooting club met late this afternoon, I wondered if perhaps an incident had occurred during that meeting which upset Miss Fennel."

"Hiram getting married?" Bitsy scowled. "First I heard of it."

"That's just it," said the pastor. "He didn't know about it either. I. . .understand Miss Fennel wasn't completely intelligible. Something about Mr. Fennel's financial situation as well, but the one thing that stood out to both men was that she clearly said Mr. Dooley didn't want to get married, and that Mr. Bane ought to do something about it."

Libby again felt color infuse her face. "Oh dear."

"What is it?" Apphia asked.

"This afternoon, before you all arrived from town, Trudy and I had a conversation about her brother. I'm afraid. . ." Libby glanced quickly at the other three. "As you say, sir, we must all be the soul of discretion. Trudy is concerned that her sister-in-law, Mrs. Caplinger, is determined to marry Hiram, but Hiram wants no such alliance. We remarked on how it would be nice if Rose would look elsewhere. Starr Tinen arrived, and she rather glibly suggested that we somehow redirect Mrs. Caplinger's affections to Mr. Bane, giving Hiram an avenue of escape. It began as somewhat of jest, and I thought it ended when the other ladies arrived to shoot. I've no idea how Isabel heard of it."

"Obviously she did from either Trudy or Starr." Apphia laid a sympathetic hand on Libby's arm.

"Well, I didn't hear anything about it," Bitsy said, "but if you ask me, I think it's a good plan. That Rose Caplinger is an overbearing, hoity-toity—"

The pastor cleared his throat, and Bitsy broke off with a shrug.

"I take it Mr. Bane isn't interested in matrimony either?" Apphia asked.

The pastor smiled ruefully. "I'm afraid Mrs. Caplinger didn't enter their heads. They thought Isabel was implying that one of them should offer for *her* hand."

"For Isabel's?" Bitsy snorted. "As if either one of them would want Cy Fennel for a father-in-law."

"Er. . .yes."

"I regret my part in this." Libby's heart ached as she thought back over her conversation with Trudy and Starr. How eagerly she'd pounced on the suggestion that Hiram would like it if Rose found some other outlet for her machinations. She'd been only too happy to participate in the plan to get Rose to stop cosseting him.

"Well, I told the young gentlemen to keep quiet about it so that Isabel isn't publicly embarrassed by her outburst. Perhaps it's one of those things that will be soon forgotten."

"I think I shall visit Isabel tomorrow," Libby said. "It was never my intent—or Trudy's or Starr's for that matter—to bring pain or sorrow to anyone."

Bitsy jutted out her chin. "Might be better to just leave it alone, like the preacher says."

"But if she harbors feelings for. . .for a certain gentlemen, and we who are supposed to be her friends scheme to match him with another lady, she must feel betrayed."

"My dear, you cannot force the man to return the lady's sentiments." As usual, Apphia's gentle observation made sense.

"But still, Isabel has confided in me lately, and I should have foreseen trouble with the course we so lightly planned. Whether we would actually have tried to carry it out or not, I cannot say, but I confess it tempted me."

"It bothers you to see Hiram annoyed and afflicted by Mrs. Caplinger's unwanted attentions," Apphia said.

"Yes." Libby looked earnestly at the minister and his wife. "Please pray about this situation. I do feel I should apologize to Isabel for my part in it, though she may not know of it yet."

She left the Bentons' house with Bitsy. "I think I might stop in at Trudy's," she said as they neared the Dooleys' home. "She can't have any idea what has happened unless her brother told her." Libby wished she could undo the afternoon's events. The least she could do was warn her friend of the flurry they'd caused.

"I doubt Hiram would string so many words together," Bitsy said. "But it might be best to talk to her, especially since the trouble began at shooting practice. She'll wonder if Isabel stops coming or won't speak to her civilly."

"I'll explain it to her," Libby assured her. Bitsy's suggestion dragged her spirits even lower. Had she helped cause a rift in the close-knit shooting society?

★ CHAPTER 18 ★

To Him be the glory, both now and forever. Amen."

Trudy opened her eyes. The Reverend Mr. Benton lowered his hands after the benediction but remained at the pulpit.

"If you would please be seated, I have an announcement."

Trudy resumed her seat on the bench between Rose and Ethan. She smoothed down her blue skirt and waited. Like everyone else, she kept her eyes on the pastor. He presented most announcements during the worship service. But now his eyes twinkled and his lips twitched as though itching to stretch into a smile.

"Ladies and gentlemen, I've been asked to issue an invitation to you all. It gives me immeasurable delight to announce a wedding to be held next Sunday immediately after our worship service. All residents of Fergus are invited."

To her dismay, Trudy felt the eyes of many people on her. Beside her, Ethan stirred. They looked at each other. Ethan gave the slightest of shrugs, as if to say, *Don't know why on earth they're looking our way.* She felt her cheeks go scarlet. It might be more humiliating *not* to be the object of speculation at a time like this, but she doubted that.

A murmur spread through the congregation, and Mr. Benton raised his hands once more. "Let me read this, to be sure I get it right." He picked up a sheet of paper and squinted at it. " 'The pleasure of your presence is requested at the marriage of Miss Elizabeth Molly Shepard and Mr. Augustus Moore' "—a choral gasp resounded across the room—" 'at half after twelve in the afternoon, Sunday, May 23rd, in the year of Our Lord 1886, in the dining room of the Spur & Saddle. Luncheon will be served afterward to all guests.'"

The pastor laid down the paper and smiled at the audience. "I understand it's been some time since a wedding was performed in Fergus. It's my pleasure to be the one officiating. I'm sure you'll all want to offer your best wishes to Bitsy and Augie. I asked them to stand with me at the door to shake hands today, but they both declined, as it's their custom to hurry home and prepare the chicken dinner they'll serve today. So I guess if you want to congratulate them, you'll either have to wait until the wedding or go around for the chicken dinner. You are dismissed."

Mr. Benton picked up his Bible and strode down the aisle, smiling. Bitsy and Augie were among the first to scoot out the door.

"Well," Ethan said. "I guess the chicken dinner will be sold out today."

Trudy couldn't help feeling just a smidgen disappointed—not that Bitsy was getting married. That was wonderful. But she'd imagined somehow that she would be the first bride Mr. Benton married in Fergus.

"A wedding in a tavern?" Rose sniffed. "I should think not."

"She's being married at her home," Trudy said. "You were married at your home. What's wrong with it?"

"You know what's wrong with it. Although I can see why the minister didn't want to perform the ceremony here in the church. If you call it a church."

"I beg your pardon." Trudy's patience had worn thinner than the knees of Hiram's gardening trousers.

"All you have is an old store building and a slew of benches. Not a proper church."

"The church is not built with human hands," Ethan said.

Trudy threw him a grateful look.

"Humph. I'm surprised he'll even conduct the wedding." Rose stood and arranged her shawl, fan, and reticule.

"Careful," Hiram said.

She smiled at him with an air of superiority. "Careful of what? She's a woman of ill repute. Why is she even bothering with a wedding?"

Hiram eyed her for a long moment then turned and pushed into the aisle at his end of the bench. He didn't look back.

"Bitsy is not a loose woman," Trudy said between her teeth.

"Hmm. If you say so. But still, being married in *that place*."

"It's a saloon. That's all." Even Ethan sounded ready to snap.

Rose watched Hiram's progress toward the door and shook her head. "Sometimes, Gert, I don't think your brother likes me."

Trudy hesitated. Their eyes met. "I go by Trudy now."

Rose flipped one end of her shawl across her shoulder, and the fringe hit Trudy in the face. "So I've been told."

She entered the aisle. Trudy stood still, fighting back tears. Ethan's hand settled on her arm. She could feel the warmth of his fingers through the fabric of her dress.

"I have a thought, sweet Trudy."

"What?"

"How'd you like to sample the chicken dinner today?"

She reached for the lace edge of the handkerchief she always kept up her sleeve on Sunday, in case Mr. Benton's sermon illustrations got too heart-wrenching. She shook it out and dabbed at her eyes. Turning to Ethan, she smiled, trying to keep her lips from quivering.

"If I hadn't cooked a big roast last night. . .besides, we can't run out on Hiram."

"I expect you're right." He picked up his hat and stepped into the aisle.

All the way to the door, Trudy felt his fingertips, warm and feather-light, at her back. They shook hands with Apphia and Phineas Benton. When they reached the boardwalk outside, Trudy automatically headed for home.

Ethan nudged her. "Hey, look."

She turned and followed his gaze. Her brother was walking slowly down the street in the wrong direction, letting other people pass him. She glanced up at Ethan then hurried after Hiram. She didn't speak until she was at his side, a little out of breath.

"Where are you going? Ethan's coming over for lunch."

Hiram stopped walking. Ethan caught up to Trudy and stood beside her. Hiram pulled in a deep breath and cocked one eyebrow southward, along the street.

"You two go on home and eat with Rose, if that's what's proper. I thought it was time I tried the chicken dinner."

Rose's presence at the wedding the next Sunday surprised Libby to no end. She had fully expected the eastern lady to boycott the event. Instead, she'd shown up wearing a watered silk gown of palest pink and a confection of a hat that Libby would have given a week's profit for.

After the simple ceremony, which the pastor performed before the bar without apparent qualms, Rose attached herself to the Runnels family. She went through the refreshment line laughing with Josiah, who was at least five years younger than she was. Libby told herself it was none of her business and she didn't care, so long as Rose's claws weren't poised over Hiram.

Trudy insisted that Libby join the Dooleys at their table to enjoy their luncheon, though she'd sat with the Harpers during the wedding. The saloon girls had transformed into bridesmaids, and the bridal couple had hired Terrence and Rilla Thistle, along with Ezra Dyer, to serve up the roast beef, mashed turnips, biscuits, and gravy.

"Don't Vashti and Goldie look sweet?" Trudy asked as they walked to one of the round tables near the bar.

Libby noted that no bottles of liquor were displayed on the shelves. Snowy linen tablecloths covered the bar, where the wedding cake and punch bowl were set out in splendor. She glanced at the huge mirror and moved toward another chair.

"Want to see your reflection while you eat?" Hiram asked, shaking his head.

"No, I want to watch everyone else without them knowing it."

He laughed silently. Their eyes met, and the warmth of the connection startled her. Feelings Libby hadn't known since early in her marriage to Isaac surged through her.

Ethan held Trudy's chair. Glad for the distraction, Libby smiled at them. They made a lovely couple. Perhaps observing today's wedding would help Ethan get past whatever kept him from making their engagement official.

She realized with a start that Hiram was holding her chair. "Oh, thank you." She sat down and avoided looking directly at him for fear she would blush scarlet. She gazed across the room to where Vashti and Goldie sat with the bride and groom. "You're right, Trudy. The girls do look fine today."

Vashti had asked Annie Harper to help her and Goldie stitch lace inserts into the necklines of their best dresses. Flounces of Viennese lace from Libby's most expensive yard goods had given the gowns a respectable "formal" length.

The bride had come to Libby for help in finding a suitable dress on short notice. Two telegrams to Boise had performed a near miracle—an elegant ivory gown had arrived by stagecoach on Wednesday, and Annie had spent all day Thursday altering it to Bitsy's form. Anyone would deem today's bride lovely and well-gowned, Libby was certain—even Rose Caplinger's snooty New England friends.

Augie had arrived at the wedding carrying a top hat, which Libby suspected was too small for him to actually wear. She recognized it as one belonging to former mayor Charles Walker—the only top hat in town, so far as she knew. Augie's plain black coat and pants, with a new white shirt and black ribbon tie, were complemented by a gold-embroidered waistcoat.

"Everyone looks well-turned-out today." Ethan gazed at Trudy as he spoke.

Griffin Bane, who had served as Augie's best man, rose and tapped on his glass with a spoon. The chatter ceased, and all eyes homed in on him.

"Folks, we're gathered for this happy occasion, and Augie asked me to tell ya all that he and the missus appreciate your friendship."

The men began to clap and whistle, but Griffin held up one hand.

"All right, thanks, but I got something else to say. That is, Bitsy and Augie have something else to say."

Bitsy stood, and Augie shoved back his chair and stood beside her behind the flower-decked table. She looked up at him, and Augie nodded and slipped his arm around her.

"Friends," Bitsy said, "we thank you all for coming. I know it's the first time some of you've been in this building, and I appreciate your being here with us today. I hope you'll consider this our home and come back often." She paused and cleared her throat. "You all know I've never served liquor in this building on Sunday for all the twenty-three years I've lived here."

"You gonna start now, Bitsy?" yelled Parnell Oxley, one of the cowhands from the Landry ranch.

"Yeah, let's have something to help celebrate," said stagecoach driver Nick Telford.

"Nope, I ain't going to do it. And furthermore, if you and the other boys come around here Saturday night, you'll be disappointed again. Folks, the Spur & Saddle is hereby closing its bar. Last night we did a good business, and I hope the fellas all enjoyed it, because that was my last evening as the owner of a saloon. Augie and I decided together that we want to get out of the business."

The room was so quiet, Trudy could hear Rose's fan flap from two tables away.

Pastor Benton rose, and all heads turned his way. "Bitsy, Augie. . ." He turned to look over the room full of people. "You've made a courageous decision, and one I'm sure the Lord will honor. I know the people of this town will support you in your new endeavors."

Augie grinned and squeezed Bitsy. "Thank you, Preacher. This decision was a long time coming, just like my darlin's decision to tie the knot."

A subdued laugh rippled across the dining room.

"Let's just say the Lord and Augie were both patient with me," Bitsy said. "As of tomorrow morning, the Spur & Saddle will serve meals, coffee, sarsaparilla, lemonade, and sweet cider."

"Amen!" Pastor Benton clapped his hands, and Libby hastened to join in. Pride welled up in her. Soon at least half the people applauded. Some of the men sat thunderstruck, their mouths set in disappointed lines.

"Good for them," Ethan said as he clapped enthusiastically.

Trudy nodded. "We'll have to come in often."

Libby smiled as she watched the newlyweds accept the unaccustomed encouragement. Bitsy's spiritual struggle had involved several more conversations with the Bentons, and after last week's announcement of the impending wedding, she'd confided to Libby that she'd believed in Christ and surrendered her heart to Him. Libby hadn't pressed her about her earlier question concerning the saloon, but she'd wondered.

Trudy leaned toward her and whispered, "What do you suppose they did with their leftover inventory of spirits?"

Libby just shrugged. She glanced at Hiram and found he was watching her. He looked away but then looked back with a sheepish smile. She hadn't felt so lighthearted in years.

When the applause petered out, Bitsy gave a decisive nod. "Well then, I hope you enjoy the cake. Augie spent the better part of the last two days working on that thing, so eat up."

"It's a work of art," Bertha Runnels called out. "Bitsy, you oughta frame that cake and hang it on the wall."

Everyone laughed, and soon Goldie and Vashti were darting between the tables, distributing slices of Augie's masterpiece. Libby got a piece with a sugar bell on it. She had to agree with Bertha, it was almost too pretty to eat.

When Vashti handed a plate to Cyrus Fennel, who sat at a nearby table with Isabel and the Walkers, he grinned up at the girl. "You sure there's nothing with a kick to wash that down with?"

"It's lemonade from here on in, Mr. Fennel."

"Bitsy can't be serious about that."

"Oh yes sir, she is."

"What will you and Goldie do for a living?" Cyrus asked. Libby didn't like to eavesdrop, but she, too, was curious.

"For now, we're staying on here to board. Miss Bitsy says we can try waiting on the customers who come to eat here and wash the dishes. Goldie's going to keep playing the piano when people want her to."

"Are you happy about the change?" Isabel asked.

"Yes ma'am. Mostly. Augie says they won't make as much money as they have been, and if business drops off, they might have to pay us less. We'll see."

Cyrus frowned as the girl moved on to the next table. Libby could almost see the gears turning in his head, like a windup music box. This place would transform nicely into an elegant restaurant, and Augie's cooking far outstripped Mrs. Thistle's. Competition for the boardinghouse. If Bitsy decided to open rooms for rent as well, she might just put the Fennel House out of business.

"Cyrus doesn't look too happy," Hiram said.

"No he doesn't." Libby decided it was time to bring up an idea she'd considered for several weeks. "Hiram, I've been thinking. You know we ladies go through a lot of ammunition at our shooting practice."

He chuckled. "Trudy's fired more rounds this spring than I've shot in my whole life."

"That's not true, and you know it." His sister scowled at him. "You used to shoot all day, seemed like, for the fun of it. You're a much better shot than I am."

Ethan leaned back and eyed her skeptically. "Everybody knows you're the best shot in Fergus."

"They *think* they know." Trudy took a bite of the wedding cake.

"So, what about the ammunition?" Hiram asked.

Libby hesitated. She'd intended for this conversation with Hiram to be private, in case he wasn't agreeable, but the others at the table had obviously heard her opening, and she couldn't back down now. "Well, I've always told the girls to gather up their empty shells. I give them a small discount on the next box when they bring me their brass or shotgun shells."

Hiram nodded. He'd often bought used shells from her to reload, as did many of the other townspeople.

"So, I wondered, would you be interested in a business arrangement with me where you reload them for me? I could resell them as reloaded ammunition, not just as empty shells. Of course, I'd supply the powder and lead as well. And if you didn't have molds for certain sizes, I'd order them for you."

His eyes took on an appreciative gleam as she spoke, and by the time she finished, his crooked, shy smile shone through. "That sounds like a good idea. I could work on them when my gun business is slow."

"I could pay you half a cent each, I think."

"That could be good for both of you," Ethan said.

Hiram nodded. "A sound business idea."

Later Libby barely remembered the rest of the afternoon. Goldie's sweet piano rendition of "Sweet Genevieve," when Augie had led Bitsy around the small piece of open floor in a waltz, had shocked those who didn't believe in dancing, and those who didn't believe in worldly entertainments on Sunday even worse. But for Libby, the most memorable moment of the day was when the quiet gunsmith gazed at her with his calm gray eyes and praised her business acumen.

★ CHAPTER 19 ★

School was finally out, and Isabel reveled in her freedom. On the Monday after the closing program, she rode into town with her father. She asked him to let her out before he turned off Main Street to leave the wagon at the livery stable. She was determined to avoid a face-to-face meeting with Griffin Bane at all costs.

Since her regrettable outburst at the smithy, she'd only seen him across the room at church and at Bitsy's wedding. He hadn't acknowledged her presence, and she'd done all she could to stay out of his line of vision. As far as she could tell, word of the incident had not reached her father, but she still held her breath every time he came home from town.

She walked to the emporium and entered. Libby looked up from arranging new merchandise in the linens section. "Good morning. It's a pleasure to see you in here on a weekday."

Isabel approached her, smiling. "Thank you. Since I've six weeks until the summer term begins, I thought I'd pick up some sewing notions. I want to make over a couple of Mama's summer dresses."

"A bittersweet task." Libby walked with her to the fabric section. "New items for your wardrobe, but constant reminders of your departed loved one."

The door opened, and Ralph Storrey came in.

"Excuse me," Libby said. "If you need any help, I shan't be far." She turned to greet Ralph. "What can I do for you today, sir?"

"Did you get any more barbed wire?" the rancher asked. "I've strung all I had, and I'm a thousand feet short."

"Yes, I did. It's on the back porch, where Josiah unloaded it for me. Do you want to drive your wagon around back, and I'll meet you out there?"

Ten minutes later, she returned to the store through the back room and jotted something in her ledger. Several other customers had come in while she was gone. Florence was weighing out dry beans for Bertha Runnels. Isabel had found all the items on her list and had stopped to examine the selection of buttons.

Libby made her way between the tables and shelves of merchandise. Isabel looked up as she approached.

"I think I've found what I need, but these darling silver buttons caught my eye."

"They can make an older dress look new."

"That's what I was thinking." Isabel slid them into her basket. "There. I suppose I'm finished, except for a pound of coffee for Papa."

She waited while Libby measured it for her.

"Any more word about your uncle?" Libby asked.

"No." Isabel glanced around at the other shoppers and back to Libby. "I haven't heard a word since that one visit. Papa doesn't talk about him. Our dinner conversation is rather strained." She had tried to put Uncle Kenton out of her mind these past few weeks, and her father hadn't spoken his name once. The entire connection with the ex-convict had a sordid feel, and she wished she could erase the memory of the night he'd come to the ranch.

"I'm sorry to hear that," Libby said. "Do you want this on your father's account?"

Isabel hesitated. "The coffee only. I'll pay for the notions." She wished she could talk to Libby again. They hadn't had much of a conversation since Libby had come to the schoolhouse to apologize for encouraging Starr and Trudy to match up Rose Caplinger and Griffin. When Libby had explained how it came about and assured her they meant no harm, Isabel was able to forgive the three ladies.

Rose swept into the emporium, followed by Trudy.

"Ladies," Libby said in greeting. Rose smiled cordially, but Trudy wore a downcast expression.

Isabel accepted her change from Libby and picked up her

market basket. "Good day, ladies." She didn't think she could remain long in the same room with Rose and not feel the pangs of jealousy rise again. The young widow was an outsider who would never understand Griffin, a man who'd grown up in the West. So far Isabel had seen no evidence that Rose had looked Griffin's way any more intently than she looked at other men. Apparently the plan had fizzled. But she still didn't want to be around the woman.

"I'll see you this afternoon," Trudy called after her.

Isabel stepped onto the boardwalk then flattened herself against the emporium's door. A short way up the street, Griffin was leaving her father's office. She stood still, her heart pounding, until he turned northward toward the livery stable without seeing her.

She felt the irony of the situation. Ten days ago, she'd longed for him to notice her. Now her cheeks burned in shame at the thought, and she was glad he'd gone the other way.

"How may I help you, Mrs. Caplinger?" Libby asked.

"Do you have any dye?"

"Yes, I have a good selection of colors." Libby led her down the room. "The newer line from the Fossett Company seems to hold better than the old ones. Emmaline Landry dyed a set of curtains with the scarlet, and she said they came out beautifully."

"Colorfastness is especially crucial in apparel," Rose said.

"Oh, are you dyeing some clothing?"

"Feathers," Trudy said with a woeful grimace. "She's going to make hats."

Libby looked at Rose and smiled. "This town could use a few more hats, and some of yours are delectable."

"Why, thank you. I've decided it's my calling."

"Oh? Are you saying you make your own hats? The pink one you wore to the wedding was exquisite."

"Thank you. Yes, I have a natural talent for it. And I've decided to stay here in Fergus and ply my skill as a trade," Rose said.

Libby looked anxiously at Trudy, who shrugged, a perfect imitation of Hiram's favorite gesture.

"No slight to your merchandise," Rose went on, "but I think

this town needs a decent millinery shop."

Libby's love of fashion struggled against her loyalty to the Dooleys. "What a lovely idea. Of course, I have to stock a wide variety of merchandise, and I only carry a limited selection of ladies' hats and bonnets. But. . .do you think there are enough ladies with spending money in this town to support such a shop?"

"I believe women are willing to pay for the best. When they find superior items that flatter their looks, they're happy to turn over their savings."

"Well, you may be right."

"I've mailed an order for supplies." Rose picked up a roll of lace edging and peered at it. Her lip curled, and she laid it down. "Feathers, netting, and embellishments."

"I wish you success," Libby said.

Trudy brought a one-pound bag of salt and laid it on the counter. She turned away, toward the spice shelves.

"I perceive that in this town, widows are required to support themselves," Rose said.

Libby felt her face color. "I would rather say that in this town, women of any marital status are able to support themselves if they so choose and if they are willing to work hard."

"Well, it seems my brother-in-law does not look for a closer relationship." Rose frowned. "No matter."

Indeed, Libby thought. To an untrained eye, she supposed Fergus might look like a fertile hunting ground for husbands. Several solvent widowers and bachelors made their home here. Without even trying, she could name a dozen, from Cyrus Fennel and Dr. Kincaid to the ranch hands and miners who populated the valley.

Rose probably considered her prospects quite good, even though Hiram wasn't interested. At least she'd finally deciphered that message. She'd been blessed with a pretty face and figure, and she could be charming when she wished. Unfortunately, a lot of the men in town already knew she could also be a harridan. Libby expected most of them to avoid Rose, if only out of sympathy for Hiram. But some gentleman might place more value on her looks than her personality and offer for her in spite of her acid tongue. And God could work the impossible, after all. Rose might, with divine intervention, change her ways.

Libby's pity collided with the knowledge that she hadn't prayed faithfully for Rose. Guilt seeped through her. The woman needed her friendship and her prayers. Instead, she had schooled her features to neutrality whenever Rose was around and had harbored her private dislike of the interloper.

On impulse, she smiled and leaned toward Rose. "Mrs. Caplinger, I know Trudy has invited you to our shooting circle, but I want to extend my invitation, as well. We'd love to have you join us on Mondays and Thursdays if it suits you."

"Hmm." Rose eyed her suspiciously. "I'm not sure that it would suit me. But I've heard so much about it, I might try it once. We shall see."

Trudy paid for her salt. Rose didn't buy so much as a spool of thread. Libby wasn't sure whether she should feel insulted. Apparently Rose planned to order her supplies for her millinery venture directly from the manufacturers and bypass the emporium. Fair enough. A dozen questions leaped to her mind. Where would Rose set up shop? Would she continue to live with the Dooleys? She decided to let the questions go until she had a private audience with Trudy. As the two women left her store, Libby thanked God for apparently solving Hiram's problem without the Ladies' Shooting Club's involvement.

Ethan hurried across the street toward the post office. Peter Nash never sent for him without reason. The summons had come by way of Peter's son, who'd popped in at the jailhouse and said, "Sheriff, my pa wants to talk to you," and left.

When he mounted the steps to the Nashes' front porch and opened the post office door, Ethan saw that Peter was deep in conversation with a stranger.

"Oh Sheriff, you're here. Thanks for coming." Peter gestured to the man, who wore spurs, work pants, and a cotton shirt. A wide leather belt slung around his waist carried a holstered gun and dozens of rounds of ammunition.

"This here's Wilfred Sterling," Peter continued. "He says he's Frank Peart's nephew."

Ethan stepped forward, scrutinizing the man. He hadn't removed his hat, but even so, Ethan recognized him.

"Sterling?" Ethan studied him carefully.

"That's right." The man made no offer to shake his hand.

"If you're Frank Peart's kin, why didn't you say so earlier? Oh, and don't think I don't know you. You're one of the rascals I ran out of the Spur & Saddle a couple of weeks ago."

"Just been getting settled in at my new job."

Ethan noted that he had his pistol back—Cyrus had taken the two cowpokes' guns away with him when he'd paid for the damage at Bitsy's. "At the old Martin ranch."

Sterling returned Ethan's gaze from beneath long lashes. "That's right."

"I've been inquiring all over the country, with some help of other folks here in town. Everything we've gotten back says Frank Peart has no living family."

"Guess they missed me."

Ethan nodded, more skeptical than ever. "And exactly how are you related to Frank?"

"My ma was his sister. She married and moved upstate. Hadn't seen her brother for nigh on thirty years."

"Uh-huh. And she's deceased now?"

"That's correct."

Ethan scratched the back of his head. He'd received replies from New Jersey indicating Frank Peart had indeed had a couple of sisters, but both were deceased.

"I'm not sure you have a legal claim to Frank and Milzie's land. But you'll have to go to Boise and do a lot of paperwork if you plan to try to inherit it. They'll expect you to prove your relationship to Frank. Can you do it?"

Sterling's eyebrows lowered and his mouth tightened. "How'm I supposed to do that?"

"I don't know. I'm not an attorney. But I'll tell you right now, you can't just squat on the Pearts' land and call it yours." Ethan wasn't sure what would happen to the land, but he had an impression the government was going to take it back. Not that the old mine was worth anything. But as sheriff of Fergus, he wouldn't let just anyone waltz in and lay claim to it. Especially someone he suspected of lying.

"We'll see about that." Sterling stomped out, his spurs scraping the porch steps.

Ethan closed the door the cowboy had left open. "So, Mr. Nash, was he here to pick up some mail?"

Peter shook his head. "Sending some."

"Where to, if I may be so bold as to ask?"

"Well, since you're the law. . ." Peter produced two envelopes and laid them on the counter. "Can't let you take them, but you can see them, I guess."

Ethan looked down at the letters. "Hmm. Written by two different people, I'd say."

"He told me one was from his boss."

Ethan bent down to decipher the addresses. "Pennsylvania. And Massachusetts."

"That's right," Peter said.

"Reckon I'll send some wires to the authorities in those towns, if Fergus can stand the expense, Mayor."

"Feel free, Ethan. I don't like that fellow." Peter scooped up the letters.

"Right. Thanks for sending your boy over for me."

Ethan stepped outside. Cyrus Fennel must be in his office now. Time for another parley.

He waited on the boardwalk while Cyrus sold a stagecoach ticket to a salesman who'd stopped overnight at the Fennel House. The man talked on and on about his recent travels. At last he came out and headed across the street toward the boardinghouse.

Ethan stepped into the office. "Morning, Mr. Fennel."

Cyrus had begun to rise from the chair behind his desk but sank back into it.

"Sheriff. What can I do for you?"

"You expressed an interest in buying the Peart place. I just wanted you to know there's a fellow in the area who claims to be Frank's heir."

"Really?" Cyrus shrugged. "Thanks, but I'm not so much interested anymore."

"That right?"

Cyrus opened a wooden box on his desk and took out a cigar.

"As a matter of fact, I'm thinking of selling off some of my property outside of town."

Ethan watched him in surprise. Cyrus usually held on to real estate like it was his life's blood. If he ever sold a piece, he made sure he took a very good profit.

Cyrus lit the cigar and took a couple of puffs. "I'm having a little cash flow problem." He grimaced. "Had some family needing a little help. So I can't buy any more land just now. But thanks for letting me know."

"All right." Ethan turned back outside into the brilliant sunshine. Odd. Very odd. And the coincidence of one of the hands at a ranch Cyrus owned claiming to be Frank's nephew—that was even odder.

★ CHAPTER 20 ★

Hiram welcomed Ethan for supper on Wednesday evening. Meals at the Dooley home had become monologues from Rose. Neither he nor Trudy had the energy to wrest the conversation from her anymore.

"Mr. Fennel showed me three buildings today. As soon as I decide which one I like best and find someone to help me clean it, I shall open my business." Rose gazed pointedly across the table at Trudy but elicited no reaction.

Trudy looked wrung out, Hiram realized. As exhausted as he felt.

Ethan smiled cordially and passed the dish of dandelion greens to Rose. "And will you continue living here when you've established your shop?"

Frown lines appeared between Rose's eyebrows. "I'm sure I've enjoyed visiting with my kin, and we have a pleasant household here. But truthfully, I'm considering another arrangement."

"Oh?"

To give him credit, Ethan hid the glee that statement must have fanned in his heart. Hiram accepted the dish of greens from Rose and nodded his silent thanks.

"Yes, I wouldn't want to impose on my brother-in-law and Gertrude. After all, this is their home. I had thoughts at one time that we might all continue as a unit, but. . ." Rose shook her head. "I've decided to become an independent businesswoman. This town seems to foster such enterprises, and I'd like to try."

"I wish you success," Ethan said. He looked over at Hiram. "I heard back from the governor this afternoon."

"About the Peart property?" Hiram asked.

"Yes. Since Milzie inherited from Frank, and then she died without a will, if no next of kin is found, the government will take possession of the property."

"But you said this Sterling fellow claims to be Frank's kin," Trudy said.

"But Milzie was the last owner of the property. Sterling's not blood kin to her. I'm not sure that matters." Ethan shook his head as he picked up his fork. "I don't pretend to understand it all. There's another complication, though. Milzie didn't pay taxes on the land for the last ten years, so it may be sold for back taxes."

"Wouldn't that be something?" Trudy rose and went to the stove for the coffeepot. "And you said Sterling hasn't proved his relationship to Frank."

"I doubt he can." Ethan held his mug up for some coffee.

Rose tossed her head when Trudy approached her. "I'll have tea, please."

Trudy said nothing but came around the table and filled Hiram's mug and her own. After replacing the coffeepot on the stove, she took down a china cup and saucer. Rose had made it clear the first day of her visit that it wasn't right to drink tea from a mug. One needed the saucer to partake properly. Lately Trudy had been waiting on Rose less and prompting her to take care of herself. Hiram wondered if her hints at moving out sprang from this. Though they'd tried to remain courteous, she must feel their reluctance to have her stay much longer.

"Well, you've got to do right by Milzie," Trudy said as she measured out tea leaves. "You can't let anyone take her land."

"I agree," Ethan said.

Hiram sipped his coffee and set the mug down. "Seems to me the law is in place, but whether Boise will bother to see that it's enforced is another question."

Trudy's eyebrows drew together. "That might fall to you, Eth."

Ethan nodded, but he didn't look happy. Hiram hated for his friend to feel pressure from the territorial officials as well as the townspeople and folks who skirted the edge of the law. But better Ethan than him. Give him a good piece of cherry wood and some sandpaper, and Hiram would be happy to stay out of public doings.

★

Ethan ate the last bite of pumpkin pudding with cream and pushed back his chair. Trudy was a powerful good cook. But Rose had stopped her flurry of baking since the Sunday Hiram made it clear he wasn't interested in marrying her. And when Trudy rose to clear the table, Rose made no offer to help.

"You folks go on into the parlor," Trudy said with a tight smile.

"Why don't you gentlemen bring your coffee, if you'd like." Rose's bright comment included them both, though Ethan had emptied his mug. "Oh Trudy, the sheriff needs a refill."

"No, I'm fine, thanks." Ethan stood. "I'll just help put these dishes through the dishpan."

"Nonsense." Rose smiled beguilingly. "You've worked hard all day. You need a chance to relax."

Ethan chuckled. "I haven't done much strenuous work today, ma'am, and I expect Trudy's done a heap more in that line than I have." He picked up his dishes and carried them to the work counter. Trudy set out her dishpan and started to walk around him, to the hot water reservoir on the stove. He touched her sleeve. "Let me get that for you."

"Thank you." Her smile was genuine now, if fatigued.

Hiram also carried his dishes over and set them in the dishpan. "How about I wash and Ethan dries? You go take a load off and visit with Rose."

Apparently that prospect didn't appeal to Trudy either. "If we all work at it, the chores will be done sooner."

"All right," Hiram said. "What would you like me to do? Whatever will help you most."

"You could sweep the floor and take the table scraps out to the chicken yard."

Rose stood uncertainly in the doorway to the parlor. "Aren't you coming, Hiram?"

"Might as well help clean up. I did my share of eating."

"You could wipe the table," Trudy suggested.

Rose's eyes narrowed. "I believe I'll work on my hat models." She disappeared into the parlor.

Ethan glanced at the Dooleys and lowered his voice. "Now that I've got you two alone, you might be interested to know that I heard back from a police chief in Massachusetts—the town where Kenton Smith sent his letter. He's never heard of anyone by that name."

"Well, you tried." Trudy finished loading the dishpan. Fifteen minutes later, the dishes were done and the kitchen back in order.

"I think I'll go 'round and see Doc Kincaid," Hiram said. "He mentioned the other day that he likes to read, and I told him he could borrow that book you gave me last Christmas."

"All right," Trudy said. "I hope he's not out on a professional call."

Hiram took his hat and slipped out the back door.

"Feel up to a stroll?" Ethan asked. "There's a near-full moon tonight."

"Yes, I'd like that." Trudy stepped to the parlor doorway. "Rose, I'm stepping out with Ethan for a little while."

"Oh. Is Hiram going?"

"He's visiting Dr. Kincaid."

"I thought his hand was healed."

"It is, pretty much. I think this is a social visit."

"Oh. I see."

Ethan took Trudy's shawl from its hook and held it for her. When she turned into it, he wrapped it around her shoulders and squeezed them. She smiled up at him.

"I expect you'll want a bonnet, too. It's still cool out evenings."

Soon they left and walked the short distance to Gold Lane. Ethan hoped she'd go with him as far as the river this time. It was quiet there and secluded. Late in summer, the river would be little more than a trickle, but now, in mid-June, it flowed fast over the rocky streambed. The sound of it reached them as they ambled past the last houses in town and down the slope toward the water. The moon peeked between the mountain summits to the east. He reached for Trudy's hand.

"What can you do about that cowboy claiming Milzie's land?" she asked.

"I expect I ought to go out and talk to him. Maybe I'll ride out in the morning. I'll tell him again that unless he can prove his kinship to Frank Peart, he can't inherit the land, and maybe not even then. He really needs to talk to a lawyer who knows the territorial statutes if he wants to pursue it."

"What will happen if he can't claim it? None of those letters we wrote have been answered yet."

"It'll sit for a while, and then it will probably be sold at auction for back taxes."

"Cyrus will buy it."

"Well, I dunno about that. Cy seems to have changed his mind about wanting it. Says he's having a cash flow problem."

"What's that?"

"Reckon it's like the river in August. Not enough liquid to keep things flowing."

"He's short on money?" She looked up at him in the moonlight.

Ethan stopped walking. "Something like that." He tugged her toward him, and she floated into his arms.

"Trudy."

"Mmm?"

He kissed her.

Trudy hurried around to the back door on Thursday afternoon. She'd stayed longer than usual at the shooting practice to help one of the ranchers' wives steady her aim. Now she'd be late putting supper on the table.

The warm, rich smell of baking hit her as she crossed the threshold. Rose turned from the stove with a sheet of hot cookies in her hand.

"That smells delicious." Trudy smiled at her. "Thank you for baking today. I'm sure the men will appreciate it." Ethan's presence at the supper table was a forgone conclusion.

But Rose turned away a bit flustered. "Oh, these aren't for supper, actually."

"What are they for?" Trudy hung up her bonnet and shawl and tied on her apron.

"I thought I'd take a basket around to Dr. Kincaid tomorrow, to thank him for the excellent job he did on Hiram's hand."

Trudy stood still with her hands behind her, on the apron strings. "He hardly did a thing."

Rose shrugged and began removing her golden oatmeal cookies from the baking sheet with a spatula.

"Wait a minute." Trudy marched around until she was in Rose's line of sight. "I thought you'd decided you liked Griffin Bane."

Rose's nose wrinkled. "I'm sure he's a nice enough man, but he smells like the stable all the time. And his voice is so loud he startles me when he speaks."

"Oh." Trudy hadn't given it much thought. A livery owner ought to smell like the stable, and a man as large as Griff was bound to have a stentorian voice. She eyed the plates of cooling cookies. Dr. Kincaid certainly would have plenty, and so far as she knew, the ingredients came from her supplies.

"Where's Hiram?"

"I'm not sure. I think I heard him out near the barn."

Trudy quickly put a pan of potatoes on to boil. "I guess we'll use the leftover chicken. I'll go out to the root cellar and see if there aren't a few carrots left."

As she crossed the backyard, Hiram came to the barn door and waved. She veered toward him.

"Did you know Rose was baking cookies for the doctor?"

He raised his eyebrows. "Smelled something good."

"Well, she's given up on Griffin. Says he smells like the barn. Now she's after Doc Kincaid."

"Maybe we should warn him."

Trudy cracked a smile. "Do we want to? Maybe she'll have a better chance with him. Griffin's too down-to-earth for her. He sees through hypocrisy every time."

Hiram sighed. "I was hoping to get a few of those cookies without any obligations attached."

"I doubt you will. Though she's baked a pile of them."

"Maybe she'll give them to more than one fella and see who comes back for more."

They both laughed.

Trudy cocked her head to one side. "How are you doing? Really?"

"All right. I feel a mite guilty."

"Whatever for?"

He shrugged. "Seems like a gentleman ought to offer her his protection."

"Oh Hiram. That's no reason to get married. Not when she's perfectly capable of taking care of herself."

"Well, I hope she snares a man soon and moves out of our house. Can't help it. I feel all kinds of sinful to think it—especially since Griff and the doctor are both nice people."

Trudy had to admit she also felt twinges of remorse for her ill feelings toward Rose. "I'm surprised she came all the way out here looking for a husband. Wasn't there anyone back home she could have married?"

"Don't know. She doesn't talk about Albert much."

They stood in silence for a moment. Trudy wondered about Rose's dead husband. Neither she nor Hiram had ever met him, but Trudy couldn't imagine he'd had any backbone.

"Why are we trying to push her off on our friends?" Hiram asked.

"So she'll leave you alone."

"Yes, but. . .isn't it wrong of us to wish her on someone else?"

"Maybe so." Trudy sighed. "You know, she can cook and keep house when she wants to. Maybe you ought to consider keeping her on as your housekeeper."

"You mean when you and Ethan get married?"

She could see that her brother was troubled. Hiram hated change. But if she did marry Ethan, he'd have to deal with it.

"I'd rather live alone than with Rose," he said. "Besides, that wouldn't be proper. I'm sorry if it's a sin to dislike her so much. I've been praying for her and that God will change my feelings if He wants me to marry her."

She stared at him in horror. "You mean you've actually thought about it?"

"Only as a—what would Pastor call it? A spiritual exercise."

"I see."

"Have you?"

"Not really. But I should probably be praying, too. She's nothing at all like her sister was, though she bears a passing resemblance to her. Violet was sweet and kind. Whenever Rose says something mean, it makes me so mad I could slap her."

"I don't think I could stand to live alone with her, and that's the truth."

Trudy nodded. She could easily gauge his agitation by the amount he had spoken that evening. He never talked more than was needful.

"I'm sorry you're in this situation. And I don't think God will blame you for not wanting to marry her. It'd be different if her heart was softer."

"She so talkative." His eyes pleaded with her to forgive him.

Trudy lifted her arms and hugged him. "I know she's not right for you. It's obvious. And it's all right. You don't need to feel bad. If you ever do want to get married again, I know you'll choose a quiet, genteel woman."

Hiram exhaled heavily and gave her a squeeze before backing away. She wondered if he would ever get to the point where he'd consider taking a wife again. There had been fleeting moments when she'd wondered, like the short time they'd sat together with Ethan and Libby after Bitsy's wedding. Hiram and Libby had talked and smiled and seemed to get along perfectly. Yet she couldn't imagine him going courting. If she knew her brother as well as she thought she did, he viewed himself as beneath Libby socially and perhaps intellectually, which was too bad. Hiram was a smart man. A near genius where mechanical things were concerned.

She patted his shoulder. "I'm going to the root cellar for carrots."

"I can get 'em for you."

"Thanks. I hope there's enough for supper. I know they're 'most gone."

"Trudy..."

"Yes?"

He looked away for a second. "You know I think a lot of you. I'm glad you've been here with me all this time."

Her heart warmed. "Thank you for saying that. I'll miss you if. . .well, if Ethan ever proves up."

He nodded. As usual, she felt they understood one another perfectly.

★ CHAPTER 21 ★

Libby smiled as Bitsy and Augie entered the mayor's parlor on Friday afternoon. She patted the settee beside her. Bitsy glanced at the men who made up the rest of the gathering and took the seat next to Libby. Augie settled in the chair beside the settee.

"Good afternoon, Mr. and Mrs. Moore," Peter Nash said. "We're pleased that you could join us today. As you can see, we've invited all the town's leading business owners to help the council decide on a matter that's been hanging for nearly a year now—that of Dr. Kincaid's situation."

Charles Walker, Maitland Dostie, Ethan, Griffin, the Reverend Mr. Benton, and Ted Hire, along with council members Libby, Cyrus, Oscar Runnels, and Zachary Harper, completed the group. Ellie Nash entered bearing a tray of mismatched mugs and teacups. She circulated, allowing each guest to choose coffee or tea.

Libby accepted a pretty, violet-sprigged cup of black tea, and Bitsy followed her lead, still darting nervous glances at various members of the gathering.

"Dr. Kincaid will join us in about a half hour," the mayor went on. "That is, provided he doesn't get an emergency call. I thought that would give us time to discuss a few things before he gets here."

"Is there a problem?" asked Maitland, the telegraph operator.

"The doc isn't happy with his living situation," Peter said.

"He's perfectly comfortable at the Fennel House."

Cyrus's defensive comment drew a sigh from Bitsy. Libby half-expected her to speak up, but for once she withheld her usually frank opinion.

"I'm sure he is, but he'd like a more permanent arrangement." Peter looked around at the others. "What happened is this: A citizen of our town, who is now deceased, invited Dr. Kincaid to come and practice in Fergus. We're glad he did, but the promises Mr. Morrell made to the doctor had not been approved by the town council, and we found them to be a bit extravagant."

"Just what did he promise?" Oscar asked. He reached into his inner pocket and pulled out a cigar. He glanced over at the ladies, as though suddenly remembering their presence. Libby frowned at him, and for once, Oscar took the hint and put his cigar back without lighting it.

Peter lifted a sheet of paper. "The doctor was kind enough to loan me the actual letter he received. In it, Morrell promised him a house, rent-free, in town, along with a horse and buggy to be maintained gratis at the livery stable"—at this, Griffin scowled fiercely—"and medical supplies to be shipped in regularly from Boise at no charge to the doctor."

"The town can't afford all that." Charles Walker spoke for the first time, his voice higher and thinner even than it had been before his grave injury the summer before.

"No, we can't, and it's not reasonable." Peter folded the letter and laid it aside. "No other physician would expect such benefits. I've discussed this with Dr. Kincaid, and he understands. However, he doesn't feel he can open an office and stock the supplies he'll need without some help from the town. So far he's been operating from the boardinghouse, going to his patients whenever he's called upon."

"But we're paying his board and room for him," Bitsy said.

Cyrus leaned forward. "Correction. The town is paying for his board. He's getting his room at the Fennel House free, which doesn't help me much in paying the couple who are running the place."

"But surely it's good advertising," Libby said. "Folks must feel safer staying there with a doctor in the house."

"Yes," said Ethan. "I expect the doc lends the place an air of respectability."

No one mentioned the boardinghouse's proximity to the Nugget saloon, but Ted Hire, who currently managed the place, sank a little lower in his chair.

The minister cleared his throat. "If I might make a suggestion, Mr. Mayor."

"Of course, Reverend."

"There are several vacant buildings on Main Street and Gold Lane, mostly owned by Mr. Fennel." He nodded deferentially at Cyrus. "Mr. Fennel made my wife and me an offer last year. We lived rent free in one of his houses for six months. During that time, the church began to pay me a salary. Apphia and I sought the Lord's direction. At the end of the six months, we approached Mr. Fennel about buying the house. We reached a satisfactory agreement with payments we can afford. Perhaps he would like to extend a similar offer to the doctor."

"I don't know how much income he has," Libby said. "Some folks pay him in foodstuffs." She didn't reveal how Kincaid had come to her asking if she could take two bushels of dried corn off his hands and apply the value to the account he'd run up at the emporium for medical supplies and sundries.

"And besides," Cyrus added, "I've already given him ten months' free rent at the Fennel House. I can't see extending it any longer."

"Hmm." Peter looked around at all of them. "Perhaps the town could afford to pay Mr. Fennel a reasonable rent on a house for the doctor. Then he could set up his office and take patients there, as well as have more private living quarters. I'm afraid we'll lose him if we don't resolve the issue soon."

"I'm sure the church members would help fix up the house, as they helped us with ours," Mr. Benton said.

Griffin straightened his shoulders. "I can let him use one of my wagons, and I can make him a good deal on a horse if he wants to buy one. Can't just give him one. I mean, they cost money. So does feed. But if he wants to arrange payments or something, I'll work with him. He's a good doctor, and I think we should do all we can to keep him here."

"I agree," Bitsy said. "Augie and I can pitch in a few extra dollars, can't we?" She looked to her new husband.

He nodded. "Guess so."

"Donations would help," Peter said, "but if it's to be a regular thing, we really ought to make it part of the town's budget."

Oscar laughed. "What's that? We've never had a budget."

"Certainly we have." Zack shook a finger toward his neighbor. "Just because we never wrote it down, don't mean we don't have one. We always collect taxes for the sheriff's pay and things like that. So, we add a dollar or two to each family's yearly bill to help the doctor out until his practice becomes more profitable."

Libby stirred. "Mr. Mayor, I think Mr. Runnels has a point. The town council hasn't kept the best records of its meetings, and we generally collect money until we have enough to pay our bills, but it really should be better organized."

"Are you volunteering, ma'am?" Peter's eyes twinkled as he spoke.

Libby smiled with gritted teeth. "I'll take part of the responsibility, but not all. I could keep official minutes at the meetings, for instance. But we really should keep precise records on how much is collected from whom and how it is spent."

"I've been saying that for years," Cyrus said.

"Well then, Mr. Fennel, would you set up a ledger for the town's local tax collection and distribution?"

"I wasn't volunteering."

Everyone stared at Cyrus.

"Oh all right." He shrugged. "Someone's got to do it, I suppose. Perhaps Mrs. Adams will assist me, to make certain I set the accounts up properly."

His suggestion surprised Libby. She'd thought she'd successfully discouraged his advances, and she had no desire to spend time alone with him. "Really, you ought to be able to do it without my help. You ran the assay office for some time, and now you run the stagecoach line. You must keep books for that and report to Wells Fargo."

Cyrus didn't look happy, but in the end, he agreed to set up the town's ledger.

Peter nodded at him. "That's the way, Mr. Fennel. Your labor in this matter will be greatly appreciated." He took out his pocket watch. "The doctor should be here soon, and we'll present this plan to him. Any other business to discuss while we wait?"

"Mr. Fennel," said the minister, "yesterday I rode out to that ranch you have northeast of town."

Cyrus's eyes flared, and he waited in silence.

"I met Mr. Smith, your tenant."

"Oh?"

"Yes, I'd heard you had a gentleman living out there and working the ranch. I invited him and his employees to the church services."

"What did he say?" Cyrus asked.

"He said he might come, but truthfully, he didn't sound committed to the idea. He also warned me not to expect his men, as they're busy stringing fence."

Libby listened with interest. That must be where the rolls of barbed wire Cyrus had ordered went.

"We have a lot of newcomers in town," Griffin noted.

"Yes, we do." Mr. Benton smiled. "My wife suggested we have a social event to bring folks together. A box social, perhaps."

"That sounds like fun," Libby said. "I'm sure the Ladies' Shooting Club would support the event."

"Thank you, Mrs. Adams. I'll ask Apphia to speak with you about it." The minister beamed at her. "Social gatherings now and then can draw the community together."

Bitsy looked askance at Libby. "I'm not sure you'd want Mr. Smith's cowhands to go to it. They might make a ruckus."

Ethan frowned. "So long as we make sure no alcohol is served, the whole town could enjoy a holiday. We could stipulate that it's a dry party when we announce it."

"We'd lose a workday," Zack noted.

"Yes, but we'd get to know some of these new people." Mr. Benton's face lit as he named them off. "There's Dr. Kincaid and Mrs. Caplinger, who tells me she's thinking of locating here permanently, and a new couple out on the Colburn place and Mr. Smith and his men. There may be others I'm forgetting."

"The Thistles," Libby said. "They came last summer."

"Yes, and we don't have many social occasions when it comes down to it," Peter said. "Folks enjoyed the Moores' wedding so much, I think they'd welcome another chance to get together without waiting for a funeral."

Bitsy's cheeks reddened deeper than her rouge accounted for.

"I'll help Miz Adams and the other women, Mayor. Just tell us what you want, and we'll arrange the refreshments and such."

A sudden thought came to Libby. "Say, what if we made this into a fund-raiser to help support Dr. Kincaid?"

After a moment's silence, Peter said, "Mrs. Adams, that's brilliant."

Ethan grinned at him. "Mayor, if you want someone to be sure everyone in town gets an invitation, I highly recommend the Ladies' Shooting Club. They helped me write some letters about the Peart property a couple of weeks ago."

"What did you find out about that?" Griffin asked.

"Nothing much yet."

Ellie Nash opened the parlor door. "Excuse me, folks. The doctor's here. Are you ready for him?"

Dr. Kincaid entered, and the discussion returned to his living quarters. By that time, Cyrus had accepted the idea of putting the physician in one of his vacant houses, even if he received a miniscule rent. *Better than nothing,* Libby thought. *He can always raise the rent when the doctor's practice prospers.*

Isabel opened the oven to check on the chicken. Papa was late for supper. He'd had that meeting with the council and business owners this afternoon, but surely that was finished by now. She poured a little water in the roasting pan to keep the chicken from drying out.

A knock at the front door startled her. She doffed her apron and hurried down the hall. She pulled the door open and stared into feral dark eyes. If asked, she'd have said Kenton Smith was the one person she least wanted to see, yet she couldn't deny the relief that washed over her when she found him waiting on the stoop.

"Oh, Mr. . . Uncle Kenton."

"Isabel. Is your father home?"

"Uh. . . ." The plaid shirt he wore was in better condition than the one she'd first seen him in, and his beard had filled in, but it did nothing to enhance his pinched face and crooked teeth. His eyelids lowered at her hesitation, making slits of the critical orbs.

She quickly cataloged how many of the hired hands were about the place and how loudly she would have to scream for one of them to hear her. "I expect him any minute. Could I...could I get you some coffee?"

"That'd be nice, thank you. And can one of your boys tend to my horse? He's mighty dry, too, after that long ride."

"Certainly. Would you like to sit here on the porch or in the parlor?"

"Oh, what's wrong with your pa's study?"

Her lungs contracted, and her breath whooshed out. Papa would never want anyone in there when he wasn't present. "I'm sorry, I haven't straightened the room today. Let me show you to the parlor."

Hoofbeats sounded on the dirt road leading to the ranch house, and she peered over her uncle's shoulder toward the sound.

"Ah, there's Papa now."

"Good. I'll go and meet him."

Papa rode his big roan gelding toward the corral near the barn. Kenton limped across the yard after him. Brady came from the barn to take Papa's horse. Isabel sighed and allowed herself to relax for a moment. Then she scurried back to the kitchen. No doubt Uncle Kenton would expect a meal. She set another place at the table then sank into her chair. She could hardly believe he was alive and well. He had indeed stayed in the area and come around to visit again. She closed her eyes. *Thank You, Lord.* It felt so good to let go of that worry. *And forgive me for thinking such an awful thing about Papa.*

Libby. She would have to tell Libby as soon as possible that her fears were unfounded. How silly she had been to think...

She refused to wonder about the hole Papa had dug. There must be some simple, mundane explanation. Shameful that she had thought otherwise.

She rose, tiptoed to the back door, and opened it a crack so that she could peek out at the barnyard without being observed.

Her father and Kenton stood by the corral fence. The sound of their voices carried to her. Papa didn't seem to care that all the hands could hear, let alone his daughter in the house.

"I told you I can't do it."

"And I say you'd better."

Kenton's tone shocked Isabel. No one spoke to her father that way. He'd fire any cowboy who dared. He glared at the shorter man with a look of authoritative dislike that she'd seen him use only twice before—once when he'd caught a ranch hand pilfering from his desk and again when he'd discovered a prairie rattler under the back stoop.

"Get out of here." She could almost see sparks fly from Papa's flinty eyes.

"You'll regret this."

"Maybe so."

Uncle Kenton whirled and strode toward the front of the house. Isabel quickly closed the door. She stood shaking for a moment, breathing in shallow gulps. Her hands shook, and she clasped them together. When they'd stopped trembling, she took the extra plate and silverware off the table.

Her father came in a few minutes later. "Supper ready?"

"Yes."

He washed his hands while Isabel took the chicken from the oven. They both sat down. Papa offered a rather curt blessing for the food.

Isabel started to speak several times but swallowed her words. As she handed him the potatoes, he squinted at her.

"Why are you staring?"

"I. . .I'm sorry. I wondered what Uncle Kenton wanted."

"Nothing."

"But he said he'd ridden a long way to see you."

Her father took a large bite of chicken and chewed it, all the while scowling and avoiding her gaze.

"Not that far," he said at last. "You may as well know, I let him move into the old Martin place. Wish I hadn't now."

Isabel's bite of potato refused to go down. She coughed and took a drink of water. "Isn't that where those awful men came from? The ones who made such a commotion in the saloon?"

"Yes, they were his hands."

"But you made it sound like you didn't know where he would be! It seems he's been out on the old Martin ranch ever since he was last here. Why didn't you tell me?"

His mouth slid into a crooked gash. "Isabel, if there are things you need to know, I will tell you. And things change. Just because Kenton is now at the Martin place doesn't mean he was the day you asked me."

She closed her mouth and sliced off a bite of her chicken. She hated it when Papa treated her this way. She was not a child.

They ate in silence for a few minutes. When Papa's plate was empty, instead of taking seconds, he sighed and pushed his chair back. "I'm going back into town. Don't wait up for me."

"But Papa, you haven't had your coffee."

She leaped up, but he was already gone. His heavy footsteps receded down the hallway, and the front door opened and closed. She began to clear the table mechanically. A few minutes later, she heard hoofbeats as a horse left the ranch at high speed.

The coffeepot was still full. She poured herself a mug and added milk, then sat down again. Papa certainly had a lot of secrets, and he wasn't about to enlighten her on Uncle Kenton's situation or the demands the man had made this evening. Could the hole behind the barn somehow be related to Kenton Smith's appearance? Or was it just the spot where Papa had buried a dead animal? He kept the spade in the barn. Should she. . .

She shuddered.

No, she absolutely should not.

★ CHAPTER 22 ★

What should I do? Do you think I should talk to the sheriff?"

Libby sat opposite Isabel in her lovely parlor and pondered. It was difficult to imagine herself in her guest's position. She had come to care for Isabel, and the young woman's plight made her heart ache.

"I'm not sure there's any need for that," Libby said. "After all, now that you're certain your uncle is well, you've less reason to think a crime has been committed—other than the disorderly conduct of his ranch hands, of course, but Sheriff Chapman has dealt with that." She tried not to think about the dead cowboy out in the cemetery near the schoolhouse. Apphia Benton had described the bleak little burial service to Libby: Only the Reverend and Mrs. Benton, the sheriff, and the two men who'd dug the grave— Griff Bane and Hiram Dooley—had attended.

"But Papa. . ." Isabel wiped her streaming eyes again with her muslin handkerchief.

"I know, my dear, but you've said last night's behavior was an aberration."

"True. Papa rarely drinks to the point of. . ." Isabel trailed off, but Libby had already heard how he'd come home after midnight and two of their trusted cowpunchers had carried him in and put him to bed, shushing each other as they tripped over chairs and banged into the bedstead, trying not to awaken her. "He often has a couple of drinks in the evening. I know this. Sometimes it makes him. . .less cordial than he would otherwise be. But last night. . ."

"He was still asleep when you left home, you said."

"Yes. When he was an hour late, I tried to wake him, but he. . ."

Libby leaned forward and patted her hand. "I'm sorry, dear. You did right to go to Mr. Bane and tell him your father was indisposed today. I'm sure Griffin will do fine with meeting the stagecoach and taking care of any passengers' needs."

"Yes. He. . ." Isabel licked her chapped lips. "He assured me he would see to things, and he had me letter a sign to hang on the office door: 'For tickets and other stage line business, see G. Bane at the livery today.' And he's a man of his word."

"Indeed." Libby rose. "Let me freshen your tea."

"Oh no. I'm keeping you from your work." Isabel rose, spilling her cotton bag and gloves to the floor.

Libby bent to help her retrieve them. "You mustn't fret about that. Florence is doing a good job. I'm actually thinking of training another clerk to give me more time away from the store."

"Business has been good lately?" Isabel asked.

"Yes, and I see it as a way to help one more woman in Fergus become independent."

"Oh? Of whom are you thinking? If it's not a private matter."

"I haven't settled my mind on one person yet, but I'm watching the Spur & Saddle. I thought that if Bitsy and Augie have a slack time when they can't afford to keep both Vashti and Goldie on, I might take one of them under my wing." Libby eyed her anxiously, but no censure met her in Isabel's face. There was a time when the schoolmarm would have been horrified and boycotted the emporium if Libby hired a former saloon girl. Now the moral judgments were left to Rose Caplinger and a few of the town's older women, Libby thought wryly. "There's Myra Harper, too. She hasn't expressed interest, but I think she might be a good candidate."

"I guess there are plenty of women in this town who'd like a chance to earn some money at a respectable establishment." Isabel drew on her gloves. "Thank you for your advice. You are a good friend."

"You're welcome," Libby said. "Speak softly to your father, and I'm sure this time of turbulence will pass. And as to that hole he dug behind the barn. . ."

"It's probably nothing."

"Probably." They looked at each other for a moment. Libby hoped they were right, but she couldn't see an advantage to stirring up more suspicion and anger between Isabel and her father. Cyrus was a proud, opinionated man. Best to ignore his occasional lapses.

"Now don't forget the box social next Saturday."

Isabel ducked her head. "I don't think I'll put a box in the auction."

"You must!" Libby squeezed her arm. "My dear, there will be dozens of bachelors bidding on the box lunches. It's a civic duty of all the single women to enter."

That drew a wan smile. "Do you think so, or are you in jest?"

Libby lifted her eyebrows. "I am entering."

Isabel's skeptical face made her burst out in laughter.

"I am, truly. So you must enter, too."

"What if we end up with a couple of crude miners?"

"Then we'll insist on eating together to keep one another safe, and rejoice in the amount of money we raised toward outfitting Dr. Kincaid's new office. But I shall pray that two nice gentlemen buy our lunches. And you must enter the pie contest, too. I happen to know you make the best lemon meringue pie in the territory."

Isabel smiled and drew Libby into an awkward hug. "Thank you so much. I've not had anyone to talk with this way since Mama died."

Tears filled Libby's eyes. "Come again soon. And if your father is cross with you tonight, ride into town and stay with me. I mean it."

Isabel opened her mouth as though to protest, then closed her lips and nodded. "Thank you, then."

She exited through the kitchen door. Libby watched over the rail until Isabel was safely down the stairs and on the back porch that served as her freight platform.

She carried their dishes to the dry sink and tidied the apartment. As she walked down the inside stairs into the emporium, she assured herself that hushing up the matter was best. What good would it do to report Cyrus's drunken spree—of which Ethan might already be aware? But it bothered her that Cyrus had set up his brother-in-law as a rancher when he'd had no contact with him for more than twenty years and didn't seem to like him much. Smith had been in prison before, and he'd hired a crew of unsavory characters.

The whole matter puzzled Libby. Cyrus was a shrewd businessman, known for running a tight ship. He wouldn't put up with laziness or drunkenness and had been known to fire stagecoach drivers for tardiness.

A vague uneasiness hovered in her chest. Kenton Smith's reappearance had not eased Isabel's fears; instead, it had substituted new ones for the old. How long could her friend continue living in dread?

The day of the social dawned bright and clear. Ethan and his two ranch hands hurried to complete morning chores so they all could attend the gathering at the schoolhouse. Spin and Johnny eagerly accepted their pay from Ethan.

"I sure hope Florence Nash tells me which basket is hers." Spin riffled the bills Ethan had handed him.

"Don't spend your whole week's pay on a lunch." Johnny shook his head at his brother's enthusiasm. "That little redhead's got you in a tizzy."

"Ain't no shame in likin' a girl. Right, Sheriff?" Spin wiggled his eyebrows at Ethan.

"No Marcus. No shame a'tall."

Spin scowled at Ethan's use of his proper name. "Hey! You better not call me that in town."

"Watch it," Johnny said. "He's the boss, remember?"

Ethan grinned. "I expect you'll be eyeing the females soon, too. I suggest you take a hard look at the Harper sisters. They're good girls."

Spin pushed his hat back and frowned. "Myra's too old for him."

"Who says? Anyway, Alice isn't. And she's not homely either." Ethan took off his work gloves. "All right, let's get breakfast and clean up. Folks will start gathering by ten o'clock."

"Are you cookin' breakfast?" Spin's eyes gleamed with hope.

"No, you are. Call me when it's ready." Ethan slapped his shoulder with his leather gloves and strode toward the house.

An hour and a half later, he and the McDade boys saddled up and rode to the schoolhouse. The school yard was already thronged. Rough tables covered with dishes stretched along one side of the meadow where the scholars played during recesses. Food for those who would not be dining on auctioned box lunches filled the plank surfaces.

Ethan tied Scout to the fence between the schoolhouse and the graveyard and ambled about the grounds speaking to the townspeople. Seemed every rancher and miner within the Owyhee Valley had gotten the word and come to join in the gala.

"Hello, Lyman," he called to a gray-haired rancher who lived five miles outside town. He hadn't seen Lyman and Ruth Robinson for at least eight months. "How'd you fare last winter?"

"We got by."

Ethan lingered a moment with the couple and strolled on. Dr. Kincaid hailed him and excused himself from a knot of gaily gowned ladies.

"Well Doc, seems you've got some admirers." Ethan extended his hand, and Kincaid shook it heartily.

"For some reason, all the single ladies seem to be competing to get my attention. It's rather distracting. Does that happen to you, Sheriff?"

Ethan chuckled. "Not since I started stepping out with Trudy."

"Ah, so that's the key. A steady girl."

"Maybe so. Have any of them told you which is their box lunch yet, to be sure you'll bid on it?"

Enlightenment brightened Kincaid's face. "Oh, so *that's* what Miss Edwards meant when she said she hoped I liked pink and green ribbons. Mumbo jumbo, I thought."

"Far from it. She's gunning for you, that's sure."

"Aha. And has the fair Miss Dooley told you which is hers?"

Ethan frowned. "No, she hasn't." Was Trudy really going to risk letting another man buy her lunch? He'd better find her soon and see if he could get a hint out of her.

"Oh, and the eldest Harper girl asked me if I like currant pie and said something about a red bow. . . ." The doctor looked anxiously toward the table set aside for the mystery lunches.

"You'd best decide which one you want and put your money on it, Doc." Ethan clapped him on the shoulder. He'd just spotted Hiram and Trudy walking into the school yard with Rose, Libby, and the Nash family.

The ladies carried large baskets with bright cloths covering the contents.

Ethan greeted them and fell into step beside Trudy.

"May I carry that for you?"

She laughed. "Oh no. No man is going to get his hands on our baskets before we deliver our boxes for the auction. Right, Libby?"

"Absolutely." Libby smiled at him. "I hope you intend to participate in the auction, Sheriff."

"Of course. But it will be difficult to remain impartial. If I only had an inkling of what to bid on. . ."

"You may carry my basket, Sheriff," Rose called.

Ethan broke stride. "Oh. . .of course. Where would you like it?"

"Just follow me, sir. You'll need to exercise discretion, however. Mustn't tell any of the other fellows which box is mine." Rose giggled and wiggled a finger, beckoning him toward the auction table.

Ethan cast a helpless glance at Trudy. She shrugged as though to say, "You got yourself into it."

Orissa Walker and Annie Harper accepted the single women's offerings under cover of a strategically hung tablecloth.

"Go on and enjoy yourselves, gals," Annie told Trudy and Libby. "We'll get a batch of six or eight before we add them to the ones on the table. That way, if the gents are watching, they still won't know whose is whose."

"What have we here?" Orissa asked as Ethan and Rose stopped before her.

"Why, it's my lunch for auction." Rose smiled prettily and lifted the linen towel draped over her box. Ethan couldn't help seeing the curled lavender ribbons and paper pansies that decorated the top of the box. "Now, Sheriff, remember, mum's the word." She winked at him, and Ethan felt the blood rush to his cheeks. Was she hinting that he should bid on her box? Or perhaps that he should tell the other men to bid on it? If he whispered about which was hers, would that in reality drive away bidders?

"I'll see you later, I'm sure, Mrs. Caplinger."

"All right, Sheriff. And thank you for your assistance."

Hiram sidled up to him. "Can you help lug out benches from the schoolroom so people can sit while they watch the shooting contest?"

"Sure. When's that going to be held?" Ethan glanced around as they walked, wondering where Trudy had gotten to. He spotted her and Libby talking with Starr and Jessie Tinen near a table covered with pies.

"After lunch," Hiram said. "The judges sample the pies and announce the winners of the pie contest, and then the shooting match will start."

"The horse race is the last event of the day?" Ethan asked.

Hiram nodded.

"You entering anything?"

Hiram shook his head.

"What's the matter? Old Hoss getting slow?" Ethan chuckled at Hiram's expression.

"You taking Scout in the race?"

"Naw, I'm just going to watch and make sure things stay peaceful."

"Hey." Hiram jerked his chin toward the road.

Ethan turned and saw several riders cantering into the schoolyard in a swirl of dust. He studied them closely and caught his breath. Eli Button, Wilfred Sterling, and the other man he'd let go after the Spur & Saddle incident had arrived, accompanied by three more men. So. Someone had extended the invitation to them, and they'd left the Martin ranch en masse for the social. He'd better speak to them immediately to be sure they hadn't brought along any liquor.

Before he could approach them, Cyrus detached himself from a knot of men and walked over to the newcomers. The oldest of the riders dismounted and fell into conversation with him.

"That must be Mr. Fennel's brother-in-law," Ethan said.

"You go ahead," Hiram said. "I'll get Griff to help me."

"All right. Oh, say, Hiram. Wait a sec." He grabbed the gunsmith's sleeve and drew him closer.

Hiram raised his eyebrows.

"Don't bid on anything with lavender ribbons and pansies," Ethan whispered.

Light dawned in Hiram's eyes, and he nodded. He smiled and slapped Ethan's shoulder before he walked away toward where Griff Bane towered over a cluster of men preparing to start a horseshoe game.

Ethan sauntered toward Cyrus and the stranger. The cowboys had dismounted and led their horses to the side of the schoolyard and tethered them near the townsfolks' mounts.

"Good day, Mr. Fennel." Ethan smiled and tried to sound friendly.

"Well Sheriff. How are you doing?" Cyrus's smile looked a little strained. "I s'pose you'd like to meet my brother-in-law, Kenton Smith."

Ethan held out his hand to the graying man. "You're the tenant on the Martin ranch."

"That's right." Smith clasped his hand briefly.

"Welcome to Fergus, Mr. Smith. Just make sure your boys behave themselves."

The older man's eyes narrowed. "Oh they will. They're good boys. They just get a little rambunctious now and then. I'm sorry about what happened earlier, but saloons have to expect a bit of action now and then."

"I don't see it that way. Were you informed that there's to be no alcohol at this picnic?"

"We got the word," Smith said.

Ethan nodded. "I hope you and your boys enjoy the day."

He walked away feeling Smith and Fennel watching him. He wondered if they had contacted the dead cowboy's family, as Cyrus had promised, but he wasn't going to ask. And he was going to do his best to find out what Trudy's box looked like. He didn't want her to wind up eating lunch with the likes of Eli Button.

★ CHAPTER 23 ★

You've got to know what she put on it. Come on, Hi. I can't let some other man buy my sweetheart's box lunch."

Hiram scowled and shook his head. His sister hadn't let him see her creation. She had taken great pains to hide it from both him and Rose. If Ethan wanted to wheedle the information out of Trudy, he should do it himself.

"They're about to start the bidding." Ethan looked anxiously toward where Peter Nash was preparing to auction off the ladies' lunches.

"Folks, and especially gentlemen, gather 'round. The single ladies have put their best efforts into preparing lunches for your gustatory pleasure. We have fourteen box lunches for our auction. Mrs. Nash is going to bring me the first one, and it's up to you fellows how much money we raise here today, but I'm telling you, if you don't bid on these boxes, you're missing out on a good thing."

Ellie smiled and carried a box wrapped in plaid flannel to her husband. "Looks like the lady who made this lunch wrapped it up in a tablecloth."

Peter took the bundle and held it up. "There you go, gentlemen. Isn't that an inviting parcel? Why, Parnell, this would go nicely with your shirt."

Parnell Oxley, one of the cowboys from the Landry ranch, guffawed. "All right, Mayor, you talked me into it. I'll bid two bits."

The other men edged closer and the bids began to fly. When they lagged at two dollars, Peter let his gavel fall. "Sold to Mr. Runnels for two dollars."

Josiah Runnels walked forward to accept the package amid applause and catcalls.

"Would the lady who made the lunch please come forward?" Peter asked.

Myra Harper came from the edge of the crowd, flushing as she peeled off her apron and tossed it to her mother. She strolled over to Josiah and looked up at him. "Disappointed it's your next-door neighbor's box, Josiah?"

"Nah. I hope you made fried chicken."

Everyone laughed.

Hiram eyed Ethan. "Whyn't you bid?"

"It didn't look like what I thought Trudy would pack."

"Huh."

They stood shoulder to shoulder while Ellie took the next box to Peter. The plain white pasteboard box was tied with a wide green ribbon. Hiram wondered whose it was. What if it was Libby's and someone like Ted Hire or one of those rough cowpokes bought it? That was scary.

Spin McDade leaped into the bidding early, and Ethan sighed. "Must be Florence's box, and she told him."

"Think so?" Hiram felt a little better. Sure enough, when the others dropped out and Spin plunked down a dollar and four bits, Florence minced toward him, her face a brilliant red that clashed with her carroty hair.

The box with pansies and lavender ribbons came up next. Hiram stood perfectly still, not moving a muscle. Ethan also stayed silent, but several men began bidding. The gavel fell at two dollars and a quarter.

Rose swept forward.

"Mrs. Caplinger, thank you for a lovely entry that raised a good amount for our cause," Peter said.

Dr. Kincaid accepted his purchase with aplomb and offered his arm to Rose. She slid her hand through the crook of his elbow with a satisfied smile.

"He almost looks happy," Ethan said.

"Think he knew?" Hiram asked.

"Oh yeah, he knew. I wouldn't be surprised if every man here knew."

The next box was wrapped in plain brown paper and tied with a black ribbon like a man's necktie.

"That's an odd one," Ethan said.

Hiram felt a strange prickle at the back of his neck. He reached to scratch it.

"Ah, this is an interesting package." Peter held it up for all to see. He tipped the top slightly toward the crowd. Fastened near the bow was a packet of primers.

Peter grinned at them. "Something tells me this box was prepared by one of the members of the Ladies' Shooting Club."

Four hands shot up, and men began flinging bids at the mayor.

Ethan leaned close to Hiram's ear. "You think that's Trudy's?"

Hiram shook his head. The brown paper was what Libby used to wrap customers' packages every day, and he'd gone into the emporium only yesterday and bought a packet of primers. Trouble was, every man in town was interested. He stuck his hands into his pockets and fingered the coins in the right one.

"Two-seventy-five," Peter called before the bidding slowed down. "And now three dollars. Who'll bid three dollars?"

Hiram reached up and lifted his hat. Peter looked his way, and Hiram nodded.

"Three dollars," Peter said. "I have three dollars from a man who knows a good thing when he sees it. Who'll bid three bucks and two bits?"

Griffin roared, "Right here, Mayor."

"Three-twenty-five. Who'll make it three and a half?" He glanced at Hiram.

How could he afford it? He had only three silver dollars in his pocket. Griff Bane would win. Hiram shook his head slightly.

"Three and a half," Peter said. "Who'll bid three-fifty?" He paused, holding up his gavel. "Going once..."

"Three-fifty." Everyone turned and stared at the cowboy who'd bid. Hiram sucked in a deep breath. It was Eli Button, the man he'd walloped at Bitsy's place.

Ethan looked askance at him. "Can't let that fella get it."

Hiram grimaced.

Ethan looked at the mayor, who was saying, "Going twice..."

"Four dollars!"

Everyone turned to stare at Ethan.

"The sheriff is in the game with a bid of four dollars." Peter grinned at him. "Do I hear four-twenty-five?"

Button shook his head and walked away.

"Well Ethan, looks like you bought yourself a lunch." Peter brought the gavel down.

Hiram exhaled and watched as Libby stepped forward. She took the box from Peter and walked toward the sheriff, smiling.

"Thanks for buying my box, Ethan. I hope you enjoy what I've packed." Her gaze slid toward Hiram. "I thought for a minute you'd be my dining partner, Mr. Dooley."

He felt his face going red. "Well I. . ." He looked down at the ground.

"Guess I'd better go pay for it." Ethan looked at Libby and then at Hiram. "Hi, why don't you join us, whether you snag a box or not."

"Oh, I don't know. . ."

"Yes, do," Libby said. "There's plenty. And I have a quilt yonder. We can spread it in the shade of the schoolhouse."

"Sounds good," Ethan said. "I'll be there in just a minute." He turned and headed for the small table where Emmaline Landry was collecting the fees from the bidders.

Libby leaned toward Hiram. "Interested in buying your sister's lunch for Ethan?"

He jerked his chin up. Her beautiful blue eyes twinkled at him. He nodded.

"A nosegay of buttercups," Libby whispered. "Yellow grosgrain ribbon."

He glanced quickly at Peter, but the box the mayor now held was trimmed with blue and red rickrack.

"Meet us over there." Libby nodded toward the side of the school building, where a narrow strip of shade would give the barest relief from the sun.

Parnell Oxley walked off with the current offering, and to Hiram's surprise, Isabel went with him. He hadn't supposed Isabel would loosen up enough to participate in the event. She'd changed a lot since she'd begun going to the shooting club.

The next box sported gaudy red, pink, and orange paper. It looked as though a child had thrown blobs of paint at it. A glittery gold cord decorated it, with several unnaturally red feathers fluttering from the knot on top.

Hiram looked about and studied the remaining widows and single women in the crowd. The two saloon girls from the Nugget giggled and nudged each other. Several men joined the bidding, and one of the cowboys won the prize of lunch with Opal Knoff, the blond from the Nugget. Another box went to Kenton Smith, and he graciously escorted the widow Daniels—whose husband had died in a wagon accident last winter—to a spot on the grass. Two cowboys and Cyrus Fennel bought boxes, and at last the one with the yellow ribbon and drooping buttercups came up for sale. The bidding slowed at two dollars.

"Come on, fellas," Peter called. "Only a few boxes left. Don't you have any cash on ya?"

Hiram looked around for Trudy, but she was keeping busy with Mrs. Storrey and Mrs. Tinen at the food tables, not paying any attention.

"Going once, going twice. . .sold to Mr. Hiram Dooley for two dollars."

Hiram accepted the box and walked over to Mrs. Landry's table.

"Who's the cook?" someone shouted.

Trudy looked up and clapped a hand to her mouth. She hurried around the tables toward Hiram. "Guess you're stuck with me."

The crowd laughed.

"He bought his sister's box," Hiram heard Cy Fennel tell someone else.

"Hey, Dooley, I'll buy it from you for two-ten," called stagecoach driver Nick Telford.

Hiram smiled and shook his head.

"You missed your chance," Emmaline yelled. "Bid on the next one." She smiled up at Hiram and held out her hand for the two silver dollars. "Thank you, sir."

He turned and found Trudy at his elbow.

"Sorry," she said.

"What for? It'll be good, I know that."

She smiled and walked beside him with her head high.

"Did you know it was hers?" Augie called.

Hiram just smiled and gave a little shrug. The crowd turned its attention back to the auction. Griffin and Nick began a battle for the next box. Hiram led his sister straight to the quilt in the shade, where Libby and Ethan were unpacking Libby's box.

★ CHAPTER 24 ★

Nearly one hundred people thronged around the pie table as the judges—Charles Walker, Bertha Runnels, and Micah Landry—sampled the entries. Much fidgeting and whispering ensued while the three conferred.

At last Charles Walker stepped forward and held up his hands. "Folks, it's a tough decision, but we've decided on the winners. The grand prize, which is that magnificent new set of bakeware over yonder donated by the Paragon Emporium, goes to Augie Moore for his pecan pie."

Everyone cheered. Augie and Bitsy stood near Ethan, and he grinned at the new restaurateurs.

"Congratulations, Augie."

The bald, muscular man blushed to the tips of his ears. "Thanks, Sheriff." He walked up to shake the judges' hands.

"Folks, the rest of Augie's pie will be sold by the slice when we're finished," Walker said. "Now, as to the best fruit pie, that was very difficult, but we've decided on a fresh rhubarb and strawberry pie by Rilla Thistle."

Again the people cheered and applauded. Mrs. Thistle, her face pink with pleasure, accepted the gift of a new apron, pieced by Orissa Walker.

"And in the cream pie division," Walker called out, "the judges are unanimous. The set of linen napkins embroidered by Ruth Robinson goes to our very own schoolteacher, Miss Isabel Fennel, for her lemon meringue."

Isabel gasped and left her father's side to retrieve her prize.

"Now, folks," Walker continued, "you know these three are mighty fine cooks. Some of the best eating in town is to be found at the Spur & Saddle and the Fennel House. And Miss Isabel showed her skills, as well, last summer during the opening of the boardinghouse. So you know you're getting your money's worth when you pay two bits for a slice of one of these winning pies. The other pies can be had for ten cents a slice. All the proceeds will go toward furnishing and equipping Dr. Kincaid's new office. So eat up and pay up."

The doctor stepped up beside Walker for a moment, and the laughter and murmuring stilled.

"Folks, I just want you to know how much I appreciate all you're doing. The town council has worked with me to help me give you the finest medical care I can. But I didn't expect the entire town to turn out and support the effort like this. All I can say is thank you, and I'll be there for you when you need medical attention."

Everyone clapped as Dr. Kincaid beamed and nodded.

"That's great," Walker said. "The ladies will serve the pies now, and I believe Miss Dooley and her helpers will be setting up for the shooting contest while that's going on." He pulled out his pocket watch. "Let's say the first round of the shooting match will begin in thirty minutes." He looked questioningly at Trudy, and she nodded.

Cowboys, miners, and townspeople lined up for pie. Ethan noted that Kenton Smith and a couple of his men were among them. He could relax as long as they kept busy. If they started getting bored, things might heat up.

He strolled toward the fence that served as a hitching rail, where a dozen wagons stood and thirty or more horses and mules switched their tails at flies. Wouldn't hurt to make sure nobody was poking around the wagons and sneaking flasks out of saddlebags. He greeted a couple of ranchers feeding their animals and ambled around the perimeter of the yard where others had hobbled their teams. Griffin and Parnell had cans of flour and were sprinkling it in a line across the road.

"You getting ready for the horse race?" Ethan asked.

"Yup." Griffin frowned as he shook the can gently. "This is the starting and finishing line. They'll ride into town, grab a flag from Ted Hire at the Nugget, and come back here. First one to cross the finish holding his flag wins."

Ethan nodded. Sounded simple enough.

Goldie and Vashti had teamed with Myra and Florence to organize games for the schoolchildren. Ethan stood for a few minutes watching the girls hand out feed sacks for the sack race. Parents and cowboys alike mingled to cheer the youngsters on. Will Ingram collected the prize of a peppermint stick. Myra announced that for the next event, the children would divide into teams for an egg-and-spoon relay. Ethan walked on to the back of the schoolhouse. Behind the building, Trudy, Libby, and Starr had set up four targets, with the shooting range facing the open prairie and the distant mountains.

Trudy came to meet him in the knee-high grass. "Ethan, we can't decide how to set up the divisions. We had planned to just let anyone enter who wanted to and not split up the contestants, but nearly thirty people have signed up. Some say we ought to separate the men and the ladies. But some of the ladies from the club want to try their skills against the men."

"How many prizes do you have?"

"Three. The grand prize, a free dinner at the Spur & Saddle for second place, and a box of ammunition for third."

Ethan nodded, thinking about the possibilities. "That Colt pistol for the grand prize is something. If I thought I had a chance, I'd enter myself."

"Libby talked the town council into buying it wholesale out of the proceeds of the day. They decided it would be a good draw for the contests, and it seems as though it worked. It's only two bits to enter, and it's for a good cause."

Ethan chuckled. "Well, in my case, it would be money thrown away, because I happen to know several ladies who can outshoot me. Probably a lot of the men can, too, but I don't think I'll stand up today and let the whole town know. If you need people who aren't competing to be judges or help change the targets, I'm willing."

"Thank you."

Libby and Starr came to join them.

"So, what do you think, Sheriff?" Starr pointed to the four

identical bull's-eye targets they'd set up. "We decided that to be really fair, we'll have to change the targets for each shooter."

"It's a good thing we brought the paper and paint," Libby said. "Twelve more people have signed up since this morning. We've got Opal and Bitsy working on more targets."

"They look good." Ethan surveyed the shooting range. "Will you be ready on time?"

Trudy's brow wrinkled. "I think so."

"Some of the men were muttering at lunchtime," Starr said. "They don't think we should let the ladies compete against them."

Libby waved one hand in dismissal. "What you mean is they don't think we ought to make them compete against us ladies."

Starr nodded with a smirk. "Guess you're right. They're afraid we'll outshoot them."

"And everybody will see," Trudy said.

Ethan raised his hands palms up, smiling. "It's up to you, but shooting's one skill that doesn't favor men or women, so far as I can see. Some have put in more practice than others, and there's always folks who have a natural talent for it."

"That's right." Starr scowled at Trudy. "Why shouldn't we be allowed to go against them?"

"Well, uh. . ." Trudy glanced at Libby. "Sometimes men get all. . ."

"Humiliated?" Libby suggested.

"Well yes. We don't want to embarrass the men that badly, do we?"

Starr let out a whoop. "Of course we do! We've been working for nigh on a year now to become good shots."

"Yes, but our purpose was to protect our families and property, not to outdo our fellow citizens." Libby arched her brows. The three ladies waited, obviously expecting Ethan to settle the matter.

"Well, if you have a first round where all the contestants shoot their rounds, then narrow it down for the next round. . . And if some of them are ladies, who can argue?"

Trudy nodded. "That's the way we were figuring to do it. If we have thirty in the first round, then we can let the ten best move on to the second round, and three for the final. Or four if it's close. We'll use fresh targets for the final go. I think we'll have enough."

"We can circle their shots on the targets from the first round and reuse them in the second round," Libby said.

Starr grinned. "Yes, and if some of them miss the target completely, we can certainly reuse those."

"Oh my, you ladies don't think much of the competition, do you?" Ethan laughed. "Are you all entering?"

"I don't know as we should," Trudy said. "We're setting up the range, after all."

"Ah, that's nothing. I'd like to see you gals shoot. I think a lot of people would. Let us see the fruits of your hard labor."

Trudy chewed her bottom lip. "Cyrus is entered."

"Is he, now?" Ethan asked.

"Yes," Starr said. "All those new cowpokes, too, and Augie and Griff and Doc Kincaid. Half the town's going to shoot this afternoon."

"Trudy, you have to enter." Libby laid a hand on her friend's sleeve, her blue eyes coaxing.

Trudy inhaled deeply and eyed the far targets. "I will if you will."

"Done!" Libby hugged her.

"We'll have to borrow a rifle." Trudy seemed to have forgotten her hesitation. "This contest is for long guns."

"You know I haven't shot much with a rifle." Libby frowned. "Hiram's is the only one I've practiced with."

"He'll let us both use it." Trudy turned eagerly to Ethan. "Do you know where he is? One of us will have to run home and get it."

"I could ride into town on Scout. I'd be back in fifteen minutes."

"Would you?" Trudy's eyes lit, and he was glad he'd offered.

"Sure. I'll find Hiram and speak to him first. I'll be back in twenty minutes, no more, I promise."

"Good," Trudy said. "Libby and I will go sign up and pay our two bits each."

"I wish we had time to get a few practice shots in." Libby looked along the barrel of Hiram's Sharps repeating rifle and squinted at the sights.

"You'll do great," Trudy said.

"I don't know. It doesn't handle like my pistol." Libby lowered the rifle.

"Here comes Mayor Nash." Trudy took the Sharps and rested it on her shoulder, pointing skyward. She and Libby walked toward the shooting line and met Peter just beyond it.

"Are you ladies all set?" He looked out over the range. "Looks good. Four shooters at a time?"

"That's right," Trudy said. "We have the list of names. And Sheriff Chapman has offered to help with the scoring and such. If he and Mrs. Runnels and Mrs. Walker handle it, we reckon it'll be all right for the members of the Ladies' Shooting Club to enter."

Peter nodded slowly. "Hadn't thought about it much, but I know my Florence wants to shoot."

Myra hurried toward them waving a sheaf of papers. "Trudy! Look! More people have signed up. We have forty-two entries now."

"That's ten dollars and a half in entry fees." Libby stared at the young woman. "I can hardly believe it."

Myra laughed and handed her the papers. "You can believe it, all right. And eighteen of them are ladies."

Trudy cleared her throat. "Mr. Mayor, we women would like to compete against the men. That is, we don't want a separate division for the women."

"I see."

"Do you?"

Peter threw back his head and laughed. "Oh yes, I think I do. Fine, ladies. When folks gather over here, I'll announce it."

Trudy nodded and scanned the papers. "For the first round, you can just read off the names four at a time, I guess. The judges will decide who moves on to the next round."

"We're setting up a table," Peter said. "Mrs. Runnels and Mrs. Walker will let the contestants draw numbers for their shooting order."

Libby nodded with approval. "That's a good idea. Then no one can complain."

Bitsy and Opal approached with Augie helping carry stacks of large paper targets.

"These things are barely dry," Bitsy called, swishing along in her red bloomers, "but I think we've got plenty now."

Libby grabbed Trudy's arm and pulled her aside. "Do you think we're doing the right thing?"

"Sure. Why not?"

"I really don't want to intimidate the men. Some of them are our friends."

Trudy frowned and placed her free hand on her hip. "Libby, if you don't want to shoot, that's fine. Just go cross your name off the list. But I've worked hard for the club, and I've taken a lot of grousing from the men of this town. I'm going to shoot today."

Libby glanced toward where Hiram and Ethan were helping the mayor set up seats for the judges. "All right. I guess." She bit her bottom lip. "Is your brother shooting?"

"Don't think so."

"Why not?"

Trudy shrugged. "Hiram hates to call attention to himself."

"Well. . .so do I. And if Hiram can be modest, so can I."

"Aw, Libby, no."

She felt the annoying blush begin under her lacy collar. "I don't think I want all those cowboys watching me shoot. And what if I miss completely?"

"Then you'll be out after the first round, and no one will stare at you any longer. Come on, Libby. Please? You're just nervous. Hi will be disappointed if you don't do it."

"You're just saying that." Libby couldn't help sneaking a glance toward the cluster of men. Hiram met her gaze from twenty yards away and smiled gently.

"I'm serious. When he came back with Ethan, carrying this rifle, he said to me, 'Libby's going to give it a try, isn't she?' I told him you were, and he grinned like a little kid with a nickel in his pocket. He wants to see you shoot his rifle."

"That's silly." Libby felt her face go a shade deeper.

"No, it's not. He's been more supportive of our club than anyone else in town. He wants to see us beat those men."

Libby flicked another glance. Hiram was moving benches and didn't see her this time. "I'll lose."

"So what? You'll be the most beautiful contestant of the day." Trudy turned toward the starting line. "Oh look! Bertha and Orissa

have set up a table and are giving out the numbers. Let's get ours."
She took Libby's arm and propelled her toward the judges' table.

"Hello, ladies." Bertha's wide frame dwarfed the chair the men
had brought out from the schoolhouse. "Would you like to pick
your numbers?"

"Yes, we would." Trudy shot a hard glance at Libby. "Both of
us." She stuck her hand into the flour sack Orissa held. "Twenty-
seven. Could be worse."

"Hey."

The soft voice in her ear sent tingles down Libby's spine. She
whirled and faced Hiram.

"You gonna shoot my Sharps?" he asked.

"Well. . ."

Hiram shoved his hat back and smiled. "It's a sight I'm looking
forward to."

She swallowed down the lump in the back of her throat. "It
seems so silly."

He shook his head. "No. This town needs some good, wholesome entertainment now and then."

Ethan stood beside him, smiling broadly. "It would be
dishonest if you ladies didn't shoot. You wouldn't let some half-
baked cowpoke take the prize, would you, when you could shoot
circles around him?"

"Come on, Libby, pick your number." Trudy's blue gray eyes
coaxed her. "Those cowboys that caused the trouble at Bitsy's
place are bragging how they're going to win the pistol."

Hiram's eyes perfectly matched his sister's and had a powerful
effect on Libby. Sometimes she thought his eyes spoke when he
kept quiet. But today he actually voiced his opinion. "You can do
it. We all want to see you put those loudmouthed hands from the
Martin ranch in their place."

Her cheeks grew warm. "Oh, I couldn't do that. Maybe Trudy
could."

Hiram nodded. "Sure. Let Trudy dig their grave with her
shooting. Then you come along and push 'em in."

Libby had to laugh. "All right, I'll take my turn. But I don't
expect to be in the final round." She stepped forward, her pulse
pounding. It still felt boastful to set herself up to shoot against

half the men in town, but how could she refuse Hiram's gentle prodding?

She thrust her hand into Orissa's flour sack and pulled it out. "Oh no."

Hiram grinned. "Number one. You'll show them how it's done."

She found herself smiling but blushing as she shook her head in protest.

A scant fifteen minutes later, Peter called, "Ladies and gentlemen, the first four contestants in our shooting match: Mrs. Elizabeth Adams, Miss Vashti Edwards, Mr. Augie Moore, and Mr. Arthur Tinen Jr."

The four walked to the shooting line carrying their weapons. Everyone in town crowded the edges of the line. Libby shoved her bonnet off her forehead and let it fall down her back.

"You will fire five rounds at your targets," Peter said. Stillness fell over the crowd.

"Ladies and gentlemen, on your marks. Get ready. Fire at will."

Libby's hands shook as she raised the Sharps. Hiram's rifle. And he was watching. Three guns cracked, and she hadn't fired with them. She inhaled and held her breath then pulled the trigger. She was sure she'd missed the target clean.

"Come on, Miz Adams!" Florence yelled from the side. Of course, Starr would root for Arthur, but the rest of the ladies would want Libby and Vashti to shine.

Then she heard it. Low and quiet, just before the others fired again, Hiram's voice reached her.

"You can do it, Libby."

She gritted her teeth and focused on the target.

"I'll now announce the names of the ten shooters who will advance to the second round," Peter shouted. "Let me say that it was a difficult choice."

Ethan looked over at Ted Hire, who had joined him, Bertha, and Orissa in examining the targets and judging the scores.

"*Really* difficult," Ted muttered. "Hope no one holds it against me."

Ethan smiled. He scanned the crowd and located Trudy and Libby standing near the other club members who had entered the contest.

Peter coughed and held up the sheet of paper Orissa had delivered to him. "I'll read the names in order of score, with the highest score first. These ten will start with a clean slate in round two. They are: Miss Gertrude Dooley."

The crowd erupted in cheers and applause. Ethan grinned as the enthusiastic shooting club women surged around Trudy for hugs.

Peter waited for the rumble of voices to subside. "Second, Mr. Cyrus Fennel."

Less ardent applause sounded.

"Mr. Augie Moore. And *Mrs.* Augie Moore."

Everyone laughed and called their congratulations to Bitsy and her husband.

"Dr. James Kincaid."

"Ooh, I *knew* it." Rose squealed and catapulted into the doctor's reluctant embrace.

"That's five." Peter paused, looking over the people. "Mrs. Arthur Tinen Jr."

"Congratulations, Starr!" Her husband good-naturedly slapped her on the back.

"Mr. Ned Harmon."

The stagecoach messenger grinned and accepted the praise of his friends.

"Miss Vashti Edwards."

The saloon girl, lately become a waitress and dishwasher, hugged Bitsy, Goldie, and the other members of the club. Peter waited until everyone was quiet again.

"I have two more names. If you're not among 'em, I'm sorry. We're going by where the lead hit the targets. So if you didn't pass muster, why maybe you should go practice more often." He nodded and looked down at the paper. "Mr. Wilfred Sterling."

The young cowboy swaggered about, shaking hands with the other ranch hands.

"And the tenth person moving on to the next round. . ."

All eyes were on Peter.

"This person missed one shot completely, but the other four shots were good enough to secure her a place in the next round."

The men exhaled, realizing a fifth woman had made the grade.

Peter smiled. "I'm happy to say it's another of our town council members, Mrs. Elizabeth Adams."

★ CHAPTER 25 ★

Hiram was so proud he thought he might need a bigger hat. His own little sister had outshot the whole town in the first round. That hadn't shocked him, but Libby—lovely, fine-boned, soft-spoken Libby—had also made the final ten.

True, she'd just squeaked into the elite ranks, but it was enough.

The saloon girls in their satin gowns and the ranchers' wives in cotton dresses milled about the five women who'd qualified, squeezing them and kissing their cheeks. Hiram stayed clear for a good ten minutes. It was only when Peter gave the call for the first four of the ten to come forward and shoot again that he edged close to Libby.

"Good shooting."

She spun and looked into his face, her china blue eyes dancing. "Thank you."

He nodded, still looking into those fascinating eyes. Her cheeks already bore a becoming flush. A few strands of her golden hair had escaped her bun and cascaded down along her smooth neck.

He inhaled slowly. "Mighty good."

"Thank you." Her eyes widened suddenly, as though she realized she'd repeated herself. "Oh. I—"

They stood for a moment, gazing at each other.

"Fire at will," Peter shouted, and four rifles cracked.

Libby leaned toward Hiram. "I froze up at first."

He nodded. "Take your time. Remember all the things you've

practiced. That's a good gun. It'll be kind to you if you keep steady."

"I'll try to remember that." She looked over her shoulder. "Oh, Trudy's shooting."

They both turned and stood, shoulder to shoulder, watching the contestants fire off the rest of their rounds.

When all the shooters rested their gunstocks on the ground, Ethan and Ted went to gather in the targets and replace them with new ones.

"The next four will shoot now." Peter called the names.

"Looks like you'll shoot last, against that cowboy." Hiram frowned as he looked at her.

"It's all right," Libby said. "I know I won't make the final. I'll just do my best and be done with it."

"Well, I'm proud of you."

"Are you?"

Her tone nearly knocked him over. Was Libby flirting with him? He smiled without meaning to. "Oh yes I am."

It seemed as though she'd leaned a little closer, and her shoulder touched his arm as they watched Doc, Starr, Ned, and Vashti prepare to fire.

Hiram reached up with his free hand and settled his hat so that the brim shaded his eyes a little better. Then he stood perfectly still, feeling the warmth of Libby's arm through the cotton sleeve of his shirt and watching the contest.

All too soon it was Libby's turn to shoot against Sterling.

"Good luck," Hiram said as Trudy handed her the rifle.

Libby looked up at him and nodded before she strode to the line.

Hiram glanced at Trudy. "How'd you do?"

"Don't know yet."

He nodded, but he knew. Even from a distance, he'd seen how close her second group lay on the target. She must know it, too, but she wouldn't say so. He sent up a silent prayer for Libby, that she wouldn't be nervous.

"Hey, Wilfred," one of Kenton Smith's men shouted, "you can't get beat by a woman. Let's see some good shootin'."

"Don't worry," Sterling replied. "I ain't never been whupped by anything in skirts, and I don't intend to commence now."

"Ladies and gentlemen, the scores in this round are very close, so we'll have four people advancing."

Libby held her breath. To her surprise, she wanted to be in that final group.

Peter consulted his notes and called out, "Those shooting in our final round will be Miss Gertrude Dooley, Mrs. Elizabeth Adams, Mr. Wilfred Sterling, and Dr. James Kincaid."

Libby clapped her hands to her face. Trudy patted her back, laughing.

"Congratulations! I knew you could do it."

"Unbelievable," Libby whispered.

"The finalists will have a few more minutes to prepare while we change the targets," the mayor said.

Ethan was busy setting up the final targets, but Hiram hovered at his sister's side.

"Can I get you ladies a drink of lemonade before the next round?"

Trudy smiled at him and leaned on the rifle with the stock on the ground. "Thanks. That would be nice."

He hurried off before Libby could even fathom his offer.

"I'm so nervous."

"Just take your time with each shot, but don't overthink it," Trudy said.

Libby wondered how she could do both. The other women clustered around them.

"Miss Trudy, I'm so proud of you." Goldie hugged Trudy, and Vashti moved in on Libby.

"You did great, Miz Adams."

Bitsy, Starr, Jessie, Florence, and half a dozen other women surrounded them, giving advice and wishing them luck.

"Pardon, ladies." Hiram's quiet voice was enough to part the waters, and a path opened for him. He handed a tin cup of lemonade to Libby and another to Trudy.

"Thank you," Libby murmured.

"Miss Dooley, do you want me to check your gun and make

sure it's ready?" Vashti asked.

Trudy's eyes widened. "How can we both shoot in the same round? We're using the same rifle."

Bitsy put an arm across her shoulders. "There, now, dearie, don't fret. One of you can use Augie's rifle."

Trudy's face cleared. "Thank you, Bitsy. I'll use it, and Libby can take this one." She held the Sharps out to Libby.

"Oh no. I wouldn't think of taking your gun. I'll accept Bitsy's offer."

"But you've never shot any other rifle," Trudy said.

Libby shook her head adamantly. "You're the best shot in Fergus, and we women all know it. It would be tragic if you lost because you had to shoot the final round with a gun you weren't acquainted with. It won't matter if I do poorly, but you've led this whole contest. I insist." She reached to take the Winchester Augie had brought over.

"Oh now—"

"Hush, Trudy." Libby glared at her. "I'm putting my foot down on this. You're representing all of us."

"She's right," Starr said. "We all want to see you win, Trudy."

"We *need* to see you win," Goldie added.

Bitsy pushed the Sharps back against Trudy's chest. "Libby will be fine with Augie's gun. Don't you let that nasty cowboy take the prize, now, will ya?"

Peter Nash stood on the bench near the judges' table. "Will the finalists please take their places?"

Trudy squared her shoulders. "If you really feel that way. . ."

"We do." Libby hugged her, rifle and all. "I'm tickled to be standing up there with you. Now, do us proud."

Dr. Kincaid and Sterling already waited at the shooting line. Libby and Trudy carried their weapons over and stood beside them.

"Everyone satisfied with his or her target?" Peter asked.

Libby, Trudy, and the doctor nodded.

Sterling squinted down the range. "I had an end target last time."

"By all means, switch with me, sir." Libby sidled around him to stand between the two men.

Peter looked them all over. "Anyone object to the new positions?"

"Fine with me," Trudy said.

The others nodded.

"Then get ready." Peter paused while they took their shooting stances and raised their rifles.

"Fire at will."

Libby squeezed off her five rounds quickly. The smoke hung thick around them, putting a bitter taste on her tongue. The others finished shooting.

"Check your weapons for safety, please," Peter said.

Libby opened the breach on Augie's gun and made sure no cartridges were left in the chamber or the magazine.

"The judges will now inspect the targets."

Ethan, Ted, and Orissa walked across the field. Tension hung over the crowd, along with the dissipating smoke. Libby walked slowly over to Bitsy and Augie and held out the gun.

"Thank you very much."

"My pleasure." Augie accepted the Winchester and held it in his beefy hands.

Libby sensed someone close behind her. She looked over her shoulder. Hiram and Trudy had followed her. Hiram smiled reassuringly. Trudy kept her eyes on the field and sucked her bottom lip.

"I'm not sure about my third shot," she muttered.

Everyone watched the three judges walk from one target to another. At last, Ethan detached them from the stands, and they ambled back toward Peter, talking in low tones.

With the mayor, the judges formed a huddle.

Griff Bane came to stand near the Dooleys and Libby.

"Ethan will give you first place no matter what."

Trudy whirled. Her eyes shot daggers at him. "You take that back."

Hiram stared up into the blacksmith's dark eyes. "You know Ethan wouldn't throw the match. He's an honest man."

Griffin smiled. "Reckon he is. I was just teasing, but your sister's got a feisty temper, ain't she?"

Peter climbed up on the bench again. His smile drooped a little.

"Folks, it's hot, and we're all eager to get the horse race started, but the judges have decided we need one last round. Miss Gertrude Dooley and Dr. James Kincaid will shoot again if they're willing, to determine the winner. Oh, and third place goes to Mrs. Elizabeth Adams."

Libby staggered. She felt as though one of Oscar's freighting mules had kicked her. Hiram reached and took her elbow.

"You all right, Miz Adams?"

She managed to breathe. "I. . .I think so."

The next few minutes blurred into a noisy clutch of women hugging, patting, and congratulating her. From the corner of her eye, Libby saw Wilfred Sterling stalk off toward the hitching rail.

"Hey, you won the box of cartridges." Goldie grinned at her.

"I guess I did. I'd rather have won the free dinner."

Hiram caught her eye. Libby had never seen him smile so thoroughly. With his long sorrow lifted momentarily from his shoulders, he looked as handsome and debonair as the doctor. Or even handsomer.

"Will the finalists please step forward."

Trudy and Dr. Kincaid went to the line.

"Come on, Trudy," Myra Harper called. "Make us proud."

"May the best *man* win," Micah Landry shouted. His wife elbowed him.

Rose, who had shared her box lunch with the doctor, stood at the edge of the crowd, breathlessly waving a lacy handkerchief.

"On your mark," Peter called.

Trudy and Doc squared up, facing the targets.

"Get ready."

They raised their rifles.

"Fire at will."

The ten shots rang out quickly, and the crowd exhaled. The contestants broke their rifles open, and Ethan and Orissa again made the trek to the targets. Bertha, who carried extra weight, sat at the judges' table fanning herself; and Ted had headed back into town to set up the flags for the horse race. Ethan and Orissa fetched the targets back to Bertha and laid them out on the table. All three judges leaned over them and consulted for a moment.

Ethan straightened and walked over to Peter, who hadn't bothered to climb down from his perch.

The mayor held up both hands. "Ladies and gentlemen, the judges are unanimous. The best shot in Fergus, and the winner of the Colt pistol, is Miss Gertrude Dooley."

The women and most of the men erupted in cheers. A few sore losers shot off disparaging remarks and went in search of lemonade or something stronger. Ellie carried the wooden box with the prize to Peter, and he called Trudy over.

"Miss Dooley, it gives me great pleasure to present you with this pistol. Congratulations. I know you'll use it well."

Trudy's scarlet face beamed as she accepted the prize.

"She deserves it," Libby said.

Hiram nodded. "She's never had a gun of her own. She was hankering to win that, but she never said so. This means a lot to her."

Libby's insides warmed, and not just from the sun. She was glad she'd chosen the latest Colt model when the council had told her to pick out a pistol for the prize, and glad Trudy had won it. She hadn't thought of how the young woman always used her brother's rifle. But Trudy gave generously of her time to help other women learn to shoot safely and accurately. She'd fired nearly every gun in town as part of her aid to her brother's business or the shooting club, but she'd never had her own weapon.

Trudy hurried to them amid the applause. She held out the box, and Hiram steadied it while she lifted the cover. Her face settled into lines of deep satisfaction, and she sighed.

"It's a beaut, isn't it?"

Hiram held the box and leaned over to kiss her cheek. "You did fine today."

Libby squeezed Trudy's shoulders. "You surely did." The day seemed nearly perfect. Her pleasure at having come in third in the contest increased when she saw Trudy's delight and her friends clustering around her. But perhaps the one element that tipped her toward giddiness was Hiram's subtle attention throughout the day.

People crowded around Trudy and Dr. Kincaid, offering their felicitations. Isabel, Rose, Myra, and the saloon girls gathered so thickly about the doctor that all Libby could see was his gleaming blond hair as he bent to receive their praise. Truthfully, the man was well-favored, but she couldn't see that he was any handsomer than...

She felt her cheeks flush once more as she looked toward Hiram and caught his smile again. Was the shy gunsmith coming out of his mournful shell at last?

★ CHAPTER 26 ★

The horse race ended with Arthur Tinen Jr. scooping up the prize of a new bridle. Ethan was glad the official doings of the day had ended. Everyone had enjoyed the contests and time of relaxation, but some of the cowboys had relaxed a little too much, in his opinion.

Smith's men left their places near the finish line, where they'd cheered on Eli Button, and headed for where their own mounts were tied. Button had claimed second place in the race, but his bay gelding wasn't fast enough to outdo Arthur's pinto. The cowboys assured Button he should have won. Ethan watched them as they neared the hitching rail. Wilfred Sterling took a bottle out of his saddlebag, tipped it up for a swallow, and handed it to one of his comrades. From their boisterous conduct during the race, Ethan guessed they'd imbibed some earlier while he was busy helping judge the shooting contest.

He hesitated. Maybe he should get a couple of friends before he confronted them. This sheriffing job held challenges he'd never imagined. But he couldn't rely on his friends all the time or he'd soon become known as the sissy sheriff. He squared his shoulders and approached the cowboys.

"Say, fellas, the town asked that no liquor be taken on the school premises today."

The four cowboys swung around and frowned at him.

Button took a step back, but the others held their ground. Wilfred Sterling especially took on a belligerent air. He passed the bottle to another man.

"You wanna make something of it, Sheriff?"

"We was just leaving." The third man hastily shoved the bottle into the saddlebag on the nearest horse. "Weren't we, Eli?"

Button had begun to untie his horse, but he shot a look over his shoulder. "That's right. The boss told us to stay out of trouble, and we're going to. Thanks for the good time, Sheriff."

Ethan nodded. "Congrats on your second-place finish in the race, Button."

Eli put his fingers to his hat brim. "Hey, a silver dollar's better'n nothing. Me and the boys thought we'd go spend it at the Nugget."

"Well, take it easy," Ethan said. "I don't want you in my jail again tonight."

"No sir." Button walked his horse away from the rail and swung into the saddle. "Come on, Wilfred. Buck. You ready?"

The other cowboys mounted and headed toward the center of town. Ethan hoped Ted Hire was open for business and ready for them. It was early yet—only four in the afternoon—but since the Spur & Saddle stopped serving alcohol, Ted had hired an extra bartender and kept the Nugget open pretty near twenty-four hours a day. Ethan rubbed the back of his sunburned neck. He'd have to stop by the saloon later and make sure those cowpokes hadn't gotten out of hand again.

He strolled back across the schoolyard and found Hiram and Griffin helping take down the tables where the food had been set out. Trudy, Libby, and a dozen other women worked at packing up all the food, dishes, and tablecloths for their men to tote home.

"Are you coming by for supper tonight, Ethan?" Trudy asked as he walked past.

"Don't know as I'd ought to. You've been busy all day."

"It won't be anything fancy."

Her eyes held a longing that drew him. He knew he couldn't refuse when she wanted him at her side. "All right. I didn't see your horses. Did you and Hi walk out here?"

"Yes. Go ahead. You probably have things to do before we eat."

Ethan collected Scout and put the saddle and bridle on him. They trotted smartly into town, where he left the gelding at the livery stable. Griffin wasn't back from the schoolhouse yet. He always let Ethan keep his horse in the stable or corral for free as part of his contribution toward the sheriff's maintenance. A bucketful of water, a scoop of oats, and an armful of hay. What more could Scout want?

As Ethan left the livery, Ellie Nash drove by in the family's wagon.

"Where's the mayor?" Ethan called.

"He went home early to sort the mail that came in on the stagecoach today."

Ethan decided to make the post office his first stop and headed up the boardwalk, past the Wells Fargo office and the emporium.

Peter had two letters for him. Ethan stuck them in his vest pocket and crossed the street. Augie was unloading his wagon in front of the Spur & Saddle.

"You folks aren't serving supper tonight, are you?" Ethan asked.

"We sure are. Had a stew simmering all day and plenty of cobbler waiting. You coming in tonight, Sheriff?"

"Thanks," Ethan said, "but I've had an invitation elsewhere."

Augie grinned knowingly. "Sometime you've got to bring your sweetheart in."

"I will." Ethan carried his letters down the street to the jail. He hung up his hat, leaned his chair back against the wall, and lifted his boots to the desktop. The first letter was from a constable in New Jersey.

Sorry, but I've turned up very little information about the Peart family. Frank Peart went west more than twenty years ago. His parents died after that, and apparently both sisters moved away, but I don't know where.

Ethan tossed it aside, opened the second envelope, and perused the message. For several minutes he sat thinking.

The sun was waning. Probably time to get over to the Dooleys' for supper. He rocked his chair forward and stood, scooping the letters off the desk.

Trudy let him in the back door. Rose was setting the table for four.

"Oh, hello, Sheriff! Wasn't it a lovely day?" She smiled at him across the room and fluttered her lashes.

"Yes ma'am." Ethan let Trudy take his hat and hang it on the rack. "Am I early?"

"No, this is fine," Trudy said. "We just need to put a few more things on the table."

"Can I help?"

"Sure, you can fill the water bucket for me."

A few minutes later, Ethan settled down for supper with the two women and Hiram. Rose was still gushing about the picnic, what a gentleman Dr. Kincaid was, and her pride in his second-place finish in the shooting match. She said nothing of Trudy's win.

Ethan looked over at Trudy and winked.

She smiled faintly. "Ethan, would you please ask the blessing?"

After the prayer, Trudy jumped in with a question for Ethan and succeeded in wresting the conversation away from Rose.

"Was the judging really that hard?"

Ethan shrugged. "Most of the time the leaders were obvious. But Trudy and Doc were so close on the next-to-last round I was afraid we'd be run out of town unless we had a clear winner. Doc slipped a little in the final shootout, and there was no question. And how about Libby Adams' shooting? She did great."

"I'm glad Libby placed. She was sure she'd be out in the first round, but she's a very good shot."

"Where's your prize?" Ethan asked.

Hiram grinned. "She's got it on display in the parlor."

Trudy scowled at him. "I'm not displaying it. I just. . .like to look at it." She twisted her napkin in her hands.

Ethan reached over and patted her arm. "I don't blame you. It's a fine pistol. I'm tickled that you got it. By the way, I got a couple more answers to the inquiries you ladies sent out for me."

"Anything that will help?" she asked.

"One had nothing new, but the second one—I'll let you read it later. It gives me serious doubts that Sterling is telling the truth."

Hiram stopped in the act of buttering a biscuit. "What will you do?"

"I'm thinking of riding out to the ranch tomorrow and talking to him."

"Need company?"

Ethan nodded. "Thanks. Wouldn't mind it."

On Sunday afternoon, Hiram and Ethan saddled up and made the long ride out to the Martin ranch. The ranch house was a rough cabin built on the mountainside, and a pole barn lay beyond it. A handful of thin cattle grazed on the sparse vegetation in the pasture. To one side of the barn sat a soddy that apparently housed the hired men. Four of them spilled out as the riders approached. The hair on the back of Hiram's neck prickled. All of them wore sidearms. Had they made a smart move by coming out here alone?

"Howdy, boys," Ethan said.

The four cowboys watched him with narrowed eyes.

The door of the ranch house opened, and Kenton Smith stood at the top of the steps and looked them up and down.

"I just want a word with Wilfred Sterling," Ethan said. "Won't take but a minute."

Smith held his gaze for a long moment and then nodded.

Sterling detached himself from the group of cowhands and shuffled forward.

"Yeah?"

Ethan dismounted. Hiram felt better in the saddle. His friend took out the letter he'd received from Frank Peart's sister.

"This is a letter that came yesterday. It concerns your claim to the Peart property. I'll let you read it if you promise to behave like a gentleman."

One of the other cowboys guffawed. "That's a laugh, Sheriff. He can't read."

Sterling whirled around. "Shut up!"

The other cowboy held up his hands, smirking. "Maybe the sheriff will read it to you if you're extra nice."

"All right, I'll tell you what it says." Ethan handed Scout's reins to Hiram and took the letter from the envelope.

Hiram sat astride Hoss and waited, keeping one eye on the cluster of men near the soddy while Ethan read the short message. Smith lounged in the ranch house doorway.

"I, being the sister of Franklin Peart, can tell you that neither I nor my sister Margaret had any children. This man you say calls himself Sterling cannot be any relation that I know of. I don't know of any people by that name. As to the property, I am too old to come out and see it, but if it is sold, I'd appreciate having the money sent to this address. Sincerely, Agnes Peart." Ethan stopped reading and looked at Sterling. "You understand?"

The cowboy nodded.

"Good. Because according to this letter, you aren't who you claim to be. This Agnes Peart isn't claiming you as either a son or a nephew. Is Sterling your real name?"

"I resent that."

"Take it easy. I just want you to understand real well that you can't inherit a square inch of that land. And if I catch you or anybody else on it, I'll have to put you in jail."

Sterling glared at him.

"You got it?" Ethan asked.

He nodded.

"All right." Ethan walked to his horse and took the reins from Hiram. He swung into Scout's saddle and turned toward Smith. "Mr. Smith, I expect this man to respect the law and keep away from what's known as the old Peart place."

Smith nodded, retreated into his home, and shut the door.

"Odd bird," Ethan said as they trotted toward Fergus.

"Smith or Sterling?" Hiram asked.

"Both, but I was thinking of Smith."

"Uh-huh." Hiram relaxed as soon as they were out of sight of the ranch. They rode in silence for a couple of miles. Finally, on a fairly flat stretch, he urged Hoss to extend his stride and trot alongside Scout. "I got to ask you something."

"What's that?"

"How long do you intend to court my sister?"

Ethan glanced over at him then back at the road. "As long as she'll let me, I guess."

Hiram digested that. Half a mile later he said, "Well, I think it's time it ended."

Ethan hauled back on his reins, and Scout stopped in the path. Hiram stopped Hoss, too.

"What? You're against me courting Trudy?" Ethan's eyes held a spark of belligerence.

"Yes. Unless you intend to marry her."

Ethan's lower jaw dropped nearly fit to hit his chest. "Of course I intend to marry her."

Hiram inhaled through his nose and leaned with both wrists on the saddle horn. "Don't you think it's about time?"

Ethan scowled at him. "I wouldn't toy with Trudy's affections."

"Prove it."

The hurt in Ethan's dark eyes stabbed him. Ethan was a good guy. Hiram hated to get after him. He sighed and lifted his reins. Hoss and Scout started walking.

"I'm standing in for Trudy's pa. You know that."

"Well yeah, but Hi, you know me. I intend to do right by her."

"Folks in town are starting to talk."

"Talk how?"

"Like you don't need to marry her."

"I could bust your jaw for saying that."

"I expect you could."

They rode on until they hit the mountain road. "How do you know what they're saying?" Ethan asked.

"Augie told me. I rebuilt the back steps over there this week."

Ethan's jaw worked for a few seconds. "I was only waiting until I could put away a little more cash. The town raised my pay a dollar a couple of weeks back. I want to have things nice for her."

"She doesn't care about nice. Besides, your place is nicer than what she's been living in the last nine years."

"You think so?"

"Yup." A mile farther along, Hiram said, "So you're sure you want to get married?"

"Oh yeah. I do. It's just. . ." Ethan glanced over at him. "It's a little unnerving."

"You're not still tied in knots over the Indian wars and your part in them?"

"I talked that out with Trudy."

"And?"

Ethan nodded. "You were right. She's a very understanding woman."

"Glad you realized that. I'm right this time, too. Quit shilly-shallying."

"I'll certainly ruminate on that."

"Good. Now let's put some miles behind us."

Tuesday evening, Isabel heard her father come in at what used to be his regular time. She dashed about the kitchen. She'd more than half expected him to be late again.

He'd left his coat and hat in the entry. When he crossed the threshold, he looked sheepishly at her. "Supper ready?"

She nearly dropped the dish of boiled greens. The flesh beneath his left eye puffed out in a red and purple bruise. "Papa! What happened to your eye?"

"Relax, Isabel. It's just a shiner."

She gulped and set the dish on the table. "It. . .looks painful. Shouldn't you see Doc Kincaid?"

"For this?" He laughed bitterly. "I've had lots worse than this when there was no doctor within a hundred miles."

They ate in silence. When she rose to get the coffeepot and her back was turned to him, she dared to say, "I can fix you a cold cloth."

"I'll be fine."

"Did someone hit you?"

"Just leave it alone, Isabel."

"Sorry. I'm concerned about you, Papa, that's all." She poured his mug full, wishing he wouldn't be so stubborn.

"Well, I don't need your concern."

"But when Paul Storrey fell on the rocks and had a shiner, the doctor said it could permanently injure his eyesight. I could have one of the men hitch up the wagon, and we could drive into town. Just let Dr. Kincaid take a look at it, Papa, to be sure—"

"Oh that's it. You just want a chance to see Doc Kincaid again. I saw you staring at him at the picnic Saturday, wishing he'd bought your lunch basket instead of Oxley."

"Papa!" Isabel stared after him. Tears filled her eyes. "I wasn't ogling the doctor."

"Oh, of course not. Saw you eyeing him at church, too." He shoved his chair back and stood, then picked up his coffee. "I'll be just fine, so you don't need to be thinking about going calling on the doc. He wouldn't look at you, anyhow. Why should he?"

"Wh–what do you mean?" She could barely believe the meanness of his tone.

"You're a skinny old maid. Kincaid's got the pick of the widows and single gals in this town. He won't likely come calling here."

Isabel gasped and pulled her apron up to her face, burying her eyes in the folds of cotton. "I never—Oh Papa, how could you say such a thing?"

She turned and ran from the room, not sure to where she would run.

★ CHAPTER 27 ★

Libby locked the door of the emporium and pulled the shade.

"Good night, Florence."

"Good night, Miz Adams. I'll see you in the morning." Florence slipped through the storeroom and out the back door.

Libby lifted the ledgers off the counter and took them to her desk in the back room. Usually she spent an hour or so on the books after closing, but not tonight. Trudy had invited her to supper. It seemed her friend's latest way of coping with Rose's overbearing personality was to have company to diffuse the conversation. Trudy had offered to hold the meal later than their usual supper hour so that Libby could join them after she closed the store at six.

She went back for the cash box and opened the safe.

Wild pounding on the back door startled her. She shoved the ledgers and cash box into the safe and shut the door then straightened, her heart thumping.

"Libby?"

She exhaled and hurried to let Isabel in.

"What is it, dear? What's wrong?"

"It's Papa. He's been in a fight or something, but he won't tell me what happened." Isabel's tears had dried on her blotchy face, and her hair hung all aflutter from her displaced hairpins.

Libby pulled her into the dim storeroom and closed the door. "Come sit down and tell me all about it."

"I. . .I didn't want to bother you, but I didn't know what else to do. He insulted me. My own father. I can't bear to stay there, Libby. I just can't."

"Oh my dear." Libby drew her into a gentle embrace and patted the back of her serviceable gray cotton dress.

Isabel sobbed on her shoulder. "I'm sorry. I'm sure you have things to do."

"It's all right." Libby considered whether she should tell Isabel of her dinner plans. If she delayed much longer, Trudy would worry and come to check on her. But Ethan was also an invited dinner guest. In his capacity as sheriff, he might be able to suggest a course of action for Isabel. "My dear, please don't upset yourself so. I'm due at the Dooleys' for supper, and I'd like you to accompany me. I'm sure Trudy and Hiram won't mind one more guest, as we're already planning a party of five."

Isabel lifted her head. "Oh no, I couldn't."

"Of course you could. In fact, I'll take a quart of milk and some peanut brittle as our contribution." Libby turned toward the main room of the emporium. "Wait right here while I fetch the items."

Isabel continued to protest, but Libby prevailed, and a minute later, Isabel's coiffure repaired, they set out together across the street. Libby carried the small milk can and a box of shells for Trudy's new pistol, and Isabel brought the box of peanut brittle.

"I shouldn't have come to you at the dinner hour."

"Nonsense." Libby shifted the cool milk can to her other hand. "One must act when the crisis occurs. Now, what do you think really happened?"

"I don't know, but when I asked questions, Papa became angry and...I cannot call it anything short of abusive."

Libby tsked and waited for more information.

"I've been desolate these past few weeks, I'll admit. Papa doesn't seem to pay attention to me anymore. Of course, if I don't have his meals ready, he notices. But he takes nearly all of his lunches at the Fennel House now. I make breakfast in the morning and supper at night. But half the time he's late for supper—sometimes very late. And sometimes...sometimes he imbibes. More than he should." Isabel's blue eyes with their pale fringe of lashes blinked anxiously.

"There, dear. It's a rare man who doesn't do so now and then." Libby recalled her own Isaac spending the occasional evening at the Spur & Saddle, much to her consternation, but she'd grown used to his habits for lack of a means to change them. "We adapt, don't we?"

"Yes, I suppose you are right. We do what we must." Isabel let out a deep sigh. "I should be used to his ways by now, but since Mama died, he's treated me rather shabbily, I think. Tonight he... he commented on my single state and hinted that no man would ever look twice at me."

Libby shook her head, new animosity toward Cyrus rising in her breast. "It's unconscionable, my dear." To think it was one thing, she told herself, but for a father to say as much to his daughter, especially a daughter who had shown her diligence and devotion, kindled her ire. More than ever, she was glad she had rebuffed Cyrus's advances in the months following her husband's death. Isabel need never learn about that. "Does he know you have fixed your affections on a certain man?"

"Oh no! If he knew that, I expect he would ridicule me even more and tell me how unsuitable I am for the gentleman."

"You know that's not true. You would make any man a good wife."

Isabel pinched up her features and shook her head. "I would try if given the chance, but that's his point—I shall never have a chance unless a blind man comes to town."

Libby's heart wrenched. While not a beauty by any means, Isabel could not be called ugly either. Many women with fewer physical charms had found husbands. Still, she had a hard time picturing Isabel happily married to the rough blacksmith. Surely the teacher needed the companionship of a more educated man. Of course, that sort of man was rare in Fergus. They reached the path that led around to the back of the Dooleys' house, and Libby led her to the kitchen door.

She prepared to apologize to Trudy for being late but caught her breath when Hiram responded to her knock. He'd forsaken his usual flannel and wore a fresh cambric dress shirt, as he did on Sundays. His damp hair lay parted neatly to the side, and he met her gaze squarely, something he'd had trouble doing a few months ago. His frank smile sent a flutter through her stomach.

"Oh. Good evening, Hiram."

He nodded. "Hello. Glad you could come." His gaze slid past

her to Isabel. "Evening, Miss Fennel."

"I hope you don't mind," Libby said quickly. "I brought another guest without asking the hosts' permission."

"That's fine. Come on in, ladies." Hiram swung the door wide and called over his shoulder, "Can we throw another plate on, Trudy?"

His sister came toward them and held her hands out to Isabel. "Of course. Welcome, Isabel."

"I apologize for barging in with Libby. If it's too much—"

"Don't be silly. We're happy to see you."

"Thank you. Oh—" Isabel held out the box of peanut brittle. "Compliments of Mrs. Adams."

"I brought some milk, too," Libby said.

"Thank you very much."

"I'll take it to the root cellar." Hiram took the can from Libby's hands and slid out the back door.

Ethan leaned against the far wall, obviously feeling at home. He straightened and nodded at the newcomers.

Libby smiled at him. "Hello, Ethan."

"Evening, Libby. Good to see you again. Howdy, Miss Fennel."

"Oh please, it's Isabel." Her face again flushed, but she looked less haggard than she had on her arrival at the emporium.

"This is for you," Libby said, handing the ammunition to Trudy. "For your new gun."

"Oh thank you. You didn't need to do that."

"I know. I wanted to."

Trudy kissed her cheek then scurried about, fetching an extra plate and cup from the cupboard and silverware from the sideboard.

"Where's Rose this evening?" Libby asked.

Trudy shrugged and laid the flatware on the table. "She's gone out to eat with a gentleman."

"Indeed?" Libby glanced at Isabel and saw that her face had paled. Perhaps she feared Rose had snared the man she had her heart set on. It would be a shame if Griffin entangled himself with Mrs. Caplinger.

"Yes, we were a bit surprised." Trudy turned to the stove, her long, straw-colored braid swinging out behind her.

"Not Dr. Kincaid?" Libby hazarded. "Did Saturday's picnic take?"

Ethan chuckled. "No, she went to eat with someone else who was at the picnic."

Trudy opened the oven. As Hiram came through the back door, she lifted out a pan that held a plump, roasted chicken. "I never would have thought she'd patronize the Spur & Saddle."

Hiram said, "Ha. She doesn't seem to object when some man is paying for her dinner."

Trudy's brow furrowed. "There, now. Let's not fuss about Rose. She's an adult, and she can decide whom she wants to eat with and where."

Libby's curiosity prickled, but her manners prevailed. Instead of inquiring outright for the name of Rose's escort, she asked, "How can I help you, Trudy?"

"I think we're ready. Just bring that dish of squash over, would you?"

Libby found the steaming dish on the back of the cookstove and took it to the table.

"Here, Isabel. You sit next to me," Trudy said. "It's lovely to have you in town this evening."

Isabel looked bleakly at Libby. In the flurry of being seated, Libby had let go the reminder of Isabel's woes—especially when Hiram pulled out a chair for her kitty-corner from his own. But as soon as Ethan had asked the blessing, she deemed it time to explain her guest's presence.

Hiram picked up the fork and carving knife and sliced a piece from the chicken's breast. "Miss Fennel?"

Isabel's hands shook as she held her plate out toward the platter.

"Trudy, I insisted that Isabel come with me," Libby said, "because I thought it was time she made known her concerns about her father—at least to Ethan, and I know you and Hiram will be discreet if she consents to tell you, too."

"Of course. You're among friends here, Isabel." Trudy shot a look at her brother, and he nodded gravely.

Isabel set her plate down before her and stared at the chicken. "I. . .I don't want to burden anyone. You've all been kind to me. . . ."

Libby reached over and squeezed her hand. "My dear, you've undergone a long period of stress and ill treatment. I think the sheriff should know."

Isabel caught her breath and flicked a glance at Ethan then stared at her plate again. Her eyes shone with tears.

Ethan leaned forward and spoke softly. "Miss Fennel, you may speak to me as a friend or as an officer of the law, whichever you prefer. Whatever you say will not go beyond these walls. Unless, of course, it bears on a crime. In that case, I can't promise."

She nodded, and a single tear fell onto the linen napkin in her lap. "It's all so complicated and. . .sordid."

Trudy caught Libby's gaze, her eyes wide with alarm. Libby's lips twitched in a rueful smile. She kept her hold on Isabel's hand until the young woman began speaking again.

"My father. . .ever since Mama died, he's acted cold and aloof toward me. He's grieving, of course, and I overlooked much, knowing that."

Trudy made a sympathetic sound in her throat.

Isabel hauled in a breath. "It's been worse this spring, though. Since my Uncle Kenton came the first time."

"Your uncle?" Trudy asked. "You mean Mr. Smith?"

"Yes."

"I first saw him at the box social. Ethan said he was a relative of yours."

Isabel nodded her assent. "I hadn't known he existed, you see, until a few weeks ago."

Everyone was silent for a long moment. At last Libby said, "Isabel told me this some time ago, but I felt it was best to keep it to myself. This Kenton Smith showed up out of nowhere, claiming to be her mother's brother, and Cyrus accepted him as such. Isabel, however, was stunned, and her father broke the news to her that they'd never told her about him because he has a criminal past."

Trudy nodded slowly, staring at Libby, then switched her gaze to Ethan.

"I met him Saturday," the sheriff said. "Cyrus introduced him as his brother-in-law, and I knew he'd let Smith settle in at the old Martin ranch. But I didn't know he'd been in prison. May I ask what for?"

Isabel stared at him blankly. "I don't know. Papa wouldn't tell me. He wouldn't tell me anything. And Uncle Kenton went away, and I didn't know where he'd gone. You see, Papa didn't tell me he was out at the ranch either. He let me think Uncle Kenton had left the valley. And I wondered. . ." She faltered and glanced at Libby. "Anyway, he came again last week. I. . .he. . ."

Libby patted her shoulder. "There, dear, it's all right. You can tell the sheriff."

"He and Papa had words. And Uncle Kenton left again. I didn't see him again until the box social."

Ethan nodded and rubbed his chin. "Hiram and I saw him again briefly on Sunday afternoon. We rode out to tell Wilfred Sterling he can't claim Milzie Peart's estate."

"Oh?" Libby asked. "You got conclusive news?"

"Seems so to me. I telegraphed the territorial governor's office in Boise after I got the letter from Frank's sister. She's married but never had any children. And there was one more Peart sister, but she died before she was twenty. Mrs. Cochran, who wrote the letter, said that despite what this cowpoke Sterling told me, Frank didn't have any nephews."

"How about that." Libby nodded thoughtfully.

"Yes. Wilfred Sterling wasn't too happy. He still claims there's been a mistake, but I let him know I'd be watching to make sure no one tries to squat on the land or anything like that."

"I wonder how he came to work for my uncle," Isabel said.

"So do I." Ethan helped himself to one of Trudy's icicle pickles. "And now Mr. Smith is courting Mrs. Caplinger."

"*What?*" Isabel stared at him.

"I'm sorry," Ethan said. "I guess we didn't mention it. The man Rose is dining with tonight is your uncle."

★ CHAPTER 28 ★

Isabel couldn't breathe. She crumpled her napkin in her fist and pressed it to her chest. How could a woman as dainty as Rose Caplinger find Uncle Kenton attractive?

"Are you all right?" Libby asked, leaning so close that Isabel could see dark violet flecks in her blue eyes.

"I—yes—no." Isabel gasped and lunged for her cup of water. She inhaled instead of swallowing and began to cough.

Libby slapped her daintily on the back. Trudy was not so gentle. She slapped Isabel smartly between the shoulder blades.

She sucked in a deep breath and held up both hands. "I'm all right."

They all stared at her. True, their faces held concern, but still she felt like a sideshow exhibit.

"I. . .I thought she was interested in someone else."

"Who? Dr. Kincaid?" Trudy shook her head. "I daresay she likes him, but he's living on a shoestring just now. Rose wants someone who can support her. The rancher came a-calling, and she accepted his invitation. I can't think it's serious, though. Not yet."

Isabel looked frantically to Libby. She smiled and said quietly, "No dear, not the one you were thinking of."

"But. . .but Starr Tinen said. . ."

"I know." Libby bent to retrieve Isabel's napkin from the floor and tucked it into her slack hand. "That incident came to naught. I'm sorry you even heard of it, but I assure you, it was nothing."

Isabel still found it hard to believe. She had stormed the smithy and humiliated herself for nothing. And Hiram Dooley had witnessed it all. He knew where her interest lay. Had he told anyone how she'd ranted at Griffin? She didn't dare look across the table at him.

She opened her mouth then closed it.

"Miss Fennel."

She snapped her eyes toward him. He'd barely spoken since they sat down.

"Yes Mr. Dooley?"

"Please, it's Hiram. And it's all right, miss." He nodded gravely, and she looked into his eyes. His expression radiated the discretion Libby had claimed he possessed. Suddenly she realized Libby would know his character well. Because this was the man Libby loved. In that moment, Isabel trusted Hiram with her secret.

"Feeling better?" Trudy asked.

She nodded. In fact, she found herself thinking that perhaps Griff Bane wouldn't make the ideal husband she'd always imagined he would.

"In that case, would you like a baked potato?"

Isabel took the dish from Trudy. "Yes, thank you. But I wonder. . ."

"What is it?" Libby asked.

Isabel met her gaze. "Is Mrs. Caplinger safe with Uncle Kenton?"

Trudy winced. "If I'd known he'd been in prison, I'd have warned her. I'm sorry."

"Should we go fetch her, do you think?" Hiram asked.

Ethan shook his head slowly. "I doubt they'll come to grief having dinner at Bitsy and Augie's. They don't even serve liquor anymore."

"I should have told you about all this when Mrs. Adams first urged me to." Isabel stared down at her untouched dinner.

Libby caught her breath. "Well. . .in light of what we all know of Mr. Smith already and the behavior of his hired hands, I think it's time you told these dear friends all."

Isabel's pulse thundered. "You mean. . .everything?"

"Yes. Your father's relationship with your uncle, and the black eye he came home with tonight, and even the incident behind the barn."

Isabel's eyebrows shot up involuntarily. "I didn't really think Papa had killed him."

Ethan's jaw dropped. "I beg your pardon."

She laughed, though it wasn't funny. "It was silly, really. I saw Papa digging a hole behind the barn in the middle of the night. It was after Uncle Kenton left from that first visit. At least. . .I didn't see him leave, but he must have. And I heard digging, and I went out there, and I thought—oh, it's ludicrous. I can see that now. I'm so silly."

But no one else laughed.

After a moment of silence, Trudy said, "And why did he dig the hole that night?"

"I don't know. But when Uncle Kenton came to the ranch a second time, I was relieved and saw that I'd let my imagination run away with me. I'm sure there's an innocent explanation, but... I don't like to ask Papa."

"Mrs. Adams said your father has a black eye?" Ethan asked gently.

Isabel nodded and licked her lips. "He came home tonight looking as though he'd been engaging in fisticuffs. When I offered to tend to it, he got angry. I just don't understand his moods lately."

Ethan looked over at Hiram. "Maybe I'd ought to drop in at the Spur & Saddle after all."

"Oh, please don't run out in the middle of supper," Trudy said. "I made your favorite cake—oatmeal."

"Wouldn't want to miss that." Ethan grinned at her.

"Well then, eat up. Mr. Smith was here to get Rose not fifteen minutes before Libby and Isabel arrived. I'm sure they're over at Bitsy's enjoying their meal."

Isabel was grateful for Trudy's practical advice, but she still wondered what her father was up to. He'd probably eaten his dinner and left the dishes and leftover food all over the table. She ought to go home. But she didn't want to.

Ethan got the coffeepot and filled all their cups while Trudy cut the cake. "I suppose I ought to see Cyrus and ask him what this is all about."

"Isabel, I'd like you to stay with me tonight," Libby said.

Isabel started to protest but realized how much she dreaded going home. "I haven't anything with me."

Libby waved her hand. "Doesn't matter. I've anything you could need in my rooms or the emporium."

"Well. . ."

"That sounds like a good idea to me," Ethan said. "I'll try to see your father first thing in the morning."

Isabel blinked back tears. "Thank you. You're all so good to me." She smiled at Libby. "I shall accept your offer."

When they'd finished eating, Hiram rose and carried his dishes to Trudy's work counter and took an apron from the peg nearby.

"What's this?" Libby called. "I don't know if I've ever seen a man do dishes."

He smiled but said nothing.

"My brother is very good about it on special occasions," Trudy said. "Especially when he thinks I'd like to visit with my company."

"Well, your company will help as well." Libby rose, and Isabel followed her lead.

"I should say so. That was a delicious dinner, Trudy."

"Thank you, Isabel. Perhaps you can help me clear the table and Libby can dry whatever Hiram washes."

"I hate to be the slacker," Ethan said, "but I ought to check in on the Nugget, and then I'll stroll down to the Spur & Saddle. Won't be long, if you'd care to take a walk after." He waited hopefully for Trudy's answer.

She smiled and stacked the remaining plates. "I'll be ready."

Hiram nodded to Ethan and kept his back turned to the ladies as he set up his dishwashing operation. He was certain Trudy was on to his feelings. Dare he hope she saw reciprocation in Libby's attitude and threw them together on purpose? Libby's face was flushed and her eyes a bit twinkly when she joined him, putting on the ruffled apron Rose preferred.

His own cheeks felt warm, but he could blame that on the steam from the water he poured into the dishpan.

"Clean towels in the drawer yonder."

"Thank you." She opened the drawer in question and took out a linen dish wiper. Trudy kept Isabel in conversation about the box social. Hiram didn't try to talk to Libby. He just enjoyed working beside her. He kept one ear tuned to what Trudy was saying about Saturday's event.

"So how did you enjoy having lunch with Parnell Oxley?"

Isabel sighed. "That man's manners could stand some improvement. But he appreciated my cooking, and overall it was not an unpleasant experience. I. . .don't often mix with gentlemen socially."

Hiram smiled at that, thinking, *If you could call Parnell a gentleman.* Not that the cowboy was a bad person, but he couldn't see Cyrus approving him as son-in-law material. No, the doctor might stand a better chance there—if he weren't so downright poor.

"How is the reloading coming?" Libby asked, and he snapped his head around. She stood there, cool and pretty as ever, watching him with a soft smile on her lips.

He realized he was staring at her delicate mouth and jerked his face back toward the dishpan. "Pretty well. I should have a couple of boxes for you by the end of the week."

"No rush."

"I'm glad to get the work. My gun business has been slow this spring." He scrubbed a plate and placed it in the pan of rinse water. He wasn't used to talking a lot, not even to Ethan and Trudy.

"I'm sure I can sell all you do." Libby used a fork to help her fish the plate from the rinse water.

The two conversations progressed quietly. Hiram gradually relaxed. He'd never supposed he could feel at ease with Libby, but somehow she chased away his nerves.

All too soon, the dishes were done. Trudy put them away quickly, and Libby and Isabel reached for their shawls.

"We enjoyed having you both," Trudy said.

Hiram looked at the floorboards. "Come again."

"Thank you so much." Libby hugged Trudy and extended her hand to Hiram. "This made for a very pleasant evening, in spite of the concerns we all share."

He clasped her hand, feeling all kinds of happy as he looked into her blue eyes. All these years Libby had been just across the street, but things had changed. Lately he felt drawn to the emporium on the slightest pretext. Where he would have dragged his feet, he now flew to fetch any item Trudy could express a desire for.

Isabel still carried a pinched, worried look, but she managed a ghost of a smile.

"I do feel better, knowing you and the sheriff know about. . . about Papa."

Trudy hugged her as she had Libby, and Isabel bent her stiff arms and tentatively returned the embrace.

Hiram released Libby's warm, smooth hand and waited to see if Isabel would also offer hers. She didn't, and the two were soon out the door.

As they went down the back steps, Ethan returned.

"Oh, Miss Fennel, I'm glad I caught you." He took his hat off and paused below the stoop. "Mr. Smith and Mrs. Caplinger are still at the Spur & Saddle, eating dessert and listening to Miss Goldie's piano concert. I expect everything's fine."

"Thank you, Sheriff."

Ethan hesitated. "I saw your pa, too, at the Nugget. Thought you'd want to know."

Isabel ducked her head. "Thank you."

"If you think he'll worry, ma'am, I could stop by there again and tell him you're staying at Mrs. Adams's."

Isabel shook her head. "He'll probably conclude that I've gone to bed when he goes home again. I doubt he'll realize I'm gone until he wants his breakfast."

Hiram wondered how much breakfast Cyrus would want if he was putting back the whiskey at the Nugget.

During this conversation, Trudy had hummed softly as she donned her shawl and bonnet. Ethan waited until Libby and Isabel had turned the corner of the path and then came into the kitchen.

"Well now, I see you're a woman of your word."

Trudy laughed up at him. "Yes, I am."

"You never keep me waiting," Ethan acknowledged.

Hiram's heart twisted just a little. Those two were so right for each other. Why on earth hadn't Ethan taken her to the preacher yet?

She turned and smiled at him. "I'll see you later."

They left, and Hiram wandered into the parlor and lit the lamp. On the mantel sat his reloading tools and bullet molds. He walked over and took one down. If he got busy, he'd have an excuse to see Libby again tomorrow.

The silent house comforted him after all the bustle and conversation. Days of hard work and long, quiet evenings had marked his life since. . .as long as he could recall. There had been a time, what seemed an eon ago, when he and Violet had looked forward to the noise and happy disturbance caused by a child. And Trudy had added some life to the house, but she had quickly adjusted to his melancholy mood and joined his detached existence without complaint.

What had happened this year to put unrest in his heart? To tell him it might not be harmful to venture out beyond the placid confines of his life?

He traced his new wistfulness back a year to the evening when Libby Adams had closed her store and come to shoot with Trudy. The old sheriff had been murdered, and Libby didn't feel safe alone in her apartment over the store. Somehow, since that day, his life had turned topsy-turvy. And a great deal of the frightening change was due to the beautiful widow.

Had the time come to alter his life in more significant ways? Trudy would leave him soon; he was sure of that. But Libby. . . he couldn't imagine her living in this weathered little house. His mind rebelled at the idea of himself living in her rooms over the emporium. Trudy had told him about Libby's elegant furnishings and expensive dishes and china. He wouldn't want her to give up the lifestyle that apparently suited her. But would he become a storekeeper? No, he could never stand behind a counter, waiting on people all day—he knew he couldn't. Neither could he let a wife run her thriving business and support him while he did. . .what? Fixed a gun now and then and reloaded spent shell casings?

For the past six months he'd made more income from carpentry odd jobs than he had at his gun business. Augie Moore had talked to him Sunday about possibly tearing the bar out of the Spur & Saddle and using the cherry wood as paneling. Hiram would like that job. His hands itched to touch the smooth, wide boards. But would Libby consider tying herself to an impoverished gunsmith and occasional cabinetmaker? Maybe she wasn't attracted to him at all, at least not in that way. Maybe she was just being friendly. She treated everyone in a pleasant, courteous manner.

But no, he was certain he'd seen something more in her expression tonight as they laughed together over the dishpan. Of all the places to further a romance. In the lamplight, he carefully measured out the black powder for the shells he was reloading, smiling and thinking all the while of Libby's blue eyes and creamy complexion.

A firm knock on the back door startled him.

Hiram laid aside his tools and stood. The knocking resounded again through the house.

He didn't pause to light a candle, but hurried through the dusky kitchen and opened the door.

"Hiram."

"Mr. Fennel?" Cyrus mounted the top step, so Hiram stood aside and let him enter. Whiskey fumes drove him back a step toward the table. "Here, let me get a light."

"Is it late?" As Hiram struck a match, Cyrus dipped into his vest pocket and hauled out a large gold watch on a chain.

"No, it's quite early," Hiram said. "I was working in the other room, so I didn't light the lamp here in the kitchen."

"Eight fifteen." Cyrus snapped the watch case shut.

"Uh. . .would you like some coffee?"

"No, I just came to tell you I've got a piece of land I'm willing to sell you."

"Me?" Hiram cocked his head to one side and tried to fathom his guest's intentions. Was Cyrus so drunk he didn't know what he was saying? He didn't sound that tipsy, but Hiram didn't have a lot of experience in gauging a man's relative sobriety. The way Cyrus was talking, and with a dark bruise shadowing his left eye and cheekbone, he might be halfway to insensible.

"You. I know you've always wanted a ranch of your own. You came here hoping to buy one, didn't you?"

"Well yes, but. . .that was a long time ago, sir."

Cyrus nodded as though he had it all figured out. "You wanted the ranch I'm living on."

Hiram cleared his throat. "You want to sell your home ranch? I'm sure I couldn't—"

"No no." Cyrus's mouth twisted in annoyance. He pulled off his hat and held it by the crown, waving it before him. "Not that one. I *live* there. It's the one out where the Logans used to live. Andy Logan sold out to me when he pulled up stakes five years or so ago. Quarter section. There's a well and a soddy."

Hiram shook his head. "I'm not interested. Sorry."

Cyrus blinked at him. His mouth drooped. "Oh. 'S all right."

For the first time, Hiram thought the man might be very drunk. "Uh. . .would you like me to drive you home, Mr. Fennel?"

"Why would I want that?" He drew himself up for a moment, tall and imposing. The fuzziness left his eyes, and they focused with anger. "Are you implying that I'm—"

"No sir, I'm not implying anything. It's just that it's getting late, and—"

"Late? You said it was early." Cyrus fumbled in his pants pocket. Hiram almost told him he was dredging the wrong pond when he pulled out another watch, this one silver. "Ha! Twenty past eight."

"Yes sir."

Cyrus nodded emphatically and shoved the watch back into his pocket. He fixed his gaze on Hiram. "You sure you don't want to buy some land? I'm short on cash. I'll give you a good deal."

Hiram shook his head. He didn't want to make enemies with Cyrus, but he certainly didn't have the wherewithal to buy a ranch, and if he did, the old Logan place wouldn't be his choice. "Maybe you could make Bitsy and Augie an offer. Or someone else with money. The Walkers, maybe."

Cyrus clapped his hat onto his head.

Hiram wondered if he ought to let him leave. And should he tell him that he'd find an empty house when he got home? Isabel had distinctly declined Ethan's offer to take the news to Cyrus. But he was right here. . . .

Hiram watched him walk to the door.

"Watch your step there."

Cyrus fumbled with the latch.

"Here, let me help you."

A moment later, Cyrus was gone. Hiram leaned against the doorjamb and gazed up at the three-quarter moon over the mountains. He hoped Ethan was making good use of that moon.

★ CHAPTER 29 ★

Ethan held Trudy's hand as they walked slowly along the riverbank.

"The water's low," she said. "Before we know it, that stream will be down to a trickle."

Ethan stopped and turned toward her. "Trudy. . ."

"Yes?"

"There's something. . ."

"What, Ethan?"

He hesitated, his heart racing. Just for a second, he wasn't sure he could do it. But the image of Hiram standing behind him with a pitchfork prodded him. *Quit that*, he told himself. *You know you want to do this.* He felt calmer then, because it was true. He did want to propose, and even more, he wanted to marry Trudy. That was all he needed to think about.

He held on to her hand and went down on one knee on the grass. "I love you so much."

She inhaled raggedly, staring down at him. Her eyes were almost luminous in the moonlight.

Ethan sucked in a lungful of air and blurted, "Marry me, Trudy. Please? I'll take good care of you."

She didn't say anything, but her face melted into sweetness so intense he feared she would cry.

"I didn't mean to make you wait. I've been saving for some things for the house, and thinking it would be nice to take you to Boise for a wedding trip, and—"

"I don't need any of that." She laid her free hand gently on his shoulder.

He gulped. "I never felt this way about anyone else. Will you. . . will you be my wife?"

"Yes."

As soon as he heard it, he sprang up and engulfed her in his arms. "Trudy, Trudy."

She raised her face to him, and he made himself calm down and lean slowly toward her to kiss her.

Ethan walked her to the kitchen door at quarter to nine. Trudy hated to let him leave, but his sweet good-night kisses would carry her through the next few hours.

She peered into the house. The kitchen was dark, but the lamp glowed in the parlor. Turning in the doorway, she let her bonnet slip down her back and slid her hands onto Ethan's shoulders. He stood on the step below her, bringing them close in height.

"Thanks so much," he whispered, drawing her into his arms.

"Tonight was lovely." She let him kiss her again, treasuring his sweet tenderness. It was new enough to set her a-tingle but familiar enough that she could nestle against his collar bone after and cling an extra moment with no fear he would think her too forward. He smelled of leather and soap and mountain wind.

He twirled a lock of her hair around one finger. "I love you, Trudy."

She smiled in the darkness and traced his badge with her fingertips. "I know. I'm glad." There was a lot more she wanted to say, but they had time. Years and years ahead. "I love you, too."

He kissed her again then pulled away. "Guess I'd better go 'round to the Nugget again. He touched the end of her nose. "I'll come by tomorrow."

"All right." She eased backward into the kitchen and watched him take the path around the corner. With a sigh, she closed the door. It was settled. She would be his wife. Soon.

She hung up her shawl and wandered into the softly lit parlor. Hiram sat near the lamp fitting a row of bullets into a small pasteboard box.

"Howdy," she said.

He glanced her way and nodded.

"Is Rose home yet?" Trudy asked.

"Yes. She came in ten minutes ago and went upstairs."

"Did she say anything?"

He shrugged. "Just that she was surprised how well that little blond vixen could play the piano."

"She called Goldie that?"

"Coulda called her worse, I guess."

Trudy sat down on the window seat. "You might do yourself a favor and start looking for a likely woman to cook and keep house for you."

"That right?"

"Mm-hmm."

"Ethan pop the question?"

"What question would that be?" She kept her voice even, but she couldn't hold back her grin.

Hiram looked her way and stood. "Well now." He crossed the room and stooped to kiss her cheek.

"What do you think?" she asked.

"I think Ethan is a fine man and you couldn't do better. Congratulations." He went back to the table and closed the box of cartridges.

"When Rose hears, she might take it into her head again that she should be the one to do for you now."

Hiram shook his head. "That won't wash with me."

"I know. But if Ethan and I get married, the two of you can't stay here together."

Hiram scratched behind his ear. "Thought she was looking for other lodgings."

"I don't know. She goes out most days, and I have no idea where she goes."

"You going to tell her tonight?"

"I think I'll keep it to myself until morning. She'll want to know when the wedding will be, and I don't know yet. But soon."

"All right. And don't worry about me. I'll be fine. You and Ethan need to be together."

She stood and headed for the stairs. "You, Mr. Dooley, are a very observant man."

★ CHAPTER 30 ★

Isabel lay awake for a long time after she and Libby returned from the Dooleys' house. She couldn't help thinking about her future.

Did she really love Griffin Bane? Or did she only long for someone to help her escape from Papa's ranch? The burly blacksmith would never be her intellectual equal. He wasn't the smartest or the cleanest man in Fergus, though the other men respected him. He lived in a little room behind the smithy, which she suspected resembled a hovel inside. When he came to church, his clothes often smelled of sweat and horses. Did she really want a life with a man like him? Had she long ago given up finding a true soul mate and manufactured affections for one of the town's more prominent bachelors? When she made herself be honest, some of his habits and traits repelled her.

And what of Papa's accusation? Had he really caught her staring at Dr. Kincaid? The physician was handsome. In truth, she had never considered that he would find her attractive, but she might have looked regretfully his way a time or two. The doctor had the education, good manners, and refinement that Griffin lacked. Most likely, he would marry one of the town's prettier girls. Isabel wouldn't know what to do if a man like him looked her way.

Only when she turned her troubles over to God would her agitated mind stop racing from one concern to another. Her loneliness must matter very little in the Lord's eternal plan, yet she thanked Him for the friendships she had lately formed with Libby and the other women in town. If her destiny was to remain single, then she could survive that. Surely she and Papa could work toward congeniality. At last she drifted off to sleep with a whispered prayer on her lips.

On Wednesday morning, Libby loaned her a clean shirtwaist and stockings. Isabel dressed and gathered her things, prepared to leave for the ranch.

When she ventured out to the kitchen, Libby was making a pot of oatmeal.

"Breakfast is ready." Libby smiled cheerfully as she ladled the thick mush into two bowls. "The tea is brewing, and I've applesauce as well."

They chatted together like schoolgirls. Isabel told her hostess about the new literature books she hoped the school board would buy for her older students, and Libby mentioned the shipment of textiles and spices she expected Oscar Runnels to bring her later in the day. They went downstairs together after breakfast.

"Are you sure you want to go home now?" Libby asked. "You could stay a bit longer if you like. I could have Florence watch to see when your father opens his office."

"I'll have to face him sometime." Despite her brave words, a weight had settled on Isabel's chest. "I'll need to do some cleaning today and tend the garden. Best I get an early start."

"Yes." Libby stood uncertainly for a moment. "Would you like to go out the back?"

"It won't matter which door I use."

They walked to the front entrance together, and Libby turned the lock. She stood on tiptoe to undo a hook higher on the door frame, then turned to face her departing guest.

"Come anytime, my dear. I mean that. And not only of necessity—come whenever you wish for some company."

Isabel smiled and held out her hand. "Thank you. It comforts me to know there's a place I can retreat to, but I must work this out with Papa."

Libby clasped her hand and opened the door. "I'll be praying for you. Godspeed."

Isabel stepped out into the early morning coolness. A breeze from the valley swept up Main Street.

"Isabel!"

Her father's harsh shout spun her around toward the Wells Fargo office. She gulped and stood her ground. He strode up the boardwalk toward her. She was glad that Libby had stopped in the act of closing the door and stood a couple of feet behind her.

"Where have you been?"

"I stayed with Mrs. Adams last night."

His steely eyes narrowed to slits. "I have never in my life known you to do something like this."

Isabel's heart thudded. She put her hand to her roiling midsection. "I'm sorry, Papa. I didn't suppose you would notice if I didn't return home."

"Not notice?" His voice rose, and Maitland Dostie, opening the telegraph office across the street, glanced their way. Cyrus looked past her and focused beyond. "Libby Adams, I wouldn't have thought you'd have a hand in this."

Libby stepped out onto the boardwalk beside Isabel. "In what, Cyrus? Having a friend over for a visit? I suggest that unless you want the entire town discussing why Isabel spent the night with me, you save your comments for later. You won't get much sympathy if you berate your daughter in public."

Isabel couldn't take her eyes off her father's face. It went from mottled gray to deep red. His lips twisted as he stared, and at last he blinked.

"I shall see you later," he barked at Isabel. "And I shall expect my supper on time." He stalked into his office and soundly shut the door.

Isabel swallowed hard.

Libby stepped closer and slipped an arm about her. "You're shaking, dear. Come inside. I'll fix you another cup of tea."

"No, I must go now. I don't want to give him another opportunity to dress me down here on Main Street."

"Then let me at least have Florence go with you. She'll be here any moment."

Isabel shook herself and gathered the edges of her shawl close. "No, I'll be fine. The walk will give me time to calm down." She reached deep and hoisted a smile for Libby. "I cannot thank you enough. I shall see you tomorrow afternoon at the shooting club."

She walked up Main Street without looking back. Folks were stirring. Charles Walker and one of his employees stood talking on the front porch of the feed store. Terrence Thistle was hanging the "vacancy" board on the bottom of the sign in front of the Fennel House. Isabel trudged past the smithy without looking toward it and continued on, out of town toward her father's ranch.

The road wound slightly uphill, and she took her time. About halfway home, she paused to admire the blue Jacob's ladder flowers growing on the slope. Probably the kitchen in the ranch house was a mess. Certainly Papa would not have cleaned up from her meal preparations last night. She doubted he'd called one of the men in to do it either.

Hoofbeats drummed in the distance. She shaded her eyes and looked northeast, in the direction she'd been walking. Between the hills, a cloud of dust sprang up, moving toward her as the sound increased. Over a rise in the road, several horsemen thundered. She stepped quickly off the way, into the grass. The five horses tore down the road, but as the leader came even to her, he pulled in his mount.

"Whoa!"

The others halted around him.

"You're the Fennel woman."

She opened her mouth and coughed at the dust hanging in the air. "I. . .yes." He looked slightly familiar.

"You're coming with us."

She stared at him and backed up a step. "I most certainly am not."

He nodded to one of the others. As the second man dismounted, she recognized him. He'd been at the box social.

She backed up again and tripped over a stone. The cowboy grabbed her arm as she stumbled and jerked her forward.

"Come on."

"No. Leave me alone."

A click drew her gaze back to the leader, and she froze. He had a pistol cocked and aimed at her.

"Do what we say, Miss Fennel."

"Where are you taking me?"

"You'll know soon enough."

The man holding her arms shoved her toward the leader's bay horse. The mounted man kicked off his near stirrup then leaned down and extended his hand.

"Hop up behind me."

"No, I—"

The man holding her slapped her so hard she recoiled and doubled over. He lifted her bodily and swung her up behind the leader. Her cheek stung, and she nearly tumbled over the far side of the horse. She grabbed for something to steady her and caught the back neck edge of the man's vest. The horse pranced beneath her, and she gasped.

"Take it easy, lady," the rider said. "This horse will be fine if you sit still."

Her skirts had hiked up nearly to her knee on the off side, and the other men were staring and smirking. She tugged with one hand but couldn't free up enough fabric to cover her calf.

"Sit still," the man in front of her said, more sharply.

She caught her breath and froze stiff, one hand still on his vest.

"That's better. Champ usually doesn't mind an extra load. How much do you weigh?"

"You insolent—"

"Stow it or we'll have to gag you." He returned his pistol to his holster.

The man who had lifted her climbed onto his horse. "She don't weigh much, Wilf. No meat on her bones."

Isabel tried to glare at him, but tears filled her eyes. Wilf. She was riding behind Wilfred Sterling, the man Libby had beaten out of third place in the shooting match.

And that other scoundrel, the one who had manhandled her—he was Button, the second-place winner from the horse race. Both Uncle Kenton's men. And Kenton was angry at Papa.

Sterling jerked his head and said to one of the others, "Go on, Chub. Make sure old Fennel gets the message."

The one he spoke to wheeled his dun cow pony and galloped toward Fergus. The other four horsemen headed up the road. A few minutes later, they passed the lane to the Fennel ranch. None of their hands were about. These ruffians must be taking her to the Martin ranch. Wonderful. A ten-mile canter behind Sterling's saddle. She looked down at the ground. The grass and stones flew by at a pace that made her feel dizzy. Staying on the horse seemed preferable to falling off and breaking her scrawny neck. But Uncle Kenton had better have a good explanation.

★ CHAPTER 31 ★

The Tinen ladies were among Libby's first customers of the day. Minutes after she opened shop, Starr and her mother-in-law, Jessie, entered the emporium, with five-year-old Hester hanging on to her grandmother's hand.

"Good morning. It's delightful to see you ladies." Libby stepped from behind the counter. "May I help you?"

Starr darted a glance at Jessie and smiled with a flush creeping up her face. "Arthur's over to Mr. Walker's buying oats, and we're here for flannel and such."

"Flannel?"

"That's right." Jessie grinned.

Libby turned toward the yard goods section. Florence, who was pricing a new shipment of tinned crackers, nodded and smiled at the Tinens as they passed her.

They reached the bolts of fabric, and Libby fanned out a red and gray plaid suitable for a man's shirt. "We just got this in."

Jesse held up a hand in protest. "Oh no. It's not for Arthur. Something for someone. . .er. . .younger." She cast a glance in Hester's direction.

"That's right," Starr said. "We're making a. . .a layette."

"Oh!" Libby hugged her. "How wonderful."

"Yes, isn't it?" Starr giggled. "Of course we haven't. . ." She jerked her head toward Hester, who walked slowly along the aisle, touching each bolt of cloth.

"She doesn't know yet," Jessie whispered loudly.

"Ah. Well, I'm very happy for you all." The little girl would be tickled to know she had a brother or sister coming, but some people waited to tell the siblings just before the new baby's birth. Libby had always thought that if she had children, she would tell them earlier so they could enjoy the anticipation with her. But that wasn't likely ever to happen. She shook off the thought and took a step to her left. "May I suggest this yellow print, or this new pale green plaid? Of course, it has a little pink stripe in it, but I think either...either could wear it."

Starr giggled. "Yes, I think so, too. I'll take a yard and a half of each."

"Oh look!" Jessie had opened the button drawer. "These little mother-of-pearl hearts are darling."

Libby's throat tightened as she carried the bolts of flannel to the counter. She didn't know why God hadn't seen fit to give her and Isaac children. They'd been married more than a decade, and she'd never lost hope until the day Isaac died, leaving her a widow of thirty-three years, childless, with a thriving business and an ache in her heart.

She measured out the flannel and folded each piece. As she jotted the amount on her slate, Florence and the Tinens approached.

"And I'll want some hooks and eyes," Starr said. "Hester was born in summer, so I expect I'll want a new woolen dress for winter this time around, or I'll have nothing to wear to church when it turns cold."

"Would you mind totting this up?" Libby asked Florence softly.

She succeeded in ducking into the back room before her tears spilled over. Why did this yearning hit her now? She'd thought she was beyond the sharp grief for Isaac, but lately she'd longed for the babies she'd never had. To hold an infant in her arms. Was it because she'd turned thirty-five this year and her chances had faded? Of course, Starr would let her hold her new baby. She pulled out her bleached muslin handkerchief and wiped her eyes. Perhaps she needed a drink of water.

Her sobbing overtook her as she reached the cupboard near her desk. She sank into the chair and buried her face in her arms to muffle the sound of her weeping. Florence came to her a minute later and touched her back lightly.

"Dear Mrs. Adams, what is it? Can I help?"

Libby raised her head and sniffed. "No, but thank you. And I'm sorry. Did anyone hear?"

"I don't think so. The Tinens left, and I came looking for you. I wanted to ask what price you want on the large biscuit tins."

Libby wiped her face. "Oh dear. I shall have to look it up. But first, I believe I'll run upstairs and wash my face."

"Take your time," Florence said with a sad smile.

Libby quickly crossed the store, avoiding the gazes of the few customers browsing her wares, and mounted the stairs to her empty rooms.

★

Ethan left the McDade brothers cleaning out the barn and rode in to town. He stopped to leave his horse with Griff at the livery and strolled over to the jail. After a quick look-in, he went to the Dooleys' back door. Hiram answered his knock.

"I've been thinking on it," Ethan said, "and I believe I ought to go and see Cyrus if he's sober now."

"He was here last night. After you and Trudy left."

"Do tell."

"Yup. Says he's short on cash and wants to sell the old Logan ranch." Hiram reached for his hat. "I'll go with you."

Trudy came to the parlor doorway. "Hello, Ethan."

His pulse picked up, but he reminded himself of his errand. "Hi's going with me over to the Wells Fargo for a bit. I want to sound Cyrus out about his brother-in-law and maybe this hole-behind-the-barn business, too."

"All right." Trudy glanced over her shoulder. "Rose hasn't come down yet. I was going to see if she'd talk about her outing with Smith, but I haven't had the chance yet. I'll put the coffeepot on, and maybe you'll get a chance to talk to her, too, when you come back."

Ethan and Hiram walked across the dusty street. A wagon was hitched before the feed store, and one of Oscar Runnels's mule teams trudged southward out of town. The OPEN sign hung in the emporium's window.

In front of the Wells Fargo office, Cyrus Fennel's big roan

was hitched to the rail. Ethan passed the horse and mounted the boardwalk. His boots thudded on the wood. The door was open, so he walked in.

"What do you want?" Cyrus sat at his desk with a ledger before him.

Ethan forced a smile. "How are you doing, Mr. Fennel?"

Cyrus frowned. "I'm busy."

Busy with a headache, Ethan thought. "Kenton Smith has begun to mix with the townsfolk, and I'd like you to tell me a little more about him."

"Like what?" Cyrus studied the ledger, moving the point of his fountain pen back and forth above the pages.

"Like where he was in prison, and what for."

That got him. Cyrus jerked his chin up and started to rise. "What do you—"

A crash of breaking glass drew their attention to the small back window of the office. It had shattered inward, throwing slivers all over the floor. A white object thunked on the pine floor.

Cyrus and Ethan stared at the rock wrapped in paper. Before Ethan could move, Hiram had slid from behind him and retrieved it. He placed it in Ethan's hand.

"Give me that!" Cyrus grabbed it and tore away the string that held the paper in place about the stone.

"That's a dangerous way to get mail," Ethan said.

Cyrus ignored him and smoothed the paper out on his desk. He bent over it, his bushy eyebrows pushed together like two colliding trains. After a moment, he shoved away from the desk and pushed past Ethan, grabbing his hat from its hook on the wall near the door.

Ethan stared after him. "Fennel!"

Cyrus untied his roan, leaped into the saddle, and galloped northward.

"Ethan."

He turned in the doorway. Hiram was studying the paper on the desk.

"It says, 'If you want to see your daughter alive again, repay your debt. Fast.'" Hiram looked up at him. "Sounds like someone's got Miss Isabel."

Ethan snatched the paper up, glanced at it, and headed for the door. "Come on. Get Hoss and meet me at the livery."

Hiram sprinted home and toward the barn behind the house. Trudy was inside the chicken yard and turned to stare at him. He dashed inside and grabbed Hoss's tack. When he headed for the barn door, Trudy blocked his path.

"What's going on?"

"Miss Fennel. Someone sent her papa a note. Sounds like she's been snatched, and they want money."

"Isabel? Kidnapped?" Trudy gaped at him.

"Lemme out."

She stepped aside, and he hurried to the corral gate and whistled. Hoss and Crinkles trotted eagerly toward him.

"Why would anyone do that?"

"It's 'cause her daddy's so rich. And he might owe someone money. He asked me last night if I wanted to buy a piece of land. Said he needed cash. And now he's got a threatening note asking for payment." As he puffed out the words, Hiram threw the saddle with its blanket on Hoss's back and reached under the horse's belly for the cinch. "Go get my rifle."

"If I do, I'm getting my pistol, too. You might need me."

"Ethan and I can handle it."

Trudy ran into the barn, not the house. Hiram shook his head and tied the cinch knot. He grabbed the bridle he'd draped over the top fence rail and fitted it over Hoss's ears. The gelding refused to open his mouth for a few seconds, and by the time Hiram pried it open with a finger tucked in at the side of Hoss's jaw, Trudy came flying from the barn with her saddle and bridle.

"By the time you get our guns, I'll have Crinkles saddled," she said.

"You're not—"

"Am, too."

"No, you're—"

"Hush! My Colt's in the pie safe."

He stared at her. She was already tightening her cinch. Hiram heaved out a big breath and trotted to the kitchen door. His rifle stood in the corner, but he knew for a fact that his sister had carried her new pistol up to her room each evening. Where she'd kept it during the day, he hadn't given much thought. Now he knew. She stashed it close by, where she could look at it anytime she wanted. He pulled it out of the pie safe and ran for the door.

She'd mounted and led Hoss to the back stoop. Hiram bounced into the saddle and handed her Colt across to her. He slipped his Sharps into the scabbard on the saddle and gathered the reins.

At the livery, Ethan sat astride Scout, ready to go. His eyes narrowed as they rode up.

"Trudy, you can't come."

"Can, too."

"Save your breath," Hiram warned him.

Ethan exhaled and shook his head slightly. He said no more but turned Scout toward the road and set out at a canter. Hoss and Crinkles managed to keep pace. When they'd nearly reached the lane to the Fennel ranch, Hiram spotted a couple of men working on the fence that bordered Fennel land.

Ethan trotted Scout over to the fence and stopped.

"Is Mr. Fennel here?"

"Nope," said the weather-beaten hand known as Brady. "He left for town this morning, same as always. Took his roan."

The horses fidgeted and shifted. Hoss tried to nip at Trudy's dun mare, and Hiram leaned forward to slap him. "Quit that."

"What about Miss Isabel?" Ethan asked.

"H'ain't seen her this morning," Brady said.

Ethan frowned and looked down the lane. "I'd like to go to the house and see if she's there."

Brady eyed him for a moment. "Help yourself."

"Something wrong?" asked the other cowboy.

"Maybe."

Brady spat in the grass and looked up at him. "I never seen Miss Isabel today, but we went down to work by the creek first thing. Just moved up here about a half hour ago. I reckon she's at the house, but I couldn't say for sure."

"Did anyone else come by here this morning?" Ethan asked. "Any riders?"

Brady scrunched up his mouth for a moment. "Seen a fella on a bay horse a while back, riding hard away from town. Nobody else."

"Mr. Fennel didn't come by, heading toward his house about ten minutes ago?"

"Nope."

Ethan looked around at Hiram. "What do you think?"

"The note said to pay his debt. That makes me think Smith is mixed up in it."

"Same here. He could have cut across country to save time getting to the Martin ranch."

Hiram hesitated then said softly, "Might be time to see what Cy's got stashed out back."

Ethan pushed his hat brim back. "Brady, I'm riding up to the house to see if Miss Fennel or her father's home."

"If they's anything we can help with, Sheriff. . ."

"Thanks. If I need you, I'll send word."

Brady looked at the other man and shrugged.

Ethan turned Scout toward the ranch, and Hiram and Trudy followed. They trotted into the silent barnyard. Ethan swung down and led Scout to the corral fence. "We'd better check the house, just to be sure."

Hiram pulled his rifle and dismounted. "You want to take the back door, and I'll take the front?"

Ethan nodded and pulled his revolver. "Trudy, you stay out here."

They met a minute later in the hallway outside Cyrus's den.

"Nobody in the kitchen, but it's a mess," Ethan said. "I checked the bedrooms back there."

Hiram lowered his gun and nodded back toward the way he'd come in. "Nobody in the parlor or those rooms yonder. I wonder where Cy keeps his shovel."

"You think we ought to look?"

Hiram shrugged. "It's a long ride out to the Martin place. I'm not against making it, but maybe we'd ought to check out Isabel's story first."

"Yeah. Might give us a better idea what we're up against."

"And whose side Cyrus is on."

Ethan's eyebrows shot up. "You think he's involved in something illegal?"

"I don't know what to think. But if we're going to end up shooting people, I'd like to get all the information I can before I decide who to shoot."

They walked out to the yard. Trudy stood near the horses. "Nobody's around," she said. "The men must all be out working. I looked in the barn. No horses in there, but there's half a dozen in the corral."

Ethan walked over to her. "Did you see a shovel in there?"

"Didn't think to look."

Hiram walked past them and entered the dark, cool barn. He squinted as he looked around. The loft was half full of hay, and the rows of stalls stood empty. Dust in the air tickled his nose, and he sneezed. Ethan came in behind him.

"Tools over there." Hiram pointed and walked toward the row of shovels, pitchforks, and dung forks hanging on the side wall. He chose the only spade and walked across the barn floor to a rear door and unhooked it. He stepped out and examined the earth.

Ethan came right behind him, and soon Trudy joined them. They walked along behind the barn, looking at the ground.

"Here," Trudy called.

The men walked toward her.

"Isabel said she came out the kitchen door and hid beside the barn and looked around the corner. That'd be over there." She pointed. "This here looks like loose dirt to me."

"As much as anything along here," Ethan agreed.

Hiram set the point of the spade to the earth and shoved the blade down with his foot. He dug swiftly, tossing the dirt aside.

"Want me to take over?" Ethan asked after a couple of minutes.

"No, I'm fine."

The spade struck metal with a clunk. Hiram's heart lurched. There really was something there. Carefully he dug around the rectangular object.

"It's a tin." He scraped dirt away from it and worked it out of the soil.

Ethan took it gingerly and set it on the ground nearby, then offered Hiram a hand and pulled him out of the shallow hole. Trudy had already bent over the tin.

"Don't know if I can get the cover off," she said.

"Careful," Ethan said, and she handed it to him. He took out his pocket knife and pried the edge of the lid until it popped off. He looked into the container and reached inside. "A paper and this." He brought out a leather pouch and passed it to Trudy. "Careful. That's heavy."

She worked at the leather thong that held it shut. "Feels like coins." She straightened, and Hiram held out his cupped hands. She spilled the contents of the pouch into them.

Hiram whistled.

"Gold coins." Trudy looked at them with wide eyes.

"Count it," Ethan said as he reached into the metal box again. He pulled out a stiff roll of paper, folded in half and smashed to fit the container. "That's all there is."

Hiram dropped the coins one by one back into the pouch and nodded as Trudy closed it. "Got it." He turned to look at the paper Ethan held, and his friend handed it to him. Hiram carefully pulled it open like a scroll and stared into water-stained drawings of two faces. "It's a wanted poster, Eth."

Ethan held one corner, and they managed to hold it open so they could view the entire page. Trudy came to peer around Hiram's arm, still holding the pouch.

"The Kentons." Ethan frowned and huffed out a breath.

"That's Kenton Smith," Trudy said.

"Yes. A very young Kenton Smith, but the face is the same."

Hiram scanned the print silently, but Trudy read it off aloud.

"Wanted for robbery, John and Abigail Kenton. Reward $1,000. Last seen in Lexington, Massachusetts, June 1853."

Hiram stared hard at the drawings. Trudy continued to read.

"John Kenton, medium height, light brown hair, blue eyes. Abigail Kenton, slight of build, medium height, light hair, green eyes."

Hiram reached out and touched the woman's likeness. "I'm not sure, but. . ."

"I think so, too," Ethan said. "Mary Fennel."

"But she and Cyrus came here. . ." Trudy trailed off and looked at Ethan.

"Cy came right after gold was discovered in these parts, '62 or '63. Him and Charles Walker and Isaac Adams, remember?" Ethan glanced at both of them, his eyebrows raised, seeking confirmation.

Hiram nodded. "And Isabel's so-called uncle is going by Kenton Smith now."

"He's got to be John Kenton." Ethan took the poster back and rolled it up. "But the Fennels came here ten years after this poster was made."

Hiram took his hat off and scratched his head. "So what do we do?"

"How much money in the pouch?"

"Five hundred dollars even."

Ethan pressed his lips into a thin line. "I think it's time to ride out to the Martin place."

Trudy touched his sleeve. "Wait a minute. Isabel's mother died three years ago. She was a good woman."

Hiram didn't like the anxiety in his sister's eyes or the turmoil in his own stomach. Breakfast wasn't sitting very well. "She did seem like a nice lady. But Trudy, we don't know what she was like thirty years ago. She could have helped her brother rob a bank or something."

Trudy shook her head. "I can't believe that. And she was a Smith. She may look like this Abigail Kenton, but I'm not convinced it's her. You've got to show me more than this drawing. I'll bet there's a thousand women who look enough like that to match this poster."

Ethan blew out a deep breath. "It's true, drawings of wanted criminals are sometimes not very accurate. They're usually made from descriptions given by people who saw the subject only for a short time, under stressful circumstances."

"Maybe she had a sister named Abigail," Hiram suggested.

"She did have a sister," Trudy said grudgingly. "That wasn't the name, though. Isabel mentioned her aunt, but she said the aunt died young."

"Anyway," Ethan said, "the fact that this man showed up here calling himself Kenton, the name on the poster, and Smith, Mrs. Fennel's maiden name, makes me think we've got cause to go after him."

Hiram had to agree, but he surely didn't want to make a mistake. He looked Ethan in the eye. "He may be this robber, but he may also have done his time for his crimes. Cyrus said he'd been in jail. So maybe he's just trying to start over and get away from his past."

"True, but what about Isabel and the note demanding Cyrus pay his debt?"

Trudy straightened her shoulders. "I think we'd better bury this again and get to the Martin ranch as quick as we can."

★ CHAPTER 32 ★

The horses raced along the packed dirt road, throwing up clouds of dust. Ethan knew trying to persuade Trudy to go back to town was useless, so he headed straight for the Martin ranch.

About halfway there, they met Cyrus on his big red roan. The horse trotted along slowly with his head drooping and his sides streaked with sweat. Cyrus sat loose in the saddle, his face a study in displeasure.

He pulled the roan in when he reached them.

Ethan eyed him and decided to skip the small talk. "Did you find Isabel?"

"Kenton's got her." Cyrus's mouth twisted.

"It's time you told me everything, Mr. Fennel."

"That's what you think."

"No, it's the truth." Ethan pressed his leg against Scout's side to urge him closer to the roan. "Cyrus, I dug up your stash behind the barn. I saw the wanted poster."

"You *what*?" Cyrus's gray eyes lowered like thunderclouds. "Who gave you permission to snoop on my property?"

"Just calm down." Ethan sat back and rested both hands on his saddle horn. "Your daughter told me last night about you digging a hole out there. As soon as you got that note this morning and hightailed out of town, I rounded up a couple of friends and rode to your ranch. You weren't there, and neither was Isabel. I figured you'd come out here to see Smith, and I also figured it was time for some answers. Time you told the truth and let somebody help you."

"There's nothing you can do."

"How do you know?" Ethan held his gaze until Cyrus looked away and gathered his reins.

"Let me pass, Chapman."

Ethan leaned over and took hold of the near rein. "Mr. Fennel, if you don't cooperate, I'll have to lock you up."

"Lock me up? That's ridiculous!"

"Is it?" Ethan tried to muster the look he'd given the cowboy, Sandy, at the Spur & Saddle on the fateful night he and Hiram had stopped the brawl. Hiram had told him later he'd looked as fierce as a general with a brigade at his back. He needed that authority now. "Let me tell you something, mister. Everyone knows you've gone all over town trying to raise cash. You offered to sell Hiram some land. Charles Walker told me a few days ago you'd gone to him with the same offer, and Augie Moore told me—"

"All right." Cyrus let out a big sigh. "All right. I do need money. It's for my daughter's life. Do you understand? I have twelve hours to raise it."

"How much?"

"Fifteen thousand."

Ethan inhaled slowly and tried not to show his shock. "Suppose you start at the beginning and tell us what's going on."

"I don't have time."

"Make time."

Cyrus glared at him, but Ethan didn't budge. Trudy had sense enough to keep quiet, though her horse fidgeted.

Hiram's silence was usually a given, but now he nudged his bay gelding forward. "Cyrus, we're your neighbors. If you've got trouble, let us do something to help."

"All right," Cyrus said at last. "You can't help, but you want the truth. Here it is: Isabel's mother was really Abigail Kenton."

"I thought her maiden name was Smith," Ethan said.

"It was. She married John Kenton. When he came to my house a few weeks ago, I called him Kenton. He insisted I tell Isabel he was her uncle, so I renamed him Kenton Smith on the spot. He was my Mary's first husband."

Ethan swallowed hard as the implications hit him. "So, was she Mary, or was she Abigail?"

Cyrus sagged in the saddle. "Her real name was Abigail.

Abigail Smith, until she married Kenton. She got involved with him, but he was bad news. I was in love with Abigail, but she had an eye for the dark, dangerous type. She jilted me and married John Kenton. I learned afterward that he was a criminal. But when I went to Abigail about it, she got angry at *me*. Didn't want to hear anything against her husband." A tear seeped from the corner of Cyrus's eye and rolled down his cheek.

"What changed things?" Ethan asked softly.

"I went away. Didn't see her for several years. When I came back, she and Kenton were both wanted for armed robbery. I couldn't believe it, but I managed to see her alone one night. She told me he'd forced her to help him carry out several thefts. She'd stuck with him because she was afraid to leave him. I. . .tried to talk her into leaving him, but she refused. Said she'd chosen her course." Cyrus wiped his eyes with his sleeve. "Then John was captured and thrown in prison. I went to her and helped her escape the authorities. I guess that makes me a criminal, too."

Ethan said nothing. The words hung heavy in the air. Only the wind and the horses' movements rooted him in the present as he imagined Cyrus on the run with a young outlaw woman. The Mrs. Fennel he'd known had been quiet and. . .well, nice. Almost genteel, as far as miners' wives went. He considered whether Cyrus might have made up the story.

"We got away." Fennel's flat voice grated on Ethan's ears. "She agreed to go west with me because she knew the alternative would mean prison. Maybe hanging. We took a strongbox full of gold they'd accumulated. Loot from their robberies. And to keep people from recognizing her, she traveled as my wife. I called her Mary. Mary Fennel." He sighed. "Those first few weeks, I was happy, strange as that may seem. I had the woman I loved with me, even though she wasn't really my wife. Everyone thought she was." Cyrus glanced at Hiram and back to Ethan. "I treated her like royalty. Showed her that I would give her a better life than Kenton had. I wanted to make sure she didn't regret going with me."

"So. . .you just ran off together."

Cyrus sat taller in the saddle and glared at Ethan. "Even though she was wanted by the law and we had to live a lie, I was happy, you hear me?"

Ethan winced. "Yes sir. And that was a long time ago. More'n thirty years, I reckon."

"Yes." Cyrus held his reins loosely, and the big gelding put his head down, sniffing for grass. "Then everything changed."

"How's that?" Ethan asked.

"Mary told me she was pregnant."

Ethan didn't dare look at Trudy and Hiram, but his face heated up. Folks just didn't talk about those things in front of ladies. "You mean. . ."

"I mean she was expecting Kenton's child." Cyrus looked out toward the mountains, blinking rapidly. "I told her everything was all right. That the baby would be mine, no matter what. We stopped in St. Louis for three months, and she gave birth to Isabel there. We put my name on the birth certificate. Later we moved on to Nebraska, and I farmed for a while, but we lived hand to mouth. Didn't want to use up all the gold she'd brought, but we had to use some of it. I wanted to give Mary a better life. Her and my daughter. But we were always going behind and having to dip into that stash. After a few years, I heard about the gold strikes up here in Idaho territory. We sold the farm. I came up here ahead of Mary and Isabel and started mining."

Trudy moved Crinkles up beside Ethan and Scout. "Mr. Fennel, does Isabel know that you're not her real father?"

Cyrus jerked his head toward her. "*I* am her father. Legally, no one can prove otherwise. I've always considered her my daughter and treated her as such."

"So. . .she doesn't know."

After a long moment of silence, Cyrus shook his head. "I know we were wrong to lie to her, but at the time, I couldn't think of another way to save Abigail. We made the story become the truth. Abigail was Mary, my wife. Isabel was my child."

Trudy looked at Ethan, but he didn't know what to say. He didn't dare to bring up the matter of Cyrus and Mary Fennel not being legally married. That was way beyond where he wanted to go right now.

Trudy cocked her head to one side. "Mr. Fennel, it seems to me that Abigail should have turned herself in."

"If she'd done that, she would have been imprisoned. I couldn't bear the thought of her wasting away in jail and giving birth to her baby there."

"But you didn't know about Isabel until weeks after you'd run away."

Cyrus just shook his head. He pulled the roan's head up. "Can I go now? I have work to do."

"Is the gold that's in the buried tin stolen money?" Ethan asked.

"Probably. It's all we had left. I never asked Abigail for particulars, but we left Waterford with more than thirty thousand dollars. We used a little on the journey. Some went for the farm in Nebraska, more for our living expenses there. We had a couple of bad crops. . . . But we made out all right when we sold that. We spent most of what we had left here in Idaho, buying land and livestock."

"I thought you made your fortune mining," Trudy said.

"Not that much. I did come out ahead, and we lived off what I earned. But I used some of Abigail's money to buy up land after the boom was over. For Isabel. And. . .I always hoped we'd have a son. But that didn't happen, so I built up my holdings for her. When I got the contract for the stagecoach line to Boise and Silver City, we had a few thousand left in the can. I used it to buy livestock and coaches. That five hundred that's left in there is the last of it. Sort of an emergency stockpile. Cash if I really needed it."

"But now you need it, and it's not enough," Ethan said. "Kenton's out of prison, and he tracked you down."

Cyrus's lips twisted in a grimace. "He didn't seem to care what had happened to Abigail. He just wanted his share of the gold. I had fifteen hundred in that tin you found at that point. I dug it up after he came that first night and took out a thousand. I gave it to him the next day. I told him that was all I had. It was a lie, but I figured if things turned out badly, I ought not to leave Isabel with nothing. As long as there was a little money in that tin and no one else knew about it, she'd have enough to get away from here—or away from Kenton—if she needed to."

"Has he got her out to the Martin ranch?" Ethan asked.

Cyrus nodded. "I need to take him the other fourteen thousand by sundown. He's got half a dozen armed cowboys—'friends' he connected with in prison. They're ready to defend the place. He said if I brought you in on this, he'd kill her."

"What are we going to do?" Trudy asked. Her eyes were gray today, no blue tints of hope.

Ethan considered several options, none of them good. "Go back to town." She opened her mouth, but he said quickly, "Hear me out. I want you to raise a posse. Get every gun you can to come out to the Martin ranch. Hiram and I will head out there now with Mr. Fennel. We'll hang back where they can't see us and wait for more men." He reached out and touched her chin with his knuckles. "Raise the whole town if you can, sweetheart. But warn them to be cautious. I don't want anyone barging into trouble. One of us will meet them a mile down the road from the ranch and tell them what we've decided to do."

She nodded slowly. "What about the noon stagecoach?"

Cyrus inhaled sharply. "Perhaps you could ask Griff Bane to meet the coach."

"We need Griffin out here," Ethan said.

"Terry Thistle, then. And tell the driver he'll have to change the team himself. Bane will have the mules waiting in his paddock."

Trudy nodded. "What if someone wants to buy a ticket?"

Cyrus hesitated. "Tell Mr. Thistle to deal with it. I can't think about that right now."

"All right, sir. We'll handle it."

Hiram edged Hoss up even with their mounts. "You might ask Libby to bring some extra ammunition, and bring the two boxes on my bedroom shelf."

"All right." Trudy looked gravely at him and Ethan then turned Crinkles homeward and put her heels to his sides.

★ CHAPTER 33 ★

Trudy galloped Crinkles into town, straight to the livery stable. "Griffin!"

The burly blacksmith came to the doorway, scratching his chin through his beard. "Hey, Gert. I mean, Trudy. Wha—"

"You've got to help me raise a posse. Men and women who can shoot. Ethan and Hi are out at the Martin ranch, where that no-good Kenton Smith is staying. They're holding Isabel Fennel for ransom. Ethan told Cyrus we'd raise the town. He wants anyone who can shoot to get out there. Can you help me?"

"Sure."

"Good. I'll get someone to change the stagecoach team for you. Start spreading the word."

She slapped Crinkles with the end of her reins and galloped over to the boardinghouse, where she dismounted and ran to the kitchen door. It stood open, and she called out as she ran up the steps, "Mrs. Thistle!"

The stout lady turned toward her, placing a hand over her heart. "You startled me, Miss Dooley. What's all the fuss?"

"Mr. Fennel asked me to get Mr. Thistle to meet the stagecoach today, in case he can't be there."

"Oh? Is he ill?"

Terrence Thistle entered from the dining room, and Trudy quickly gave him Cyrus's instructions about the stagecoach team and tickets. With his one good arm, Mr. Thistle pulled on a jacket. "I'd better go over to the livery and make sure I can find the right harnesses for the mule team."

"But isn't Mr. Bane there?" Mrs. Thistle's forehead wrinkled like a washboard. "Is something going on?"

"He's going to help the sheriff. I can't stay long enough to explain it all, but there's trouble out at the Martin ranch."

"Oh, those no-good cowpokes." Mrs. Thistle shook her head and went back to stirring her bowl of cake batter. "The night your brother came for the doctor, I knew no good would come out of that bunch."

"I really must go. Thank you both! Oh, and tell Dr. Kincaid if you see him." Trudy dashed out the door and scooped up Crinkles's reins. She was close to the Bentons' house, so she turned her mare down Gold Lane. Apphia was in the front yard, bent over her tiny flower bed.

"Trudy! What brings you out on horseback?" She stood and brushed at the stains on her skirt.

"The sheriff needs help. Is your husband home?"

"Yes. He's studying."

"Tell him I'm raising all the men and women I can. Isabel Fennel's been kidnapped by that awful man who calls himself her uncle. Ethan and Hiram are with Mr. Fennel out at the Martin ranch. Anyone who can help is to bring a weapon and meet them a mile down the road from the ranch house."

"We'll both come." Apphia hurried toward the house and called over her shoulder, "Don't wait! Go tell the Moores. Augie will get the word out."

Trudy turned Crinkles and cantered back to Main Street. She stopped at her own house only long enough to run inside and snatch the extra ammunition. Rose jumped up from her chair in the parlor and stared at her.

"Where are you going?"

"The sheriff needs everyone who can shoot out at the Martin ranch." She ran back out to her horse and stuffed the cartridge boxes into the saddlebag before she mounted. Already, word had spread up the street, and men were saddling their horses. She caught a glimpse of Griffin hurrying out of the feed store with Mr. Walker.

At the Spur & Saddle, she jumped down, threw the ends of the reins over the long hitching rail, and pounded up the steps.

"Augie! Bitsy!"

Bitsy and Goldie were working together in the dining room, setting the tables. They set down the dishes and napkins they held and came toward her. Augie popped out from the kitchen, wiping his hands on a linen towel.

"What is it, girl?" Bitsy asked.

"The sheriff needs you. All of you. Anyone who can shoot. Kenton Smith and his men have kidnapped Isabel and are demanding a ransom from her father. Ethan wants anyone who can help to ride out to the Martin ranch."

Goldie tore off her apron. "I'll run across the street and tell the Nashes, the Harpers, and anyone at the emporium. Miss Bitsy, bring my pistol, would you? And tell Vashti!"

Before Bitsy could reply, the girl was out the door. "I'll go down this side of the street and tell Dostie and—"

"I've been to the boardinghouse and the Bentons'. Anyone else you can reach. . ."

Augie grabbed his shotgun from behind the bar they now used as a serving counter. Bitsy ran to the bottom of the ornate staircase and shouted, "Vashti!"

"Yes'm?" came a muffled reply.

"Come down and bring your pistol and Goldie's. It's shooting club business."

Augie turned in the doorway. "You best be letting men into the club, then."

"The sheriff needs all of us," Trudy assured him.

Augie nodded and went out.

"Wait and ride back with us, Trudy. Do I have time to change into my bloomers?"

"I don't think so."

"Right." Bitsy planted her right foot on the seat of a chair and hiked her skirt up. Strapped to her garter was the tiny pistol she cherished. She drew it and checked the load then slipped it back into its diminutive holster. "That's good. Gotta get the rifle, too, though." She disappeared through the kitchen door.

Vashti scurried down the stairs, carrying her revolver and Goldie's, her long, dark hair floating about her shoulders.

"Do you ladies have horses?" Trudy asked.

"Augie's is over to the livery," Vashti said. "Maybe we can get a wagon." She peered out the front door. "Say, that looks like the Harpers. And Goldie's with them. We can catch a ride with them."

"Go," Trudy said. "Ask them to wait for Bitsy."

When Bitsy returned carrying the rifle, Trudy told her, "Hurry. Zach Harper's out there, and his wagon's nearly full."

They dashed outside. Down the street, Oscar Runnels and his son, Josiah, came from behind the feed store driving freight wagons. Each was pulled by a team of six sturdy mules.

"You shooting club ladies, pile in," Oscar yelled. Charles Walker, Pastor Benton, and a couple of other men climbed into the wagons, as well. Libby and Florence ran from the emporium carrying their weapons and hopped onto the back of Josiah's wagon.

Trudy mounted Crinkles and tore for the livery. Terrence Thistle bustled about, helping men find mounts and bridles. Doc Kincaid and Ted Hire quickly saddled their own horses.

"Just don't take the stagecoach mules," Thistle shouted to one of the freighters who ducked between the rails of the corral fence.

Kincaid mounted and rode over to Trudy. "I'm ready. Do you know the way, Miss Dooley?"

"I sure do. Let's go."

An hour later, Hiram lay on his stomach, looking over a knoll toward the ranch house. Ethan had given orders to the townspeople as they arrived, and now he ducked low and joined Hiram, sliding in next to him on his belly.

"If all goes well, we'll have the house surrounded in about fifteen minutes. Can you believe how many folks came?"

"Nope. It's almost like the day of the picnic." Hiram glanced over his shoulder. Rose sat on the tailgate of Josiah's wagon handing out cookies. "What'd she come for, anyhow?"

Ethan shook his head. "The entertainment?"

"I guess so."

"Maybe she cares about Smith. Kenton, that is."

"I don't think so. Trudy told me she said some mean things about him this morning—like how his teeth are all brown and how bad his grammar is."

"Well, why'd she go out to dinner with him last night?"

Hiram shrugged. "Bored?"

Ethan shook his head and slid up to where he could see the ranch house, barn, and corrals. "I guess the next thing is to try to talk to Kenton and demand that he release Isabel."

"I wondered."

Ethan sighed. "I'm not very good at this, Hiram."

"Been praying."

"Thanks." Ethan lifted his hat, wiped his brow with his sleeve, and settled it again. "It gives me the shivers to think one of our ladies could get shot. But I think we need numbers to make this fellow back down."

"He's been in prison before. Won't want to go back."

"That's the way I look at it. All right, I'll get Cyrus to go down with me. Maybe Griffin, too. Do you want to go?"

"What good would I do?"

"Some of those cowboys saw you lay Eli Button out. They probably think you're as tough as nails."

Hiram barked out a little laugh. "Likely." He slid back until he could stand without being seen over the mound. "Let's go."

He and Ethan rounded up Griffin. The three walked over to where Cyrus stood near his horse. Libby was talking to him, her back to them as they approached.

"We're all praying, Cyrus. The Lord can get her out of this."

Cyrus's face was gray as he looked down at her. "She got involved in that trouble last summer, and I vowed I'd see she had a good life. But. . .but lately I haven't been able to get along with her. Somehow we can't see eye to eye anymore. She started going to the shooting club—"

"No, Cyrus. Don't blame this on the shooting club. Things have been tense between you and Isabel since Mary died."

He hung his head. "I suppose you're right." He looked up as the others stepped forward. "Sheriff, when are you going to do something? We been here over an hour, just standing around waiting."

"We're going down there now," Ethan said. "You, me, Griffin, and Hiram. I want you to call out to Kenton and see if he'll parley."

"What if they shoot at us?"

Ethan scratched his chin. "Think we'd ought to carry a flag?"

"He told me not to bring you." Cyrus stood tall. "I think I should go down alone."

"Alone? No, come on, Mr. Fennel. We can't let you walk into a trap."

"All right, I'll take Dooley."

Hiram gulped.

"You'll what?" Ethan scowled at him.

"Kenton told me he'll kill Isabel if I bring in the law. All right, so I go down with a friend instead. I'll tell him Dooley's staking me the money."

Ethan frowned.

"I'll do it." Hiram was so startled at his own words that he jumped. He looked at the other three men to see if they'd heard him. Maybe he hadn't actually said the words aloud.

"Hiram, you must be cautious," Libby said, and he knew he'd blurted it out, all right.

"I will. We will. Won't we, Mr. Fennel?"

Cyrus nodded.

"We'll ask them to let us see Isabel," Hiram said.

"That's good." Ethan looked keenly into his eyes for a moment. "All right. But you've got to stall him. Tell him you're trying to raise the money but you don't think you can come up with the cash that fast."

"What's the point in that?" Cyrus asked.

"Get him talking and ask to see that Isabel's alive and well. If he's cooperative, maybe you can get a count of his men and see how their defenses look. Tell him you can't get the full amount, but maybe you can come up with less. See what he says—if he's willing to deal or not."

"And if he's not?"

Ethan's dark eyes narrowed to slits. "That's when you back off, and we show our hand. Forty guns trained on them."

Cyrus grabbed his hat from his head and threw it on the ground. "I knew I shouldn't have waited for you. They'll kill my daughter."

★ CHAPTER 34 ★

Here's your white flag." Trudy placed a long stick in her brother's hand. Fluttering from the top end was a white petticoat. He didn't want to know whose.

"Mr. Fennel, there's one more thing." Ethan looked around at Hiram, Trudy, and Cyrus. Griff Bane stood a few yards away, checking his saddle. The rest of the townsfolk had dispersed in a large cordon around the ranch. Libby had set up an ammunition station on the back of Josiah's wagon. Even Rose had stationed herself with the Harper ladies several yards away.

"What do you want?" Cyrus stood by his roan with the reins in his hands.

Ethan dropped his voice. "You said Isabel doesn't know Kenton is her father. Does Kenton know that she is his daughter?"

"No. So far as he knows, Isabel is mine and Abigail's."

Ethan let out his breath. "So he's not apt to spill the beans to her in there."

"No. I suppose he could tell her he was married to her mother." Cyrus's face twisted, and he looked away, toward the mountains.

Trudy touched his arm. "I'm sorry this is happening, Mr. Fennel. Do you think it would help the situation if Kenton did know that?" She looked at Ethan. "I mean, he might be less likely to hurt Isabel if he knew she was truly his kin."

"It's too risky," Ethan said. "If Isabel learns it from him, she might be overwrought. There's no telling what she would do."

Cyrus clenched his fists. "Besides, if Kenton knew, he might try to take Isabel away with him and force her to do things she shouldn't. That's what he did with her mother thirty-five years ago. Why would he do any differently now?"

Ethan nodded reluctantly. "All right. We won't tell him. Just go in to where he can hear you and see if you can get him to release her."

Griffin walked over, leading his big gray gelding. "I'm going, too."

Cyrus hesitated then nodded. "All right then. The three of us."

Ethan looked at him, Hiram, and Griff. "Godspeed."

Hiram walked to Hoss. His stomach churned, but the docile bay gelding stood still for him while he mounted and shifted the flag to his other hand. He thought about taking his rifle from the scabbard and using it as a flag holder, but he might need his Sharps. And he couldn't ride in there with it drawn. Kenton might not think that was neighborly. He pried a spot for the end of the flag stick between his right boot and the stirrup.

Cyrus led the way, and Hiram followed, with Griff trotting along behind. The sun neared its zenith, and Hiram's cotton shirt stuck to his back. The breeze had died down. He could feel perspiration forming on his forehead along the sweatband of his hat.

The ranch house lay quiet, baking in the heat. The walls were built of logs, with only one small window on the front. Beyond the house lay the barn, corral, and the old soddy they used for a bunkhouse. Hiram remembered the Martins who had built the spread—two brothers. One of them had a skinny wife and two young'uns. They must have sold out to Cyrus and moved on five or six years ago. The isolated location was too far away from civilization for most women.

Cyrus's horse slowed to a walk, and Hoss broke stride as well. Hiram urged him up beside the roan. A magpie flew from under the barn eaves and swooped toward the corral. Griff closed in on Cyrus's other side, and they continued slowly toward the house, with the petticoat flag hanging limply over Hiram's head. A glint of metal caught his eye. Someone crouched behind the farm wagon near the corral fence.

He started to speak, but the door to the house opened.

"Don't come any closer."

They halted and stared at the door. It stood open only a couple of inches, and Hiram couldn't tell who had spoken. He saw a flicker of movement at the window to the left of the door frame as well.

"Tell Kenton I want to talk," Cyrus yelled.

The door opened wider, and Kenton Smith—or John Kenton—stood in the shadowed opening with a rifle in his hands.

"Why are those men with you? I told you to keep your trap shut. This is between you and me."

"Oh yeah?" Cyrus stood in the stirrups. "Then why have you got all your men guarding the house? Don't tell me you threw that rock through my office window personally."

Kenton shifted his gun so that the barrel pointed straight at them. "Have you got my money?"

"Not all of it. I told you—I can't raise that kind of cash that fast."

"Then go away until you've got it."

"Even if I had the resources, there's not that much hard money in Fergus. I'll have to send to Boise City. It'll take at least a couple of days."

"No deal. I've been waiting a long time, Fennel. I want my money now."

Cyrus's hard gray eyes narrowed. "Let Isabel go, and give me a few days. I promise I'll get the money."

"Why should I believe you? I told you not to tell anyone, and you've brought two men with you. Next thing I know, the sheriff will ride up."

"That's your own fault," Cyrus shouted. "I wasn't alone when the rock came through the window. Mighty hard to keep something like that secret when you've got folks in the room with you."

Another man appeared in the doorway behind Kenton, and they spoke in low tones.

"How much you got on you now?" Kenton yelled.

Cyrus hesitated. He looked askance at Hiram. "What do I say?"

"Ask to see Isabel."

Cyrus leaned over and unhooked a canteen from his saddle. He took his time uncorking it and tipping it up for a drink. Hiram could almost taste the water running down his dry throat, and he looked away. The second man had come out where he could be seen. Eli Button.

Cyrus cleared his throat. "Kenton, I'm not going anywhere until I see my daughter."

Kenton stared at him, his bushy eyebrows low. "What for?"

"To prove you've got her, for starters. And to see that she's all right."

Kenton turned his head and spoke to Button. The cowboy lumbered into the house, and they waited in tense silence.

After half a minute, Griffin said, "You think it's possible they don't have her?"

"It entered my mind." Cyrus started to put his canteen back and paused. "You boys want a drink?"

"Thanks. I was wishing I'd brought something." Griffin took the canteen and tipped it up for a swig. He passed it back to Cyrus, who relayed it to Hiram.

Hiram shook it. Half full. He took a mouthful and handed it back to Cyrus. "Thank you kindly. She wasn't in your house when we went there, sir. Your men said they hadn't seen her."

"Well, you just never know. She could still be over at Libby Adams's place. I'd hate to be doing this for nothing."

"No sir, Mrs. Adams came along with the other folks from town," Griffin pointed out. "She told us Miss Fennel left for home just before she opened the store this morning."

Near the corral, a cowboy stood up behind the wagon, showing himself openly. He rested a shotgun on the side of the wagon and stared insolently at them. Hiram caught a suggestion of movement again at the window of the house.

Isabel burst through the door of the ranch house in a flurry of gray skirts. Hiram caught his breath. Button held her around the waist with a revolver pointed at her right ear. Hair fluttered about her face in disarray. Her frantic, pale eyes focused on her father, and her mouth opened in a silent plea.

Kenton looked her over and turned toward the horsemen.

"All right, you seen her. How much you got on you?"

The creases at the corners of Cyrus's eyes deepened as he squinted. "About three dollars."

"What?" Kenton limped toward them, brandishing the rifle. "You get outta here right now and get me the money. You're a-wasting time! Be back by sundown, or Miss Isabel is a bye-bye. You get me?"

Hiram's heart pounded in his throat.

Cyrus's face went beet red. He stiffened in the saddle, and his horse pawed the ground.

"We'd best be going," Griffin said softly.

"Boss," yelled the cowboy near the corral.

Kenton turned his way. "Yeah?"

"They's men out there." The cowboy swept his arm in an arc, indicating the terrain toward the road and on each side.

"You double-crosser!" Kenton swung his rifle toward the horses and let off a charge.

★ CHAPTER 35 ★

W e could pick off some of the men." Trudy jerked her bonnet back and let it slide down her back. She itched to do something. Studying the scene before them, she made a few mental calculations. "Dr. Kincaid and Libby and me. Bitsy, too. I'm sure we could get that one behind the wagon, and maybe the one peeking around the side of the house. There's got to be two or three more men in the house, though."

"Patience." Ethan kept his eyes on the three horsemen and the people standing before the ranch house below. From the length of the lane, he could make out the figures near the house but couldn't hear what was said.

Kenton whirled around, spoke to one of his men, then faced Cyrus and his friends and fired a bullet. Dust plumed near the horses' feet. All three horses jumped. Griffin's bucked and dumped the big blacksmith in a heap on the ground. Hiram's bay turned completely around and lunged a few steps away from Kenton, but Hiram quickly got him under control and brought him around to approach Griffin. Fennel's roan, meanwhile, turned and tore away from the gunman, straight toward where Ethan, Trudy, and Libby watched.

Cyrus never looked back until he reached them. He pulled the roan in and glared at Ethan. "He wants the money now. And he knows you're up here. The men saw you."

"If they know I'm here, I guess it won't matter if I go help Hiram." Ethan ran to his paint gelding and mounted.

Cyrus turned his horse and looked back, down the slight

decline toward the ranch house. Griffin slowly rose with Hiram supporting him and limped to where his horse stood, grabbing a mouthful of pale grass.

"What happened?" Cyrus asked.

Trudy scowled at him. Trust Cyrus to think of himself first and everyone else last. "Griff's horse dumped him when Kenton fired."

"He's not shot, is he?"

"How should we know? At least he's alive."

Dr. Kincaid came running from his post along the fence row. "Is Mr. Bane hurt?"

"Don't know," Trudy said. "Hiram's helping him get on his horse. Just wait here, and we'll see."

Ethan had reached the other two now and dismounted to help boost the huge blacksmith onto his horse. The gelding was skittish, but Hiram held his head firmly while Ethan loaned his shoulder and a shove. Griffin rose in the stirrup and swung his right leg gingerly over the saddle.

"Looks like his arm's hurt," Libby noted.

"Yes." Dr. Kincaid gritted his teeth. "Maybe I should go and meet them."

"No, wait here," Trudy said. "Let them come to you, out of range of those roughnecks."

Griffin's horse came toward them at a choppy walk, lifting each hoof high and fighting the bit. Griff held the reins in his right hand and let his left arm dangle at his side. His dark beard was coated in dust, and he held his mouth in a grimace as the horse's steps jostled him.

Hiram and Ethan mounted and trotted up on either side of the gray horse. After a moment, Ethan left Hiram and Griff behind and cantered toward the watchers.

He pulled his pinto in when he reached them and hopped to the ground. "Doc, Griff thinks his arm's broken."

Trudy exhaled heavily. "Didn't think Kenton shot him, but it was hard to tell from here."

"Hiram says Kenton fired to scare them, but it worked too well, and Griff's horse threw him."

"I'll tend to him." Doc looked around. "I'll have him lie down in the shade of that tree."

"Maybe you should take him back to town in one of the wagons," Ethan said.

Trudy shook her head. "Griff won't want to go."

Rose came running from her observation post, her pink and white skirts swaying. "Doctor, is there anything I can do to help?" She fluttered her lashes at him, but the gesture was lost on Dr. Kincaid as he strode toward his horse.

"Perhaps so, Mrs. Caplinger. I may be able to use an assistant."

Rose smiled triumphantly at Trudy and Libby before scurrying off after him.

Hiram and Griffin topped the rise, and Ethan and Cyrus went to help Griffin dismount.

"I'm sorry, Bane," Cyrus said as the big man slid from the saddle with a moan. "Didn't realize you'd gone down."

Trudy went to her brother's side. "You all right, Hi?"

He nodded.

Ethan stood close to Griffin so the bigger man could lean on him. "Where you want to sit, Griff?"

"Doc says to put him in the shade over there." Trudy pointed.

The men hobbled off together toward one of the few scrubby trees in the fencerow.

Libby stepped closer and eyed Hiram. She said nothing, but a glance passed between them that almost made Trudy blush. Her curiosity drew her gaze to Hiram's face.

He lifted his hat, wiped his brow with his cuff, and put his hat back. "I'm fine, ladies. Wish I could say the same about Griff and Miss Isabel. But I'm just fine."

"Is Isabel hurt?" Libby asked.

"Don't think so. But she looked like death."

Trudy reached for his elbow. "Maybe you should sit in the shade, too." She flicked a glance at Libby. "I'm sure Libby could find something for you to drink. I saw Annie passing a jug of water."

"No time," Hiram said. "We got to help Cy raise some cash. That or put some pressure on Kenton and his men."

Libby cleared her throat. "I wasn't in on the discussion when Cyrus told you about Mr. Smith's demands, but. . .I could lend him some money."

"Before sundown?" Trudy stared at her friend. "He needs fourteen thousand dollars."

Libby cleared her throat and shot a glance at Hiram. "Well, I don't have that much, of course, but I have"—she leaned toward them and dropped her voice—"about two thousand in my safe. I was planning to send most of it to the bank in Boise City by this afternoon's stagecoach."

Trudy tried not to let her eyes bug out. She'd always known Libby had a good income from the Paragon Emporium, but she would never have guessed she had that much cash on hand at any given time. How would this knowledge affect Hiram's feelings toward her?

Hiram cleared his throat. "If you want to offer that as a loan to Cyrus, it might help him some. And I'd be willing to escort you in to town to fetch it if you decide to do that."

Libby's sweet smile beamed for Hiram. "Thank you. That's kind of you. I would certainly want an escort I could count on."

Trudy saw that ardent look in Hiram's eyes—almost the same intent look Ethan had for her when he moved in to kiss her. She gulped.

"Why don't I fetch Cyrus so you can ask him if he thinks that would help?"

★

Isabel cowered against the wall farthest from the four men in the kitchen and rubbed her sore wrist. Eli Button had bruised her when he took her outside. Now he slouched against the front window frame, watching the lane. Kenton and two of the cowboys lolled at the table, playing cards.

"What if he don't bring you your money by suppertime?" asked the one they called Buck.

"He'd better." Kenton glanced her way. "Get on with the cooking, girl. We're powerful hungry."

"Yeah," said Eli. "We ain't had no woman's cooking for weeks and weeks."

She moved along the wall, keeping her distance, until she reached the work area. It consisted of a rough bench at waist height and a small heating stove with a flat top. No oven. No dry sink—just a dishpan and a bucket of water with a tin dipper floating in it. Dirty dishes lay strewn on every flat surface.

She rolled up her sleeves. *This is just like at home. Fixing dinner for Papa.*

Even as she thought it, she knew it was a lie. This was nothing like home, and these men had nothing in common with her father. She blinked back tears and looked about in vain for an apron. If only she could go back to the big, airy kitchen at home and clean up the dirty dishes she'd left last night. Could Papa ever forgive her for her outburst? His face had been like stone today as he'd gazed at her across the yard.

He'd come this morning and then gone away for an hour or two. Why hadn't he returned with the money Uncle Kenton wanted? Had he truly tried to raise it without success? Or didn't he intend to pay? Didn't he care about her?

And Griffin Bane had been with him, of all the odd things. He and Hiram Dooley had accompanied her father. She wasn't sure what to make of that. One of the ruffians had said they observed more men at a distance. So Griffin's appearance didn't necessarily mean he cared about her. She suspected the ladies of the shooting club harbored stronger feelings for her than the blacksmith did. For once, she didn't care.

She opened a crock that sat on the floor beneath the bench. Wheat flour. Another held rolled oats. Methodically, she surveyed the jars and tins on the bench. Nothing fancy, but she could make a bean soup and biscuits. She set a pan of dry beans to soak. Lifting the heavy kettle made her wrist ache.

Behind her the men began to bicker over the card game. She looked at them, and one of the cowboys caught her glance and grinned. He winked with a leering eye. She shuddered and turned away.

How could Papa owe Uncle Kenton so much money? He was asking for a fortune. Papa had a lot of property, and he never seemed to lack for cash, but surely he didn't have that much. Suppose Uncle Kenton was lying?

She went to the stove and opened the door. Ashes and charcoal filled the bottom of the firebox.

"You ain't going to light a fire, are you?" asked Buck. "It's hot enough in here already."

True, the day promised to be a scorcher. The gloomy log house offered some shelter, and Isabel had found it much cooler inside than out when Eli Button had pushed her back through the door.

She straightened and looked over at the card players. "How else do you expect me to cook?"

Uncle Kenton dealt the dog-eared cards rapidly. "Leave her alone. I'm hungry."

"Well, make it a little fire," Buck muttered, picking up his hand.

"Ain't there a fire ring out back where Sammy cooks sometimes?"

"Shut up, Red. I don't want her outside where they can see her." Uncle Kenton leaned back and studied his cards.

The man with carroty hair scowled but said no more on the matter. She found only a few sticks of wood in the box by the stove. No one offered to fetch her any kindling. She cleared her throat.

"Would there be more firewood about?"

"In the lean-to." Kenton nodded toward the door at the back of the room. "Eli, go with her."

"Thought you wanted me to keep guard."

Kenton swore and shoved his chair back, scraping the floor. Isabel's pulse pounded. She shrank toward the back door.

"Go on," he snarled. "I'm right behind you. Let's have some of that pie you served me and your daddy."

She gulped. "I'd need mincemeat. Do you have—"

"No, we ain't got mincemeat. I shoulda had the boys raid your larder when they grabbed you. Get moving." He nodded toward the door.

Isabel turned and walked the three steps to the door made of weathered boards. She swung it open and peered into the lean-to. A stack of firewood on one side of the door reached to her waist. Straight ahead was daylight. She could see part of the corral, and a ways from the house, where the land sloped sharply upward, a dilapidated outhouse.

"Quit lollygaggin'."

She chose an armful of sticks from the woodpile and carried them past him, back into the kitchen. It would be a shame to heat up the place.

She dropped her load into the wood box and moved a crusty frying pan, a tin cup, a filthy towel, and a box of shotgun shells from the top of the stove to the workbench and knelt on the rough board floor. At least they had matches handy. When the kindling caught, she put a few sticks in and closed the stove door. The men ignored her as she bustled about to start a pot of coffee and get their dinner cooking.

At the back of the bench, she found a jug of molasses. A golden powder half filled a small, unmarked tin. When she sniffed it, her nose tickled. Ginger. She was halfway to a pan of gingerbread. Baking powder? Hmm. She poked about, setting dirty dishes into the dishpan. She'd probably have to wash those or the men wouldn't have plates enough to go around. She picked up the box of shotgun shells. Uncle Kenton apparently kept his supply of ammunition on a shelf beyond the table. If the boxes there were full, these men were prepared for a fight—or a siege.

"Hey, boss." Eli turned from the window. "Sammy's coming—"

The front door burst open. "Mr. Smith!"

"Right here, Sam." Uncle Kenton folded his cards and laid them facedown on the table. "What's the matter?"

"You know you told me and Chub to watch the hills out back?"

"Sure did. So why ain't you out there?"

"'Cause I seen people up there. With guns."

"Whyn't you come in the back door then?"

Sammy spit on the floor. "I didn't want to get shot at."

Uncle Kenton and the other two cowboys stood. "They's that close?" Red asked.

Sammy nodded. "Looked to me like they was sneaking closer. Wilfred's still out near the barn watching 'em, and Chub's out beside the wagon. I told them I'd come in and report to you."

"Those men out near the road are still there, too," Eli said from beside the window.

Kenton strode to his position and peered out. "You mean to tell me Cyrus ain't gone to get the money?"

"I don't know if he went or not," Eli said, "but there's somebody out there. I keep seein' 'em move."

Buck went to a corner and lifted his rifle. "Maybe the whole town is having another play party."

Isabel's heart leaped. Had the sheriff raised a posse to get her back? How many members of the Ladies' Shooting Club were out there right now, prepared to defend her? She surely would hate it if anyone got hurt helping her.

The men crowded around the one small window, all trying to get a better view. In the momentary silence, the fire in the stove crackled. Isabel jumped.

A stray thought took root in her mind. She glanced at the men with their backs to her. She reached across the workbench and opened the cartridge box. A half dozen shells stood inside it. She tucked them into the pocket of her skirt and closed the box.

"You think they've got us outgunned?" Eli sounded worried. Maybe he was thinking about the shooting match in the schoolyard.

Isabel tiptoed to the stove and opened the door. The men paid no attention. The fire had taken hold and had begun to burn down. She tossed a couple more sticks in.

"Uncle Kenton?"

"What do you want, girl?" He had a rifle in his hands now and was easing the front door open a crack.

"I need to use the necessary." She fingered the shells in her pocket and held her breath.

"What? Oh. Not now!"

Isabel swallowed hard. She thought of how little Millie Pooler's plaintive wail always got to her during school. "But I have to *go*, Uncle Kenton."

He turned and glared at her. "This ain't a good time, Isabel."

"I don't think I can wait." Her face flushed. Bad enough if it were true, but she'd never made a habit of lying.

"Sammy, take her out there. Watch yourself. And then resume your post."

Quickly, Isabel pulled out a handful of shotgun shells and tossed them into the firebox behind the cover of the stove door. She slammed it shut and stepped away.

"All right, let's move," Sammy said, waving his gun barrel toward the back door.

Gladly, Isabel scurried to the lean-to. When they'd left its cover and stepped into the open, she wondered if she'd done something wrong. Hiram Dooley had made it sound like you only had to drop the bullets into the stove and—

Behind them, gunfire erupted inside the house. Without looking back, Isabel lifted her skirt and ran for the outhouse.

★ CHAPTER 36 ★

Somebody's shooting! Let's go! Quick!" Ethan ducked low and ran toward the house with his rifle pointing at the front door. The stark terrain offered no cover. Footsteps thundered behind him as a dozen people followed. For a moment, it felt like his old army days, only now he was the officer leading the charge into battle.

Cyrus pounded past him on the lane.

"Mr. Fennel! Wait!"

"My daughter's in there!"

Fennel tore forward. Ethan was surprised the older man had such speed. Movement at the window distracted him, but someone behind him fired and broke the windowpane.

Cyrus slammed into the door and shoved on it, but it didn't open. He put his shoulder to it and rammed it again. The door flew open. Cyrus and Kenton stood face-to-face for an instant. Kenton raised his gun and fired. Cyrus let off a round as he staggered off the step. More shots came from within. Ethan leaped aside and flattened himself against the log wall beside the door.

Hiram and Doc Kincaid, with half a dozen other men behind them, stopped ten yards from the house and peppered it with bullets. Farther back, a cluster of women approached.

Hiram walked steadily forward, aiming his rifle at the front of the ranch house. They must be crazy, attacking like this. Didn't the British lose the whole country because they fought in the open and refused to skulk behind trees like Indians?

A few shots came from inside the house, but most of the gunfire came from his contingent. He looked around uneasily. What had happened to that cowpoke near the wagon? No one seemed to be crouched behind it now.

As the door opened and Cyrus went down, Hiram's hat flew off. He whirled toward the barn, his Sharps at his shoulder. Above them, through the cloud of gun smoke hovering over them, he saw a figure in the door of the hayloft. A heavyset man with a beard stood above the posse, taking aim at those below.

Hiram hated to use his rifle to harm another human being. He also hated to reveal his well-concealed shooting ability. But unless he acted quickly, one of his friends would likely be killed. They were sitting ducks for the sniper. He hesitated only an instant before he pulled the trigger. The man in the hayloft dropped his rifle. It fell to the ground below. He staggered back and disappeared into the dark loft.

Ethan held up his hands to stop the townsmen's shooting. Doc drew a bead and fired once more before he noticed the signal. The noise subsided. Cyrus lay still on the dirt at the bottom of the steps.

From a distance, Josiah Runnels shouted, "They're jumping out the back!" Several shots followed.

"Go ahead, Sheriff," Hiram called. "I'll cover the door."

Cautiously, Ethan took a quick peek around the doorjamb. Kenton Smith lay on his back just inside the door. Another man had crumpled beneath the window. Ethan couldn't see anyone else, but a thick haze of smoke obscured the room.

"Doc, tend to Cyrus." Ethan dove into the house, leading with his Colt. Eerie quiet buzzed around him.

From the doorway behind him, Hiram called, "All clear?"

"Reckon so." Ethan continued to scan the dim room.

"Art Tinen winged one of them that ran out the back door, and Doc says he hit one in here. The rest ran to their horses and got away clean."

Ethan jerked his head toward the man lying beneath the window. "That'd be Doc's target, I guess."

Hiram stepped over to the inert form and stooped to pick up the fallen man's weapon. "That's the fella I got into it with at Bitsy's."

"Yup. Eli Button." Ethan lifted his hat and wiped the sweat from his brow with his sleeve. "Where's Isabel? Did they take her?"

"Nobody's seen her. She wasn't with them when they ran."

Ethan stared at him. "That's crazy. We saw her an hour ago. She was in here with them."

"Maybe she's still in here."

Ethan looked around again. "Miss Fennel?"

No answer. The house appeared to have only one large room with a loft over part of it. He crossed to another door and opened it. The lean-to held a woodpile and a few tools. "All right, get a couple of people in here to search the loft. She could be tied up in a corner. You don't suppose she got away from them and ran?"

"Don't see how she could have," Hiram said. "We had the place surrounded."

Ethan called again, "Miss Fennel?" He stepped out into the lean-to. No one cowered behind the woodpile. Josiah, Augie, and several of the shooting club members had fanned out over the barnyard and corral. Ethan called to Augie, "Miss Fennel's not in here. Search that barn and the bunkhouse." He walked back through the house, stepped over Smith's body, and went out the front door.

Doc Kincaid and Bitsy knelt beside Cyrus, while Rose stood by, knotting her handkerchief. Ethan walked over to them.

"How is he, Doc?"

Kincaid glanced up at him. "I'm losing him."

Ethan grimaced. They were lucky no one else had been killed, the way things had erupted.

Augie came out of the barn and crossed the yard. "Funniest thing, Sheriff. I found a rifle lying on the ground in front of the barn, and up in the hayloft there's a dead cowpoke shot in the heart."

Ethan eyed the front of the barn. "Somebody must have shot him through that door to the loft."

"That's what I figure," Augie said. "Don't know who did it, though. Oh, and Art Tinen says he got a shot at that Sterling fella when he grabbed a horse out of the corral. Thinks he may have nicked him, but he got through our lines."

Ethan scratched the back of his neck. The sun beat down on them. "Go in and help Hiram tear this house apart. Isabel's got to be here someplace. We saw her less than an hour ago."

Kincaid sat back on his heels and looked soberly at Ethan. "He's gone, Sheriff."

Ethan let his shoulders sag. He'd handled everything wrong today. He should have let Cyrus scramble for the money and borrow what he could from Libby and the other business owners.

Josiah came tearing around the corner of the house. "Doc, there's a wounded man out back."

"One of Kenton's men?" Ethan asked.

"Yup. Looks like he fell off his horse and the others left him."

Dr. Kincaid stood and reached for his bag. "There's nothing more I can do here." He followed Josiah.

Ethan met Hiram's gaze and sank back against the wall. "Don't know what else we could have done when they started shooting in here."

Hiram's brow furrowed. He looked down at Kenton's body and over at Button. "That was an odd thing. All our people were holding back. Who started the shooting?"

Ethan shook his head slowly. "I thought some of our people got too close. Around back, you know? Where we couldn't see them."

Hiram shook his head. "Augie said they heard shooting here before they moved in. According to him, it sounded like the first shots were inside the house. The fellows around back thought you'd started something out front."

Ethan closed his eyes. Had he moved in too fast? Was it his fault that lives had been lost?

Lord, how could I have been so wrong? Now we've lost Cyrus and Isabel both. Those no-accounts must have gotten her out of here—don't ask me how. Show me what to do now, Lord, 'cause I'm not much good on my own.

No shots had sounded for a good ten minutes. Isabel had stopped shaking and had almost stopped noticing the stench of the privy.

Maybe it was safe to go out now. She reached for the rusty steel hook that held the outhouse door shut and pushed it out of the staple. Slowly she opened the door an inch and peered out.

Dr. Kincaid and Josiah Runnels were walking across the overgrown barnyard behind the ranch house. She opened the door farther, and the hinges creaked.

The men swung toward her, Josiah, bringing his gun around to point at her. The doctor's face changed from surprise to concern, and he hurried toward her.

"Miss Fennel? Is that you?"

She opened the door wider. "Yes. Is it safe to come out now?"

"Yes ma'am." He offered his hand as she stepped down from the little shack.

"Thank you." She stumbled a little, and he steadied her.

Josiah had lowered his gun but still stared at her. "Should I tell the folks you're all right, miss?"

Isabel managed a shaky smile. Josiah had been one of her students not so long ago. "Yes, please. I'm fine."

He turned without another word and ran toward the ranch house.

Isabel looked up into Dr. Kincaid's somber blue eyes. "Is my father all right? I heard a lot of shooting."

The doctor glanced uneasily back toward the house. "Ma'am, there was a big dustup, and. . ." He hesitated, and she studied his face. "I'm afraid the news is not good."

"Papa's been shot?"

"Yes."

"Then why aren't you with him? Is it serious?" The regret in his eyes told her more than she wanted to know. "Oh no. He's not—Tell me, Doctor. Is my father dead?"

Before he could speak, Josiah's whoop reached them. "She's found! Sheriff, Miss Fennel's found!"

Kincaid's quiet words sliced through her heart. "I'm afraid so, ma'am. I'm so very sorry."

Isabel reached for him, her head swimming. She clutched at his neat black vest as her knees buckled.

★ CHAPTER 37 ★

Hiram and Ethan met Josiah at the ranch house steps. Hiram had just spread a blanket over Cyrus's still body.

"Is she alive?" Ethan asked.

"Yeah, she's fine," Josiah said, his eyes glittering. "Doc and I walked out back and saw her coming out of the outhouse. Funniest thing—but she's right pert."

Ethan looked at Hiram. "She'll want to see her pa."

Hiram searched for his sister and saw her talking quietly with Libby, Bitsy, and Augie. "I'll get Trudy."

"Good. And Josiah. . ." Ethan turned back to the freighter's son. "Can you bring your wagon down here? We'll need to carry the bodies back to town. Tell your pa, too."

Hiram strode quickly to Trudy's side. "Miss Isabel might need you ladies when she finds out about her father."

Trudy and Libby took a hasty leave of the Moores. As they walked toward the steps, Dr. Kincaid rounded the corner of the house, carrying Isabel in his arms. Her gray skirts flapped about his legs as he bore her toward them, and her head lolled against his chest.

"Is she all right?" Trudy ran forward, and Hiram followed. Ethan and a dozen others joined them as they clustered around the doctor.

"She's had a shock. I need a place to put her down where she can rest." Kincaid caught Trudy's gaze. "Perhaps you could attend to her?"

"Yes, certainly. Mrs. Adams can help me."

"Should I take her inside?"

Ethan shook his head. "I don't think so, Doc. Why don't you lay her down here by the house? Josiah will bring a wagon down in a minute."

Kincaid stooped and lowered Isabel gently to earth.

"Can we get a blanket?" Libby asked. "What about a pillow?"

Ethan looked uneasily toward the house. They'd moved Cyrus off the steps, but Kenton's boots were visible through the doorway. "I'm not sure that's a good idea, ma'am."

"I'll get them." Hiram ran for the steps. He hopped over Kenton's body and looked around. On the bunk against the side wall he found one more musty wool blanket but no pillow. He carried it outside, shook it, and walked over to Libby. "This is all I could find."

"Thank you. We'll make do." She squinted at his battered hat. "Are you all right?"

"Yes ma'am. I'm fine."

She nodded soberly, and he wondered if she knew about the shooter in the barn.

"There's a hole in your hat brim," she said quietly.

He inhaled deeply. He'd noticed that hole when he retrieved his hat after the gunfire had ceased. Not much he could do about it. "Yes ma'am. I gave thanks to the Almighty."

"So did I," she said.

"Hey, Doc?" Arthur Tinen Jr. strode over to the knot of people, and Kincaid looked up at him.

"Yes?"

"That fella out back. . ."

Kincaid grimaced. "I confess I forgot about him. I'll come right away."

He started to stand, but Arthur put his hand on the doctor's shoulder. "No need."

Kincaid sighed. "I'm sorry."

Ethan stood. "It's all right, Doc. You need to see to Miss Fennel now. I'll go take a look at the cowpoke, and you can check him over later and do what you have to do."

Hiram looked from the huddle around Isabel to Ethan's retreating back and decided to tag after him. He followed Ethan and Art behind the house and out to the far edge of the corral, where the ground sloped up sharply into the scrub pines.

Griffin Bane stood over the body, his face set in grim lines and his right arm cradled in a sling improvised from Annie Harper's paisley shawl.

"He's a goner, Ethan," Griff said as they approached. "Nothing you can do for him."

"Would it have helped if the doctor got to him?"

"Doubt it." Griffin looked down at the body. "I met this fella once, in the Nugget."

"Oh?" Ethan asked. "Does he have a name?"

"Red. On account of his hair, I reckon."

"Too bad we didn't catch any of them alive," Hiram said.

"Yeah." Ethan pushed his hat back. "We might have trouble identifying some of these fellas. We don't even know most of their names, and some of them we do know are false."

Hiram looked down at the dead man's face. "Guess you'll have to write some more letters before Doc can make out all the death certificates."

Ethan knelt and gingerly checked the man's pockets but found only a few extra cartridges, a nickel, and a pocketknife. "Hiram, would you ask Josiah to pick this one up after he gets Kenton and Button?"

"Sure. What about Cyrus?"

"He oughta ride in a different wagon from the others, I'd think."

"That's fittin'," Griff said.

Isabel moaned and put her hand to her aching temple. "What happened?"

"You swooned, dear," Libby said, "but you'll be all right. Dr. Kincaid has been attending you."

Dr. Kincaid. The privy. Papa.

Isabel struggled to sit up, and Trudy got her arm beneath her and gave her a boost. Her head ached. Isabel looked around and spotted a form lying by the steps that was covered with a dirty woolen blanket. Her stomach clenched. "That's Papa, isn't it?"

"Yes dear," Libby said. "I'm so sorry."

The men within earshot ducked their heads and removed their hats.

Libby reached both hands toward Isabel. "Come sit in the wagon and let Dr. Kincaid examine you."

"I want to see Papa." Tears gushed from Isabel's eyes, and she fumbled in her pocket for her handkerchief but found only a shotgun shell she'd missed when loading the stove. She stared down at it, her innards still swirling. Had her bid for freedom sparked a fatal shootout?

Libby put her arms around her. "There, now. Maybe you'd best wait until. . ." She glanced up at Hiram, who stood nearby. "Until the men take him home and. . .and clean him up, dear."

"No." Isabel found the hankie in her other pocket and held it to her eyes. "Please. Let me see him now."

With Dr. Kincaid on her left and Libby on her right, she tottered to the doorstep.

"Are you certain you're ready for this?" the doctor asked.

"I'm sure."

Kincaid looked toward Hiram. "Would you, Mr. Dooley?"

Hiram stepped forward, stooped, and grasped a corner of the blanket. He pulled it back a few inches, and Isabel could see her father's graying hair. Hiram shot a glance at the doctor. Kincaid arched his eyebrows and nodded, though he tightened his hold on Isabel's arm. Hiram laid the blanket back as far as her father's waist.

Blood drenched the front of Cyrus's clothing. His head was thrown back, his eyes shut. Isabel's lips trembled as she viewed him, so unnaturally still.

"Papa," she whispered. She plucked at her skirts and lifted them a few inches so she could kneel beside him. She glanced toward the open doorway of the house. A man's feet in worn boots lay just within. "Is that. . .Uncle Kenton?"

"Yes ma'am," the doctor said softly. "He's left this world as well."

She shivered.

Dr. Kincaid quickly wrapped his arm around her waist. A vague uneasiness swept over her. No man had ever touched her in so personal a manner. . .not until the vile cowboys, anyway. "Come, Miss Fennel. I think you've seen enough. You need to sit down and take some water. I want to check your pulse as well."

He pulled her gently toward the nearest wagon, and she let him guide her. He kept his arm about her, and the sensation was not unpleasant, though the back of her bodice was damp with perspiration where his arm encircled her. Josiah lowered the tailgate. Isabel wobbled a bit, and Dr. Kincaid braced her with his other arm.

"All right?"

She sized up the wagon bed. It seemed impossibly high. "I don't think I. . ."

"Allow me." Dr. Kincaid bent and lifted her, depositing her on the back of the wagon.

"Thank you." Isabel shut her eyes for a moment then opened them.

"I fear you've overtaxed yourself." The doctor took out his pocket watch and reached for her wrist.

"I shall be fine." Isabel looked over at her father as the doctor checked her pulse. Hiram had laid the blanket back over the body. She sucked in a breath and looked at the doctor instead. His blond hair gleamed in the brilliant sunlight.

Trudy moved in with an open canteen. "Here, Isabel. This is probably warm, but it will do you good."

Her hand shook as she took it and tipped it up. How many people had drunk from it before her? As she lowered the canteen, she eyed it critically. "This is Papa's."

"Is it?" Trudy asked.

"Yes." She took another swallow then handed it to her friend.

Kincaid looked around. "Where's Runnels? We need to put this wagon in the shade."

"I'll get him," Trudy said. "There's a strip of shade yonder, by the barn."

Libby climbed in over the wagon seat and came to sit beside Isabel. Dr. Kincaid looked into Isabel's eyes for a moment, frowning.

"Why don't you lie down and rest, Miss Fennel?" he asked as he put away his watch.

Isabel started to protest, but his suggestion made sense. From out of nowhere, Annie and Bitsy appeared beside the wagon and offered a shawl and a horse blanket. Libby arranged them so that Isabel could have a cushion for her head. She soaked a handkerchief in warm water from the canteen and dabbed at Isabel's forehead. It felt good, and Isabel closed her eyes.

"That's it," the doctor said in his melodious voice. "Try to rest. I have some other duties I must see to, but Mrs. Adams will stay with you. I'll come back and examine you again before you leave."

Leave? Where would she go? She pulled in a breath, fighting panic.

"What else you want done, Sheriff?"

Isabel's eyes flew open at the shout. That sounded like Micah Landry. When had he arrived? Was the entire town here? She must have slept, but she was roasting. The rays of sun seared through her cotton blouse. She wanted to be at home, in her cool, wallpapered bedroom, on the double feather bed. But then she'd have to listen to the empty house.

"They're going to move the wagon," Libby said. A few moments later, the wheels creaked, and they lurched several yards. Blessed shade crept over Isabel, and she shivered.

"Better?" asked Libby.

"Yes." She heard Ethan say something about the livestock. She would have to think of Papa's cattle, too. A little moan escaped her lips.

"It's all right, dear. You're going to be all right." Libby leaned over her.

"Papa. . ."

"Yes. He's gone."

Isabel puffed out a breath and shut her eyes again.

"I'll help you in any way I can," Libby said softly.

"It's so hot."

"We'll take you back to town soon."

"What happened?" Isabel asked. "Who killed him?"

After a short pause, Libby drew a deep breath. "Your father confronted Mr. Smith. It seems they shot each other." She blotted Isabel's brow again with the handkerchief.

"What will they do with him now?"

"Your father?" Libby touched her shoulder gently. "Shall we carry him into town, or do you wish to have him laid out at the ranch?"

Isabel shuddered. "I. . .don't know."

"If you'd like, the men can take him to the livery stable. Mr. Bane has offered to help care for him. Mr. Dooley will build a coffin, and they'll fix him up nicely for the funeral."

Isabel nodded. "I suppose that's best. Put him in here with me. I want to ride with him."

Libby squeezed her hand. "I'm so sorry, dear Isabel. So very sorry."

"Papa wasn't a bad man."

"No. No, he wasn't." Libby set her jaw and nodded firmly. "He came here to get you away from those evil men. He loved you very much."

"Our men at the ranch will want to see him."

"We'll pass by your home on the way to town. We can send a rider ahead to tell them. If they want, they can accompany the. . . the body to the livery stable."

"Good. I think they'd want to help get him ready." Isabel pressed her lips together. As dry as she felt, a new flood of tears sheeted down her cheeks.

Libby foraged in her pockets but came up empty.

"Will this help?"

At Hiram's soft inquiry, Libby turned. He stood beside the wagon offering a folded bandanna. She took it and held out the faded, soft square to Isabel.

"Th–thank you."

"The doctor's coming back," Hiram said.

Isabel sat up slowly. Libby reached to help her inch over to the tailgate. Trudy hovered on the other side and reached to help. Isabel let her feet hang over the edge of the wagon.

The physician had almost reached them when Rose ran out from a knot of people near the house, carrying her parasol.

"Doctor, my ears are still ringing from all that shooting."

Kincaid paused and eyed her pensively. "I'm sorry, Mrs. Caplinger. It will pass after a time."

Trudy rolled her eyes skyward and called, "Rose, Dr. Kincaid needs to tend to Miss Fennel."

"But I can barely hear you." Rose's face crumpled up. "Doctor, you don't think it could be permanent, do you?"

Kincaid shook his head. "I doubt it, ma'am. You weren't close to the gunfire. I expect you'll be fine by evening, if not before." He walked the last few yards to the wagon.

"I told her not to come," Trudy muttered. "But no, she heard about the posse and insisted on riding along."

Rose stood for a moment with her mouth pursed, but when the doctor paid her no more attention, she swung about and stalked back to the shade with the fringe on her shawl fluttering.

The doctor stood facing Isabel. "I'm glad to see you're feeling better, Miss Fennel. I couldn't see that you had any wounds."

"No. My wrist aches, but I think that's the only thing wrong." She shuddered, and Libby patted her shoulder again. So very much was wrong, after all.

"Let me see." Kincaid took her left hand gently.

Isabel winced. "It's quite tender. That Button man twisted it."

"I'm sorry. May I unfasten this cuff?"

Inexplicably, she found herself blushing. "I can do it." She fumbled with the button and extended her arm again.

He bent over her hand and pushed the sleeve up a few inches. "Mmm. I see the redness. A little swelling." He probed the wrist joint. "Turn your palm up, please. Uh-huh. Does that hurt?"

"No more than before."

"And when you make a fist?"

She tried it. "Yes, that hurts."

He felt the joint again. "I don't think anything is broken, but you should take it easy for a few days. It might help to wrap your wrist to support it for a day or two. Would you like me to bandage it for you?"

"No, thank you. I'm sure it will heal." She rubbed the sorest spot with her fingertips. "Doctor. . ."

"Yes?" Kincaid looked gravely into her eyes.

"Did you examine my father's body?"

"Yes ma'am."

"Could you please tell me. . .anything?"

Kincaid cleared his throat. "He died swiftly. One fatal wound to his heart."

She nodded. "He didn't suffer, then?"

"I think not. It was nearly instantaneous for both of them."

"Both—" Isabel glanced at Libby then back to the doctor. "You mean my uncle, don't you?"

He nodded. "The sheriff was right behind your father. As near as we can tell, Smith pulled the trigger as he opened the door, and your father returned fire. It was the last act for both of them."

"I heard someone say the rest of his men got away."

"Three were shot down. The others—three more, we think—escaped."

Isabel nodded, mentally counting the men she'd seen hulking about the ranch.

"Which ones?"

"One man was killed by a shot through the window. I believe he's the one who brought you outside when your father insisted on seeing you."

Kincaid avoided looking directly at her as he spoke. Isabel wondered if he'd taken part in the shootout, but she didn't ask. He was one of the best marksmen in town. Perhaps she would ask Libby sometime. Not now. It might be best if she didn't know who fired the fatal bullets.

"The other dead men are a large, heavy man with a beard and a red headed man."

"He was in the house when Papa and the others came. They were playing poker—Uncle Kenton, Red, and Buck—while Button kept watch at the window. I only saw the others from a distance."

"The one called Buck must have gotten away."

"Yes." Isabel gazed toward the ranch house and the mountains beyond.

"I think you should rest some more, ma'am," Kincaid said. "Is there anyone at home who can stay with you tonight?"

"No, I . . ."

"She can stay with me," Libby said. "Isabel stayed at my home last night, and I'd be delighted to have her again. We can stop briefly at her father's ranch on the way to town, and she can pick up a few things."

Isabel caught her breath. Did she want to do that? She certainly didn't want to stay alone at the ranch. She exhaled in a sigh. "Thank you. I believe I'd like that if it's not too much trouble."

"No trouble at all." Libby squeezed her shoulders gently. "You may stay as long as you like."

"Poor Papa." Isabel pushed back a loose wisp of her hair. "I wasn't there to fix his breakfast this morning."

★ CHAPTER 38 ★

The motley procession started for Fergus. The Harpers' wagon pulled out first, loaded with townspeople. Libby sat in the back of Josiah Runnels's wagon with Isabel and the Bentons. They'd persuaded Isabel to let Arthur Tinen Jr. transport her father's body in the wagon behind them. Libby was glad she didn't have to sit close to the corpse, but she would have if Isabel had insisted. Hiram and Trudy rode their horses alongside them. Ethan rode at the head of the procession with some of the other men. The wagon bearing Kenton and his dead ranch hands followed several yards behind.

Within a mile of the Fennel ranch, several riders galloped toward them. Cyrus's men paused to speak to the sheriff then rode on back and clustered their horses around the wagon in which Isabel rode.

The oldest of the cowboys lifted his hat and eyed her sorrowfully. "Is it true, Miss Isabel? Is your father dead?"

"Yes Brady. I'm having him laid out at the livery in town, where folks can stop in and see him before the funeral. I'll be stopping at home for a minute to pack a few things. I'm staying in town tonight with Mrs. Adams."

Brady touched the brim of his hat. "All right, miss. If you need anything, you let us know. The boys and I will go into town and make sure they tend to your papa right."

"Thank you."

Brady turned his horse and trotted back to the wagon behind them. He and the cowboys gazed into the bed then fell in behind.

At the lane to the Fennel ranch, Josiah turned in. His father and Arthur continued on, driving their grim burdens toward Fergus.

Ethan called to the freighter, "We'll be just a few minutes, Oscar. Head for the livery, and I'll be along before you get there."

Most of the townspeople went on, but Ethan and the Dooleys followed Josiah's wagon to the Fennel house.

Apphia Benton slid toward the back of the wagon. "My dear, I can go in with you and help you gather your things."

"Thank you." Isabel climbed down.

The pastor got out of the wagon, too. Libby stayed put and watched the three go into the house. Ethan and the Dooleys dismounted and walked their horses over close to the wagon.

Ethan said, "We thought maybe we'd ought to have a little discussion while Miss Isabel's inside."

"What about?" Libby asked.

"Her uncle Kenton."

"What about him?"

Ethan pushed his hat back and looked around at them. "Hiram, Trudy. . ." He glanced toward the wagon. "You know about this, too, Miz Adams."

Libby gathered her skirts and hopped to the ground. Josiah had climbed from the wagon seat and was checking his team's harness. Libby glanced at him and walked a few steps away with the others.

Ethan scratched his jaw. "The way I see it, we four are the only ones besides Isabel who know about that metal box her daddy buried behind the barn."

"Metal box?" Libby looked quickly from one face to another. "He buried a box?"

Trudy shrugged. "You knew he buried *something*. Isabel told you."

"Yes, of course, but I didn't realize you'd learned what it was."

"We went and dug it up this morning when Cyrus got the note and tore off," Trudy said. "When we got to his ranch, he wasn't here, so we decided to settle the question of what he'd buried."

"And you uncovered a can?" Libby asked.

Ethan nodded. "A tin like crackers and things come in. There's a pouch of coins in it and a wanted poster showing Kenton Smith and Mary Fennel—under different names."

Libby opened her mouth then closed it. Her brain whirled as she tried to make sense of that.

Trudy squeezed her arm. "Isabel's confided in you more than anyone else in town. You're probably her best friend right now. This morning we three rode out and met Cyrus and told him we'd dug up his secret. And he told us some shocking bits of family history."

"Isabel's not his daughter," Libby said with sudden certainty.

They all stared at her.

"How did you know that?" Trudy asked.

Libby puffed out a breath. "Something happened many years ago—it's not important what—but Mary Fennel said something to me I've never forgotten. She said Cyrus wanted a child of his own."

"That fits." Ethan gritted his teeth and looked toward the ranch house.

Hiram reached down and plucked a grass stem and stuck the end in his mouth.

"So do we all agree that it wouldn't do Isabel any good to know that?" Trudy asked. "Cyrus said Kenton didn't know she was his daughter."

"And Isabel certainly didn't know," Libby said. "It explains a lot of things, though. Why Cyrus has acted so strangely, and why he let Kenton stay on his land."

"Kenton was blackmailing him," Ethan said. "When he was arrested for robbery and put in prison, Mary took off with Cyrus—and the loot they'd collected from Kenton's robberies. Sounds like she may have helped him in some of those crimes. When Kenton was released, he tracked them out here. He wanted his share, and Cyrus didn't have it. That's why Kenton grabbed Isabel—to put pressure on Cyrus."

Libby's heart ached at the sordid sadness of it. "You mean. . . they weren't legally married."

Trudy winced and nodded.

"I never would have guessed Mary could take part in anything like that."

"Well, we've only Cy's word and an old wanted poster," Ethan said. "But why would he lie about something like that?"

Trudy straightened her shoulders. "Since Kenton and Cyrus are both dead, why not let this secret die, too? Why should we give Isabel more reason to grieve?"

Hiram nodded. He arched his eyebrows at Ethan.

"But if they were criminals. . ." Ethan looked around at his friends.

Trudy scowled at him. "All the criminals are dead, Ethan, except for the three cowpokes that escaped this morning. And we don't know that they did anything but follow their boss's orders."

Ethan sucked air in between his teeth. "I guess. But I'm supposed to uphold the law."

"And so you do, sweetheart." Trudy slipped her hand through the crook of his arm. "It's a shame about Cyrus, but I suspect the other men who were killed have a lot of dark deeds in their past."

"One of the others is hurting, thanks to you," Hiram said.

Ethan eyed him testily. "We should have gone after them."

"No," Libby said. "The most important thing was finding Isabel. By the time we knew she was safe, those cowpokes were halfway to Nampa."

"I expect you're right." Ethan sighed. "All right. I'll go along with you, though I'm not sure it's the best thing to do. But I'm telegraphing the authorities in Boise and Nampa when we get back to town."

"Not a bad idea," Hiram said.

"Libby, you okay with that?" Trudy looked to her friend with arched brows.

Libby spread her hands. "At this point, I'll do anything that will help Isabel, so long as we don't have to lie to her. She'll be more at peace burying Cyrus if she goes on believing he's her father."

Trudy gazed up into Ethan's face. "I feel the same way. At least. . .she'd be *less* at peace if she knew who her real papa was."

Ethan rubbed the back of his neck. "All right."

Hiram slapped him on the back. "There you go."

Trudy leaned close to her brother's face and said sternly, "But this is something none of us four can ever tell anyone, and we'd do best not even to talk about it amongst ourselves ever again. As far as we know, well. . .we don't. That is, we don't know anything."

"Agreed," Libby said quickly.

The door to the house opened, and Pastor Benton emerged carrying a valise.

"The ladies will be right out. Miss Fennel wanted to tend to a few things in the kitchen."

"Let me take that bag." Ethan took the valise and hefted it into Josiah's wagon.

As Libby turned to follow, she darted a glance at Hiram. Despite the day's grim events, he gave the appearance of a man at peace. He met her gaze, and just before he turned toward the hitching rail, she could have sworn he winked at her.

★ CHAPTER 39 ★

Ethan climbed the stairs at the back of the emporium building before seven the next morning and knocked on the door to Libby's apartment. In spite of the early hour, Libby greeted him pleasantly.

"Good morning, Sheriff! Can I help you?"

"I wondered if Miss Fennel is up. I'd like to speak to her about the time she was held hostage if she's feeling up to it."

"Why, yes." Libby stepped back to give him entry to her kitchen. "We just finished breakfast. I need to go downstairs and prepare to open the store, but perhaps you'd like to interview her here. There's some coffee on the stove, and it's quiet here. No one will bother you."

"Thank you. . .if you think. . ." He looked around cautiously. It felt a little odd, standing in an unmarried woman's home. Almost as awkward as the first time he went into the Nugget.

Libby smiled, and he suspected his ears had turned red. "I see nothing wrong with conducting official business in a friend's kitchen. And I'll be only a few yards away, after all."

He couldn't argue with that. He nodded, and she hastened into the next room.

Ten minutes later, he and Isabel sat across from each other at the little maple table. Sun streamed in through the eyelet curtains at the window on the back of the kitchen. The excellent coffee and the occasional quiet sounds of Libby moving about in the store below took away all Ethan's apprehension.

"You say the men talked some amongst themselves while you

were their hostage. Can you tell me what they said?"

Isabel set her cup down and frowned. "Let me see. . . . I recall Uncle Kenton talking to the man they call Sterling. That was before Papa showed up the first time, when he came alone."

Ethan leaned forward. "What did they say?"

"It was something about a piece of land that they'd wanted to get for free. I wondered at the time if they were talking about the Peart property."

"Maybe so."

Isabel took a sip of her coffee. "Uncle Kenton said something like, 'Well, it's too bad that plan didn't work. That sheriff—'" She broke off and set the cup down, not meeting his gaze. "I'm sorry."

Ethan smiled. "It's all right, ma'am. I already know Smith didn't like me much, nor Wilfred Sterling either."

She shrugged and gave a little cough. "Well, if you must know, he said you might be smarter than he'd given you credit for."

"Do tell." Ethan sat back, rather pleased with her revelation.

"That was about the time I gathered they were demanding a ransom from my father." Her forehead wrinkled, and she picked up her spoon. "Why would my uncle demand a ransom? Did my father give you any idea?"

Ethan rose and got the coffeepot, though he didn't need more coffee. He poured a small amount into his cup. "Would you like more?"

"No, thank you."

He set the pot back on the stovetop and sat down again. "Miss Fennel, I was with your father when he first learned you'd been kidnapped."

"You were?"

"Yes. Hiram Dooley was there, too, at the Wells Fargo office. Someone tossed a rock wrapped in a note through the window. Your pa took off. Hiram and I read the note and rode off after him. But we had to stop and saddle up, and Trudy joined us."

She raised her pale eyebrows.

"We. . .uh. . .met him coming back from the Martin place. He'd been out there and talked to Mr. Smith."

"Yes, he came alone that first time, and Uncle Kenton told him to go and get some money and to come back with it by sundown."

She shivered. "I confess I didn't take to my uncle when I first met him, but I had no inkling he would do violence to our family."

"You know he had been in prison, I believe."

"Papa told me. But still. . ."

Ethan sipped his coffee while thinking through what he knew and what he could reveal. "Well ma'am, I think it's obvious that when Mr. Smith was released from jail, he didn't give up his criminal ways. He may have pressured your father into giving him a place to live and then gathered some of the no-accounts he knew around him."

"His ranch hands? I suppose you're right. They could all be felons he met while in prison. And he might have seen Papa as an easy way to get some money, rather than earning it."

"Less risky than robbing a bank, or so it might seem. Of course, in the end. . ." Ethan shrugged.

"I wonder if he was jealous of Papa's success."

Ethan decided his best course was to avoid talking about money where Kenton and Cyrus were concerned, so he sipped his coffee without answering. A knock at the kitchen door startled him. Isabel caught her breath and looked to him expectantly. Ethan rose and walked to the door. He opened it and found Phineas Benton and his wife on the landing outside.

"Reverend."

"Sheriff. Mrs. Adams told us you were here. We wondered if Miss Fennel was up to discussing funeral arrangements for her father."

Ethan looked over his shoulder toward Isabel. "Ma'am, the parson and Mrs. Benton are here."

Isabel rose and came to the door. "Thank you for coming, Pastor."

The Bentons entered, and she accepted Apphia's embrace.

"Libby said we could sit up here with you and talk about your Papa's service if you're up to it." Apphia drew back and appraised Isabel. "Did you sleep last night, dear?"

"Not much. I did drop off toward dawn."

Ethan reached for his hat. "I'll get going, but please feel free to call on me if you need anything, Miss Fennel."

"Thank you, Sheriff."

He went out the door and down the back stairs. Isabel seemed to accept his train of thought about her so-called uncle's motives, and he was glad she hadn't mentioned the hole behind the barn. At some point he'd have to retrieve the money for her, but that could come later. Maybe he could arrange it somehow so that she received it as part of Cyrus's estate, and its source could remain secret.

Isabel prepared a light luncheon for herself and Libby. It was the least she could do for her hostess. To her surprise, when they sat down together, she found her appetite had returned.

"That's a very good red flannel hash you've made," Libby said with a smile. "Thank you. I don't usually take time for a hot meal at noon."

"The air is cooler today, and I thought it might taste good. After all, you've done so much for me."

"Think nothing of it." Libby sliced off a bite of leftover chicken. "Did you have a good visit with the Bentons?"

"Yes, I...we've decided to hold the service in the church."

"I think that's wise," Libby said. "If it rains, or even if it doesn't—it's been so hot lately—it will be nice to be under cover."

Isabel detailed the plans they'd made for the service while they ate. When she'd finished, Libby stood.

"Forgive me for running out so soon, dear. I like to get back to the store quickly and let Florence go home for her dinner. Is there anything I can do for you before I leave you again?"

"No, I think I'll take a nap," Isabel said. "I fear I didn't sleep much last night."

"I'm sure it will do you good. Thank you for the delicious meal." Libby started to gather her dishes.

"Oh, just leave those. I'll take care of them."

Libby had hardly gone down the stairs when a knock came at the kitchen door. Isabel jumped and hurried to open the door. Dr. Kincaid stood on the landing, holding his black bag and smiling.

"It's good to see you looking so well, Miss Fennel. May I come in? Mrs. Adams said I would find you here."

"Why, yes, Doctor." Isabel stepped back and let him enter.

He removed his hat and stood looking at her expectantly.

"Oh, let me take that." As she reached for it, he smiled down at her, and Isabel felt suddenly at sea. She'd never been alone with such an attractive man. A hint of guilt buzzed about her mind, like a horsefly zipping in and leaving, only to return a moment later. Was it wrong to think a man pleasant to look at or listen to? She turned away and carefully placed his hat on a rack near the door.

"I shan't take long," Dr. Kincaid said. "I'd like to count your pulse and respirations if you don't mind, and ask you a few questions."

"Oh, of course." Isabel felt her cheeks flush. "Would you like to come into the parlor?" Now, why did she ask that? Surely the physician could listen to her heartbeat just as well in the kitchen.

"Thank you."

He didn't seem to think it odd, so she led him into Libby's parlor.

"Won't you sit down?" She took one of the straight chairs near the window.

He set his bag on the sofa and opened it. "I'll stand. How do you feel today?"

"Quite well, thank you."

"I'm sure yesterday was trying."

She nodded and lowered her gaze. "I met with Mr. and Mrs. Benton to plan Papa's funeral."

"Ah. And when is that to be?" He took a stethoscope from his bag and hung it about his neck.

"Tomorrow. The pastor thought it not wise to wait longer."

"I see."

She looked down at the carpet, feeling a bit queasy. Neither of them spoke of the heat that made the hasty service necessary. "I'm still. . .getting used to the idea that Papa is gone."

"Shall you stay here with Mrs. Adams?"

"For a while, I think. She's invited me to remain with her indefinitely, and I've decided to stay a few more days. I don't wish to impose on her, but—"

"I'm sure she finds your company stimulating." He took out his watch and approached her. "May I?"

She held up her wrist, and he took it gently, focusing on the timepiece.

"Your pulse is a bit rapid and thready. You haven't felt dizzy, have you?"

"No, but. . .when I think of all that happened yesterday. . ."

"Of course."

She didn't look at him. The touch of his warm hand contributed to the frantic pace of her heartbeat, she was sure.

He lowered her hand to her lap and stood back a bit. "Now, if you'll just breathe normally, I shall count your respiration."

Again she sought something else to look at. His compassionate blue eyes could make a woman think all sorts of things. Just the concept brought the flush to her cheeks again. *Oh dear, this will never do. He'll think I'm ill when I'm merely behaving like a schoolgirl—swooning over an attractive man. The idea!*

"Miss Fennel?"

She jumped. "Yes?"

"How was your sleep last night?"

"Fragmented, I fear."

"I'm a bit concerned. Do you have a strong constitution?"

"Certainly, under normal circumstances."

He nodded thoughtfully. "I'd like to prescribe a tonic for you."

She straightened her back, wondering whether she ought to protest that she was fine.

"I assure you it's mild, but it will help you sleep. Take it just at bedtime. And if you wish to lie down this afternoon, take a spoonful then, as well. I know it's difficult to keep the mind from racing when you've had a shock. The memory constantly replays the unfortunate events and the tragedy that ensued."

"Why, yes. That's exactly how it was." She looked into his eyes. They radiated a serene kindness.

"And how is your left wrist? Still sore?"

"A little, but it's much better today, thank you."

"I'm glad to hear it." Dr. Kincaid sat down on the sofa, sliding his bag over a few inches. "Do you plan to return to your teaching post?"

She blinked at him, surprised at the inquiry. "I hadn't considered not doing so."

"And when does the next term begin?"

"In about three weeks. We'll have a two-month summer term,

then a break of three weeks during harvest, and then begin the fall term."

"May I suggest that you take these next three weeks to rest? I know the temptation is there to busy yourself and forget about all of this—to prepare for school and perhaps overhaul the ranch house. But you need to build yourself up physically. You'll have your father's affairs to settle, too. He had a lot of business concerns, I understand."

"Well yes, there's the stagecoach line and the boardinghouse, in addition to the ranch. And he owned considerable property."

He leaned back on the sofa. "You'll have to think about those things, of course. But take time to rest your mind in between." He looked around at the pleasant room, and his gaze landed on Libby's cherry bookcases. "I see Mrs. Adams has quite a library."

"Yes. She has more books than anyone else in town. She's told me I may borrow any I like."

"That's good. It may seem frivolous right now, but if you can lose yourself in a novel for a few hours, it will help you stop thinking of your own troubles for a while."

"I thought I might try the latest one by Henry James, though Papa might. . ." She broke off and smiled in apology. "I was going to say, 'Papa might think it quite daring for a mountain schoolteacher.'"

Kincaid smiled. "I think you would enjoy it. I'm reading Turgenev's *Fathers and Sons* right now."

Isabel raised one hand. "Oh, those Nihilists!"

"You've read it?"

"Yes, but I'm not sure I understood it. I rather liked it, but I felt as though I shouldn't."

He chuckled. "We'll have to discuss it when I've finished it. That is, if you'd care to do so. . . ."

He must be lonely, Isabel thought. *That wistful look could mean nothing else.*

"I should be delighted." She swallowed hard and lowered her lashes. Papa's words had suddenly bounced back into her mind. *I saw you staring at him at the picnic. . .saw you eyeing him at church, too.* Should she say something to assure Dr. Kincaid that she wasn't pursuing him? No, if he hadn't thought such a thing, mentioning it might make him wary. And she would dearly love to discuss Turgenev with an intelligent person.

"Are you well?" He leaned toward her and reached for her wrist again.

"Why, yes. I only. . . Oh, it's silly, but I was thinking of the books we might discuss. You've no idea how much I've longed to do that. My father isn't much—*wasn't* much of a reader for pleasure, and while I'm sure Mrs. Adams indulges, she is so busy that we rarely meet except at church or the shooting club."

"I should be delighted to engage in literary discussions." He fingered his stethoscope. "I was going to listen to your lungs—"

"I assure you, my breathing is fine. I shall recover soon from all of this." Her face must be as scarlet as a radish by now. There was no chance she would let him get any closer with that stethoscope without another female present. It would be too, too unsettling.

He took the instrument off and tucked it into his bag. "All right. Let me just write down the name of the tonic. Mrs. Adams stocks it in the emporium." He took a small pad and a pencil from his coat pocket and began to write.

"There you go. And if you don't mind, I'd like to come by and see you before the service tomorrow, just to be sure you're up to it."

"You may come, sir, but I shall be fine."

He nodded and stood. "In that case, I'll be off. I have a patient to visit at the Storrey ranch. But if you feel the need of my ministrations, send someone to the boardinghouse. I'll be back there in an hour or two."

"Thank you. I'll do that." Isabel looked down at the sheet of paper he'd handed her. They said doctors had terrible handwriting, but she could read his script perfectly. She rose and saw him to the door, trying to keep her breathing steady and willing her heart to stop hammering like a frenzied blacksmith.

The blacksmith. She paused with her hand on the doorknob. "Doctor, there is one thing that troubles me. I wonder if you might give me some advice on a financial matter."

"I'd be happy to, though I'm not an expert in that field."

"It's my father's business with the stagecoach company. He had a contract running through next spring. I suppose the logical thing is to ask Mr. Bane to see it through if he's willing. He already keeps the horses and changes the teams."

"He seems a good businessman. Didn't he start out with just the smithy?"

"Yes. He bought the livery when the former owner moved out of town."

"From everything I've seen of Mr. Bane, he's trustworthy. If he's not too busy to take it on, he would probably do well with the stage line."

Isabel nodded slowly, amazed that she could discuss Griffin Bane without becoming agitated.

"Do you know whom I should discuss it with if I were you?" Kincaid asked.

"No sir."

"Your friend Elizabeth Adams. She's the shrewdest woman I've ever met. And she's known Mr. Bane much longer than I have. She could tell you if he'd do well in the position."

"Yes, you're right." Isabel smiled as she swung the door open. "Thank you so much, Doctor. I shall put the matter to her this evening."

She closed the door behind him and stood for a moment, puzzling over the thoughts whirling through her mind. Dr. Kincaid would call again tomorrow. She must be ready to receive him graciously. But she mustn't throw herself at him. Indeed, she mustn't even think of pursuing him. How unladylike and vulgar that would be. Shades of Rose Caplinger and her mass distribution of cookies to the single men of the town. And Papa was surely right that the handsome doctor would never look her way. On the other hand, Dr. James Kincaid had expressed interest in discussing books with her.

She caught her breath. She'd better dust off that volume of Turgenev and refresh her memory of the story line and philosophy between its covers. Slowly she walked into Libby's parlor and stood gazing into the mirror between the windows. Papa was quite right. She was too thin, and her hair had always been a nondescript brown. Her pale eyes held none of the allure of Libby's sparkling blue ones. And yet. . . She strode toward the bookcase but stopped in the middle of the room.

First things first. She must fetch the tonic. Surely the doctor would inquire tomorrow whether she had followed his instructions.

★ CHAPTER 40 ★

On the Monday after Cyrus's funeral, Hiram plied his hoe in the corn patch behind his house. So much had changed in Fergus that he needed a few hours of solitude to sort it all out. His shirt stuck to his skin, wet with perspiration. He hoped this heat would break. As soon as Oscar hauled the lumber from the sawmill, Hiram and his crew would start on the new church building.

"Mr. Dooley?"

He looked up in surprise. Isabel made her way daintily across his garden, holding her skirt up as high as her shoe tops.

"Help you, ma'am?" He leaned on his hoe. The send-off they'd given her pa Saturday afternoon would have made Cyrus proud. Hiram hoped Cy had been able to look down and see them all honoring him at the haberdashery building and then out at the graveyard for the burial. He'd rest near the schoolhouse, where his daughter could walk over and visit the grave anytime she wanted.

"Mr. Dooley—Hiram—"

"Yes?"

Isabel's face, beneath the brim of her gray bonnet, seemed rather pinker than the warmth of the morning accounted for.

"I wonder if I might discuss a matter with you."

He waited, curious and a little on edge. Would this turn out like the evening she'd gone to the smithy? He pulled his bandanna from his back pocket and blotted his forehead so the sweat wouldn't trickle down his face while he talked to her.

She cleared her throat. "I've been staying with Mrs. Adams all week, and I find that I can't face moving back to the ranch, where

I lived so long with my father."

Hiram frowned, trying to fit her words with her nervous twisting of her reticule's strap.

"And so I wondered if it's possible—well, I happen to know that at one time you had considered buying the ranch where we lived. Before my father bought it, that is."

"Yes ma'am, I did."

"I. . .don't suppose. . ."

Hiram swallowed hard. Here it was again—the opportunity he'd wanted, and again he'd have to say no. "Miss Isabel, I don't have much money put by."

"Oh, I understand that."

A horrible thought suddenly came to him. She wasn't implying—was she?—that perhaps he'd consider marrying her and moving to the ranch with her? This had to be worse than that night at the smithy, when she approached Griffin. They'd all decided to ignore that outburst. But now she'd gotten desperate, since her father died.

"Ma'am, I. . ."

"I realize you've got your sister-in-law visiting and all, but with Trudy planning to get married. . ." Her eyes darted about as though seeking something less objectionable to gaze at than him. "Since the parson announced yesterday that Trudy and the sheriff will be married soon, I got to thinking you might rather live closer to them, and if you still want to try ranching, why maybe the solution would be for you to swap houses with me."

Hiram stared at her for a long half minute, remaining outwardly still while his heart pounded and leaped. Was she nuts? His little house in town with a couple of acres out back was worth far less than Cyrus's ranch. That fine, big ranch house outshone this little frame dwelling by far. And Cy had a big pole barn, and corrals and pastures, and a bunkhouse for his cowboys. And the cattle. What did she intend to do with all those beef steers? He certainly couldn't ante up for all the livestock, and what good was a ranch without cattle? But. . .swap houses?

"Well Miss Fennel, I don't know. . . ." He pushed his hat up in the back and scratched where the band had hugged his head. His hair was damp all around where the hat had rested. "Maybe you'd ought to wait a while before you decide something like that. Go through your pa's papers and such."

Isabel puffed out a breath and looked at the ground. It had been so dry lately, the grass was all brown and wilted. Cyrus's ranch bordered the river on the southwest. Hiram wondered how many cattle were running Cy's range right now.

"Maybe we could talk about it later." He wiped his forehead again. "After you know what's what with your pa's property."

"Papa had a lot of land." Her dull eyes shifted uneasily. "Honestly, I don't know what to do."

Hiram tucked the bandanna back into his pocket. He clasped his hands over the end of the hoe handle and leaned on it again. "I wonder if the sheriff and some of the town council members couldn't advise you a little."

She nodded. "They might. I've talked to Libby some. . . ."

"You must realize that your father's ranch is worth a lot more than my house."

"Well. . .I thought perhaps we could work it out somehow. I. . .don't want to live there anymore. I'm certain of that. I'd like to live in town, but I don't wish to impose on Libby much longer." Her head drooped.

Hiram couldn't help feeling a rush of sympathy for her, all alone in the world as she now found herself. "Say, don't you own the boardinghouse now? You could stay there for a while. Until you have time to make some decisions."

Her chin came up an inch. "Yes, I could."

"And your pa had some more empty houses in town."

"That's true. I could probably fit one up to live in. But even so, it's on my heart that you should have the ranch. Papa didn't do right when he bought it out from under you. I've heard people talk about it, and I think it's time you had the land you wanted."

Hiram pulled in a long, slow breath and looked down the rows of his garden. "Well now, that's kind of you to say so. The truth is, that dream has faded since my wife died. Violet and I, we thought we'd get us a ranch and work it together. Raise our family there. But without her, I'm not sure I could resurrect that vision."

They stood for a long moment in the hot sun, saying nothing.

Hiram's thoughts spun off on a new dream's track. Would Libby consent to live on a ranch? The very idea enchanted him, but he couldn't picture her without the emporium. Libby, riding the range with him? Cooking up supper for a bunch of cowpokes? The idea began to grow on him. But could she be content living outside town, not seeing folks every day, away from other women? Not too far away, of course. Close enough to walk into town. And there was the shooting club. But what about the store?

Isabel sighed, and her shoulders sank again.

It occurred to him that her attitude might change if she found a husband. He eyed her uneasily. He'd about discounted the notion that she hoped he'd pop the question and marry her. But maybe this offer to swap property was an attempt to draw it out of him and make him think it was his idea.

"Miss Isabel, someday you might want that ranch. It's a good piece of land."

She shook her head. "It holds too many sorrowful memories. I shall never live there again. And I shall consider your advice about the boardinghouse. It might be a good place for me to stay while I consider my options."

"Didn't your pa have a lawyer or somebody like that to draw up papers and such?"

"Well yes." Her pale blue eyes brightened. "There is a man in Boise. I suppose I should telegraph him."

"Sure. He might be able to advise you on what to do about the property."

She nodded slowly. "And maybe—it just came into my mind that maybe you'd consider managing the ranch for me. You could still do your gun work. We could apply your wages to buying the property if you wanted."

Hiram frowned. It would take a ranch foreman a lifetime to save enough to buy that spread. And he was committed to overseeing the building of the new church.

She twisted the strap of her bag again. "I've so much to consider. There's the stagecoach line, for instance. I need to find someone who can fulfill Papa's contract."

"I expect Griff Bane might help you there."

"Do you? I don't like to ask him any favors."

Hiram shrugged. "If it's profitable for him, it won't be a favor."

"That's true." She gritted her teeth as though steeling herself to do something unpleasant. "All right, I'll ask him. And will you think about the possibilities at the ranch? If you won't move out there, I'll have to sell it, and it seems property in Fergus is hard to sell just now."

That was true. Cy had tried to sell property just last week with little success. "I guess it can't hurt to think about it."

"Thank you." She turned and walked away, her shoulders slumped. She'd seemed almost handsome that night at the smithy when she'd raged at Griffin, but now she looked gray and tired. Hiram watched until she turned the corner of the house. The satisfaction he'd felt in the sunny day and the waist-high corn had fled. Why did he feel guilty?

The kitchen door opened, and Rose stood on the stoop staring toward him. He poked halfheartedly at a weed with the hoe.

"Hiram! Didn't I just see Miss Fennel go past the window?"

He sighed and turned toward the house, walking slowly through the rows. When he was ten feet from the back steps, he stopped and looked up at her. "Yes, she came to discuss some business with me."

"Business?"

"She has her father's estate to settle."

Rose's smooth, creamy brow wrinkled. "Why should she talk to you about that?"

Hiram drew in a deep breath, quickly running through and discarding possible answers. He gave up and shrugged.

"Ooo! You're so maddening! Why can't you speak like a normal man?" Rose gathered her skirts and stormed back into the house, shutting the door firmly behind her.

Hiram eyed the closed door helplessly. Yes, why couldn't he speak? Sometimes he kept quiet because he had nothing to say. When he was a boy, his father had often quoted Proverbs 17:28: *"Even a fool, when he holdeth his peace, is counted wise: and he that shutteth his lips is esteemed a man of understanding."* That made sense. Lincoln had put it another way: *"Better to remain silent and be thought a fool than to speak out and remove all doubt."*

There were other occasions when Hiram felt tongue-tied and fearful that what he said would be rejected—moments when he'd stood face-to-face with Libby came to mind. But you couldn't go all your life regretting what you never said. Perhaps it was time.

Griffin set the pritchel precisely where he wanted it on the branch of the red-hot horseshoe and hammered away. The jarring hurt his arm, but Doc had said it wasn't broken, so he gritted his teeth and kept at it. Three holes on each side of the horseshoe would do it. The metal cooled before he could do the last one. With his tongs, he lifted it from the anvil and stuck it back into the glowing forge.

"Mr. Bane?"

He jumped and looked toward the door of the smithy. Isabel stood there, much as she had that evening a few weeks back. He swallowed hard, trying to force back the sour taste in his mouth. He didn't even have Hiram here to deflect her anger today.

"Mr. Bane, I've come to talk to you about the stagecoach business. First of all, thank you for handling things for me the last few days."

"No problem." He turned and poked at the horseshoe. It glowed orange. He worked the bellows a few times.

She was still standing there. "I wondered if you could continue doing it—that is, if you would be in a position to fulfill my father's contract with Wells Fargo. He was to continue as division agent for this line until next May. I telegraphed the company the day after Papa died, and they've approved my finding a replacement for the duration of the contract. We're so far off the main line that I suppose they don't want to take the trouble to come all the way up here."

Griffin turned and eyed her suspiciously. "You want me to take on his duties as division agent?"

"That's right."

"I'm awful busy."

"Yes, I know, but I can't think of anyone else as qualified."

Griffin looked back at the forge. The side of the horseshoe he needed to work was white-hot now. He seized it with the tongs and carried it to the anvil. As he positioned the pritchel and picked up his hammer, he could feel her watching him.

A few blows did the job, and he plunged the shoe into the bucket of water at his feet. "We've got no one else in town who can run this smithy, ma'am. This and the livery keep me going all day."

"What if someone else could run the livery for you? Couldn't you hire an assistant?"

Griffin pulled the horseshoe from the water and squinted at it. "Maybe." Josiah Runnels came to mind immediately. He hated freighting with his father's mule teams. Griffin didn't say so, but he reckoned Josiah would jump at the chance. "Your pa did a good job of keeping the stages running on time."

"Yes, he did. You understand what's needed."

"What would you pay me?"

"You could collect Papa's salary. I would ask nothing of you other than fulfilling the contract in an efficient manner. The job would be yours."

Griffin stood for a long moment, thinking about that. How could he be sure she meant that? Nothing else required. Would she expect him to be grateful?

"I would also give you one of Papa's pocket watches to help you in the job."

He tossed the horseshoe into a bucket of finished shoes and scratched his chin through his beard. He'd never owned a watch but had never viewed it as necessary. "I dunno. It might work."

"You can think about it for a couple of days if you want. I'll continue at Mrs. Adams's lodgings a few more days. And can you see to the stage line until you give me your decision?"

"I s'pose I can. Maybe you could ask Josiah Runnels to sit in the office mornings and sell tickets? That way I can get my smithing and barn chores done."

"That's a good idea. Thank you. I'll ask him right away. Please let me know when you've made your decision."

Griffin stood ruminating after she'd gone. He still didn't want to hitch up with her, but if she was serious. . .

He had an inkling that Cyrus collected a hefty salary for running the branch line. He wouldn't have kept doing it year after year if he hadn't been making money.

Certainly he'd clear enough to hire a stable hand or two. He'd have to oversee the drivers and messengers. Probably would have to ride the line now and then and check out the other stops between Fergus and Boise to make sure things ran smoothly. If it worked out and he could get the contract on his own next year, he might even advertise to sell the smithy. And he'd be shoveling less manure. The more he thought about it, the better it sounded.

But he wouldn't rush over to the Paragon Emporium to tell Isabel. Not yet. He had a stagecoach team to switch out in an hour. And besides, he didn't want her to think he was too eager. She could get all sorts of notions.

✮ CHAPTER 41 ✮

The Paragon Emporium experienced a lull most afternoons. Patrons did their shopping early and stuck close to home during the heat of the day. Libby had ordered a thermometer from New York, and Josiah had posted it on the back porch, out of the direct sunlight. This afternoon it registered one hundred degrees. She'd sent Florence home at lunchtime and told her to take the rest of the day off. No sense having two of them in the store when only a handful of people would come in.

She'd thought about ordering a dozen of those mercury thermometers to sell in the emporium. But would people like to know how hot it really was, or would that just disturb them more? People like Hiram, who had a scientific turn of mind, would probably appreciate the device. Knowing how hot it was wouldn't keep him from working, but it would give him something to think about.

Bertha Runnels, on the other hand, often complained about the heat. Some days she declared that if it got any hotter she would surely die of heatstroke. So if she had a thermometer and it told her that the heat really had increased, would Bertha be more likely to keel over and die? The sobering thought kept Libby from stocking weather instruments. Maybe she would ask Dr. Kincaid his opinion. After all, he had a medical thermometer. Did he tell people when their fever was high enough to damage their organs? Or would that adversely affect the patient?

As she pondered the question, she sorted the nails that had fallen into the wrong buckets. The hardware section of the store took as much of her time as the yard goods. Isaac used to keep it organized, but now the chore fell to Libby—unless she delegated it to Florence.

After bending over the buckets for five minutes, she stood and stretched her arms and back. Some days she wished she hadn't married a storekeeper. She hardly got outside except for the shooting club. Not that she regretted coming out here in response to Isaac's plea, but it would be heavenly now to be out on the prairie away from town, where the breeze would reach her. If the good Lord ever gave her a chance for a different life, she'd choose to live out away from town. That and children. Of course, a thirty-five-year-old single woman was unlikely to see that opportunity.

The bell on the door jangled. She pasted a smile on her face before turning to greet the person brave enough to come out in this heat.

Hiram nodded soberly and closed the door behind him.

Libby's chest contracted, and she reached out to steady herself against the table of hinges and stovepipe. "Good day, Hiram. How is your garden taking this weather?"

"I'm hauling water."

"Of course." No one in Fergus would see a harvest this year without irrigating their crops. But wells were going dry. Going to the river to fill barrels and hauling them back to the fields took a lot of energy. "May I help you with something?"

He took two steps toward her then stopped. His eyes held hers, and he swallowed hard. "Would you. . ."

Her heart tripped. Instantly, she cautioned herself. *Don't assume anything, Libby. His next words might be, "Would you have any dung forks?"*

For a few breathless seconds, they stood eyeing each other. Libby refused to speak. Though she'd developed a fondness for Hiram, she would not go about completing his sentences for him and explaining his actions to other people, the way his sister did. Let him speak for himself.

"I. . .wondered if you'd. . .like to take dinner. . .with me."

He gritted his teeth and waited. Libby drew in a tight breath. In this moment, she could change their lives. If she declined and sent him away, he would never approach her again. But if she encouraged him—even if they only spent one evening together—

her life would be different. Perhaps very different. Rockets of possibilities exploded in her mind. A new love. A new home. Trudy for a sister-in-law. A gentle husband. Children.

"I should be delighted."

He exhaled audibly. "I thought. . .maybe Bitsy and Augie's? Or the boardinghouse if you'd rather. . ."

"I've wanted to dine at the Spur & Saddle, but I hadn't the courage to go alone."

He nodded. "Tonight, then?"

Little pricks in the back of her throat made it hard for Libby to breathe, but she managed. "Yes. Thank you."

"Shall I come by after closing?"

She did some rapid calculations. She usually closed at six. "Would six thirty be too late?"

His rare smile came out like the sun sliding from behind a cloud. "No ma'am. That's perfect." He nodded and went out. The bell jangled as he shut the door.

Libby pulled in a deep breath, straightening her shoulders.

"I'm having dinner with a gentleman this evening." Saying it made her pulse throb even faster. And he was not only a gentleman, but a hero. She'd kept quiet and listened after the shootout at Kenton Smith's ranch, but Hiram had never owned up to shooting the man in the hayloft. If not for his quick action, at least one of their townsfolk might have been killed. The sheriff, perhaps. But Hiram didn't ask that anyone recognize his prowess. In fact, if anyone asked, he'd probably insist his sister was a better shot than he was. But Libby knew better.

She hurried to the apparel section and eyed the merchandise critically. Perhaps Rose was right and Fergus needed a milliner. She scooped up a pair of spotless white gloves with tiny seed pearls stitched in a floral design on the wrists. She would wear her best Sunday hat, though Hiram had seen it many times. At least she would have new gloves.

⭐

Hiram whistled as he loaded his tools and paintbrushes into a box. The heat no longer seemed oppressive. Clouds flirted with the sun, bringing welcome shade off and on.

As he headed out of the barn, carrying his toolbox, Griff Bane rounded the back corner of the house.

"Howdy, Griff."

"Hiram. Brought you something to work on. My rifle's jammed. Didn't want to do too much prodding for fear I'd blow my toe off, so I brought it to you."

"Fine. I'll look at it tomorrow if you don't mind. Got a little job to do for Augie and Bitsy this afternoon." Hiram set down the toolbox.

"Oh?" Griff handed him the gun.

"Yup. They want me to repaint the sign at their place."

"Huh. What's wrong with the old one?"

"It says, 'Beer & Whiskey.'"

"Oh right." Griff shook his head. "Don't seem right with only one saloon in town. Main Street's not balanced anymore."

"Oh, somebody'll open up another watering hole soon. Wait and see." Hiram broke open the gun's breech and peered into the chamber. "Looks jammed, all right." He closed it and set the rifle inside the barn, leaning against the wall. "I'll get to it tomorrow, for sure."

Griffin frowned at him in silent study.

"What?" Hiram asked.

"I dunno. You just. . .you talk more than you used to."

Hiram chuckled and picked up his toolbox. "Listen, I want to ask you something." He walked slowly across the barnyard toward the path, and Griff kept pace with him. "Isabel Fennel came by this morning and offered to sell me her pa's ranch. She even offered to swap houses with me."

"Wow. Good opportunity for you."

"Yeah." Hiram shook his head in doubt. "I told her I don't have the money, and then. . .well, she asked if I'd think about living out at the ranch and acting as foreman. She'd pay me. Trudy says I should do it, but I don't know. . . ."

"Well, I'll help you move if you do it. And I'll help Miss Isabel move her things, too."

"Chances are she'll go live in one of Cy's empty houses here in town, or at the boardinghouse. I got the impression she doesn't like living out at the ranch, at least not now that she's alone."

They'd reached the boardwalk on the street, and Griff stopped. Hiram paused, too.

"She asked me to keep the stage line running. Offered to let me take over her pa's contract with Wells Fargo."

Hiram whistled softly. "You going to do it?"

"Don't know yet. I kind of feel sorry for her."

"Yeah. She seems a lot more mellow since her father died." Hiram smiled up at his friend. "Maybe you ought to think about calling on her."

"Oh no. Not a chance." Griff held up both hands and backed off a step. "You're not going to marry me off, so quit thinking that way. I like my life just fine the way it is."

Hi chuckled. "Aw, Griff, she's a nice young woman. And Trudy says she's coming right along with her shooting lessons. She may not be the prettiest gal in town, but she's not so bad."

Griffin laughed and shook his shaggy head. "Not me, mister. I'll start courting a lady the day you do."

Hiram eyed him soberly. Griffin stopped laughing and peered at him suspiciously. Hiram felt a blush washing up from his neck to his hairline.

Griffin's eyes popped wide. "You wouldn't."

"Yes, I would. As a matter of fact, I'm going calling tonight."

"No."

"Yes."

Griffin stared at him. "Might I ask who?"

Hiram couldn't help it. He must look like a fox that just raided the henhouse, but he couldn't stop grinning. "The prettiest woman in town. She's a good shot, too." He swung his toolbox by the handle and headed up the sidewalk whistling.

From behind him came the stunned words, "I don't believe it. I just don't believe it."

Bitsy came out the front door of the Spur & Saddle and walked over to admire Hiram's work. He had repainted the sign and was adding a gold stripe around the edge of the board.

"Oh, that's fine." Bitsy grinned at him. "Can you hang it back up tonight?"

"The paint's not dry, and one of the screws is stripped. I don't have quite the hardware I need."

"Hmm. The emporium's still open."

Hiram glanced up at the westering sun. "Not much longer, and if I ask Mrs. Adams to stay open to sell me hardware, she and I will both be late to dinner tonight. I'm bringing her here."

Bitsy stared at him for a moment then playfully shoved his shoulder. "Go on."

"It's true."

"Well, I never." She eyed the sign critically. Beneath the shaded Gothic lettering of "SPUR & SADDLE" and Hiram's rendition of a roweled spur, smaller block letters spelled "FINE MEALS SERVED" and "MR. & MRS. A. MOORE, PROPS."

"I like it," Bitsy said. "Looks dignified."

Hiram nodded slowly. "Refined."

"The picture really looks like a spur, and the gold stripe gives it an aristocratic touch." She chuckled. "Who'd have thought it?"

"Bitsy, your place is as proper as a church now."

"Well, thank you. I don't need folks to feel all inhibited, but I want them to know we're decent now."

"How's business?"

Bitsy scrunched up her face. "I'm not sure yet. We don't make nearly so much as we did when we sold liquor. I probably shouldn't have bought so many new dishes. Might have to cut the girls' pay, but I hate to do that."

Charles and Orissa Walker strolled over from their house across the street.

"New sign?" Charles asked as they mounted the steps.

"New paint on the old one," Bitsy said.

Orissa eyed it closely. "Looks fine."

"What's the special tonight?" Charles asked.

"We've got chicken and dumplings or roast beef." Bitsy watched the Walkers enter the building. She looked anxiously at Hiram. "Do you think we ought to put, 'No LIQUOR' on there, too?"

Hiram twitched his lips back and forth, thinking about it. "No, I think it's good."

"Magnolious. I'm going to go get Augie so he can see your handiwork. Of course, he'll say he's too busy and want to wait until the dinner rush is past."

"Say, I'd better get moving." Hiram gathered his tools.

Bitsy headed for the door grinning. "I'll be looking for you a little later."

★ CHAPTER 42 ★

Ethan ambled down the sidewalk toward the Dooleys' house. The sun had sunk behind the mountains, leaving the valley in soft twilight. Across the street, Libby shut the door to the emporium and turned the placard in the window. Ethan strolled around to the kitchen door and mounted the steps. When he knocked, Trudy let him in.

"Am I late?" he asked.

"No. At least no later than anyone else."

To his surprise, the table was set for only three. A vase of fresh wildflowers stood on a doily in the middle.

"Isn't Rose joining us tonight?" He hung his dusty hat on the peg rack.

"Yes—at least I think she is. She went down to the store beside the telegraph office."

"What store?"

Trudy scowled. "The empty one between the telegraph and Bitsy's."

"Why'd she go there?"

"That's the one she wants to lease from Isabel for her millinery shop. Isabel told her she could go in and measure the windows for curtains."

"Rose is really planning to do it?"

"I guess." Trudy set a plate of sliced, cold ham on the table. "I didn't want to heat up the oven today."

"Can't say as I blame you." He eyed the place settings. "Er. . .if Rose is going to be here, am I one too many?"

"What? Oh no." Trudy pushed her hair back. "Hiram's going out."

"Out?" Something wasn't right. Ethan frowned, certain he had missed something.

Trudy smiled and peeked around the parlor doorjamb. She turned back and whispered, "With Libby. He finally asked her. I think he's going to court her."

Ethan's jaw dropped.

She laughed and went to the stove. "Don't look so shocked."

"Sorry. I just didn't. . ."

"Didn't think he'd have the nerve?"

"Something like that."

"Well, he found it someplace. Maybe you inspired him when you asked me to marry you."

Now, that was something worth discussing. Ethan stepped closer and wrapped his arms around her from behind. For a moment, she leaned back against his chest. He bent and kissed her cheek.

"Hey, now." She gently disentangled herself from his embrace. "I do think Rose will be home any minute, and Hi might finish with his preparations and come out here, too."

"What's he doing?"

"Having a bath. Though he came home later than I expected. He'll have to make it a quick one. I had the water ready for half an hour before he showed up. Didn't want to keep the stove going, so it was only lukewarm when he got to it."

Ethan laughed.

"Why is that funny?" Trudy placed her hands on her hips. "Don't you dare make fun of him. You've been known to bathe once in a blue moon yourself."

"I know it." He grinned. "I think it's great."

"Good. He can't pick Libby up until a half hour after she closes the store."

"She getting a bath, too?"

Trudy slugged his shoulder and picked up the bread plate. "Maybe you could run out to the street and see if you can tell whether she's closed shop yet."

"Don't need to. I saw her closing up right before I got here."

"Good. I can tell Hiram when he's dressed."

Ethan followed her to the table. "Hey, listen, I've got some news for you. They caught Wilfred Sterling."

She whirled to face him. "*Who* caught him?"

"The marshal in Boise. They're holding him in a bank robbery. And he did have a wound that hadn't healed. Guess Arthur Tinen was right when he said he thought he'd hit him."

"Well, what do you know?" Trudy said.

Ethan nodded in satisfaction. "I might ride up to Boise when Sterling goes to trial. I wired the marshal some details about Isabel's kidnapping. And I told him to ask Sterling why he was so interested in Milzie Peart's land."

"Did they get anything out of him?"

"Sterling said Kenton put him up to it, thinking he could get Frank's mine and make some featherhead think it was worth something and sell it to him. But when I started all the inquiries, it wasn't worth the trouble, so they gave up on that."

"Hmm. If he's telling the truth."

"Right."

"I suppose it fits with what Isabel told you she heard them talking about."

"Trudy, can you—" Hiram appeared in the parlor doorway, his hair damp and his face pink and clean shaven. "Oh hello, Eth. Trudy, I can't make this tie sit right." He fumbled at the black ribbon below his collar.

"Here, let me." She untied the ribbon and gritted her teeth as she set about tying it correctly. "There. But you can't go yet. You're too early."

"You sure?" Hiram glanced anxiously toward the window. "I don't want to be too early. But I don't want to be late either."

Ethan chuckled. "Maybe you need a watch."

"Can't afford one."

"Well, maybe for Christmas." Ethan closed his mouth, but he couldn't help where his thoughts led. If Hiram succeeded in wooing Libby, he'd probably have a very nice pocket watch by yuletide.

"Ethan says Libby closed up about ten minutes ago," Trudy said. "Relax and give her time to prissy up."

Hiram glared at her and went to the stove. He hefted the coffeepot and reached for a mug.

"So. . ." Ethan watched him. "I thought maybe we could ride out to the Fennel ranch this evening and dig up that tin for Isabel. I asked her if she wanted me to check the place where her pa had buried something, and she said she'd be grateful if she didn't have to do it herself. But I don't suppose you'd want to go now. I mean, you'll probably be tied up till all hours, and—"

"Yes, he'll be busy," Trudy said. "You and I could go, though."

"Yeah, I like that idea." Ethan smiled at her. Trudy and moonlight, always a good combination.

"What are you going to do with the paper that's in there?" Hiram asked.

"Get rid of it," Ethan said.

Hiram nodded. "Probably best."

"And I'll take Isabel the money. I was thinking I could tell her that when I dug up the hole, I found that pouch in the tin. She doesn't need to know it wasn't the only thing in there."

"That's a good idea." Trudy beamed at him. "That way she'll stop fretting. Let's do it tonight."

Hiram sipped his coffee and looked at them over the rim of his cup. "You kids have fun. But just remember, Ethan—you might be getting married in a couple of weeks, but I still expect Trudy home at a decent hour."

Ethan saluted. "Yes sir. We'll be in by curfew."

Hiram grunted and set his mug down. "Guess I'll get going."

"Wait!" Trudy lifted the flowers from the vase and wiped the dripping stems on a linen towel. "Hold on. Let me wrap a handkerchief around these." From her apron pocket, she produced a white square of cotton edged in blue tatting. "There, now." She held the bouquet out to Hiram.

He swallowed hard and stared at them.

"Take it. And don't ask me what you're supposed to do with them." Trudy scowled at him.

At last he raised his hand and took the posy. "Thank you. Shoulda thought of it myself."

"Yes, you should, but I wouldn't say so." She nodded firmly.

Ethan hid a smile by turning to open the back door for him.

"Have a pleasant evening, my friend."

"No doubt." Hiram walked down the steps and around the house.

"I was afraid he wouldn't go through with it," Trudy whispered.

From outside, Rose's high-pitched tones reached them. "Why, Hiram, where *are* you going? And just look as those delectable blossoms!"

Hiram muttered a reply.

Before Rose came into their line of sight, Ethan leaned down and kissed Trudy. "You're a good sister."

She smiled and nodded. "He makes it easy, but yes, I am."

★ CHAPTER 43 ★

Libby turned before the beveled mirror, anxiously regarding as much as she could see of the back of her dress.

"Are you sure I'm all buttoned correctly?"

Isabel smiled at her in the mirror. "You look marvelous."

"Thank you." Libby put a hand to the smooth wing of hair at her temple. "I'm nervous, I guess."

"I could tell."

"Yes, well it's been a long time since I've had a gentleman caller."

Isabel sat down on the cherry-framed settee and picked up the skirt she was sewing. "I hope you and Mr. Dooley have a very pleasant time."

"I hope so, too." Libby glanced in the mirror again then made herself move away from it. "You know, I think it's a good idea for you to rent Rose that little shop near the telegraph office. It will be income for you, and she'll be out of Hiram and Trudy's hair."

"I'm glad you think so." Isabel frowned as she pushed her needle through the fabric. "I don't like to admit it, but sometimes I find it difficult to think charitable thoughts toward Mrs. Caplinger. But she is a sister in Christ, and I'm sure her business will be an asset to the town. I told her she could fix the rooms above the shop and move in if she wants and live there."

Libby tried not to let her face show the full extent of her delight. Seeing Rose move out from under Hiram's roof would be pure pleasure. "That sounds good. She has such a flair for decorating, I'm sure she'll improve the building's value for you."

"Yes, if she doesn't pester me about repairs and such." Isabel waved a hand in dismissal. "What am I saying? I shall have to educate myself on what it means to be a landlady. I have several tenants, after all."

"I'm sure you can hire someone to make repairs to the buildings your father left you."

"True. And I'm thinking of reserving one of the houses on Gold Lane for myself."

"Oh! You'd be right near the Bentons. How delightful."

"Yes. I don't want to live at the ranch anymore. I've made that decision, at least. And I'm trying to negotiate with a gentleman I'm sure would like to have the ranch."

"That's good." A quiet rap sounded on the kitchen door, and Libby caught her breath.

"That must be your gentleman caller." Isabel laid her sewing aside and rose. "Shall I let him in?"

"Oh! Yes, I guess so." Libby tried to breathe evenly as Isabel walked briskly into the next room. She glanced again at the mirror then resolutely turned her back. Too late to change anything now. As Isabel's greeting rang throughout the apartment, she clenched handfuls of her embroidered pink muslin skirt. She'd loved the fabric when it first came in and had hired Annie to stitch her a gown. Then she'd wondered if she'd have a place to wear it. The dress was too fine for workdays in the store. She'd decided to wear it to church on Sunday—and then Hiram had invited her to dinner.

He stood in the doorway, beaming at her and holding the dearest nosegay of bouncing bet and fleabane she'd ever seen. His freshly shaven face fairly glowed, and his hair was neatly parted and combed. Libby's stomach fluttered. She would be proud to be seen on his arm tonight.

"Evening," he said.

She let go of her skirt and crossed the room to meet him, trying to rein in her smile so she wouldn't look foolish. "Good evening."

"You look fine, Elizabeth. Mighty fine."

"Oh thank you." She felt the blood rush to her cheeks. He'd given her Christian name a lyrical lilt, and suddenly she was glad to be wearing pink again and to hear a man say *Elizabeth* in that deep, profound voice.

He thrust out the flowers and opened his mouth then closed it.

"For me? How lovely!" Libby took the bouquet, noting that the stems were folded in one of Trudy's handkerchiefs. The blossoms in varied pinks and mauves complemented her gown. "Thank you so much. I shall wear a sprig if you don't mind." Isabel hovered in the doorway behind him, grinning at her over his shoulder. "Perhaps dear Isabel would put the rest in water."

Libby pulled one of the fuller stems free and took it to the table beneath the mirror, where she found a pin. After fastening it to her bodice, she turned.

Hiram gazed at her, unblinking. His usually mournful eyes seemed younger. Libby even thought she glimpsed a bit of a twinkle there. His mouth curved in a fetching smile that demanded an answer. How long they stood like that, she couldn't tell, but Isabel entered the room with the posies in a small, milk-glass vase.

"These are delightful. I'll set them here on the side table."

"Thank you, Isabel." Libby sucked in a breath and reached for her gloves and handbag. "I'm ready if you are."

In reply, Hiram offered the crook of his arm.

"Good night," Isabel called as they went through the kitchen.

"Good night, dear," Libby said. Somehow they went through two doorways and started down her rear stairway, and she was still holding on to Hiram's arm. She shot a glance at his face. He was only three inches or so taller than she was, but she felt he was just the right size. They stepped across the back porch and down to the ground, then rounded the corner and entered the alley between the emporium and the stagecoach office.

"Griffin seems to be doing a good job keeping the stages running on schedule," she said.

"Yes."

She smiled. One word from Hiram was as good as ten from any other man.

★

After supper Rose retired to work on her plans for the millinery shop, and Trudy quickly did the dishes with Ethan's help. The two of them sauntered out to the barn, and Trudy hummed as she saddled Crinkles. Ethan untied Scout's reins and led his mount away from the fence.

"You all set?"

"Sure am." Trudy swung into the saddle and stroked Crinkles's neck as she looked up at the almost-full moon. "Going to be a pretty ride tonight."

The horses trotted side by side, snorting now and then. When they reached the Fennels' barnyard, a man came from the bunkhouse.

"Evening, Brady," Ethan called.

"Sheriff. Can I help you?"

"Miss Dooley and I have a bit of business for Miss Fennel."

"Anything I can help you with?"

"You could bring me a shovel."

Brady's eyes widened, but he nodded and turned toward the barn.

"They'll want to know what's going on," Trudy said.

"I'll just tell them Isabel knew her daddy had a stash behind the barn, and I'm digging it up to see if he left any cash there for her."

Trudy nodded and smiled as Brady came from the barn hefting the spade.

Fifteen minutes later, they left the ranch and rode back toward town. Ethan carried the tin box in his saddlebag.

"Thought we wouldn't get away without opening it in front of Brady," Trudy said.

"Me, too. He sure was curious."

"Good thinking to tell him he could ask Isabel all about it when he sees her."

Ethan grinned over at her. "She'll tell him she found a pouch of hard money, and that was all."

"Right."

As they passed his own ranch, Ethan said, "I don't s'pose you want to stop in and take a look at your new kitchen?"

"Well. . .it's tempting." *Too tempting*, Trudy thought. If anyone else in town heard she'd gone into Ethan's house alone with him before they were married, the gossip would fly. "We'd probably best go home. Rose will be there even if Hiram's not back yet."

"All right." They rode along in companionable silence to the Dooleys' house. A light shone in the front bedroom window.

"Rose must be upstairs," Trudy said as they rode behind the house to the barnyard. The oppressive heat was gone, but the breeze that flowed down from the mountains was almost too cool.

Ethan halted Scout near the corral fence. "I'll take care of Crinkles. You take the box inside and stoke the fire." He dismounted and opened the saddlebag.

Trudy lit beside him on the ground and exchanged Crinkles's reins for the tin they'd unearthed. He came in five minutes after she did. By then she'd lit the lamp and had the kindling snapping. She added a couple of good-sized sticks to the firebox and smiled at him.

Shadows lay dark under Ethan's eyes. He looked tired, and she knew the outcome of the shootout still bothered him.

"It wasn't your fault," she said.

He didn't ask what she meant. He only set his lips together and shrugged. "Shoulda been some way to get Isabel out without killing anyone."

Trudy put the lid on the stove. "You can't let that nag at you. It's over."

"I know." He exhaled in a puff and shook his head. "And I know that God is in control. He could have stopped it." He still stood by the table, staring off at nothing.

"You sure you're ready to get married? Next Saturday, I mean. It's not too soon?" Trudy's own question appalled her. Why was she giving him the chance to back out?

He focused on her, his dark eyes glittering in the lamplight. "Trudy, it's not too soon. I don't want you thinking that way."

"What way?"

"That I don't want to tie the knot."

"I'm not thinking that."

"Good. Because the closer it gets, the happier I am that we're going through with it. A week from Saturday is *not* too soon."

She shivered as his voice cracked with emotion.

"I love you, Ethan."

He stepped closer and pulled her to him. She wrapped her arms around him and met his kiss eagerly, hoping her lips would transmit her own anticipation and joy.

After a long moment, he pulled away. "Guess we'd better get down to business."

She ducked her head and ran a hand over her hair. Her face must be five shades of red. Why hadn't anyone ever told her how wonderful it was to kiss the man you loved?

Ethan picked up the tin and worked the lid off. The pouch of coins clinked as he set it on the table. Carefully, he took the rolled-up paper out.

Trudy opened the stove lid. "Let's not even look at it again. Those pictures are burned into my brain, and I need to forget about them."

"All right." He brought it over and paused a moment, holding the paper above the open firebox.

"This is the right thing to do," she whispered.

He tossed it into the stove, and the blaze flared up. She closed the lid.

"Trudy, is that you?" Rose came into the parlor doorway. She saw Ethan and pulled her wrapper closer around her. "Oh, excuse me. I didn't know Mr. Chapman was here."

"I'm just leaving, ma'am." Ethan tucked the tin under his arm.

Trudy saw him to the door. "Good night, Ethan."

He winked at her as he clapped his hat on. "I'll see you tomorrow." He nodded vaguely at Rose over Trudy's head and went out.

With the door shut behind him, Trudy turned to face her sister-in-law. "What is it, Rose?"

"I've decided to rent the shop from Miss Fennel, and I wondered. . ." She looked down at the floor for a moment. "It's just filthy. All dust and cobwebs. And. . .well, I wondered if. . .do you know someone I could hire to help me clean it?"

Trudy smiled. That certainly wasn't what Rose had intended to ask, but for whatever reason, she had changed her mind and her approach.

She walked across the room and squeezed Rose's arm gently. "I'd be happy to help you without pay, and I know a few other gals who might pitch in, too."

Rose's eyes flared. "Really? I hated to ask you with the wedding coming up and all. I know you're busy."

"Yes, I am, but I can give you a day's work. Rose, there's something else. Would you consider making me a new bonnet for the day of the wedding?"

"Why. . .I'd love to."

"Nothing too fancy, now."

"Of course not. You're not a modish person. Yet I think we can come up with some fetching design befitting a new bride that will bring out the blue in your eyes."

Trudy nodded. "That'd be nice. Thank you."

They stood for a moment watching each other.

"I don't believe I've thanked you for your hospitality in putting me up this summer."

"You're welcome." Trudy smiled and walked toward the stairs.

★ CHAPTER 44 ★

At the Spur & Saddle, quiet music floated from the piano in the corner. Hiram sat across from Libby at a small table, carefully eating his soup. It wouldn't do to be sloppy this evening or to accidentally make slurping noises.

Sitting opposite Libby was distracting enough, but he knew all the other patrons—not to mention Bitsy, Augie, and the two girls waiting on tables—kept an eye on them. The Walkers lingered over their cake, and Dr. Kincaid ate alone at a small table near the piano. Someone probably watched them every second. It wasn't exactly the quiet, romantic dinner Hiram had imagined.

Vashti set their plates of roast beef, mashed potatoes, gravy, and fresh peas on the linen tablecloth. Oscar and Bertha Runnels came in, greeted the Walkers loudly, and pulled chairs over so they could share their table. Hiram could tell the precise instant Bertha spotted him and Libby. She turned and leaned close to Orissa Walker's ear and whispered something. Orissa cast one of her pinched glances in their direction. Hiram looked away.

They ate in silence for a few minutes.

"This is delicious," Libby said.

"Mm. Do you need anything?" He probably should have thought to ask sooner. He was too used to his sister waiting on him all the time.

"No, I'm fine." A moment later, Libby said, "Trudy stopped at the store today, after she'd been to see Annie Harper about her wedding dress."

"Oh?"

"Yes. I've never seen her so happy. These days she might as well be walking on air. If her feet touch the ground, she's insensible of it."

Hiram smiled and wiped his lips on his napkin. The china and linens looked new and very elegant. Bitsy and Augie must have laid out a lot of cash to refit the restaurant. "I'm glad she and Ethan are getting married."

"So am I, but I'll miss having her right across the street. You'll miss her, too."

"I expect so." Hiram laid his napkin in his lap and leaned forward a little. "Elizabeth?"

Her shapely eyebrows flew up. "Yes?"

"There's something I'd like to discuss with you. Maybe this isn't the time. . . ." He glanced around. Everyone seemed to be eating and enjoying themselves, but even so, two or three people caught his gaze.

"Is it a private matter?"

"Yes."

"Hmm." She looked around. "I would be surprised if folks could hear you over the music."

He gulped in a big breath. "Isabel invited me to be foreman at her daddy's ranch. That is, she suggested swapping houses first, but when I said that wouldn't be fair, she came up with this other plan."

Libby cocked her head toward her right shoulder and studied him. "She's told me she wants to move into town, but I didn't know about this. Is it something you'd like to do?"

He shrugged. "I haven't worked for someone else for a long time. I did want to ranch when I came here, but. . ." So many things to consider. Did he know enough about it to do a good job? Could he boss the men and not look like an idiot? Could he live contentedly on his wages? And could he stand being farther from Libby now that they'd stepped into a different relationship? "There's a lot to think about."

"Indeed." Libby took a bite of roast beef.

Hiram just watched her and waited. Libby did everything delicately, even chewing. He wished he could look at her all the time. Her golden hair shimmered in the lamplight.

After a minute, she took a sip from her water glass. "You'd be closer to Trudy and Ethan out there."

"And farther from Rose." He could feel his ears going red. "I'm sorry. I shouldn't have said that."

"If it's important to you. . ."

"I don't mind her, I guess, but I'd rather not be under the same roof with her."

Libby nodded thoughtfully. "You'd be good at ranching."

"Would I? I don't know. If I'd worked with cattle the last ten years or so, maybe. But I don't want to do it and lose a lot of money for Isabel. And I might go crazy out there by myself."

She didn't answer for a long time. Instead, she cut off another piece of beef and slowly put it into her mouth and chewed it. Hiram took a bite, too, but his appetite had dulled. *I'd be farther from you,* he wanted to say. The bite of potato didn't want to go down, and he reached for his glass.

"If you were lonely, you could do things with the ranch hands," Libby said. "Invite them into the house for coffee and checkers, maybe."

Hiram thought about that. "I don't know."

"You could ask Isabel for some time to think about it."

"Maybe I should."

"Good evening, folks." Dr. Kincaid stood by their table with his hat in his hands.

"Well, hello, Doc." Hiram stood.

Libby favored the doctor with one of her glowing smiles.

"Sorry to interrupt, but I thought I'd inquire about Miss Fennel. Is she still staying with you, ma'am?"

"Yes, she is. She's making plans for a place to live here in town, but I've told her she's welcome to stay with me as long as it's convenient and agreeable to her."

"That's kind of you. Is she feeling well?"

Libby's whole face softened. "She's grieving, of course, but physically, I'd say she's doing well. And her father's estate is a good distraction for her."

Kincaid nodded. "She's an interesting woman. Very well read for a woman in this territory."

"Indeed," Libby said.

Hiram felt a sudden pang of guilt. "I reckon we should have invited her to come and eat with us tonight."

"I'm sure she wasn't offended," Libby said. "However. . ." She looked expectantly from him to the doctor and back. "I do wonder if she'd enjoy having a piece of Augie's chocolate cake with us."

Dr. Kincaid smiled. "Now, that sounds like a good idea. I'd decided to skip dessert tonight, but if Miss Fennel could be persuaded to join us, I might change my mind."

Hiram had been puzzling in his mind ever since he'd noticed Doc eating at the restaurant, and his curiosity got the better of him. "Say, why are you eating here, anyway? I heard Mrs. Thistle is a good cook."

"Oh, she is. But I, uh. . ." Kincaid glanced around and leaned closer. "I did a little professional consultation here yesterday, and Mrs. Moore asked if they could pay me in meals. I didn't want to embarrass her, so I said yes."

Hiram nodded. Doc wouldn't be one to point out that he already paid for three meals a day at the boardinghouse. But if Bitsy and Augie were short on cash, that might mean they were hurting even more than Bitsy had let on this afternoon.

"Well, say," Libby said with a broad smile, "I think it would be delightful to ask Isabel to come and join us. What do you gentlemen think?"

Hiram nodded and looked toward Doc.

"If you agree, I could step over to your lodgings and invite her," Kincaid said.

"Sounds good." Hiram resumed his seat as Doc headed for the door. He looked across at Libby and chuckled. "Well, what do you know about that?"

"It was unexpected," Libby said. "At least on my part."

"Mine, too."

Vashti approached, her satin skirt swishing. "Can I give you folks some coffee?"

"Yes, thank you," Libby said. "And we expect two more people to join us momentarily for dessert."

"Why, ma'am, that's lovely. I'll bring over a couple more chairs." The girl brushed her dark hair back and poured both their cups full.

"The place is busy tonight," Libby said.

"Yes ma'am. This is the way we like it."

Vashti went off with the coffeepot.

"You don't mind that I suggested we invite Isabel and Jim Kincaid, do you?" Libby asked.

"Not a bit."

"I hope Isabel isn't too overcome when he shows up at the door. I don't know if she's ever had a gentleman caller before." Libby's face went pink. "Oh dear. I just thought—what if she decided to retire early? And she might be frightened if someone knocks on the kitchen door."

Hiram tried to imagine the schoolteacher's reaction to the unexpected arrival of a man on the doorstep. "If you think we ought to, we could step over there and..." He let it trail off. Libby was already shaking her head.

"No, Isabel is not overly timid. I know she's been through a lot recently, but I think Dr. Kincaid is intelligent and polite enough to overcome any awkwardness."

Hiram let out a sigh. "That's fine, then. Because if we're going to have company soon, there's something else I'd like to say."

"Oh?" She fixed her vivid blue eyes on him with an air of expectancy.

"Yes. That is...Elizabeth..."

Her lips curved in a gentle smile. "Yes Hiram?"

His heart pounded like the hooves of a running pony. "I wondered if you ever thought about...about a different life."

"What sort of life?"

"Away from the Paragon."

She was silent for a long moment. Goldie ended her song at that instant, and the entire room seemed breathless.

"Yes," Libby said. "I often think of it."

Hiram felt a warm wave of satisfaction wash through him. The music began again, a slower tune. A rogue thought crossed his mind of dancing with Libby to that music. Of course, they didn't have dancing in here, and he wasn't sure his strict New England upbringing would allow him to come here if they did.

She still watched him. "As a matter of fact," she said, "the last time I was in Boise, I received an inquiry about my business."

He had to breathe carefully to keep his chest from hurting. "I've been thinking of life at the ranch," he said, barely above the music.

She nodded.

"But not alone. Isabel's right about that. It's not a life for the solitary."

Her lips parted, and his pulse soared.

At that moment, the door to the Spur & Saddle opened, and Isabel walked in wearing her gray schoolroom dress, her spine as stiff as a ramrod, followed by dapper Dr. Kincaid. She darted nervous glances about the room while he closed the door. When she located Hiram and Libby, her back seemed to unkink and let her stand like a normal woman.

"I believe our guests are here." Hiram stood beside the table and gave Isabel a slight nod.

Isabel noticed and nodded back. She looked behind her for Dr. Kincaid. He caught up to her and touched her elbow lightly, looking toward Hiram.

Just before they reached the table, Libby said softly, "Indeed, that is a topic we should discuss further."

Hiram glanced at her, not wanting to plunge into conversation with Doc and Isabel. But there would be another time. Libby's approving eyes told him that.

"Yes," he said, "and soon."

He found it easy to work up a smile for the new arrivals.

On a fine day at the end of August, Hiram stood outside the haberdashery building with Trudy and Libby. Too bad the new church wasn't ready for the occasion, but his crew had only begun to hoist the rafters for the building on Gold Lane.

From inside the makeshift sanctuary came the strains of the hymn "Savior, Like a Shepherd Lead Us." Goldie had a way with the piano. Oscar Runnels and a crew of volunteers had hauled the instrument over from the Spur & Saddle for the wedding. The effort expended probably wasn't worth it, especially considering the men would just have to move it back again after the celebration. But Bitsy's gesture in lending the piano and pianist showed her love for Trudy, and that's what this day was all about.

Libby, too, hovered over the bride, brushing a bit of dust off Trudy's powder blue dress. "All set?" she asked.

"Yes." Trudy's smile was more eager than anxious, and Hiram's own butterflies settled down a little.

Libby held on to her own bonnet and ducked under the edge of Trudy's astonishingly wide-brimmed hat to kiss her cheek. Wearing the same pretty pink gown she'd worn to her first dinner with Hiram, Libby made a perfect companion for Trudy. The two of them ought to sit for portraits.

"I'll see you inside," Libby said softly.

Trudy squeezed her hand and nodded.

Hiram realized the music had changed to a slow, solemn tune he didn't recognize. Libby smiled at him and headed for the door. It closed behind her, and he exhaled. Wait thirty seconds—those were their orders.

Trudy adjusted her bouquet of wildflowers.

"Trudy?"

"Hmm?"

He sucked in a deep breath. What would Pa say now if he were here, not back in Maine at the boatyard? "I. . .love you."

Her blue gray eyes glittered, mostly blue from the reflection of the dress's fabric, but a watery blue. "Don't make me all weepy now. I love you, too."

He nodded and crooked his arm. She grasped it firmly, and he patted her hand. "Guess it's time."

They walked down the aisle slowly. Goldie laid on the trills and arpeggios. Ethan stood at the front of the room waiting for them with Pastor Benton. On both sides of the aisle, the people of Fergus stood and stared at them, grinning. Some of the ladies already had their handkerchiefs out. Libby had reached her position opposite Ethan and watched them with her chin high and her cheeks flushed. The thought that she was the most beautiful woman in the room caused Hiram a pang of guilt—but Trudy wasn't far behind. His little sister had never looked better.

They stopped before the pulpit. Hiram stood between Ethan and Trudy as Pastor Benton puffed out his chest and began the "Dearly Beloveds." Not looking over at Libby took all Hiram's concentration.

When it came to the question, "Who giveth this woman in matrimony?" Hiram caught his breath. That was his cue. He gazed down at his little sister. Her eyes gleamed. He nodded and spoke up.

"Her parents and I do."

Over Trudy's head, Libby smiled at him. Hiram stepped back, placing Trudy's hand in Ethan's, and stood on the other side of his friend to act as Ethan's best man.

As the pastor recited the vows, Trudy and Ethan responded as they should. Hiram couldn't help imagining another wedding— one that would take place in the new church. And after that, a new life with Libby at the ranch...

Suddenly Ethan was kissing Trudy, and everyone clapped.

"Ladies and gentlemen," the pastor intoned, "I now present to you Mr. and Mrs. Ethan Chapman."

Hiram grinned as the couple walked down the aisle. Time for the reception over at Bitsy and Augie's, with the Ladies' Shooting Club serving cake and punch. He moved over and crooked his elbow for Libby. She smiled up at him as she took his arm.

"Well Mr. Dooley," she murmured.

Hiram winked at her with his right eye—the one no one but the pastor could see, if he were looking—and straightened his shoulders. He and Libby strode smartly down the aisle and out the door together. Ethan was kissing Trudy again, right there in the street.

Hiram looked down at Libby. Well, why not, he thought. He bent toward her and kissed her, and a jolt of fire shot through him. But by the time the haberdashery door opened, they stood discreetly next to the bride and groom, ready to accept good wishes with them.

About the Author

SUSAN PAGE DAVIS is a Maine native writing historical novels, suspense, and romance by the grace of God. She's married to Jim, a retired news editor, and they have six children and six grandchildren. Susan loves horses, books, and anything old. Visit her Web site at www.susanpagedavis.com.

Coming soon from

SUSAN PAGE DAVIS

THE BLACKSMITH'S BRAVERY

Book 3 in the Ladies' Shooting Club series

Coming November 2010